SWEETER THAN SIN

Y0-AQP-599

SARA ORWIG

WARNER BOOKS

A Time Warner Company

This book is dedicated to
Jeanne Tiedge-Lafranier

WARNER BOOKS EDITION

Copyright © 1992 by Sara Orwig
All rights reserved.

Cover photograph by Steve Lovi
Cover lettering by Michael Sabanosh
Cover design by Jackie Merri Meyer

Warner Books, Inc.
666 Fifth Avenue
New York, N.Y. 10103

 A Time Warner Company

Printed in the United States of America

First Printing: March, 1992

10 9 8 7 6 5 4 3 2 1

Alette fought against him, pushing against his chest.

Jeff kissed her, holding her until her struggles ended.

When he released her, they both were breathing as if they had been running. "You think that isn't real?" he asked gruffly.

"It's physical!"

"The hell it is. It goes deeper than just something physical when we kiss. You know damned well it does!"

"Rutger was right about you. I'm gullible. I want you to leave, Jeff."

He closed his eyes. Her request hurt. "All right. I'll go, because I know you're shocked, but you think about what I've said."

"If you stir this up for Cheramie, don't come back. Don't call me. I'll have to believe Rutger if you continue to pursue this, because there could only be one reason for it—to hurt the Lachmans. Get out, Jeff."

★ ★ ★ ★ ★

"The multi-faceted talent of Sara Orwig gleams as bright as gold."
—*Rave Reviews*

"Sara Orwig is unquestionably one of the best romance writers in the country today."
—**Judith Henry Wall, author of *Love and Duty***

"Compelling and richly drawn . . . thoroughly enjoyable!"
—**Catherine Coulter on *Favors of the Rich***

★

Also by Sara Orwig

*   *   *

FAVORS OF THE RICH
FAMILY FORTUNES

Published by
Warner Books

With many thanks to:
Sandy Northern
Leon Hooker
Harry Lemmerman
Penny McKenzie
Earnest Dixon
Bill Golliher

And for questions answered, thanks to:
Jim Slater
Mary Ellen Lee
Mitchell Lee
Warren Edwards
Susan Keeley
Office of the district attorney, San Francisco
Board of Landscape Architects, California
Board of Landscape Architects, Oklahoma
Chuck Rutherford, Oklahoma County deputy sheriff
Brooke Edmonds
Larry Huffman
George Orr
Bo Rhoades
Janie Reece
Tim Orwig
Sam and Mary Jane Noble
Caral McCall

Prologue

March 14, 1990

"To the next president of the United States!"

The toast echoed in Alette Lachman's mind as she stretched against the seat in her family's Falcon. Cruising at 435 knots at 39,000 feet, the plane flew above the snow-covered Sierra Nevada. Ignoring the spectacular view, Alette had thoughts only for the party that had kicked off the presidential campaign of her brother-in-law, Senator Phillip Walcott.

She could imagine Phillip in the Oval Office; with his political background *President* Walcott was conceivable. It was First Lady Cheramie Walcott that gave Alette pause. Her volatile sister hardly seemed like White House material. Cheramie was perpetual motion—and perpetual emotion. If Phillip could handle Cheramie, he should be able to run a nation.

Her sister was socially ambitious with a vengeance. Cheramie's golden eyes would sparkle as she greeted and danced with heads of state. She would thrive under such a spotlight, and their father would see his political ambitions fulfilled through his son-in-law.

Reflecting that she preferred the comparatively quiet life she would share with Bill, Alette recalled their personal party after the political gala. Bill's lithe body never ceased to thrill her. As she remembered just how his hands had moved over her, his fingers winding in her black hair as he pulled her to his chest, Alette wished with all her heart that there were fewer miles between them.

"Miss Lachman." The Lachman pilot interrupted her thoughts. "We're approaching for a landing."

She fastened her seat belt and looked out at San Francisco as rush hour approached. The bay was fogged in, clouds rolling over the hills to blanket the city. The Garrett engines whined as the jet lost altitude, dropping until Alette saw the green of eucalyptus and pine trees, as well as traffic on the freeway.

After stopping at her office at Lachman Landscape Architecture even though it had closed for the day, Alette arrived in front of her Victorian home in Pacific Heights at ten minutes before six. She parked on the steep pavement that sloped at a 15 percent grade down to the bay, its view now obscured by the fog that had settled since her arrival. The mist softened outlines and blurred shapes, giving everything a mysterious haze. Alette thought it was one of the city's most charming and romantic features, though she knew others who would disagree.

Upstairs in the silence of her white-and-beige bedroom, Alette kicked off her shoes, her toes sinking into thick white carpet as she walked into her closet. In an hour she was scheduled to attend a cocktail party for the opening of a gallery. Without hesitation she selected a deep blue Armani silk suit, tossing it on the bed just as the telephone cut into the quiet. Expecting to hear Bill's deep voice, she hurried to answer it. When there was no greeting, only heavy breathing, she frowned.

"Hello?" Alette spoke firmly, on the verge of replacing the receiver if obscene words came from the caller. As she started to hang up, she heard a raspy whisper bearing traces of a southern accent.

"Miss Lachman?"

She pressed the phone to her ear, wondering if the caller was in need of help; she could barely make out the words. "Yes?"

"Do you want to see your sister again? Do you want her to live?"

Alette's breath caught and held, but for only a moment. Reason replaced fear; this had to be a prank. She could still hear ragged breathing. It sounded as if the caller had been running.

"This is a joke," Alette snapped, her anger stirring. Cheramie was home with Phillip. They would be in San Francisco for the next two weeks before their planned return to Washington. Thoughts spun through her mind like leaves caught in the wind. It was early evening. If this were a kidnapping, the captors would call the husband, not a sister. It had to be a prank.

Alette slammed down the receiver. She counted to ten to make certain the connection was broken, then punched the single digit that would connect her with Cheramie's private phone. It was getting dusky in the room, and she switched on a lamp. She felt chilled, aware of the forbidding silence and emptiness of her house. She switched on another lamp. "Cheramie, answer," she whispered, each ring causing her apprehension to intensify.

Alette punched another digit and waited while the Lachman family phone rang without answer.

An insistent buzz signaled another call was waiting. She pushed down the button and lifted it to hear silence and then the same raspy, uneven breathing.

"Don't hang up again."

"You don't have Cheramie. She's home with her husband," she lied. "I just talked to him, and your call interrupted. She—"

"Listen!" There was a clatter and rustle and then a noise, like something scraping.

"Alette, please help me—"

The voice sounded like Cheramie's.

"Cheramie! Cheramie, are you all right?"

Something clattered again, and the whisper returned. "Do you want to see her again?"

"Of course. Let me—"

"Shut up!"

Alette caught her lower lip between her teeth as the voice gave her instructions. She tried to think while she listened, as her world was transformed by a brief phone conversation, a change as quick and sharp as the thrust of a sword. And then the voice was gone, the line went dead, and Alette was left with only the few bizarre instructions that had to be followed immediately.

1

San Francisco, 1968

The small wooden door on a carved cuckoo clock opened, and a yellow bird slid out. Four notes broke the silence in the bedroom. Without a glance at the familiar clock, Alette packed furiously, cramming her belongings into a leather suitcase while tears streaked her cheeks.

After tying her black hair in one long braid and tucking it beneath a cap, she pulled on a jacket over jeans and sweatshirt, stuffed her brown bear inside the suitcase, and glanced around: one last look at her wide canopied bed, the four-foot-high rocking horse, and all her bears and dolls and books.

Her room was her world. She adored it and didn't want to leave it. Wiping her eyes, she opened the bedroom door a fraction. Her heart thudded violently, a pounding in her ears that she felt could be heard in her father's master bedroom.

Listening for the moment when her father would wake and discover her, she descended the stairs. She knew the burglar alarm was on, but during the afternoon she had opened a window so she could now slide out without discovery.

Beyond the yard was the forbidding darkness of the street. Squaring her shoulders, she climbed over the sill. She dropped to the ground and picked up her suitcase, then hurried around the house. She walked headlong into someone.

With a cry, she jumped back. A boy swore and stared at her. "Alette! What are you doing here?"

"I'm waiting for the paper," she said to Chuck Dayton, the paper boy and a friend of Aubrey, her brother.

"With a suitcase?"

"I planned to put it inside the suitcase."

"You're running away from home!"

"No, I'm not! I'm going inside. Want to give me the paper?"

"Yeah, sure." He handed her a paper, and she walked toward the back of the house. When she'd stepped behind a well-trimmed fuchsia shrub, she peeked around the corner and her heart skipped. Chuck stood on the porch, pushing the doorbell. In a panic, leaving her suitcase behind in the bushes, she scurried to climb back into the library.

Lights came on all over the house, and shivers of fear raked through her, because when he was angry, her father could be terrifying.

"Aubrey! Cheramie! Alette!" From the sounds of his call, Alette knew her father was in the hall. "Aubrey! Cheramie! Alette!"

"What is it, Rutger?" Aubrey's voice came from upstairs. He called his father by his name, as they had been taught to do.

"I'm sleepy," Cheramie grumbled.

"Come down here at once. Where is Alette?"

"I'm here," she said, stepping into the hallway.

Rutger wore his blue monogrammed robe over silk pajamas. His golden hair was awry, his blue eyes filled with anger as they focused on her.

"All three of you—into the library."

Alette waited as they filed into the room. Aubrey stopped beside her, giving her a questioning look.

"Sit down!"

All three sat down instantly, Cheramie raking her hand through her thick black curls, her amber eyes growing round with fear while she gave Alette a curious stare.

"Where have you been, Alette?" Rutger asked, pausing in front of her.

Terrified, she lifted her chin and stared back at him. "I was running away," she answered.

"Why in God's name were you running away from home?"

"Because you're sending me away!" she said, bursting into tears, emotions surging to the surface.

"That makes sense," he said with sarcasm. "I'm sending you away so you run away! Dammit!" He slammed his fist on the desk, and they all jumped.

"I don't want to go to Boston to school! I want to stay here at home with my friends," she cried, terrified to defy him yet determined to convey her feelings.

"Rutger," Aubrey said, standing up. Rutger glanced at him while Aubrey sat beside her and took her hand in his.

"She's only ten and she doesn't want to leave home," he said, and as she cried, Alette heard the quaver in his voice.

"I don't mind leaving, because it's exciting!" Cheramie said smugly.

"Quiet! All of you, quiet! Aubrey, you and Cheramie go to your rooms."

"She's a baby, Rutger," Aubrey said bravely. His face paled as he stared back at his father, and Alette felt better knowing that her brother was her champion.

"Dammit, you get to your room!" Rutger said in a cold voice. Aubrey gave Alette one more worried glance.

"Running away wouldn't have done you any good," Rutger said as soon as they were alone. "It would have been an embarrassment to me and to the family. It was a stupid, inconsiderate thing to do."

"Yes, sir," she said, trembling. "Please let me go to school with Cheramie!"

"No. If the three of you go to different schools, it will make you more independent. God knows you need it. For the next two weeks you're not to go anywhere or have any company."

"That's when I have to leave for school! I can't see my friends—"

"You should have thought of that before you tried to run away. Go to your room."

She turned and ran, crying as she went, knowing it was
useless to argue with Rutger. Her father was implacable. She
sat down on her rocking chair and gathered up a teddy bear
to hug. Aubrey thrust his head into the room.

"Rutger's gone to bed," he said softly, crossing the room
to sit at the foot of her bed. "Did he hit you?"

"No," she said, trying to stop crying. "I can't go anywhere or have my friends over before I leave for Boston."

"Well, hell," he said, pushing curly sandy hair off his
forehead. "How'd he catch you? I didn't hear the alarm go
off."

"It was that miserable Toad who's your friend—Chuck. I
ran into him."

"Chuck ratted on you? I'll kill him," Aubrey said, his thin
chest expanding. The door opened, and Cheramie slipped into
the room, her eyes sparkling.

"What happened?"

"She's grounded until she goes to school," Aubrey answered. "Big help you were!"

"Trying to run away was sappy," Cheramie said in smug
tones. "All you did was make him angry. You'll get put on
a plane to Boston by one of the maids while Rutger will take
me to lunch, buy me something pretty, and put me on the
plane himself."

"Don't pick on her, Cheramie."

"You always take her side."

"You always take Rutger's!" he rejoined, glaring at her.

Cheramie smiled and swished around the room. "That's
because it makes life much nicer. You just need to grow up,
Alette." She pulled out a cigarette case. "Look what I can
do at school."

"You smoke?" Aubrey said, shocked.

"Yes," she answered eagerly. "I'm fourteen years old
now. Besides, don't you?"

Alette stared at Aubrey and was amazed to see him blush.
"Yes, but it's different for boys."

"The hell it is," Cheramie said.

"And you shouldn't swear."

"You do. I've heard you. And don't tell me it's different

for boys. At your old military school I'll bet you smoke and swear and do all sorts of things.'' She scooted close to Alette and sat on a footstool. "You'll like school. You'll have new friends and freedom, and you can smoke—''

"I don't want to smoke. And I want my old friends.''

"You're the biggest baby!" Cheramie stood up and headed for the door. When Aubrey started after her, she laughed and disappeared into the hall.

Alette looked up at her thirteen-year-old brother. "I'll be all right, Aubrey.''

"It might not be so bad," he said, flinging himself onto his stomach on her pink velvet chaise longue, balancing a pillow in the air with his toes.

"You hate military school.''

"Yeah, but that's because it's military. You'll get used to being away. And you'll make friends that are really super.''

"My friends are here. Aubrey, sometimes I hate him so much. I wish we had a family like Mary Jenkin's.''

"We don't. We have each other," he said, holding up the palm of his hand. "Let's call each other once a week. Every Wednesday night.''

"Good idea.'' She placed her palm against his in a ritual that was a secret between the two of them.

"Then it's settled. I'll call the first week," he said, dropping his hand.

She looked into his eyes, and fear overwhelmed her. She remembered the last big loss in her life, her mother's death— the funeral and the baskets of sweet-smelling white roses. Four months later Cheramie and Aubrey had been sent away to school. Now she was to go far away where she didn't know anyone. She burst into tears, unable to stop and knowing it would annoy Aubrey, who always told her crying was for sissies.

"Aw, gee whiz, Alette," he said. "Stop crying and I'll tell you a secret. You have to stay stopped until I've gone to bed.''

She cried a second longer, sniffed, and looked at him through tear-filled eyes. "All right," she said. "I stopped.'' Her curiosity grew as she followed him to the attic.

"What are you going to get up here?" she asked, gazing at the orderly room with dusty trunks. She heard a whine.

"Here's my surprise. I was going to show you tomorrow anyway. Come look." He led the way to a box and picked up a brown puppy.

"Oh, Aubrey!" she exclaimed, her worries evaporating as she took the wriggling bundle from his hands. The puppy was warm and soft, gazing up at her with brown eyes. "He's marvelous!"

"Hank Brownwood and I found him. I tried to find out where it lives or who the owner is, but I couldn't."

"He's beautiful!" she exclaimed, holding up the puppy and letting it lick her face. "Rutger won't allow you to keep it."

"Hank is going to take him next week. His folks said he can have a dog, but I can keep him until then."

"Can I take him to my room?"

"Gosh, no!"

"Please. I promise to bring him back early in the morning. Please, Aubrey."

"All right, but you better not get caught."

"I won't," she answered happily, holding the puppy close as they left the attic. At the door to Aubrey's room, she paused. "Thanks, Aubrey."

"Just don't get caught," he whispered gruffly, but he looked pleased.

"I didn't mean just about the puppy. Thanks for taking up for me." She hurried to her room, and sat down in the middle of her bed to play with the dog. Her father had always been cold and formidable, but he had grown more so in the last year. She pulled the pup onto her lap and vowed that someday she would have a family to love.

2

Lugano, Switzerland 1977

The air was crisp, the sky blue, as Alette hurried away from campus down a street lined with chalets and bright flowers. An American academic institution established in Switzerland, Jefferson University drew children from families who could afford to offer their progeny an education abroad. Now in her sophomore year, Alette planned to earn a degree in landscape architecture.

Her mind wasn't on courses, but on a luncheon date with her father and Paul Simmons. Knowing the kind of man Rutger admired, she didn't expect her father to be impressed, but she hoped he would accept Paul.

Paul stood in front of the quaint restaurant with its peaked roof, flagstone terrace, and baskets of flowers. Her heart skipped when he saw her and smiled. Sunlight highlighted his straight brown hair, and there was no mistaking the warmth in his brown eyes when she walked up to him.

"We can get a table outside to watch for your father."

"He will be here exactly at noon. He's never late."

"I hope I pass inspection."

"You will," she said, her gaze raking over his lean frame.

"I want his friendship and approval."

"Just hope for approval. My father is a cold man."

The maître d' seated them at a round metal table in the shade of an umbrella, and promptly at twelve Alette saw her father stride up, his golden hair glinting in the sunlight, his walk purposeful. In a town populated with people of wealth and position, Rutger still stood out. Pedestrians stepped aside for him, the maître d' rushed forward to greet him, and Alette wondered what it was that made her father command attention so effortlessly. She realized Paul noticed it too when she heard him draw a sharp breath.

"Look at the maître d'. You'd think your father is a regular patron from the way he's treating him."

"People react to him that way."

"Lord, this may be a long lunch," Paul said under his breath.

Surprised by Paul's nervousness, she squeezed his hand. "Don't be ridiculous. It's only my father. He isn't royalty," she said, trying to wipe the worry from Paul's expression.

"Does he know that?" Paul asked quietly.

"Here he comes," Alette said, waiting, knowing there would be no hug or kiss, for seldom did Rutger touch any of his children. She nodded in greeting and introduced Paul.

"Rutger, this is Paul. Paul, I want you to meet my father, Rutger Lachman."

The men shook hands and sat down. A waiter came directly to Rutger to ask about drinks, and Alette realized she should have warned Paul that Rutger was a wine connoisseur.

"What are your white wines?" Rutger asked the waiter, who listed Les Murets, L'Arbalete, and Ruffino Soave.

"Do you have a bottle of Ladoucette's sauvignon blanc? I think everyone will like that," he said, giving Paul a questioning glance.

"Fine," Paul answered while she nodded. She knew Paul preferred dark German beer.

Rutger approved the wine, and as soon as it was poured, Paul immediately downed his, and Alette realized just how overwhelmed he was by Rutger. After they had studied the menus and ordered, there were perfunctory exchanges about her classes and Rutger's flight. Then Rutger focused on Paul. "Alette tells me this is your senior year. What do you plan to do when you graduate?"

"I'm majoring in landscape architecture, the same as Alette, and I plan to return home to San Francisco to work."

"Your parents live in San Francisco?"

"They're divorced. My mother lives there."

"I don't recall meeting her."

"It's a big city, Rutger," Alette said, realizing that time and the distance between Switzerland and San Francisco as well as her love for Paul had caused her to forget how cold Rutger could be. He gazed now at Paul with a frosty disdain that was unmistakable.

"You probably haven't met her," Paul said evenly. "She works at Mason's department store in the shoe department."

"She did well to send you here to school," Rutger said, his brows arching.

"No, sir. My grandparents helped, and I had an art scholarship."

"Thank God you don't plan to be an artist. You'd starve to death."

"Rutger, you have no idea how talented Paul is!"

"In spite of the scholarship, I think my talents lie more toward landscape architecture than drawing, Alette. I'll be the first to admit it."

"You were in art and now you've changed to landscape architecture?"

"Yes, sir," Paul said, sounding young and subdued.

"So if you marry my daughter, as you two say you plan to do someday, you'll go into business together and Alette will give you the contacts you need to succeed."

"Rutger—" she began, seeing that the meeting was taking a disastrous turn and knowing she shouldn't have expected anything else.

"Mr. Lachman," Paul cut in, "I'm not marrying Alette for her business contacts. We both enjoy working in the same field, so it seems best to work together."

"I'm sure it does," Rutger rejoined with unmistakable sarcasm. "Best for you without a doubt. Whose work do you prefer, Thomas Church, Garrett Eckbo, or Dan Kiley?" he snapped.

"I don't remember that much about them," Paul replied stiffly.

"Which firm have you worked for in the summers when you were home?"

"I haven't worked for landscaping companies in the summers. I plan to go home and do my apprenticeship then."

They paused as lunches of *Geschnetzeltes*, thin strips of sautéed veal in a cream-and-wine sauce, were placed before Paul and Alette while Rutger received grilled shad. The waiter refilled Paul's glass with wine, which he drank as quickly as the first. She wanted to reach over and squeeze his hand for reassurance, but she resisted the impulse.

"My drawing class is going to Bellago next week for the day," Alette said, hoping to stem Rutger's interrogation.

"I'm sure you'll enjoy that. You've always liked to travel," Rutger said.

"Do you remember when you took us to Zurich when I was twelve?" she asked Rutger, and turned to Paul. "They were filming a movie, and the second day we were there, Aubrey wangled his way into the background of the movie."

"Do you know anything about the market for landscape architects in the Bay Area?" Rutger asked Paul, returning to the subject with the single-mindedness Alette knew too well.

"No, but I expect to find work. I have to work for someone else for two years. It's required before I can take the state test for a license."

"Have you contacted anyone yet?"

"No. I'll do that when I get home."

"You never did say—where have you worked in summer?"

"At my uncle's dry cleaning shop. Jobs aren't easy for college students home for the summer," Paul said in a tense voice, his face flushing.

"He'll be getting experience soon," Alette said, trying to smooth things over.

"Have you traveled much while you're here in school?" Rutger asked him.

"I've been to Italy."

"Rome?"

"No, sir. Just across the border, where we go on weekends to dance. I can't afford to see Europe."

"I hope you both aren't already living on Alette's allowance," Rutger said quietly.

"Rutger!" she exclaimed, aghast at his bluntness.

"No, sir, we're not," Paul replied, color flooding his face as he put down his fork. "I think I need to go in order to get to class on time."

"Paul, please—"

He stood up. "Thank you for the lunch, sir. I'll see you later, Alette."

She gave Rutger one angry glance, tossed down her linen napkin, and rushed after Paul. She caught his arm.

"Paul, please. What can I say? I can't help what kind of man my father is, and I warned you he would be this way."

"Alette, you need a different type of man," he said, and started to walk away.

"No!" She stopped in front of Paul to block his path. "All my father can see is money! Do you think I'm like him?"

Suddenly Paul's features softened, and she exhaled in relief as he reached out to take her hands.

"No, I know you're not like him. But if I marry you—"

"We can move to the ends of the earth. We don't have to live in San Francisco. Just don't be angry."

"Go back and eat lunch with him. I'm fine, and I do have class shortly. I'll see you tonight for dinner if your father still plans to leave town this afternoon."

"He does. This was just a brief stopover on his way to Stockholm."

Paul leaned forward to kiss her lightly. She stared at him as he walked away, and then she returned to the restaurant. Rutger was leaning back when she faced him.

"You don't like him. You don't want me to see him."

"No, but I know that won't stop you. He's weak, Alette, and whether you realize it or not, you're my child, and you're a strong woman. He'll never make you happy."

"Right now he makes me supremely happy," she answered, wondering vaguely when her father had decided she was strong.

"Go ahead and eat."

"I've lost my appetite," she answered stiffly.

"Over my questions? Alette, he's a grown man. If both of you can't take a few questions by an interested father, then you're in for a rocky future."

"It wasn't merely a few questions—asking him if he shares my income!"

"I think that was a valid question."

"He doesn't share it, if it makes you feel better."

"I'm glad he doesn't. I hate to see my children make mistakes. Time is as valuable as money, and when you waste it on bad marriages, you can't get it back."

"I love Paul and think he's wonderful," she said, wondering if Rutger ever made an effort to see anything from someone else's point of view.

Rutger stared at her as he inhaled deeply. "You have to live your own life, but you'll see I'm right."

"You don't know him!"

"No, I don't. But I know you."

He finished his lunch, and she was tempted to get up and walk out without speaking to him further about Paul, but she knew that wouldn't accomplish anything.

She stared beyond him at the town that was full of charm, with palms on the lake's edge that were a startling contrast to the wintry peaks of the snow-capped mountains beyond them.

"What time does your plane leave?"

"Rushing me away, Alette?" he asked, tilting his head to study her.

She faced him squarely, lifting her chin. "I don't think you've been fair to Paul. You could have given a little time to him, made a little effort to try to discover what I see in him."

"You're young and in love for the first time."

"Were you ever in love?" The question came out angrily, and the moment it was said she knew she had crossed a boundary drawn in early childhood. No one questioned Rutger about his actions. A shuttered look came over his face, a chilling coldness shone in his eyes; otherwise there was no change to his expression. He sipped his coffee and gazed at the street.

"Insolence doesn't become you, and I won't tolerate it. I'd like to walk around the campus in the short time I have left. I'd like to see some of your work." He focused on her again, and she felt the challenge to his authority and was tempted to refuse him.

Instead she nodded, because if she defied him, it would only cause her trouble. She finished lunch in silence.

"Which class do you enjoy most?" Rutger asked in a pleasant voice as they strolled toward the campus.

"My drawing class," she said, knowing the remainder of their time would be spent in innocuous questions and conversation; the subject of Paul was dropped.

She didn't wait and watch Rutger's plane leave but returned to her apartment, anger boiling at Rutger and his cavalier dismissal of Paul.

As they had agreed before Rutger's arrival, Paul waited after her last class. They had planned to go to his apartment and study together. The moment she left the classroom and met his solemn gaze, she felt the strain between them. "Rutger's gone now."

"And so I'm safe," Paul said bitterly. "On campus I forget the differences between us. They become minimal because we have the same interests and we're away from our homes, but today the differences were pointed out to me clearly."

"We won't live with Rutger. It doesn't matter," she argued, determined that Rutger not continue to rule her life.

Paul took her arm. "Let's go to my place to talk." They walked in silence the four blocks to his apartment, where he faced her. "You can be much happier married to someone else, someone . . ."

"Someone like Rutger?" she finished for him. "I know what I want, Paul. I know what's right."

"You're young. I'm not the man he wants for you, Alette," Paul repeated stubbornly.

"It doesn't matter to me," she said.

"It'll matter to him." Paul's brown eyes met hers. "I need your friendship. I want marriage; I want you for yourself, not because you can help me in business—you do believe me, don't you?"

"Of course. And you don't have to keep reassuring me." She took his hand and squeezed it while studying him. Paul was tall, handsome by any standards, with a strong jaw and wide brown eyes, a full mouth. His face was slender, giving him a deceptive appearance of leanness, yet he had solid muscles. She loved the peace and comfort she felt when he held her, and if theirs was not a passionately sexual relationship, Alette appreciated their deep friendship and sense of camaraderie more.

"You have a very strong-willed man for a father."

"He's as cold as marble." She gazed up into Paul's eyes. "In you I've found the reassurance and love I never had," she said. "I was sent to boarding school when I was ten. I cried nights on end and had nightmares."

He pulled her close in his arms. "We need each other, love. I need your strength. I'll make you happy, Alette. I promise."

She knew they hadn't heard the last from Rutger. It was years before they planned to marry. Her father was patient enough to hold back now, thinking time might solve the matter for him.

But four years later when she recalled that first meeting between Rutger and Paul in Switzerland, Alette realized she should have known then what would happen. At first she had expected Rutger to interfere, but as time passed and he didn't, she relinquished her fears. Paul went home to California to work for Dade Wells, a landscape architect in Sacramento. She finished school and started her apprenticeship. They planned to marry as she neared the completion of her two years as an apprentice. They wanted to take their state tests together, become licensed, and start their own business. She planned for her wedding and her future as Mrs. Paul Simmons.

So eight months before the tentative wedding date, when Rutger summoned her home and closed the door to his study to talk to her, his orders came as a shock.

She sat on the burgundy leather wing chair, the same chair she had sat on for lectures as a child when her feet dangled in the air. The hand-tooled leather-bound volumes on the shelves looked as untouched as museum pieces. A Jan van Eyck painting was placed above the broad stone fireplace, a Vermeer on another wall. The paintings and matching wing chairs were the only touches of color in a room decorated in shades of brown, the dark tones a reflection of the somber man who used it.

As he had done when she was a child, Rutger stood in front of the long windows, gazing out at lighted grounds. As a child Alette had always thought he was trying to curb his anger before he spoke. Now she wondered if he were summoning his thoughts in the efficient manner he had. The years had done little to change him. His shoulders were broad, giving the impression of force even when he stood in repose. To many he was probably handsome; since childhood she had seen women fawn over him like glittering butterflies flitting around a stone lion in a garden.

She had long ago given up yearning for his love, stopped aching to win his approval. She faced him in silence, the old ripples of fear and awe still plaguing her. They were so different—her blond, strong father who was taciturn, bound in his own thoughts and endeavors—while with her black hair and dark eyes, Alette resembled a faded picture of her French mother. She often wondered what he had been like then, the young man with the French bride, the young father. Had his heart died along with his wife, leaving only the ambitious businessman? Many times Alette had wanted to think so, but in her heart she suspected all there ever had been in Rutger was the ruthless, determined man who needed power above all else.

Never given to nervous mannerisms, he stood absolutely still. Had the worst possible crisis precipitated, she suspected he would remain as calm and logical as in his most relaxed moments. The only indication of his anger was the quiet in his voice and the glacial look in his blue eyes, which he finally turned on her with all their force.

"You can't possibly marry this man."

"I am going to marry him," she answered in a firm tone that she hoped hid the flutter in her pulse. "I'm grown—twenty-three now—and I've completed my education. I love him and think he's a wonderful person, the right person for me," she answered, aware their words were soft-spoken. No heated passions would rise in the Lachman household, where only the iron will of its owner would prevail.

Rutger turned to face her fully, gazing down his sharp, straight nose at her. "He's had a male lover."

"I know that. But that was all long ago when he was a teenage boy away at boarding school. He experimented a little—just like lots of young boys. Besides, no one had heard of AIDS then, and Paul grew up to be completely heterosexual," she answered stiffly, finding the discussion of this topic so personal as to be odious.

"It isn't just AIDS. It's the man."

"Paul loves me and wants what I want."

"He's not the man for you, Alette. I've said it before—you're a strong woman, whether you realize it or not."

"Perhaps strength is best tempered by gentleness." How polite their argument sounded, yet Rutger's arguments never stopped with mere words; they were always followed by decisive action.

"Wait a year. One more year can't hurt, and you might thank me later."

"I've known Paul since my sophomore year, four years now. That's long enough."

"Most of the time you were away at school and he was here. He's worked in Sacramento and you work here. It's an unrealistic relationship. You see him only on weekends or holidays. Look at Cheramie. She goes out with the right type of men. But with this man you'll have nothing but heartbreak."

Alette drew a deep breath and glanced away. She knew what Rutger didn't—the men Cheramie dated who weren't the right kind were kept hidden from Rutger. "Paul is a wonderful friend. We're totally compatible."

"You're a young, naive woman; men like Paul never change. He'll always have a streak of the androgynous in him. If you insist on this matter, then I want to talk to both of you. He's not the sort of man I want in this family."

Her head snapped up, because she realized the crux of the matter. "You don't want him interfering in your campaign for governor!"

"I damned well don't. What a circus the press will have when they find out my future son-in-law is gay."

"He isn't gay."

"That's part of his life. It's like arguing that his skin isn't white because he's been out in the sun."

"I love him whether he interferes in your becoming governor or not!"

His eyes narrowed, and she faced a look that would make many men cringe. "I'll disinherit you, of course."

She had known that would be a threat, and she merely nodded.

"You pass that off lightly, which shows your immaturity."

"Money—"

"Is the most important consideration. And someday you'll agree with me. Right now you're wrapped in security. It's all you've ever known. What date have you set for your wedding?"

"We haven't reserved the church yet, but I'd like December twenty-seventh, a winter wedding."

"And you're making the decision, of course."

"It's what we both want."

"He'll do whatever you want. He's quit his job, moved here; he's just waiting for you to set him up in business. You'll regret this marriage if you go ahead, Alette."

She stood up. "I need Paul. He's gentle and compassionate," she said, wondering if Rutger knew what the words meant. "I hope you'll come to the wedding."

"I have no intention of lending my approval to such an obvious disaster," he snapped, an edge coming to his voice that surprised her and gave her pause.

She left the room, knowing the dispute wouldn't end with their conversation. Rutger was a man of action and few words. He would do something, but she couldn't think what. Cheramie had had boyfriends when she was younger whom Rutger had eliminated from her life easily with money or threats, or by talking to their families. But they were younger than Paul. He couldn't be swayed by her father.

She hurried to the solarium, picking up a phone to call Paul. His deep voice was reassuring. She glanced over her shoulder and lowered her voice. "I'm leaving Rutger's now."

"Want me to come pick you up?"

"No. I'll come to your place."

"Alette, I love you," he said calmly, and his words increased the urgency she felt to get away from the mansion and her father and to the haven of Paul's arms.

She swung the Jaguar away from the curb, glancing back in the mirror at the granite-and-stone Gothic mansion perched at the top of one of the highest hills, a home as forbidding and overwhelming as its owner. She drove swiftly through quiet streets until she reached a main thoroughfare. She drove too fast, feeling as if she had to escape Rutger's presence. As soon as she entered Paul's apartment, she walked into his arms.

"Hold me."

"He can't do anything to us," Paul whispered, his arms tightening around her.

"I know him so well. He'll do something." She gazed up into brown eyes. "He'll disinherit me."

"We've discussed that. You expected it. Have you changed your mind how you feel about it?"

"No. We're starting together, and between us we should do all right. I don't need the Lachman money."

He smoothed her collar with long fingers. "He's already given each of his children enough that you won't ever have to work. You'll always be wealthy, Alette, but if you inherit, you'll be immensely wealthy. You're casually giving up what is almost a kingdom."

"Paul, I don't think he'll stop at threats of disinheritance."

"I'm not afraid of him. Have some sherry and relax," he said softly. "I have dinner in the oven, the table set, and we can forget the world, your father . . . everyone."

They reserved the Episcopal church for December 27, and Alette hung her wedding dress in the spare bedroom in her condominium. Made of douppioni silk and Alençon lace with seed pearls, the dress had a cathedral train and a rosette headpiece. Cheramie would be maid of honor, and there would be eight bridesmaids.

On Tuesday night, the last week of May, Paul disappeared.

3 ～～～

When Paul was an hour late for dinner, Alette called his house and received no answer. She had grown up in a household with a man who never accounted to his family for his whereabouts, but while dating Paul she had become accustomed to his constantly letting her know his schedule.

She decided he had been detained, but after an hour and a half had passed, she became worried. By eleven o'clock she was frantic. She phoned his friends, trying to find him. Paul's mother was visiting relatives in Ohio, so she wouldn't know where he was.

Frightened, Alette knew before she called the police that a man who hadn't shown up for a dinner date would be no cause for worry to them. The officer explained politely why he couldn't yet put out a missing persons bulletin on Paul.

Terrified of what might have happened, she spent a sleepless night, and by midmorning the next day she drove frantically to Paul's apartment. When she saw a car parked in front and his car at the curb, relief washed over her. Wondering what had happened, she rang the bell. The door opened and Paul faced her.

With shock she stared at him. He was bare-chested, his belt unfastened. One eye was puffed almost closed, his cheek bruised. He had a day's growth of beard, and he reeked of whiskey.

"Paul, I've been so worried! What happened?" Visions of a mugging, of Paul unconscious in an alleyway, came to her, but his response wasn't the indignation or fright of a man who had been mugged. Hot sunshine warmed her shoulders while Paul stared at her.

"Come inside, Alette," he said solemnly. A bare-chested

man stood behind Paul. He was pulling on his shirt and had a faint smile on his face as he gazed at her.

"I'm going, Paul," he said, picking up a wallet and car keys and moving past her as she stepped into the entryway. Making no effort to introduce them, Paul waited while the door closed. When he faced her, she felt as if she were staring at a stranger.

"I should have called," he said, his words barely audible.

"Why didn't you? I've been going crazy."

His gaze slid away from her, and he clenched his hands. He crossed to the fireplace in the front room, and she followed. When he knocked over a vase, she realized he was drunk. He straightened it, glancing at her; the look in his eyes agonizing.

"What happened?" she asked, dreading his answer.

"I haven't changed," he snapped, his voice rough, so unlike him. "I think too much of you, Alette, to deceive you."

She felt the sharp pain of anger and betrayal. "How long have you been seeing him?" The words seem to come from a distance while she stared at him, trying to reconcile what she surmised he was saying with the man she thought she knew.

"I can't be faithful to you." He turned his back and covered his face with his hands. Aghast, she realized he was crying.

Her anger disintegrated, and she rushed to him. "Paul, don't."

He grabbed her, pulling her to him and clinging. "God, I'm sorry, Alette! When I met you, you wanted someone gentle, kind. I thought I could be that for you. I needed your strength; you needed my gentleness."

She didn't want to know, yet she had to hear. "Is it one man? How long have you known him?"

"I haven't been seeing someone without telling you!" he cried, pulling back. "I wouldn't do that to you." Self-loathing laced his words. "This only happened once—just last night." He turned as if he couldn't bear to face her. "He came to my apartment. I just couldn't . . . resist. I thought I had changed for good. It's been so many years. But he knew just how to get to me," he finished lamely.

"When did you meet him?" Her words were sharp, anger mixing with shock.

"I met him yesterday afternoon when he came to my apartment," Paul said.

"*Yesterday?* You just met him. How did he know—" She stopped abruptly. "My God. *My father sent him.*"

"Yes, your bastard father, who knew what you didn't," Paul said, and she had never heard such bitterness. "He saw my weakness. I'm not strong like him, Alette. Your father sent money, so much money, and he sent that guy, and I succumbed to it all."

"How much did my father pay you?" she said, aghast that she had to ask such a question. The silence lengthened, and she raised her voice sharply. "Dammit, how much? I have a right to know. I'll ask him if you won't tell me."

"Two hundred thousand."

"After all you promised me and told me . . ." Her voice trailed away. She wanted to scream at him. "Here's your ring," she said, closing her eyes, feeling betrayed and angry.

"Alette, I never meant to hurt you."

"Don't whine!" She threw down the ring and fled the apartment, slaming the door behind her. When she reached home, she stood in the empty apartment, shaking violently. Her first reaction was to confront Rutger; then she remembered he was out of the country. She moved purposefully, packing swiftly, making calls to change appointments, finally calling Aubrey.

"I'll be right over," he said.

"No. I'm going to Utah," she replied, thinking of the secluded Lachman home in the mountains.

"Then I'll go with you. I can help with the driving."

"No, thanks, Aubrey. You don't have to hold my hand."

"Would you rather stay on my boat?"

She smiled. "No, thanks. I'll be all right."

"I'm on my way. Don't leave without me."

"Aubrey—" She stared at the phone because he had hung up. She shook her head, but forty minutes later when he appeared, she walked into his arms.

When she regained her composure, he took her arm. "I'll drive, and no protests."

As he drove she talked, glancing occasionally at her brother's profile, his thin, straight nose, his broad, firm Lachman jaw, the hair that in childhood had been sandy but, with all his boating, was now bleached almost white.

"I'm sorry," he said when she finished. "Be thankful you found out now."

"Rutger told me this would happen."

"And our father is right too damnably often, which he lets you know in no uncertain terms. I don't miss being around him."

"I don't know how you manage to avoid it."

"Yes, you do. He won't associate with a son who lives on a houseboat and races and brokers yachts for a living."

She smiled and felt better. "You always help cheer me up."

"I recall a few times you've done the same for me. Besides, that's what a brother is for. My stomach is riding on empty, and I see golden arches ahead."

"I know you have hollow legs. If I ate what you eat, I would weigh as much as the car."

"Sure, Alette. I can smell the fries from here."

Her gaze ran down his lanky body and thin legs, and she laughed. "You don't burn it off in restless energy; I don't know what you do with the calories."

"Loan them to my lady friends. They're always complaining."

Alette settled back, thankful now that he had insisted on coming along.

During the first day she talked and cried some more while Aubrey listened. They sat in the wide living room that had floor-to-ceiling windows with a panoramic view of spruce-covered mountains.

"I know you love Paul," Aubrey said, "but if this had happened later, it would have been worse."

She ran a hand over her eyes. "I feel betrayed, and I feel as if I can't trust my own judgment."

"To hell with that. You're young, vulnerable because of all the lonely years. But the time will come when you won't have regrets."

She stared at Aubrey. He was unbound by convention, a free spirit who would have no qualms following his inclinations. His curly hair was shoulder length, his frayed jeans were white with wear, the shirt had sleeves ripped away, his long arms were deeply tanned, his beard thick and curly. He was sensitive, as soft-spoken as Paul, but beneath the quiet exterior was a man as iron-willed as Rutger, probably the one man on earth Rutger hadn't been able to buy, bully, or mold.

Aubrey moved to the window. "I prefer the ladies, but I know men like Paul, and their sexual preferences run deep."

"In a month I may be able to calmly accept that, but right now I just hurt. I really believed his flirtation with his sexuality was just an adolescent fling."

"It might have remained that if Rutger hadn't interfered." He nodded. "You're a survivor. We all are. Cheramie is, you are, even I am in my own modest way."

She gave him a faint smile. "Not so modest when you think of the money you give away."

"Ah, the money. I make a good living doing what I want to do. I don't really give so much to charity when you think about how much I keep. Let's sail down to the Caribbean. To do nothing would be good for you."

"Thanks, Aubrey, but I'll go home in a few days. I've passed my state test and I'm licensed, and I want to start my business."

"I wish you luck, sis, but just don't let it make you too tough. Don't turn into a ballbreaker."

"That will hardly happen in the landscape business," she said with dry amusement.

He shrugged. "It happens. Uptight women are a nuisance."

"Since when have you had uptight women in your life?"

"As seldom as possible. Speaking of which, where's Cheramie?"

"In Paris with friends. She wants some new dresses."

"Any particular man in her life?"

"Cheramie?"

He shrugged broad shoulders. "Sometimes it happens to the wildest of them."

"No. Cheramie still just loves men. And money."

Aubrey winked. "Ah, the great puzzles of life. Men and money."

4

A Fendi sable-trimmed blue silk dress flew through the air. Cheramie Lachman walked over it barefoot to her closet. She had no interest in Rutger's political future, but she knew it would be best for her if she appeared at his parties anyway.

Trying to ease her conscience and her headache with a whiskey sour, she had bathed and changed with the help of Gretchen, who now worked for Cheramie instead of Rutger. Gretchen always put the Lachmans first, but she was failing dismally on this occasion. Her lips firmed as Cheramie crossed the room in a staggering walk that caused her to bump into the bed.

"Ma'am, here's a cup of hot coffee."

"I don't want any damned coffee!" Cheramie snapped, sipping her cocktail. "It'll be one of those boring political evenings, my head is pounding, and I'll have to wait hours to escape. I don't have anything to wear, and I just want to go to bed. Find me a dress, Gretchen."

"Yes, ma'am. If you drink the coffee, ma'am, you might feel better. Begging your pardon, Miss Lachman . . ."

Cheramie gritted her teeth, because when Gretchen started a sentence with "Begging your pardon," trouble was coming.

"Your father is not going to be pleased. He may be quite angry," Gretchen said, helping her into a burgundy Karan beaded dress that clung to Cheramie's voluptuous figure.

"Ma'am, I brewed a pot of coffee," Gretchen said in haughty tones. Cheramie fished out a beaded evening bag, leaving the drawer open, knowing Gretchen would straighten everything.

"Ma'am, if you'll just wait a moment for the coffee—"

"To hell with that! I'll be sober by the time I get there." She took another sip of whiskey and glared at the maid, who had the temerity to glare back. "I'm going."

"Yes, ma'am. I think you should stop downstairs at the hotel and have a cup of coffee. I can call ahead—"

"Fuck the damn coffee, Gretchen!" she snapped.

"Your father would not want his daughter ridiculed by the press. Not on the eve of a gubernatorial campaign," Gretchen said stiffly, spots of color rising in her cheeks.

The words chilled Cheramie, breaking through her alcoholic haze. She scooped up her mink coat and swept out of the room. Henry, a Lachman chauffeur, waited to take her to the party at the Fairmont, and she rode in stony silence, mulling over Gretchen's last words. When Henry held open the door, he took her arm and started for the door of the hotel.

"I'm fine, Henry!" She yanked her arm free and swept into the Fairmont. Instead of navigating the doors, she miscalculated and bumped into the doorman, who turned scarlet and apologized.

"Miss Lachman, I'm sorry—"

She ignored him and entered the hotel. Glancing at the coffee shop, she swayed in indecision, realizing she'd had too many drinks, too little food. She lurched to the elevators and stepped inside just as the doors were closing. The only passenger was a handsome man in a tux. She dropped her purse, and he stooped to pick it up.

The swift rise of the elevator made her head spin, and she clutched the handrail and closed her eyes.

"Here's your purse. Are you all right?"

"Yes, thank you," she said abruptly. The elevator

stopped, and he waited. She started out, brushed the doors with her shoulder, and missed a step. A firm hand steadied her, and she looked up at the stranger from the elevator.

"Want to join me? Let's have a cup of coffee before you go to the party." She looked at a face that seemed vaguely familiar. He was handsome with a thatch of brown hair, blue eyes, and a faint smile lifting the corners of his mouth.

"I'm late."

He leaned closer, a twinkle in his eyes. "Maybe better late and sober."

"Are you saying I'm drunk?"

"Never in the next million years would I say that to a beautiful woman. Let's get a cup of coffee," he said, his fingers cupping her elbow.

"I really should—"

"You really should have a cup of coffee. Trust me," he said in a cajoling, sexy voice that ended her protests.

"You'll be more interesting than the dull politicians I have to meet."

He laughed, steering her to the elevator. She was amused and curious. He stirred her interest with his aggressive confidence. She usually gave the orders, but he had easily gotten his way. In the restaurant he led her to a table, and in seconds steaming cups of coffee lay before them.

"This is a terrible way to meet someone. You'll think the worst of me."

He grinned, with even white teeth showing. "Because you're late for your father's party?"

"You know who I am?"

"Of course." He held his hand across the table. "I'm Phillip Walcott."

"Should I know you? I seem to be doing everything wrong." When she took his hand, his strong fingers closed around hers, and then he suddenly looked at her palm.

"I read palms." He held her hand in his, gazing up with a lowered head. "Want yours read?"

"Yes," she answered, her curiosity stirred once again, aware through the alcoholic fog of his thumb running lightly back and forth across her knuckles.

"You're impulsive, beautiful. There's a man in your future who has brown hair and blue eyes and wants to take you to dinner tomorrow night. And you'll go with him."

She laughed, enjoying his smile. His voice changed. "What about it, Cheramie? Want to go to dinner?"

"I know you now—you're in the assembly. Oh, God, you're a—"

His eyes twinkled. "A dull politician," he said, quoting her. "I'll try to change your opinion of us."

"You're Phillip Cade Walcott the Third. Your grandfather founded the Walcott hotels. And your father is Judge Walcott," she said, seeing a family resemblance now, thinking of Judge Walcott, whom Rutger claimed was one of the most powerful judges in the state.

"That's right. I've heard about you, but we haven't officially met until tonight."

Phillip's hand still held hers, his thumb moving over her fingers. She withdrew her hand and sipped the hot coffee.

"You're going to think the worst of me. I've been to a party, but I know that's a poor excuse." She shrugged.

"I don't think the worst. Far from it, Cheramie. But reporters might make something of it. Your father should have a good campaign."

She tilted her head to study him. "Spoken like a man who has a personal interest."

"I'll support your father. I may want his support soon."

She didn't want to admit that she knew nothing about Rutger's campaign except the fact that he was running for governor. "I hear Salvadore Giavotella will be difficult to beat."

"He's a popular man, particularly in northern California."

"And he has charisma."

"Brains and drive can overshadow charisma."

"Said by a man who has more than his fair share," she said, enjoying flirting with him.

A faint smile played across his mouth as he watched her. "Thank you. That's a compliment I'll treasure."

"So you're into politics."

"It's a challenge," he answered. "What challenges you,

Cheramie?'' he asked in a soft voice, making her intensely conscious of his appealing good looks.

"Exciting, powerful men," she replied evenly.

"And do we have a dinner date tomorrow night?" he asked, giving her another lazy come-hither look while he waited for her answer.

"Yes. And I better go to the party now. Rutger will be furious as it is.''

"I suspect you can handle the situation. You aren't exactly trembling with fear." He stood up to take her arm.

Phillip Walcott moved close to her, his fingers light on her arm. She was aware of his height, glancing up at him as they talked while they went to the elevator and rode up to the ballroom. Band music could be heard above the noise of several hundred people talking. At the door she stopped him. "Thank you, Phillip, for taking me for coffee. It helped immeasurably.''

He ran his fingers along her arm lightly. "Let me take you home after the party.''

"I'd like that. If you want to be a white knight one more time, come with me to greet Rutger. He'll be far less scathing if someone is with me.''

"Here he comes, and he's all smiles. Good evening, Mr. Lachman.''

"Phillip, good to see you. And finally, Cheramie. Do you and Phillip know each other—I suppose you do, since you were standing talking.''

"We met downstairs," she said. Within minutes she noticed that Rutger was on his best behavior, whether for Phillip's benefit or for anyone observing his actions, she didn't know; but she realized he liked Phillip.

When Rutger left them Phillip steered her toward the long tables ladened with ice sculptures of swans and fish and with steaming silver bowls of food, platters heaped with shrimp and golden chicken, sparkling crystal compotes of fruit. They paused to talk to Senator Welby and then Cecily Britt, the golden-haired actress, who tried to monopolize Phillip.

White-coated waiters passed silver trays of drinks, and

after half an hour Cheramie separated from Phillip. Several times during the evening she saw him in serious discussion with Rutger. When she had a chance she observed Phillip unobtrusively, deciding he was more handsome than any other man present. When he laughed, his smile was dazzling. He had perfect white teeth, and appealingly masculine creases bracketed his mouth. He was a natural with people. As he worked the room, he attracted attention. Women hovered near him, men listened to what he had to say, and Alette decided the wrong man was running for governor.

Intrigued and stirred out of the haze of boredom that usually possessed her at one of Rutger's parties, she wanted to know Phillip Walcott better. She knew he was the oldest son of a family who had hotels all over the world. He was one of the youngest men ever elected to the California State Assembly, a conservative like Rutger. She was accustomed to wealthy, powerful men, charming men, but seldom had she met a man who was all three at once until Phillip Walcott. And their meeting was a bad start—she drunk and he helping her sober up enough to attend her father's party. She groaned inwardly, smiling at something Lars Mason was saying to her even though she didn't have the slightest inkling what it was.

Phillip Walcott was taking her home after dinner.

Later she was talking to Deke Martin when Rutger joined them. She watched Phillip talking to a group of men. "Rutger," she said, "I'd like to work on your campaign. Is there something I can do at your headquarters?"

He stared at her. "Cheramie, I've never known you to give a damn about politics."

"You don't want me to help campaign for you?"

"Of course, I do. You've been on enough charity committees. I'll ask Lydia Ritter to find you a job."

"I'd like that very much," she answered, and Rutger looked beyond her. She followed his gaze to see him studying Phillip.

"I'll find you a place," he said, and his shrewdness surprised her.

"Thank you. Alette is in Utah."

"Is that right?" he asked. "She'll come around." He gazed over her head, and she suspected that was all he was going to say on the subject of Paul Simmons.

"If you two will excuse me, I need to speak to Sally Carson." She moved away, leaving them to discuss polls while she talked to Sally about lunch tomorrow. As Sally left Phillip appeared, his fingers touching Cheramie's arm.

"There you are. I thought perhaps you had forgotten me."

"I doubt if there's a time in your life when a woman has forgotten you," she said lightly, and he laughed.

"Ready to go? If you are, we'll say good night to Rutger."

She nodded, and in half an hour they drove to a supper club in Sausalito, where they could look across the water at the lights of San Francisco. A few couples danced while Cheramie and Phillip lost themselves in conversation. When he finally asked her to dance, she rose eagerly. He held her close as they swayed together. She was aware of his warmth, of a scent that was inviting, of the soft wool of his suit.

It was two in the morning before they drove to her home, and Cheramie's mind was racing as she listened to Phillip talk. She sensed that she should be cautious. He already might have a warped opinion of her because of the way they met, so when he walked her to her door, she turned to face him, offering her hand.

"Thank you for rescuing me earlier this evening. Now that I'm cold sober, it's very embarrassing to look back, but you saved me from trouble."

Amusement tinged his voice as he took her hand in his. "I'm not invited inside?" he asked softly, brushing his fingers along her throat.

His touch made her tingle, and she wanted to close her eyes and yield to impulse, but she also wanted more than one night with Phillip Walcott. He intrigued her in a way few men had.

"It's very late, but I really do appreciate what you did."

"White knights usually get to kiss the fair damsel they rescue," he said, tilting up her chin and leaning down to brush her lips with his. Cheramie closed her eyes as his mouth settled firmly on hers. His arms held her lightly while he slowly kissed her.

Breathless, she pulled away. She wanted to walk back into his arms and stay, but caution prevailed. "It was fun, Phillip."

"And we have a dinner date tomorrow night. I'll pick you up at seven."

She nodded. "Good night." She went inside, locking the door and smiling in anticipation, thinking about Phillip.

The next afternoon she began work at her father's head-quarters, but to her disappointment Phillip Walcott did not appear. She went home early to get ready for her date. By the time she had made a decision to wear a red wool Ungaro, the chairs were littered with dresses.

When the doorbell rang, Cheramie was waiting eagerly. Her heartbeat quickened when Phillip flashed his winning smile. A dark suit added to his handsome appearance.

Cheramie stepped back. "Come inside. You know where I live, but I don't know where you live."

"You will before the evening's over," he said, his gaze raking over her. "I like your dress."

"Thank you," she said, moving ahead of him into the spacious living room that looked out over the bay.

"Nice view," he said from the living room doorway, leaning his shoulder against the jamb as he watched her.

"You're not looking at the view," she said with a laugh.

"I'm looking at the one I want to see," he said in a seductive voice that made her anticipation grow. As she picked up her purse, he glanced around. "This is nice, Chera-mie."

"It's comfortable and close enough to home."

She locked up, and as he held open the car door, he asked, "How about dinner in Sausalito?"

"Fine," she said, sliding onto the seat of his black Porsche. Campaign flyers for Rutger lay on the seat, and she picked one up. Phillip took it from her hands and tossed the stack into the back.

"You have more campaign literature than Rutger does. I don't know how much he'll campaign for himself."

"He's campaigning. I think he'll win by a big margin."

"If he loses, I'm packing and going to Europe until he cools down. You can't imagine how much he wants this."

"He's very businesslike in his approach to the campaign, but he doesn't look like a man desperate for victory. He may expect to win without question."

"No. I know my father. He won't expect it to fall into his lap without work."

"He's got a good staff. He'll carry his party and win in the primary. Then I hope he can destroy Sal Giavotella."

"I don't ever remember meeting his opponent."

"Another dull politician, eh?" Phillip asked with a grin. The light from the dash highlighted his cheekbones, and she was intensely aware of him, her gaze drifting down over his chest and long legs while she wondered what he would be like in bed.

She laughed. "Will I ever live that down! After meeting you, never again as long as I live will I talk about dull politicians!"

"Thank you. Sal Giavotella moves in different circles from the Lachmans," Phillip said, returning to the subject. He drove fast, weaving through traffic. "I knew him in high school; we both played football. He was tough then, though I didn't know him very well. Don't let his size fool you— he's a natural athlete. He played baseball, too. He went to USC."

"I've heard he's much younger than Rutger and has five small children, which may appeal to voters."

"He's one year younger than I am. Thirty-three. And I've been told his father once worked for your father."

"I don't know," she answered with a shrug. "That's so much younger than Rutger."

"Rutger's experience will offset that."

"Will you run for another term?"

"I'll run again for some office. I told you, I like the challenge of politics. What do you like to do, Cheramie?"

While she answered, he parked and took her arm to enter an Italian restaurant perched over the water, where they sat on the deck and watched the lights across the bay. They talked and let most of the enticing Caesar salads, Milanese stuffed veal, and Sicilian cheesecake go untouched. Afterward he took her to the Carnelian Room, and over drinks they talked and looked out at the glittering city and the tall spire of the Transamerica Pyramid. He parked on the street, and they entered his third-story condominium on Telegraph Hill. She moved to the window of the darkened living room; the only light shone from the entry hall.

"Your view is better than mine," she said dryly. "No wonder you didn't bother to look out."

"That isn't why I didn't look out your window," he said softly, coming to stand behind her, his hands on her shoulders and his breath fanning the back of her neck. He brushed his lips across her nape. "I'll get us a drink."

He moved to the bar, and she glanced around the elegant room at the Louis XV giltwood furniture, matching ormolu-mounted commodes flanking the marble fireplace. She knew his family was as wealthy as Rutger and his father had connections all over the state and in Washington.

She watched Phillip mix drinks after tossing his jacket over a chair. Loosening his tie, he handed her a drink.

"Here's to a fun evening."

"It has been," she said, touching her glass to his and taking a drink of Scotch and soda.

Setting his glass on a table, he took hers from her hands. Cheramie's heart raced as she gazed up into his eyes. His arm slipped around her waist, and he pulled her close.

She wrapped her arms around his narrow waist and lifted her mouth to meet his. She was impressed with him, more so than other men she knew. But she felt a need for caution. She didn't want Phillip Walcott to lose interest. She intended to stop his lovemaking soon, but when he tugged the zipper to her dress, she was lost in his kisses. Her dress fell around her ankles.

"Phillip, I must—" She broke off her words when she gazed into his eyes and saw the expression on his face. He slipped his finger beneath her bra and pushed it down, bending his head to kiss her breast, taking a nipple in his teeth. She closed her eyes and gasped with pleasure, winding her fingers in his thick hair.

They made love on the carpet, her climax coming quickly and wildly as she clung to him. Later she lay with her head on his chest while his breathing slowed to normal.

"Want to go to lunch?" he asked.

"Now?"

He chuckled and ran his fingers through her curls, pushing her up so he could look at her. Cheramie gazed down at him, thinking he was the most handsome man she had known and one of the most sensual.

"No, Cheramie, love, lunch. As in noon tomorrow." He stroked her lightly while his gaze roamed over her. "And dinner tomorrow night."

"I have a date," she answered with a faint smile.

"Break it."

She wondered just how important Phillip Walcott would be in her life. "All right," she said. His smile vanished as he pulled her down; her soft breasts pressed against him while he kissed her.

They had lunch and dinner, but when he asked her out the following night, she said she had another date. Other men paled in comparison to Phillip, and late Monday afternoon when he walked through the door of Rutger's campaign headquarters, her heart missed a beat. He crossed the room to her desk.

"Hard at work to elect the next governor of California?"

"Yes indeed. I was beginning to think you'd never darken the door."

He sat on the edge of her desk, his foot swinging as he looked down at her. "How about dinner?"

"That would be nice."

"How soon can you get off?"

"Since I'm the daughter of the candidate, I think I can leave right now," she replied.

"Good. Let's go."

She picked up her purse, told her fellow workers good-bye, and saw her friend Helen's gaze drift over Phillip before they turned for the door. She caught him winking at Helen.

"How long have you known Helen?" she asked as they stepped outside.

"Since the campaign started. Jealous, I hope?"

She laughed. "Not exactly. My father needs eager volunteers like her. I just saw you wink."

"I do that with all pretty women. It's a natural reflex." He linked his arm through hers and winked at her, making her laugh. She felt bubbly with him, a feeling no man had stirred in her for a long time. Phillip Walcott was a challenge, and she intended to make him a part of her life.

On the eighth floor above the streams of traffic on Market Street, Jeff O'Neil leaned back in his chair while he studied several brochures. He pushed them aside and ten minutes later left the office and made his way through the crowd along the sidewalk. As he walked he enjoyed the spectacular view of the bay snapped by tourists who had a tripod blocking the walk. Cable cars clanged at the next intersection. He saw his reflection in the windows of crowded shops he remembered as a kid while his long legs took the steep hills in an effortless stride.

In front of a corner restaurant he waited in the sunshine. He grinned when he caught sight of a familiar head of black curly hair in the throng of pedestrians.

Darkly handsome with swarthy skin and black eyes, Salvadore Giavotella approached Jeff, his white teeth flashing in a broad grin as he extended his hand.

"Good to see you. I didn't think you'd ever be back here. But then I didn't guess I'd be running for governor."

"It's home, and I'm going to help you win."

"I'm glad. We'll have a hell of a campaign. The city is a little fancier than when you left, I imagine."

"It looks the same, it smells the same, and it sounds the same," Jeff replied as they went inside. He spoke to the hostess, who seated them at a table beside a smudged window. As soon as Jeff sat down and ordered black coffee, he gazed at Sal. "How's Gina and the family?"

"They're fine. I told her I'm having lunch with you, and she wants me to ask you for Saturday night dinner."

"That would be nice, but please, no blind dates. How old are the kids now? And how's Jeffie? I still can't believe there's a little kid named after me."

"Gina and I got an early start, remember. Jeffie's twelve. Here are their pictures," Sal said, pulling out a wallet that was filled with photographs of his five children. He glanced up. "I'm really glad you came back to help with the campaign."

"Texas didn't hold much for me anymore. There were more reasons to come home."

"I'm damn glad my campaign was one of them!" His features sobered. "Governor Giavotella. I want it, Jeff, just as much as I used to want money. If I get through the primary next week, and if Rutger Lachman wins, we'll be running against each other."

"I'll campaign like hell for you against that bastard."

"Hey, Friday night is a fund-raiser, a black-tie dinner dance. I bought several tickets to support the cause and for political exposure, but we can't go because one of Gina's cousins is getting married that day. We both think you should go."

"Black tie?"

"It'll do you good to meet people if you're going to live here. Here are the tickets."

"Sure. Thanks."

They paused to order, and then Sal studied Jeff. "Sorry about your arm. You had a career and a half in pro ball."

Jeff shook his head. "Like father, like son."

"Only your injury won't incapacitate you for life. You've been good to your folks, Jeff. I hear about them from Dad."

"It's better for them now."

"Understatement of the year. Sometimes I wonder how we survived as kids. See, I still have my scar from that fight with the King brothers." He turned his head and pointed to a faint mark along his neck behind his ear. "You still have yours?"

Jeff held up his hand to expose a scar from wrist to his knuckle. "That and others. I had more fights than you did because you were older, bigger, and you moved away from the neighborhood when you were sixteen."

"Do you remember the night the warehouse burned?" Sal asked.

"I think I do, but I was only three. I remember flames and smoke, my mother crying. The ambulance came, and I remember my father lying still while men leaned over him and then took him away." Jeff looked out the window. "That's partly why I came back. I've always thought that someday Rutger Lachman should pay for that night. Maybe now I'm in a position to fix that."

"You better have an army if you're going after him. Unless you take out a contract."

Jeff smiled at Sal. "No contract. I want to go after him myself. A man like Rutger Lachman is vulnerable somewhere."

"You've never really known if he set that fire; they never caught the arsonist."

Jeff arched an eyebrow. "What do you think?"

"Hell, all I know is what my dad says. I was just six years old myself. You and I really don't know anything about it."

"I know my Dad was crippled that night after chasing the arsonist inside a burning building, and I know that Rutger Lachman bought him out of the partnership at the rate they had paid when they went together into the business. Dad got his half of the insurance money, but Lachman wanted out of the partnership and talked Dad into selling cheap, for almost nothing, when actually Lachman had new business lined up. He cheated Dad out of a big commission, an account Dad had called on before the fire. Dad has always said Rutger Lachman set the blaze.''

"That's what my pop has said, too. Lachman is one of the most powerful men in the country now. From a failing jelly business, he's the largest food wholesaler in the state. And that's only part of it.'' Sal wiped his mouth, and his eyes twinkled. ''Well, helping me beat him in the gubernatorial race is one good way you can get back at him.''

"I want more than that. And I'll get him.''

"Unless you do something physical or help me beat him in politics, I can't think of anything vulnerable about Lachman. He's like the rock of Gibraltar. Invincible.''

"No, he's not. No business is invincible.'' Jeff paused while a platter of steaming ribs was placed in front of him and fries and a hamburger in front of Sal, who grinned at him.

"Sure it wasn't your head that got the blow and not your arm? You're talking about the biggest food wholesaler in the state, plus he has land holdings, the original jelly business, and I've heard he's into oil now. There's also the Lachman Real Estate chain. No way you can touch that.''

"I have an idea. I've been looking at several companies to buy, and I think I've found a likely prospect. Jayton Foods.''

"Jayton Foods is for sale?''

"Richard Jayton wants to retire.''

"That's a big company. It's territory goes to the Mississippi, doesn't it?''

"Not every state, but they're in fifteen. I can swing it. It would be a direct competitor of Lachman Foods.''

"Jayton is probably giving him competition now. I'm surprised Lachman isn't trying to buy it.''

"I don't think it's public knowledge yet that Jayton may be on the bargaining block. What I'm wondering is whether there is a possibility you and I can work out a deal. If you're interested in politics, are you interested in selling your trucking company?''

"Jesus, how much money did you make throwing a ball?''

Jeff laughed and gazed out the window. "It was good. And

I was fortunate in my investments. I haven't touched a lot of what I made. My injury earned me more."

"Do you know how large my company is now?"

"Yes," Jeff said, "as a matter of fact, I do."

"Okay," Sal said, scratching his jaw. "I don't want to sell. I don't want out completely. But it's true that I don't want the day-to-day running of the company. My future is politics."

"What do you think about a merger?"

Sal stared at him, and Jeff waited, thinking his friend had changed little since their days at USC. "How do I know you can run a business?"

"You don't, except for my investments, which I handled. The only other thing I've ever done is play baseball."

Sal stared at him, and Jeff waited quietly. He took the check when the waiter came, and as he placed some money on the tray, Sal drummed his fingers on the table.

"Jeff, I'll give it thought. You won't want to merge and my men run the company. I know you want control."

"You're right. A reasonable amount. A food wholesaler and a truck company could do well together. And the part that isn't concerned with food, you can leave to your men. If you like the idea, we'll get down to figures."

Sal grinned. "I'm always open to suggestion when it comes to making a buck. Let's talk next week. How about my office next Wednesday? You bring your proposal. In the meantime, I'll see you Saturday night about seven."

"Tell Gina I'm almost engaged to a woman in Texas."

"She has some good-looking friends."

"Sal."

"Okay. It's your life."

Jeff strode back to his new office, glancing at the tall building that offered him a view of the bay from his small room on the eighth floor. He turned to look at the tall spires of the Golden Gate Bridge thrusting up through a long white streamer of fog. He raised and lowered his arm several times, wondering if he could ever straighten it out again completely and if the dull aches would end. Reaching for the phone, he

thought about the fund-raiser and the few women he still
knew in San Francisco.

Within minutes he had a date with Mitzi Corning, an old
friend from high school and someone who loved sailing as
much as he did. He had already joined the Sausalito Yacht
Club, and he had signed on a crew to race Saturday.

Friday night he held Mitzi's elbow lightly as they entered
the ballroom for the dinner dance. A vision in blue, with her
blond hair piled high on her head, Mitzi took his hand as she
introduced him to all the people she knew.

Thirty minutes later he caught her arm. "Stop. I've met
more people than I can remember."

"I know how well you remember names. And you need to
get settled here."

"I don't have to meet everyone in an hour."

She laughed and accepted a martini from a waiter while
Jeff ordered a vodka and tonic.

"Mitzi—"

Jeff turned to see a dark-haired woman gazing at him with
a look of blatant speculation in her eyes.

"You have someone new with you," she said in a throaty
voice that was as inviting as the look in her eyes.

"Cheramie, meet Jeff O'Neil. Jeff, this is Cheramie Lachman."

"How do you do," he said quietly, letting his gaze run
swiftly over her shapely curves. With a sensuous curiosity in
her brown eyes, she offered her hand.

"How do you do, Jeff O'Neil. Have you just moved to
San Francisco?"

"He played ball, Cheramie," Mitzi said.

Without taking her eyes from Jeff, Cheramie said, "I don't
know much about football."

"It was baseball," Mitzi answered impatiently.

"I grew up here," he said, amused that she didn't have
an inkling who he was or that their fathers were once partners.

"What a shame we haven't met before then," she said,
smiling at him. "Have you found a home?"

"I have an apartment."

"When I moved back a couple of years ago after college, I had a dreadful time finding the right place, but now I'm on Green Street in an old house I've done over. I had to have a house. Apartments make me feel caged; do they you?"

"No, but then I grew up in a small apartment."

"Oh?" She blinked and glanced around. "I see Milton, and I think he's searching for me. Please excuse me."

They nodded as she left, and Mitzi wound her arm through his. "I thought she was going to put you in her purse and take you home with her."

"I thought so, too, until I told her I lived in a small apartment," he said, laughing and draping his arm across Mitzi's shoulders.

"Wait until she finds out more about you."

He watched Cheramie walk away from him, her hips twitching in an inviting manner. "Would that be so bad?"

Mitzi shrugged. "It depends on your taste. Unless you changed a lot when you were gone—you'd love it. I haven't seen many men who weren't taken with Cheramie if she wanted them to be, but they have to have Papa's approval if they last long."

"He runs his children's lives?"

"You know the Lachmans?"

"I know about them," he said carefully.

"Cheramie is the oldest. Aubrey next, and then Alette. He doesn't run Aubrey Lachman's life. I know he does the girls'. I don't know Alette very well, because she's younger and she doesn't socialize like Cheramie. But I do know she doesn't draw men like a magnet the way Cheramie does."

"Not all men. Want to dance?"

"I thought you'd never ask!"

Saturday morning, with Mitzi cheering on the sidelines, Jeff crewed on a yacht, the *Ingrid*, which got off to the best start, but on the last leg of the course on the choppy bay, a blue-and-white boat, the *Catbird*, passed them. Within minutes the *Ingrid* caught up, the two sailing side by side. The skipper of the *Ingrid* called out orders to tack when Jeff wouldn't have, and he watched the *Catbird* do exactly what he would have done, sail straight on. Within minutes the

Ingrid tried to compensate, but it was too late. The *Catbird* was ahead and crossed the finish line.

"Who's skipper of the *Catbird*?"

"Guy named Aubrey Lachman."

"One of *the* Lachmans?"

"Sort of," Kyle Davis, the skipper, answered as he handled the tiller. "He's the son, but he doesn't get along with the old man. He's disinherited and unacknowledged. Knows boats. He's a good broker."

Jeff gazed at the other boat, watching it being maneuvered toward the dock in Sausalito. Later in the day in the yacht club, Aubrey paused beside him at the bar, and Mitzi introduced them. "Aubrey, meet Jeff O'Neil. Jeff, this is Aubrey Lachman."

Jeff offered his hand. "Congratulations on winning the race."

"Thanks. It was close," he said in an offhand manner that was so far removed from his father's imperious manner, Jeff was surprised.

"It wasn't really close, but you did what I would have done if I'd had my own boat," he said, gazing into blue eyes and seeing only a faint resemblance to the father. Aubrey's features were less bold, his nose was thin, his face longer and freckled, yet he had the same jaw, the same golden looks.

Aubrey tilted his head. "You're *the* Jeff O'Neil. I saw you play once in the Astrodome, and you were good."

"Thanks."

"Sorry about your arm. Want to look at the *Catbird*?"

"Sure."

They walked outside, and wind buffeted them. It was chilly coming off the bay in spite of bright sunshine and a clear afternoon. The water was choppy, and the yacht bobbed in its slip. Halyards clicked and rattled all along the row of berths as the tall masts rocked slightly.

They stepped on board a Reliance 12. Aubrey talked about the light displacement and the high-performance laminate with thirty layers of Lyasil at the keel bolts.

"Your other boat is close. You should see it, Jeff," Mitzi said.

"If you're interested—"

"Sure," Jeff answered, and the three strolled down the dock to a yacht named *Easy*, a Hatteras 65.

"The *Catbird* is my weekend racer. This is home," Aubrey said. The three looked at the elegant salon with a foam-padded mast, Oriental rugs, and cushioned settees. The over-size master stateroom held a king-size bed.

"This is marvelous. No wonder you live here," Jeff said.

"It's designed to be a heavy-displacement boat that will sail well. It's damned comfortable, and I can go where I want."

While the men talked, Mitzie prowled the boat on her own. As the two men looked over the extra-large engine room, the twin diesels with reversible-pitch propellers, Jeff was aware of a close scrutiny from Aubrey.

"This is a damned fine yacht."

"I think so. Funny you're here. We're the Lachman-O'Neil Jelly Company kids. That was before my time and yours, too, but I remember hearing about those days."

"I'm surprised your father talks about us."

"He doesn't. I heard from others and from my mother before she died. Our fathers didn't get along."

"You could say so, yes," Jeff said with sarcasm.

"Well, I don't get along much better with Rutger, so we have that in common."

As they continued touring the boat, Jeff studied him, wondering what had alienated him from his father. When they finished the tour he turned to Aubrey. "Thanks for showing me the yacht."

"Aubrey sells them," Mitzi said, joining them. "He's not your typical salesman," she added, and received a grin.

"When I have more time, I'd like to talk to you about buying one," Jeff said. "I've always dreamed of owning my own."

"Sure. I'll be happy to try to find what you want."

They walked back to the club and parted, and Jeff took Mitzi home. He couldn't help thinking about the Lachmans. He was glad Aubrey didn't get along with his father because he had liked Aubrey in the first meeting, and he wanted to contact him about a boat.

The Giavotellas' house, atop a steep hill, was almost an hour's drive from the city. The yard was landscaped with neat plantings, and fancy boxes of flowers with toys tumbled across the grass. He stepped over a tricycle and went up the walk.

The chimes rang, the door opened, and he faced a short, slightly plump, dark-haired woman. Gina Giavotella hugged him, her black eyes sparkling as she took his hand. His glance raked over her red dress and frilly white apron. "You're prettier than ever."

"What a liar the man is!" she said, laughing and patting her rounded hip. "Pounds and pounds since I saw you. Here's Jeffie, Doreen, Ladd, and Tommy. Children, I want you to meet Mr. O'Neil."

He shook hands with a solemn, black-eyed Jeffie as he said hello to ten-year-old Doreen, six-year-old Ladd, and a chubby four-year-old Tommy, who was more concerned with a toy truck in his hands.

"The baby, Melissa, is in bed," Gina said, taking Jeff's arm and leading him to a spacious living room that reflected Sal's taste. The furniture was Spanish, large carved pieces of dark wood that were as rugged and flamboyant as Sal. A gun rack lined one wall, and Jeff remembered Sal's love of guns, a hobby Sal couldn't afford when they were younger. When he glanced at the expensive, bold paintings and masculine decor, Jeff wondered if Gina had selected one thing in the room. Tempting aromas of lasagna and baked bread assailed him as he faced a slender blonde who was seated on the sofa.

"This is my friend, a neighbor, Linda Ford. Linda, meet Jeff O'Neil."

"Hi," he said, glancing at Sal, who rolled his eyes toward the ceiling.

"I've been hearing about you," Linda said. "I saw when you played against New Orleans one time. Your team will have a tough season next year."

To his surprise, she was interested in baseball and was knowledgeable about the teams. Sal fixed drinks, and in a short time Jeff held Tommy on his lap while Linda told him about her job as a real estate broker.

Once, after dinner, when he was in the kitchen pouring another cup of coffee, Gina came into the room. She moved close to him. "See," she whispered, "I told Sal you'd like Linda. She loves baseball, you love baseball—"

"And you're a hopeless matchmaker," he whispered in return.

Shaking curls away from her face, she laughed and punched his side. "Maybe. Everyone should have somebody. I'm lost without Sal."

"You both look great," he said, knowing Sal and Gina had gone together since ninth grade and married two weeks before they graduated from high school.

She looked up at him solemnly as he stirred in a teaspoon of sugar. "Any chance you can talk him out of this governor's race?"

Startled, Jeff studied her. "You don't want him to run?"

Her face flushed and she glanced at the door in a furtive manner that added to his surprise, and he realized things between Gina and Sal might have changed in the years he had been away from them. Her dark eyes were filled with worry when she turned back. "You know Sal. Once he wants something, he goes after it one hundred percent. This scares me."

"He was that way about his business and you both did fine, Gina."

"Yes, but it was business. It wasn't women groupies and the public and all kinds of commitments. People wanting him twenty-four hours. Can you do something, Jeff?"

"I don't know," he said, wishing she weren't trying to put him in the middle. "How often has anyone changed Sal's mind?"

She bit her lip. "I guess never."

"Maybe you're worrying needlessly. A campaign is strenuous."

"It hasn't even really started," she said with such bitterness that his surprise deepened.

"Gina, have you really let him know how you feel?"

She looked away. "I shouldn't pull you into this, but don't encourage him, Jeff."

"Tell him exactly how you feel."

"Sal says you might have a business deal," she said as if she wanted to change the subject.

"I hope so."

"Want us to throw in four kids and a baby?"

He smiled, but he was worried about her, and he felt the jest was an attempt to return to a lightheartedness she didn't really feel. "I know how long you'd agree to that. They're cute kids."

"I'm going to keep them. Take the lady home, Jeff."

"I was going to offer."

"Sorry. Sal says I'm too bossy. He says I'm the one who should run for governor. Let's get back." As she started out, he touched her arm lightly.

"I like you both. Tell him you don't want him to run. Do it soon, Gina."

"You know Sal. I might as well try to stop a charging bull." She moved ahead of him to the living room.

They talked until midnight, when Jeff took Linda home. He meant to kiss her good night and go, but it was dawn when he left. He drove through empty streets and on impulse turned and headed down to the pier, where restaurants and gift shops were dark and closed; a derelict was asleep on a bench. In the silence, Jeff's shoes on the concrete were loud, the only other sound the steady lap of waves against the pilings. He paused to lean his arm on a fence and stare at the spot that now held a warehouse. Years ago on that spot had stood a dilapidated jelly factory with three wooden buildings. He had lived with his parents in one of them until the night the factory burned.

He gazed out to sea, the water blurring with sky along the horizon. He had met two Lachmans, a son and daughter, but he hadn't seen Rutger Lachman since his return to San Francisco. He remembered the old frustrations, the anger and hurt of seeing his father incapacitated and growing bitter over the years, his mother working hard to give him an education. He remembered the times spent along the wharves, the fights, the games, later the girls. He had wanted to escape that life. He took a deep breath, smelling the sea, remembering and relishing the knowledge that not only was he out of the old way of life, but he had been able to get his parents out, too. Wind swept over him, carrying the smell of fish and water while he stood quietly lost in memories. Despite all the hardships, he was a man for the sea. He loved it, and he loved his hometown. And it was time to right some old wrongs.

Jeff turned away to climb back into his car and drive home.

Wednesday he met with Sal. One month later he bought Jayton Foods, and two months later he sat down with Sal to sign papers that would merge the two companies, the food wholesaler and the trucking company. Jeff became CEO of Jayton Foods while Timothy Kramer, one of Sal's top men, was promoted to president of Sunshine Trucks.

In October Jeff attended a political meeting between opposing candidates speaking to the longshoreman's union. He was in the meeting hall when the camera crews arrived from the first television station on the scene.

Jeff thrust out his hand. "I'm—"

"You're Jeff O'Neil, aren't you?" the man said, studying Jeff as he shook hands.

"Yes. Who's in charge here?"

"I am. John Kincaid. I heard you're living here now. Ever think about an interview? We'd like to have you on our early morning show."

"Thanks. Let's worry about that after the campaign. I'm part of the Giavotella staff. We didn't know which auditorium would hold the meeting. There are two—this one and another one on the east end of the building."

"It's this one. The west end. At least that's what my letter said. There's plenty of time yet," Kincaid said. "Once we get set up, everyone will know which auditorium."

"Sal Giavotella is in the other auditorium. Would you like an interview before we start the meeting?"

"Yes, we would. I'd like it if you'll talk to us a few minutes, too."

"Sure, but focus on Sal. He's the man of the hour."

Jeff left in long strides, knowing Sal would welcome the exposure and knowing that Rutger Lachman and his men should have arrived and probably were ensconced down the hall, where a crowd was gathering. Howard Westerman, Sal's press secretary, came striding toward him.

"KTOB is here," Jeff said. "The meeting is in the west auditorium."

"Shit."

"Howard, get Sal there right now, and they'll interview him before the meeting."

Howard's frown vanished and he was gone down the hall at a jog. "Will do!" floated behind him.

Jeff went back to wait, swinging shut the auditorium door behind him, wondering how long Sal would have on camera.

"He's on his way here," he said to John as the cameraman hoisted a minicam to his shoulder.

"We can start taping with you, Mr. O'Neil. Okay?"

Jeff answered the usual questions about leaving baseball, getting in a plug for Sal. Within minutes Sal, accompanied by Hal and Blake Dorth, his stocky campaign manager, came striding in. Jeff introduced him to the cameraman and went into the hall to wait, exultant that Sal would get the extra exposure.

Almost five minutes later a tall man in a navy suit strode toward the door. "Is the meeting here?" Gold cuff links flashed as he waved his hand.

"Yes, but right now they're busy in there."

"But the meeting is going to be in here?" he persisted, looking around impatiently.

"Yes," Jeff answered, leaning back against the wall.

"Who's in there now?"

Jeff gazed at him blandly, waiting a moment before he answered. "One of the candidates."

"Giavotella? He's *busy*? What's he doing? Can I go in there?"

Stalling for every second he could give Sal, Jeff looked at his watch. "He's talking to the men from station KTOB."

"He has an interview?" the man asked sharply.

"No. He's here for the meeting. The crew was setting up—"

The man swore and rushed away. In minutes men came

hurrying down the hall, some of Sal's men trailing along with the Lachman supporters.

Even if Jeff hadn't seen his picture on the news and on political signs, he would have recognized Rutger instantly. He had changed little from the man Jeff remembered, only now he didn't loom as a giant. Jeff was now as tall as Rutger. Still handsome, aloof, with an arrogance that showed in his walk, Rutger Lachman looked as if he owned the world. He brushed past Jeff and strode into the auditorium, and in seconds he was on camera along with Sal.

When the meeting started, Jeff stepped to the back of the auditorium while cameras taped the talks. The door squeaked and Cheramie Lachman entered, casually dressed in a yellow skirt, sweater, and a leather jacket. She moved down the center aisle and slid onto an empty seat beside the Lachman man Jeff had talked to in the hall. For the next few minutes the two carried on a whispered conversation.

As the candidates got into questions and answers, Jeff sat in the back row, deciding that Sal was reaching the audience better than Rutger. There was a rough element to Sal that made him more of an ordinary guy than Rutger Lachman, who looked and sounded as if he belonged on Wall Street. Sal could talk about the lean years and hard, physical work, and when the issue of new taxes was raised, Sal was on home ground.

"We can make changes elsewhere in the budget. We need to concentrate on better mass transit for the state, more port development here at home—"

This brought a cheer, and Sal waited for several seconds before continuing, "But we can find the money in the budget!" Cheers came again.

When they were almost finished, Jeff went outside to wait until Sal wanted to leave. A mist fell, and he watched the shadowy shape of a tanker glide toward open water. Soon men poured out of the building. Only the union leaders remained behind with politicians and their supporters. The television crews filed out. The double doors burst open and a man came out beside Rutger Lachman; Cheramie was on the far side, and she didn't glance Jeff's way.

"Who the hell got him in for that interview?" Rutger snapped. At that moment he looked up at Jeff.

"Lachman!" Sal called, stepping outside.

Frowning, Rutger Lachman spun around, and Jeff wondered how often any man addressed Rutger in such an audacious manner.

"I want you to meet one of my campaigners. Actually, you know him. Jeff O'Neil." Sal approached, and Rutger glanced again at Jeff. He grudgingly thrust out his hand, and Jeff shook hands, feeling his gripped tightly, his aversion seeming to heighten with the physical contact.

"Jeff, you should remember Rutger Lachman," Sal said with a jovial voice.

"Barney's son?" Rutger's frown vanished, and he seemed to make a quick assessment as his glance flicked over Jeff. "You've grown up. I think of you as a kid. You did well pitching."

"Thanks."

"I've read about you. This is my daughter, Cheramie, and Assemblyman Phillip Walcott."

"We've met," Cheramie said as Jeff shook hands and greeted Phillip. "You know each other?" she asked, looking at Rutger.

"Yes, of course, Cheramie. Jeff is Barney O'Neil's son. From my first jelly plant. Lachman and O'Neil."

Cheramie focused curious brown eyes on Jeff. "We knew each other as children."

"You were only a baby."

"And now you're on the campaign trail," Rutger said, glancing momentarily at Sal. "You'll be busy with politics." He turned away, dismissing Jeff.

Jeff watched the sway of Cheramie's hips below the short jacket. As she turned to get into the waiting limo, she glanced back at him.

"I didn't even get introduced to the family," Sal said dryly. "She doesn't look like she's related to him."

"She is, though. It doesn't pay to forget."

"You've met before."

"Yes. But then she didn't pick up on the name. He didn't even tell me to say hello to my dad."

"You're expecting a lot. Made him mad as hell that I got the TV time." They headed toward the cars.

"You won the votes back there. You speak the same language as those men."

"It's odd how he seems to separate himself from the public. He came up the hard way."

"Icebergs are warmer if today was any indication. I hated him so much as a kid, I don't think I ever saw him as anything except a monster. If today is any example of how you're reaching voters, I think you're going to win."

Wind ruffled Sal's thick cap of curls. "Do you now?" he asked with amusement as they settled on the backseat of the car. "Since when did you reach that opinion?"

"Rutger Lachman seems formidable. You're young, inexperienced in politics, don't have some of the old politicians behind you. But after watching you on the road and during the campaign, I think people feel a tie with you. I know your stand on taxes is more popular than Rutger's vague answers. He knows how to field questions."

"I'm surprised he wants the office. He doesn't seem that much of a people person."

"He isn't. It's not people he's interested in. It's power. Election day is only two weeks away."

"Join us in the hotel suite at five. You can bring a date."

"Sal, if Gina fixes me up with any more women, I'll have to give them name tags to keep up with them."

"She wants you married and happy."

"She doesn't think I can meet women on my own?"

Sal laughed. "I can't control the woman."

"And so I have to be burdened with good-looking women. Okay, I'll be there on election night."

6

In the hotel suite Jeff watched television with the others while Sal paced the floor and popped his knuckles loudly.

"Sal, sit down. You're a wreck," Gina said.

"It helps to move around. Damn, this is going to be a long night." He paused beside the windows. "I wonder if the Lachmans are celebrating yet?"

"They don't have anything to celebrate," Howard said.

Sal looked at Jeff. "Still have the same opinion?"

Jeff nodded. "It'll be close, but I think you'll win. I think you'll carry northern California."

"I have to have more than northern California."

"The way you campaigned, you better win," Jeff said half in jest. He had joined Sal in several cities but would fly home often to see about business. It was a killer tour that took the stamina of someone robust with bulldog determination.

The local networks were all covering the election, and the polls would soon close. The news replayed the tape of Sal and Gina going to vote this morning.

They became silent as Rutger Lachman appeared and said a few polite words to the newsman before disappearing into the voting booth.

"It's time to go downstairs," Howard said, and they all stood up. Sal pulled on his coat, and Jeff watched him put on a confident air at the same time. His shoulders straightened, he combed his hair and stood tall while he adjusted his tie and smiled at his reflection.

In the big ballroom a mob of supporters cheered when Sal appeared. He moved through the crowd, shaking hands and hugging people, while Jeff worked his way to the sidelines where Linda waited. He glanced up at one of the monitors posted high so the crowd could view the election results. The polls had closed, and the first precincts were reporting. The Lachman party was on the other side of the block at the Marriott. Sal appeared confident and relaxed; Gina stood off to one side, her gaze on Sal, and Jeff wondered if she had ever let Sal know her feelings about his campaign. It was irrelevant now, but looking at the both of them, he wondered about their future. Gina's brow was furrowed, and lines bracketed her full mouth. Sal was radiant, with a white-toothed smile, moving constantly as if he had too much energy to stand still. A gubernatorial victory would change Gina's life. Looking at Sal, Jeff wondered how much it would change him.

A brief interview of the Lachmans came on television. A dark-haired woman stood beside Rutger Lachman and Cheramie. Jeff decided he was looking at the two Lachman daughters. There was a definite resemblance between them, but very little resemblance to their blond father. Jeff focused on the younger woman; she was slender, tall, and willowy, with a wholesome beauty that held none of the earthiness and come-hither look of her shorter sister. Even though their looks were different, both women would turn heads. The younger one had the same cool, detached, go-to-hell air about her that her father always exhibited. She seemed completely at ease, remote, and if it hadn't been such a gala occasion for her father, Jeff would say she appeared annoyed.

Rutger Lachman took the lead when the first precincts came in, and the exuberance of Sal's crowd diminished somewhat; but after the first thirty minutes the gap between the two men narrowed. While Sal looked self-assured, Jeff knew how he hated the moments when something was beyond his control.

By ten o'clock, with eighteen thousand votes in from three hundred and eighty-nine precincts, Sal led by four thousand votes. Linda had to go home early because she was catching an eleven-thirty flight to Los Angeles, and Jeff walked her out to her car, glad to escape the tension-filled ballroom. Cool wind blew against them as they stopped at her car, and he turned her to face him.

"I hope Sal wins. I wish I could stay to see, but I have an appointment in L.A. at seven-thirty in the morning."

"He'll win."

"It's close. You can't be sure about it. You're an optimist."

"It makes for a nicer life," he said lightly. "I'll call you when you get to the hotel and let you know." He leaned forward to kiss her until she pushed him away.

"I'll miss my plane." She unlocked the door, slid behind the wheel, and drove out of the lot. He stood watching her, his coat pushed open, his hands on his hips. He noticed some people across the lot and realized it was Chad Vickers, a boating friend, and his wife, Elena, walking with the youngest Lachman daughter. She parted from the couple a few seconds later and headed Jeff's way, the Vickers striding ahead. Chad caught sight of Jeff, and Jeff waved.

"Congratulations," Chad called. "See you Saturday at the race?"

"Thanks," Jeff answered, staring at the woman walking toward him. She was as willowy as she looked on television. She held herself gracefully, her long hair swinging with each step, her dark-eyed gaze finally meeting his. She looked at him, but instead of congratulating him, she walked past with her chin lifted, over to a Jaguar parked four spaces away.

"Congratulations. Your man won."

"It was close. I'm Jeff O'Neil."

He had rehearsed what he'd expected to hear and say in his mind. Now he watched her, half hoping her car wouldn't start and she would be compelled to acknowledge his presence. She was either very cool and distant like her father or very angry over his loss.

The motor kicked to life, and she drove away without another glance in his direction.

In the Marriott Cheramie leaned against Phillip as the screen flashed the news that over twenty thousand precincts had reported and Sal held over fifty-four percent of the votes. Rutger kept a frosty smile, but his eyes were fiery, and Cheramie knew her father was furious.

"I didn't think Giavotella would do this well," Phillip said.

"Do you think Rutger might win?" she asked.

"There are only some four thousand precincts left," Phillip replied; his brow was furrowed, and he gazed at the television returns.

Half an hour later Sal's lead widened, and he won with fifty-one percent of the votes. Rutger made a concession speech before they headed home. Within fifteen minutes after their arrival, drinks had been served and men stood in clusters, rehashing the campaign and the election. Phillip separated himself from one and approached Cheramie.

"When can you escape?"

"This minute. I long ago learned it pays to get away from Rutger when he's angry."

"I'll speak to him, and we'll go."

Within the hour they walked into Phillip's condo. As he mixed drinks, Cheramie sat on the white sofa. He built a fire and sat down beside her. Closing her eyes, Cheramie leaned her head back against the sofa. "I can't believe he lost."

"He can't, either. If we had it to do again, there are things I'd suggest we do differently. His big drive last year to replace the Embarcadero Freeway with a waterfront parkway was farsighted but costly, and I think it scared some people. Even more damaging, he's said repeatedly he supports a raise in taxes."

"He had a lot of support."

"But not enough. Rutger should have made more public appearances. Giavotella hit the campaign trail like Sherman marching through Georgia. He went to every town possible."

"Rutger hates that part of campaigning."

"It's necessary, and he was told it was necessary. O'Neil drew votes for Giavotella—the wholesome, all-American boy with his 'aw, shucks' grin. Both of them are like two tigers dressed as lambs. I wonder if O'Neil will accept a political appointment now," Phillip said.

"Rutger said Jeff O'Neil bought Jayton Foods and merged with Sunshine Trucks, which belongs to Giavotella. Jeff O'Neil is CEO of Jayton. When he heard the news, Rutger came as close to losing his temper as I've ever seen."

"O'Neil can't run Jayton and take on a political job."

"I can't imagine a baseball player in the food business. He doesn't know anything about it. I'm not a businesswoman, but that doesn't sound threatening to Lachman Foods."

"It isn't threatening," Phillip answered, running his fingers along her nape and through her soft curls. "Just damned annoying to Rutger. Except word's out O'Neil has a shrewed mind when it comes to money. And you don't make the big league without a competitive spirit and an unholy drive. This Jayton-Sunshine deal was a big one. The man must have come out of baseball well fixed." Phillip leaned over to kiss her throat. He set aside her drink and scooted off the sofa to the rug in front of the fire, pulling her beside him. He removed his coat and tie and rummaged in his pocket.

"Cheramie, I thought we'd be celebrating a victory tonight."

"I know. I did, too," she said, touching the corner of his mouth with the tip of her tongue.

"Are you sad?"

"I'm sorry he lost, but Rutger has enough confidence that he won't be hurt badly. He lost an election, nothing more."

"Then the night isn't ruined?" Phillip asked in a husky voice, pushing the skirt of her dress high and sliding his fingers beneath her lace panties.

She gasped with pleasure.

"Want to make tonight special?" Phillip said, watching her.

"Yes," she whispered eagerly, her hands unbuttoning his shirt.

Moving back, he caught her hands and smiled when she looked up in surprise. "If tonight still can be special, I don't want to wait." He placed a small box in her hand.

Inside the box nestled a six-carat sparkling marquise diamond. Cheramie looked up at him as he removed the ring. "Will you marry me?"

She paused. They hadn't known each other more than a few months, but as she looked at the handsome man in front of her, she knew he was all she would ever want in a man.

"It's been only months since we met at the fund-raiser," she said softly. "Are you certain about what you want?"

"Cheramie," he whispered, "I know what I want. Will you marry me?"

"Oh, yes!" she cried, throwing her arms around him, overjoyed in the proposal, thinking instantly of the wedding she could have.

He caught her in his arms and kissed her a long time before moving away and slipping the ring on her finger. Then he pulled her to him again; his hands unfastened the buttons at her neck and pushed away her red dress as he lowered her to the floor, his hands moving to her full breasts.

Thursday morning at work, Jeff faced his vice-presidents in a meeting. He was still learning names and the structure of the company. Black-haired and slender, Harry Matsui was the senior vice-president of distribution, in charge of warehouses and production. Balding John Bernhard was senior vice-president of marketing. The oldest employee was his chief financial officer, Bob Knight, who was a year away from retirement. Two more senior vice-presidents sat at the long table: Isaac Starr, head of merchandising, and the senior vice-president of information systems, who was one of the best-looking women Jeff had met in San Francisco. Golden-haired Nancy Holiday was divorced, and he admired brainy, successful women; but he didn't believe in office relationships, so when they were alone he kept his conversations businesslike. Three of the key officers were within two years or less of retirement. Jeff planned to look for the right men to fill their jobs, knowing that with hefty bonuses they would take early retirement and leave the positions to his choices.

During the next few days, as he listened to reports from his vice-presidents, Jeff familiarized himself with the four divisions, the twenty distribution centers, and their regional managers. He felt as if he were taking a crash course in wholesale distribution, but eventually he felt more confident for all his hard work.

One morning as he glanced through the paper, he spotted a picture of Cheramie Lachman. A series of photographs in the society section depicted a party honoring Cheramie Lachman and Phillip Walcott. Skimming the article, Jeff paused to read:

> Walcott says he will stay in politics, setting his eye on the next congressional race. Recently the Assemblyman was an aide in Rutger Lachman's gubernatorial campaign.

Jeff picked up the phone and called Sal's private number. His booming voice came over the line.

"Have you read the morning paper? Cheramie Lachman and Phillip Walcott are engaged."

"I know that isn't why you called."

"Walcott has congressional aspirations. You may not have seen the last of the Lachmans."

"Right now I'm getting ready for an inaugural and a move to Sacramento, and I don't have to worry about running against a Lachman for four more years. I'm not afraid of Phillip Walcott. He's as pompous as his future father-in-law. How's business?"

"Making changes. I'm working on bonus plans, incentives. I want to enlarge our territory."

"You're asking for a fight, and you'll get it. You would have been better off if Lachman had won and was busy with this office."

"It's more of a challenge this way. How's it going?"

"Busy. Damned busy. Gina is already complaining. I don't think she was cut out for politics."

"She'll adjust. She isn't the politician in the family," Jeff said, surprised at the tenseness that came into Sal's voice. "I'll keep you posted on business." Jeff hung up and rushed to shave, dress, and get to the office. Late in the afternoon he drove to Aubrey Yachts for his appointment to look at boats with Aubrey Lachman.

When Jeff entered, Aubrey was stretched in a hammock and got up in a supple unfolding that made it seem as if he didn't have a bone in his body.

"Maybe that's what I need in my office."

"I love that hammock. Keeps me from worrying."

"I forget how different you are from your father until I see something like that."

"He's only been here once. The sight of my hammock probably drove his blood pressure up twenty points."

For the next half hour the two men discussed boats, and Aubrey listened closely. "I have a couple of possibilities here I can show you. One's a bargain. Owned by a guy for six months."

Outside, Aubrey jammed his hands in his pockets. "I was astounded Rutger lost the election. He doesn't usually lose."

"Was that your sister I saw with him on election night? Tall and dark-haired."

"Probably was Alette."

"She's the only one I haven't met. You don't look alike."

"If Alette comes in while you're here, I'll introduce you. I'm trying to interest her in sailing."

"You must have succeeded if she's out alone."

"No. A friend of mine is with her, giving her a lesson. Do you have brothers or sisters? I don't remember."

"No, I don't."

"That has its advantages," Aubrey said with a grin. "Here's a dandy yacht. It's a Sabre thirty, one of the best for its size." He stepped aboard. "I know you're going to want to race, and this is sleek, easy to handle." He motioned to the companionway. "It's elegant and roomy for its size. Handcrafted teak interior. The bulkheads are taped to the hull with biaxial roving," Aubrey said, leading Jeff around the yacht. "It's good for cruising or racing. Over six feet standing headroom. Thirty feet, seven overall length, the beam is ten six."

"Looks great," Jeff said, rubbing the smooth bulkhead.

"I've got a Sabre thirty-four if you want something larger."

"This is all my budget allows."

"You might be surprised what kind of deal I can make. Let's look at the Sabre thirty-four."

For an hour Jeff looked at yachts, finally asking Aubrey if he could take the Sabre 34 for a trial run.

"Sure. I'll go with you and help if you'd like."

"Can you get away now?" Jeff asked.

"All I have to do is lock the door. That's the joy of owning your own business."

As they readied to shove off, a yacht powered by motor approached slowly. When they were at right angles with Aubrey and Jeff, Aubrey waved.

Alette Lachman, in cutoffs and a blue shirt tied high around her tiny waist, stood by the mast. Her dark hair was pinned on top of her head, a sailor hat perched on the mass of black hair.

"How was the sail?" Aubrey called to the blond man beside his sister.

"Great," he answered, grinning.

"Alette, Gene, this is Jeff O'Neil. Jeff, meet Gene Krell and my sister Alette."

Jeff waved, giving Gene only the barest glance, his gaze going to Alette, who met his with the same coolness she had exhibited on election night. She nodded in acknowledgment of the introduction and turned away as the man waved and they continued past.

"Is she engaged, too?" Jeff asked as Aubrey pushed away from the dock. Jeff started the engine.

"Alette? Not any longer," Aubrey answered. "She recently broke up with a guy."

Jeff looked back over his shoulder. The yacht was in its berth now. As she moved around the boat, Jeff's gaze drifted over her long legs and back to her face, raised in a haughty tilt. "I can imagine why," he mumbled under his breath, knowing Aubrey, in the bow of the boat, couldn't hear him.

7

Alette studied the empty office in downtown San Francisco. Two bay windows would give her good lighting. It was tiny, expensive, and old, yet this was a good location, and equally important, there was a small parking lot at the rear of the building.

Aubrey prowled the empty room with her, and she smiled at him. "You've gone beyond the call of brotherly duty today."

"I'm overcompensating for our father."

She laughed. "He'll be here, you can bet on that. He'll be watching to see if I can succeed."

"With the Lachman contacts and your brains, you will."

She laughed. "I should take you with me more often to bolster my ego."

"How is the ego?"

"Fine. I've long since gotten over Paul."

"Maybe you weren't as in love as you thought."

"If not, that's scary, too, because I was ready to marry him."

"It was the first time you were ever in love. You might be a sucker for a gentle, understanding man. Did you ever think about that?"

"No. Well, maybe. That's what appealed to me. There isn't any particular thing about women that appeals to you, is there?"

"Lord, yes. Looks, first, foremost, and all."

"Aubrey! There must be more to you than just shallow lust."

"The only requirement I have is that they don't mess with my life," he said, placing his hands on his hips. His bleached hair was a tangle of curls tied in a ponytail at the back of his neck.

"This place is perfect."

"Seems as if you should have a place where you can have a nursery."

"Aubrey, I'm a landscape architect. I initially work with architects as well as homeowners, not the actual bushes! My basic job is to draw up plans."

"I'll look at office space with you, but you can't landscape a boat, so I'm out as a client."

"I really hadn't planned on you as a client," she said, thinking of his houseboat. It was a hopeless jumble of unidentifiable objects with not a patch of dirt in sight.

"What are you going to call this company?"

"Lachman Landscape Architecture," she said, smiling. "I'm not above using connections to get started."

"Hell, no. If you have to work for a living, you might as well do the best you can."

"You didn't stoop to that."

"No. Rutger would have meddled if I had. Ready for food?"

"Yes."

During lunch two men and one woman came over to talk to Aubrey, and another man nodded at him from across the restaurant.

"I am constantly amazed by you," Alette exclaimed. "You avoid all society functions. I know you sail around alone; you live like a hermit—"

"Not so. I'm a very social animal in my little water world. And a lot of people are around boats and water, and some of the acquaintances who eat here I've known for years."

"I'm glad. It worries me sometimes to think about you sailing alone."

"Put your mind at rest. I'm supremely content when I'm sailing. Gene says you're a good pupil."

"He's as patient as you are."

"He's a damned good sailor. I can get away Saturday morning to sail with you if you want."

"Sure. I'd like that if the weather is good."

"Do you like sailing?"

"Yes," she answered cautiously, "but I don't have a love affair with it the way you do. You know I love mountains better than water."

"Well, it's a way to get out, and that's good for you."

"Thank you, big brother," she answered, amused and touched by his concern. "And thanks, Aubrey, for going with me today. It's good to have another opinion."

"Besides our father's, which you will get whether you want it or not. I'll take the check," he said, pulling it out of her hand.

Alette moved into her new office the following month. Her first client was a friend of her father's who'd recently remarried and was moving to a suburban area across the bay to the northeast of the city.

She made an appointment to meet the Southlands at their new home to take measurements and find out what they wanted. As she drove up the narrow curving road to their house, she noticed the natural setting and envisioned how she might enhance it.

Harriet Southland, George's new wife, opened the door and waved Alette inside. For a moment, as she followed Harriet and gazed at the older woman's austere hair style, practical shoes, and plain sweater and slacks, Alette wondered if her client would want the yard as unadorned; but when they stepped into an elegant room filled with antiques and ormolu mirrors, Alette relaxed. The living room had floor-to-ceiling windows on the north and west, giving a panoramic view of the hills. The yard sloped away in a tangle of weeds and trees.

"Ah, there you are," said George Southland, coming into the room and shaking her hand. His gray hair was combed straight back from his ruddy face, and although she knew he was her father's age, he looked ten years older. "I see you've met. Harriet, I've known Alette since she was a toddler."

"You have a lovely place here," she said, feeling a fluttery nervousness that she hoped remained hidden. This was her first job, and it was critical. She knew Rutger would be watching, and if she failed to satisfy his friends, he would start to interfere.

"The yard will be a challenge, Alette, but you're a Lachman, so I know you'll be up to it," George Southland said, leading the way to an upper deck that overlooked the yard.

"What do you have in mind? Something formal or a more natural setting?"

"Let's keep it natural looking," George said, moving toward wooden stairs that led down to the yard. "I want a patio, and I'd like some kind of fountain, but no little flower beds that take maintenance."

As they talked and Alette took measurements, she began to get an idea of what the Southlands had in mind. She stepped off various areas, keeping everything proportionate, making notes in a tablet and writing down all the measurements. She took snapshots.

They discussed costs only briefly in general terms. Alette was elated to learn that George Southland was unconcerned with price, so for this first job she was fortunate enough to not have to worry constantly about a budget.

"I'll draw up plans and estimates, get an idea what we can do, and then I'll call you for an appointment."

"Sounds fine," George said, draping his arm across his wife's shoulders. "We'll leave it all up to you."

"I don't have a shred of imagination when it comes to a yard," Harriet said, smiling at Alette, who suspected that Harriet Southland might not have any imagination, but she had a good idea of what she liked when she saw it.

Alette returned to town to get a legal description of the property, then spent the rest of the afternoon laboring over a drawing board. She plotted out the territory on a twenty-four-by-thirty-six-inch sheet of graph paper, using the same scale she had always used. She spotted all the trees on the lot.

The next day she began planning what she could do for the yard, and gradually a layout developed. Since she had an ample budget, she drew plans for fifteen-gallon shrubs. Two twisted junipers dominated the northeast corner, and she planned to leave them, to plant alta fescue for ground cover, pink rhododendrons along the north side of the house, and golden bamboo behind the fountain. She sketched circles for three lemon-scented gum trees with stone mulch on the west side of the house. For the patio she planned a large container with a pygmy date palm and four single-gallon containers of annuals, perennials, and bulbs to give color.

When she had the rough sketch finished and her plans readied, she redrew the sketch on vellum paper with the permanent plants and house in ink, the possible changes and landscaping in pencil.

She met Aubrey Saturday morning for another sailing lesson. She had sailed with friends many times but never learned to handle a boat alone, and it amazed her to see her slow-moving brother handle a large yacht with ease. She realized where Aubrey acquired some of his muscles.

He waved to someone in a passing yacht, and she recognized Jeff O'Neil's yellow hair. "How did you two get to be friends?"

"He bought a boat from me and we race each other in competition sometimes. Why? You don't like Jeff?"

"I don't know him, but I know Rutger dislikes him. And during Rutger's campaign, he supported Giavotella," she said, glancing back over her shoulder to see O'Neil standing in his boat, hands on his hips, staring back at her. He faced her direction, it was too distant now to tell if he were really staring at her, but she knew that was what disturbed her about him. He always stared at her in a disconcerting manner; it wasn't an appraising look men often give women or a stranger's idle glance. Instead it was as if he were trying to see inside her head and read her thoughts, a bold gaze that conveyed a sense of animosity. "His father is the one who worked with Rutger when Cheramie and you were babies."

"Alette," Aubrey said with a grin, "haven't you ever heard of Jeff O'Neil any other way?"

"No? Should I have? Did he date Cheramie?"

"No, but she probably wishes he had. He was a star pitcher for the Astros. He's one of baseball's greats."

"You know I don't follow baseball, and if he's so great at baseball, what's he doing sailing here?"

"He was in a car wreck and it smashed up his arm. He can't ever pitch again."

She glanced back at the boat that was sailing away from them. "Now," Aubrey continued, "he's giving Rutger competition. He bought out Jayton Foods."

"Did he really?" she said, turning in surprise to stare at Aubrey. "I've never heard Rutger mention it."

"I don't think it's any real competition. I'm going to turn. Get ready to move."

He pushed the tiller, the boat swung around, and she shifted quickly to the opposite side.

"When do I take the tiller and learn to do this?"

"Come on. You can sail."

They exchanged places, and after fifteen minutes Aubrey stood up. "You're doing great! Gene said you're an apt pupil. I'll get me a beer. Holler if you need help."

She took the tiller and practiced various maneuvers, enjoying herself until she realized the wind had come up and she was having a difficult time keeping control. Without noticing what was happening, they were far from land and the water had grown much rougher, the sky obscured now by clouds. She turned to head back and in minutes saw O'Neil's boat approaching behind her as he also headed toward shore. For a moment a competitive urge made her try to outmaneuver him and beat him home.

In minutes he drew abreast several yards away and glanced over to grin at her. He pulled ahead and swept in front of her to sail ahead, and she felt foolish for trying to race with him when she knew so little about sailing.

"Aubrey!" she called, able to see him sitting on a bunk, untangling fishing gear. "We're in bad weather."

He glanced over his shoulder at her. "Where are we?"

"Heading back toward the dock. Your friend O'Neil is just ahead."

"Yeah, well, don't plow into him. Call if you need me."

"I do need you!" she exclaimed. "Can you come here? He's going to get home an hour before we do. Come look at the gap between us."

"What difference does that make?"

"I don't want to drag behind as if I don't know how to sail," she replied in exasperation, glancing at Aubrey, who was carefully winding a line on a reel. To her relief he set it down.

"All right, we'll catch O'Neil."

In minutes they drew close, and then both boats went the same speed. "He knows we're racing him," Aubrey said happily, and she realized her lackadaisical brother had his competitive moments. She followed his orders and felt a rush of satisfaction as they drew abreast and then ahead of O'Neil.

"We have an advantage. He's alone. I couldn't have passed him alone."

As the breakwater loomed in sight, the *Bluebonnet* drew alongside, and both raced toward the dock until they had to slow for safety. Jeff waved as he turned in the opposite direction, where he kept his boat. Aubrey returned the wave, but Alette merely stared at him. She wondered if Rutger would eventually buy out Jeff O'Neil's business or if he'd force him out.

Along with two smaller jobs, for the next month Alette was involved in the Southlands' yard. When she learned from them that Rutger had stopped by once to see her work, she hoped he'd been impressed. She knew she'd hear from him otherwise, and the last thing she wanted was another confrontation with her father.

8

A resounding blare of trumpets rose over the organ notes as Cheramie linked her arm with Rutger's and moved forward. Resplendent in a white satin Dior gown with hand-beaded Alençon lace, Cheramie glanced around the church. Banks of white roses and red anthurium filled the room with a heavy, sweet scent. Everything looked perfect. As she walked down the long aisle, Cheramie smiled serenely. Phillip Walcott was the catch of the year. Handsome and politically ambitious, he came from a family as wealthy as her own. He could give her everything she wanted, and his insatiable appetite for sex made her feel loved and desirable. Ten bridesmaids were lined up in red dresses, an unconventional color, but one that made an excellent backdrop for Cheramie's white dress and dark coloring. Alette gazed at her with shining eyes, and Cheramie made a mental note to introduce her sister to the *right* kind of men later. Alette seemed drawn to gentle souls who were great buddies and nothing more.

Aubrey smiled when she met his gaze, and she dismissed him as hopeless. Aubrey was a social misfit and seldom entered her thoughts or her world except on such family occasions as funerals and weddings. He was almost as bad as Phillip's eighteen-year-old brother, Edwin, who caused the Walcotts trouble and looked petulant and impatient in his tuxedo as he watched her walk down the aisle.

She smiled at Phillip's mother, Katherine, who gazed back with approval. Katherine, with her shiny brown hair and good figure, was lovely in an Oscar de la Renta gown, but it was her new father-in-law who gave Phillip his handsome looks. Phillip was a younger version of Judge Phillip Cade Walcott II. Cheramie had made a concentrated effort to win Katherine's approval, knowing that she had Judge Walcott's from the first moment she'd met him. But it wasn't difficult to win the approval of any man she had ever known.

Rutger placed her hand in Phillip's, and they turned to repeat their vows.

They honeymooned high on the cliffs in Sorrento with the blue waters of the Gulf of Naples below. Phillip had arranged for them to stay in the bridal suite of the Walcott Inn, and whole days would pass when Cheramie didn't put on more than lacy lingerie. After two weeks they went to Monte Carlo for a week and then to Paris for another, and finally home to a new condominium on Russian Hill.

Cheramie became busy with her volunteer work on charity

drives while Phillip assembled his staff to enter the state senate race in the next election. The first time she was tempted to flirt with another man was fourteen months after her wedding, when she was dancing with Bryce Wolfe at the country club on Saturday night.

"Let me take you sailing Monday afternoon." His brown eyes were warm as he gazed at her. "You can't believe how slick my new yacht is until you've sailed with me."

"And how would I explain the afternoon to Phillip?" she asked with amusement.

Bryce's arm tightened, pulling her closer against him. "You can get away," he said, breathing in her ear. "I know Phillip doesn't question your every move."

She moved her hips against him. She liked to know men wanted her; it gave her a rush of pleasure.

"Come on, Cheramie, we'll have fun."

She moved back. "Sorry, Bryce. Maybe another time."

"I'll keep asking. You're going to get bored playing house. That wasn't meant for a woman like you."

She laughed. "You don't know me that well!"

"You've got the moves, honey," he said in a husky voice. "You're a woman meant to be adored by men."

"That's foolishness," she said softly, running her hand across his chest, glancing at Phillip, who was talking to two women and standing at their table. "Phillip is looking for me."

"I'll come back when you've been married a couple of years."

She laughed as she moved ahead of him to join Phillip. She enjoyed mild flirtations, but she kept them harmless, because Phillip gave her his undivided attention when he was home.

The company bought another chain of hotels. When they signed the contracts closing the deal, Phillip was gone for a week, and Cheramie grew restless. Grandfather Phil was relinquishing more of the hotel business to Phillip, who was the oldest grandson, the only one to step in unless Edwin changed drastically. With the campaign looming, Phillip was involved in hiring men to take his place, because as soon as he announced he was running, he would leave private business.

Within a month he was into the campaign full swing, working long hours, sometimes traveling the state. Cheramie tried to adjust to seeing him less, but it made her restless and edgy, and she had never been a homebody.

One evening in April Phillip called, and the moment he told her he had to work late, disappointment filled her. It took great effort to keep from arguing with him while she stared at the calendar and saw he had worked until midnight the past three nights.

"You think you'll be home by midnight?" she asked.

"Sure, honey. I'm sorry, but I'm tied up. We're going to the hotel and have dinner sent up and work on my ad campaign."

"Phillip, I hope being senator is worth all this."

He laughed softly. "If I'm elected, I'll make this up to you. We'll take a trip the first chance we get. I have to run."

She replaced the receiver and paced restlessly, trying to think what she could do to occupy her time. Evenings and weekends were the worst time to be left alone. Two hours later she stood in the bedroom, brushing her hair and staring in the mirror at herself, her thoughts on Phillip in the penthouse suite of the hotel. She thought of nights she had spent in that suite with him and wished she were there now instead of his campaign staff.

Suddenly she decided to surprise him. She lowered the brush, frowning as she mulled over the idea. Around midnight she could drive to the hotel, take the private elevator to the suite, wait in the foyer—she rejected the idea. That would be too blatant when the men came out. She mulled it over and decided she could park and wait for everyone to leave and *then* surprise Phillip. They could spend the night in the suite. The notion appealed to her, and she ran a hot bath to soak and perfume.

She dressed in filmy underwear and slipped into black silk slacks and a shirt. Humming a tune, she sacked a chilled bottle of Chardonnay while she thought about surprising him.

The section of the parking lot reserved for the Walcotts

held only Phillip's car and one other. Cheramie parked in the shadows on a back row to wait until the occupants of the one car left. She didn't know the kinds of cars driven by the men who worked for Phillip, so she had no idea who was with him, but she didn't want to barge in and embarrass her husband, so she settled to wait. She leaned forward, switching on a light, and saw it was exactly midnight.

Twenty minutes later her patience and enthusiasm wore thin, and she wondered how late they would work. Twelve more minutes passed, and Cheramie decided the whole notion was foolish. Phillip might work until two in the morning, and she had no intention of sitting in a dark parking lot until two A.M. She decided to give him ten more minutes before going home. Then the door to the Walcott private entrance opened, and she smiled, her good humor returning.

Phillip stepped outside with a woman at his side. He laughed at something she said.

In the few moments it took Phillip and the woman to walk from the door to her car, the night changed for Cheramie. It became indelibly etched in time with a clarity to her surroundings. She heard a distant horn, the slam of the car door as the woman climbed into her car. She felt the chilly night air on her skin and inhaled the faint diesel odor as the car across the lot started up its engine.

Phillip leaned down to say something, laughed, and stepped back as the woman drove away. Without glancing around, he reentered the hotel.

Feeling numb and remote, as if she were a spectator at a play, Cheramie turned on the ignition. She drove home, and in the short distance her emotions ran wild. Shock was replaced by rage; within minutes logic came, and she wondered if she had misjudged and acted in haste. The woman could have been a campaign secretary. Phillip hadn't kissed her; he hadn't had his arm around her. She parked and hurried into the house, knowing Phillip would be home any minute. She put away the wine and changed.

Thinking back over the past month, she struggled to recall the excuses Phillip had given for being late. Until four or five weeks ago he had been home around six every night, but a month ago that had changed. Until today she'd attributed the change to the campaign, accepting what he said without question. The image of Phillip emerging from the hotel with the blonde haunted her. It could be meaningless, yet Phillip had an intense need for sex; he liked women, and they flirted with him constantly.

Twenty minutes later she heard the door slam. Phillip called to her, and she stared at the door as she answered him. In minutes he appeared, shirt unbuttoned, tie and coat in hand. He dropped them on the chair and crossed the room to take her in his arms. "You waited up for me?" he asked in a husky voice.

She looked into his eyes as his gaze lowered and he pushed the straps of the diaphanous gown off her shoulders. She saw desire flare in his expression, and as he pulled her into his arms, she forgot her fears.

Jealous suspicions were alleviated by his lovemaking, but with the light of day and long, lonely hours in the early evening while he worked late again, her suspicions returned. He was home by eight and the weekend came, and she stopped worrying over the incident.

Tuesday at ten minutes before six, the phone rang. Her heartbeat quickened at the sound of Phillip's deep voice as he told her he was at the hotel, something had come up, and he would have to work late. All the worry she had suffered the week before came back. She clutched the phone. "Phillip, come home."

"Is something wrong?" he asked.

"It's been too long since we were in bed."

There was a husky laugh. "Not since last night."

"I want you," she said breathlessly, meaning it, feeling an aching need, a deep-rooted fear.

"Hey," he said softly, "you're making me have more regrets than ever that I have to work late."

She stiffened and heard a buzzing in her ears. "Phillip," she said, speaking carefully, feeling as if she were losing him, "come home. Just tonight let the work go. I've been thinking about you all day."

There was another pause. "Honey, I swear I'll try to get

away as early as possible. You go ahead and eat without me. I'll do what I can.''

"What's so important it can't wait until tomorrow?'' She knew her voice was sharp and nagging, but she couldn't keep from asking him.

There was a pause of silence. "I'm planning campaign strategy. What's the matter with you, Cheramie?''

She heard the change in his tone of voice, a cold flatness that alarmed her. "I just want you home with me," she said.

"Honey, I'll make it up to you,'' he said, the warmth returning. "I'll get there by midnight, I promise. Wait up for me, okay?''

"Sure, Phillip,'' she answered. "Don't work too hard.''

He laughed and told her good-bye, and the connection was broken. She replaced the receiver on the phone and stared at it. She felt caught in a current of suspicion; nagging doubts wouldn't stop. Most nights no matter how late he came home, they made love, but Cheramie knew that wasn't proof of anything.

By ten o'clock Cheramie decided she would see for herself. She would drive to the hotel, wait, and see. If the blonde appeared again, she would face that problem.

Two hours later she drove into the hotel lot. Only two cars were parked, in the same places again. Her heart beat faster while she swore softly.

Near midnight he came out with the same woman. As they stepped through the door Phillip dropped his arm from around her waist and walked at her side to her car. Cheramie gripped the arm of the car so tightly that her nails dug into the soft leather, and it took all her will to keep from jumping out of the car and screaming at him. Rage seemed to come in hot waves; perspiration broke out on her brow, and she shook as she stared at them. Then she scooted down in the seat. She did not want Phillip to spot her. She heard car doors and motors start, and as the sounds diminished she sat up to see Phillip's taillights as he turned the corner of the lot.

Moving with an angry determination, Cheramie climbed out and hurried to the entrance. Fumbling in her purse for her key to the suite, she punched the button in the elevator.

With a purposeful stride, she moved through the suite to the spacious bedroom that offered a panoramic view of the city and bay and bridges, but all Cheramie looked at was the rumpled bed. She picked up a vase and pulled back her arm to throw it, then paused and stopped. She set down the vase, her mind racing. Phillip was on the way home, expecting to find her in bed.

She hurried back to the car and drove as quickly as possible, knowing she risked a ticket and a wreck as she tore through a red light.

Taking a deep breath, she strode into the house.

"Cheramie!"

"Here I am. Sorry. I went to a movie with Francie."

"I expected to find you in bed," he said, his gaze running over her. "I'm disappointed about that, but I'm glad you didn't sit home. We had more reports than I realized. I'm beat. Let's have a drink, a hot bath, and go to bed," he said, taking her in his arms. She gazed up at him and thought how little she really knew him. She wanted to scream at him that he was a deceiving bastard. Not trusting herself to speak, she placed her head against his chest.

"I'll get us a drink. Go start the water."

He left her, and she watched him walk away. He was oversexed, incredibly handsome, successful, full of energy, and she should have guessed. Lord knew she had seen women flirt with him shamelessly. In the large bathroom she turned on the faucets of the sunken pink marble tub. There was a buzzing in her head, and her thoughts seemed to swirl in a jumble of random notions. She dropped her clothes in a pile. The phone was beside the tub, on a marble shelf beside a potted palm. She thought of Bryce and his constant flirtation. With a glance at the doorway, she picked up the phone and dialed information to get his number. She punched the numbers quickly and continued to watch the door.

"Hi," came a mumbled answer.

"Did I wake you?" she asked in a sultry whisper, amazed that she could act in a normal manner when enveloped in rage.

"Hell, no," he answered, sounding more alert.

"I'd like to go sailing."

"God, now? Hey, that's great!" Now he sounded fully awake. "It'll take me half an hour to get down to the boat—"

She laughed with a bitter satisfaction. "Not tonight. Tomorrow morning about eleven."

He groaned. "Shit, I can't get free until four."

"Four's fine. Where shall we meet?"

"The yacht club," he said, a note of curiosity in his voice. "Four o'clock in the bar."

Phillip came through the doorway.

"Right," Cheramie whispered, and replaced the receiver. She looked up at Phillip. "I called Alette. I'm supposed to meet her for lunch tomorrow." She moved slowly to meet him. His gaze raked over her, and he sucked in his breath.

"Lord, you're beautiful."

"And I've missed you," she said, unbuckling his belt and tugging down the zipper of his fly.

They made love once in the water and then again in bed. But all the while anger burned in Cheramie like a smoldering fire. He hadn't slept more than twenty minutes when she rolled over to kiss him again, rubbing her bare body against him as she moved down, her head going between his legs. She felt him get hard again.

"Cheramie, the honeymoon is over," he whispered, but in minutes he was holding her, his hands roaming over her while he kissed her wildly.

She woke him again when it was almost dawn. He caught her hands and looked at her, a quizzical smile on his face.

"Maybe I should work late more often if this is what it does to you. Honey, I won't be able to crawl out of bed if we go again."

"Of course you will, Phillip. I know your strength."

"You're going to know my weakness. All night when we were on our honeymoon and nothing else to do was one thing, after a long day and night at the office is another."

"Just go to sleep and let me touch you and caress you and look at you," she whispered, her tongue playing over his stomach. "I can't get enough of you, Phillip," she said, her hands stroking him, playing with him.

"God, Cheramie," he whispered, his hands caressing her as he groaned and kissed her.

He had a total of three hours' sleep before the alarm went off and she bounced out of bed. He rolled over, reaching out to turn off the alarm.

She went around the bed to turn it back on. "Phillip, you're supposed to go to work," she said flatly.

"I can't move."

"Of course you can." She climbed astride him and wiggled against him.

"Cheramie, have a heart. You've demolished me." He rolled over and looked at her. "Are you trying to prove something?"

"No, I'm madly in love with the sexiest man on earth," she said, smiling at him sweetly.

"Well, the sexiest man on earth is fading fast. I feel stuffed with jelly, and I don't know how I can face a committee meeting in an hour."

"Better hurry. I'll see if Jolene is here to fix breakfast."

She pulled on a robe and went to the kitchen to see if their cook had arrived. Cheramie kissed Phillip good-bye before eight, and at three, dressed in a navy sweater and navy slacks, she left for the yacht club. She was well aware of the risks she ran, because many of their friends belonged to the same yacht club and any of them might see her meeting Bryce, but Phillip was running risks giving her excuses night after night during the week. Cheramie dismissed worries; she wasn't going to sit home and wring her hands over Phillip. She wondered if Bryce had any idea what woman was going to meet him this afternoon. She hadn't given her name, and she suspected he had no idea with whom he had made a date.

He sat alone perched on a high stool at a table in the dusky oak-and-brass bar. A tight blue T-shirt and jeans revealed trim muscles. He was a handsome man with his thick gold hair and strong jaw and deep brown eyes. When she appeared, he called to her.

"Cheramie, hi." He waved his drink, and she crossed the bar to sit down beside him.

"Hi, Bryce," she answered, excitement racing. Risk and revenge were heady, making her give him her best smile.

"How're you doing?" Bryce asked politely. "Are you meeting Phillip?"

She laughed, and he gazed at her with curiosity while she put her chin on her hand and leaned closer. "No. Phillip isn't coming."

He stared at her, a puzzled expression in his eyes, and then he blinked and she suspected comprehension finally dawned.

"Cheramie?" Pleasure and obvious surprise lighted his eyes. "I'll be damned."

"Bryce, don't disappoint me. I never took you for a slow man," she said, twisting on the stool slightly so her knee pressed against his.

"Well, hell, a voice wakes me after midnight, whispers a few words, no name, and hangs up. I'm not going to question the lady."

"Suppose it had been someone you didn't like?"

"I'd dump her. I don't have to get out my"—he paused and gave a suggestive emphasis to the word—"boat." He grinned as his gaze raked over her. "My day just improved enormously."

She smiled and watched Bryce as the waiter reached their table.

"I'll have a whiskey sour," she said, remembering Phillip mixing them drinks last night.

"Two," Bryce told the waiter, and then they were alone. "If I'd known—"

"I'm bored."

"This is a perfect day to sail," Bryce said, reaching out to stroke her wrist. "There's a little cove up the coast that has a gorgeous beach. I can show you things you've never seen," he added in a husky voice.

"Maybe I can show you a few," she answered in the same tone.

"Let's get out of here," he said, and she slid off the stool eagerly, glad to get out of the yacht club. Fortunately, at four in the afternoon on a weekday it was quiet, and as they walked to the yacht, she didn't see anyone on the dock.

Using power, Bryce headed north, where he maneuvered
the yacht into a secluded cove and then jumped out to wade
to shore. He held her hand, and they walked along a sandy
deserted beach that was blocked by a rugged precipice behind
them.

When they returned to the boat, he led her down to the salon.

"All the comforts of home," he said as he mixed more
whiskey sours, sitting close to her and leaning forward to kiss
her throat.

"Bryce—"

He turned his head to cover her mouth with his, and his
arm went around her, pulling her close. Cheramie slipped her
hands up his muscular arms and around his neck, clinging to
him while she returned his kiss. Her pulse pounded when she
remembered Phillip's arm around the blonde.

One weekday at noontime aboard the yacht as she lay in
Bryce's arms after having sex, he lit a cigarette and blew gray
smoke rings that floated and disappeared into the air.

"Are you doing this to get back at Phillip?" he asked, his
voice casual.

She turned to look at him. "What do you mean, 'get back
at Phillip'?"

He rolled on his side to prop his head on his hand and look
down at her. "I get a feeling of hostility sometimes when I
mention his name."

"You just know he's having an affair, so you think I'm
angry."

He gave her a level look before he took another drag on
the cigarette. "Okay, I do. He's careful, but word gets
around. He's a little more circumspect than you."

"I'm careful."

"Like hell. A lot of mutual friends know you go out with
me."

"Can you think of one who would tell Phillip?"

"No. That's more something a woman would do. Did a
woman tell you about him?"

"No."

Bryce raised his eyebrows. "I thought Phillip would be
cagier than that."

"I have a private detective following him."

"Jesus!" He sat up and frowned. "You're a cold bitch, Cheramie."

"That wasn't what you called me half an hour ago."

"Remind me never to get married," he said, pulling on his white briefs. "How can you do that to Phillip?" A frown creased his brow, and his eyes widened. "Are you getting a divorce?"

She laughed loudly and rolled away to get up and gather her clothes, stepping into bikini panties that were tiny bits of lace held together by a band of elastic. "You look terrified. Relax," she said, leaning forward as she cupped her breasts in a red silken bra, bending over so her face was inches from his. "I'm not after you, Bryce. I'm perfectly happy married to Phillip."

"Then why the detective? That's a real bitch. You stir things up and he'll lose the senate race, and right now he's the leading contender."

"Men," she said contemptuously, pulling on her garter belt and stockings. "If anything ever happens, I want all the information possible. I learned long ago from my father to get all the facts. In the meantime, I'm happy screwing around. It gives me excitement and retaliation. You look as if you found a scorpion in your bed."

"Remind me to stay friends with you."

"Bryce, are you afraid of me?" she asked with amusement, suddenly finding it intriguing to think she might have more than just sexual power over men.

He turned to face her. "No," he answered, his voice firm and his gaze impassive. Yet she wondered about his reaction. "Like you said, we're friends. No ties, only fun. I guess that's why I'm still single."

"Are you going to tell Phillip about the detective?"

"Lord, no!" he exclaimed in such haste that she knew she was getting an honest response this time. "I don't tell husbands anything."

"Who's his latest?"

"You should know. You're the one with the detective."

"They're just names. I don't recognize any names."

"Might be a secretary. I'd think you'd know."

She smiled at him. "I do know. I know everything."

Bryce stared at her as if he had never seen her before, and she could see that he was afraid of her. She widened her smile. "Tomorrow night we're going to the club for dinner."

"Yeah. I'll see you there. If you play tennis tomorrow, I'll see you."

"I have lunch with Rutger tomorrow," she said airily. Later she left in a jaunty stride, a feeling of power exhilarating her along with an intense satisfaction that she was getting revenge for Phillip's unfaithfulness.

The next day she went shopping and was at the restaurant promptly at noon, arriving the same moment Rutger pushed through the glass doors. Dan, Rutger's usual waiter, brought cups of hot, black coffee immediately. As soon as he was gone, she looked into Rutger's blue eyes and wondered if she could ever guess what went on in his mind. Lately their lunches had been taken up discussing Phillip's campaign, and Cheramie suspected Rutger took a vicarious pleasure in seeing his son-in-law succeed in politics.

"How is Phillip's campaign?" he asked, as she had expected.

"I imagine you know the answer to that better than I do. I haven't involved myself in his campaign yet."

"Maybe it's time you did."

They paused to order.

"I think you should involve yourself in your husband's campaign," Rutger said. "I think he's going to have a strong campaign, and I expect him to win."

"That makes two of you. He expects to win," she said, smiling. Rutger gazed at her without a flicker of emotion, and she realized he was angry with her. She lowered her cup of coffee.

"What's wrong?" she asked, knowing she had displeased him and wondering what she had done.

"You're going to defeat him. You're going to ruin a damned good campaign."

"What are you talking about? He can win without my help. I've already posed for pictures with him."

"You'll destroy him. Phillip can go far. He has the backing, the personality, the money, and the ambition. I don't want you to pull him down," Rutger said, speaking with clipped precision.

Cheramie drew a sharp breath, paying full attention to him because she realized he was furious with her. "I have no intention of pulling him down!" Then she went cold as she realized what was making Rutger angry. She blinked and leaned back, thankful the waiter arrived with their lunches and she had a moment to think.

As soon as the waiter left, Rutger leaned forward, and he seemed to swell in size. His voice was soft, yet it held the force of his steel will. "Your affairs will ruin him, Cheramie."

She wanted to look away from Rutger's condemning gaze, but she couldn't. "What about *his* affairs?" she snapped, raising her chin, her anger flaring at the unfairness.

"I'll talk to him. Both of you are running stupid risks," Rutger said with scathing contempt. "I'm surprised at you, Cheramie, because you've always had a head on your shoulders. Of all my children, you are the practical one, the one most like me, the ambitious one. This is so damnably stupid!"

"I did it to get back at Phillip," she said stiffly, her terror mounting because Rutger's fury was demonic.

"Don't lie! You may have the first time, but not to the extent you've carried it."

"Are you having me followed?" The moment the words were out, she wished she could retract them. She saw the red flood his cheeks. His tone didn't change, but she knew Rutger: He was in a rage. And when he was goaded to a rage, action usually followed.

"Cheramie, stop jeopardizing your future. I'll see to it Phillip stops."

"Okay," she said quickly, hoping to forestall the threat that she knew was coming. "I give you my word."

"If you don't, it'll cost you."

"I keep my promises. You know I always have," she said, hoping he had no inkling when she hadn't.

"I'll cut your inheritance," he said slowly and distinctly.

"Everything will go to Alette and her heirs only. Every cent, if you cost Phillip this election with your indiscretion."

"I'm your child! How can you take his side?" she said, momentarily stunned.

"I'm not taking Phillip's side. If you'd stop to think, which I don't believe you've done for months now, you'd see I'm not. I'm interested in your welfare. Judge Walcott is one of the most powerful judges in the state. What do you think would happen if you went to court in a divorce case?"

She had thought of the possibility, and it terrified her. "I'll never divorce Phillip."

"But you're doing something to make him divorce you! Phillip has a promising career ahead of him. Very promising. Both of you seem hell-bent on ruining it for the pleasure of the moment or the pleasure of getting back at each other."

"He started—"

"I don't want to know, Cheramie," he said, and she clamped her mouth closed.

They ate in silence while she vowed that never again would she be so reckless and careless. Hiring a detective to follow Phillip seemed shrewd, yet forgetting to take precautions to see if one followed her was utmost folly. She had lost all appetite and sipped her coffee while Rutger ate. "It hurt to discover Phillip was unfaithful."

Rutger gave her a stormy glance. "It may have, and you're a modern woman, but there's still a double standard. He'll never be hurt as badly as you will be if the truth comes out."

She bristled and bit back the retort that came to mind, staring at him and wishing she had used more care. Fury consumed her, but it was directed at men in general, Phillip in particular, and her own carelessness. She should have known better after years of hiding things she didn't want Rutger to know. She had assumed that with marriage he would no longer involve himself in her life. The idea of Alette getting her inheritance because of her affairs made her want to scream in anger. Instead she ate quietly, forcing down each bite, until Rutger paid the check.

"You'll have everything if you do your part," Rutger said as soon as the waiter was gone. "Phillip shouldn't have any limitations, and he's damn well not going to have them put in front of him by his wife. I won't stand by and watch you ruin your future, Cheramie.''

"I won't, but it's unfair—''

"I'll see that Phillip stops. He's ambitious and he's not stupid. The matter is closed.'' Rutger stood up, and she picked up her purse, knowing there wouldn't be another word said to her about it unless she disobeyed him.

He nodded and turned to walk out of the restaurant without looking back.

Anger made her want to pick up the plates and toss them at the wall. She walked out briskly, climbing into her car and driving home. The moment the door slammed behind her, Jolene appeared from the kitchen.

"Ma'am, you're home early. You had a call—''

"Get out, Jolene. Go home. Come back tomorrow.''

The woman blinked, and her face turned red. "Yes, ma'am,'' she said, and scurried into the kitchen. Cheramie threw her purse across the room and hurled her shoes down the hall into the bedroom.

Once the bedroom door was closed behind her, she screamed. She rushed across the room to the dresser to pick up the framed wedding picture of her smiling up at Phillip. She smashed it on the corner of the dresser, beating it until the picture was in tatters.

Breathing hard, she sat down on a chair and stared into space. She had learned a lesson she would never forget. The phone rang, and she picked it up to hear Bryce's voice.

"Hi, Cheramie. Want to play tennis?''

"It's over, Bryce. I can't see you again.''

"Hey, what happened? Dolly, what's wrong?''

"My conscience is bothering me.''

"It isn't bothering Phillip.''

"Fuck you, you son of a bitch.''

"For chrissakes, Cheramie, what the hell did I do?''

"Good-bye, Bryce,'' she said firmly, and replaced the receiver, feeling no remorse where Bryce was concerned. Kneeling on the floor, she picked up the pieces of glass, carried the shredded picture to the trash compactor, and covered everything with newspaper so Phillip would never notice. She listed the things she needed to do. She didn't intend to anger Rutger further. She started to call the detective and tell him his assignment was terminated, but she paused with her hand on the phone. Rutger was forceful, but she didn't know if he really intimidated Phillip.

She removed her hand from the phone and stared in the mirror at her red-faced reflection. She took a deep breath and vowed that never again if she did something clandestine would she be so careless as to get caught.

9

"Twenty, nineteen, eighteen, seventeen—" Aubrey stretched in the hammock and watched the second hand of the clock, counting down the seconds before it reached six o'clock. The moment it ticked past one second before six o'clock, he heard a footstep outside the office, and then the door opened. Rutger paused to scowl at Aubrey, who unfolded from the hammock and sat up, dropping his book on the floor.

"How in hell you earn a living, I can't imagine."

"It's the Lachman blood in my veins," Aubrey replied, curious what would bring Rutger to call. "What happened to 'Hello, Aubrey. Hi, Rutger'?"

"Where do your customers sit?" Rutger asked, eyeing the small cluttered room that was filled with tools, boat parts, books, and papers.

Aubrey stood up. "Here, sit down," he said, moving to perch on top of his cluttered desk. Two papers fluttered to the floor.

"I have no intention of sitting on a hammock," Rutger

snapped. He faced Aubrey with his hands on his hips. "I wonder if you'll ever grow up."

"I hope not. Childhood is delightful. Especially when it arrives after you're twenty-one years old."

"I knew I would waste my time, but for the sake of the family—"

"Ah, the old sake-of-the-family time. What's the present crisis?"

"I'm sure you wouldn't know. You have a brother-in-law, Phillip Walcott."

"I know Phillip," Aubrey said, suddenly becoming solemn.

"He's running for the senate, and he has a damned good chance of winning."

Aubrey's solemn expression changed, and he smiled, realizing why he was being paid a visit. "You surely don't expect me to get out and campaign. You have the rest of the family's support. Alette takes time from her business to campaign for her brother-in-law, and she's as respectable as a church choir."

"Yes, and I'll see to it she's rewarded for her time and efforts."

"I'm sure you will. We all learned that fact of life by the age of five."

Rutger pulled out a checkbook, and Aubrey inhaled deeply. "I want Phillip to have everything possible going for him. I don't want rumors of an estranged boat bum brother-in-law."

"I'm not on the outs with Cheramie or Phillip Walcott. I don't see them often—you know we don't move in the same circles, and Cheramie doesn't understand my life-style much more than you do, although she is more tolerant about it. But there is no quarrel between the Walcotts and me."

"But there's no visible support, either. The public doesn't know the situation, and if you are never seen or heard from, the press will pick up on it."

"Rutger, other than when I win races, the press lost interest in me when I graduated from college and stopped raising hell on campus. A man who sails and lives a solitary life doesn't make for headlines.''

Rutger leaned over the desk and wrote in his checkbook. "I want you to appear at a rally next week and at Phillip's watch party. Both will be highly visible occasions—"

"Hell, Rutger, Phillip won't know or give a damn. That's asinine."

Rutger straightened up and gave him a withering look. "I see you haven't changed in the slightest. Two thousand dollars is yours if you appear. One thousand dollars for each hour you put in an appearance."

For a moment Aubrey felt a faint twinge of the old anger, but he had removed himself so far from Rutger and from old hurts and frustrations that he laughed. "You think my presence will be worth two thousand dollars to Phillip Walcott? You sound as if you think he can't win without me! Damn."

"There's no way I can order you to go."

"Rutger, Phillip doesn't need me. I won't cause any ripples by not appearing."

"You make enough money with this"—he paused and waved his hand—"to ignore two thousand dollars?"

The bell on the door jingled and an auburn-haired woman in red shorts stepped inside. "Hi, Aubrey," she said.

"Get out," Rutger ordered. "We'll be finished here in a minute."

"Hey, hey, Rutger," Aubrey said, another flare of anger coming as he moved quickly to Pat Reiner's side. She blinked and backed out the door.

"Sorry," she mumbled. Aubrey followed her out, catching her arm to turn her to face him. Sunshine splashed over them, and she shielded her eyes, frowning as she looked up.

"Come back inside," he said quietly. "He's my father, and you can ignore him. This is my place, not his, and he can't order you out."

"Aubrey, I'm going home. I'm not going back inside," she said, her dark eyes flashing.

"Oh, hell, go around to the boat and wait for me. He'll be gone in a minute."

"Jeez!"

"Yeah, see why I'm so lovable?" he said, relaxing, seeing that she was going to capitulate.

Her frown vanished and she smiled, revealing a crooked eyetooth. "All right. I'd hate to waste my day off. I'll wait."

Aubrey returned to the office. Rutger stood behind the desk, looking down at paper scattered over its surface.

"Doesn't it bother you to treat people like that? Pat's a pleasant, attractive lady. You scared the hell out of her."

"She was intruding, and I mean nothing to her."

"What you're really saying is, she means nothing to you," Aubrey said, stretching in the hammock and keeping one toe on the floor to move gently back and forth.

"I know better than to ask if you are engaged or married. You can't handle responsibility of any sort."

Having learned long ago to stop taking his father's barbs to heart and suffering from them, Aubrey continued to rock in silence.

"I wonder what happened. Why you're like you are," Rutger said, studying his son.

"Environment versus heredity. I think environment is the big influence. God knows it made me what I am today."

"Here's a check and the times and addresses of the rally and party," Rutger said, letting them flutter down on Aubrey's chest. "Will you put in an appearance?"

Aubrey sat up and picked up the list and check without looking at them. "Rutger, Phillip and Cheramie won't give a shit whether I'm there or not."

"It will help Phillip. I know politics. You're going to hurt him otherwise."

Aubrey stared at his father and tore the check into pieces as he gave a sigh. "All right. I'll go kiss the press's ass, because I have no intentions of hurting Cheramie. You can keep your money."

"That's a damned stupid thing to do, Aubrey, but then you never did have any business judgment."

"This doesn't fall under the heading of business. It has something to do with a thing called family or principles," he said, wishing Rutger would go. "Want to apologize to Pat?"

"Your friends are of no consequence. I don't have time to

waste." Rutger slammed the door and strode away while Aubrey got up, jumped over a basket of laundry, and went to his boat.

"Here I am, hopefully not a chip off the old block."

"Okay, Aubrey. I'm beginning to understand you a little better. How do you stand him?"

"Who? Rutger? A child doesn't have choices."

"You're not like him. I think you're fun," she said, sliding her arms around his narrow waist. He put his arms around her, gazing into her brown eyes.

"Let's see how much fun," he said softly, bending his head to kiss her parted lips, his hand sliding up her warm thigh while Rutger's remarks echoed in his mind.

10

On the day of the election Cheramie strode confidently through Phillip's campaign headquarters, crowded with volunteers manning phones. She had driven straight from the salon to see him, and excitement made her pulse race.

They had never discussed their affairs, and she wondered if Phillip had any idea she had been unfaithful. To her satisfaction, she knew he had stopped seeing other women. After talking to Rutger, she began taking an active interest in her husband's campaign. The blonde she had seen at the hotel with Phillip was his campaign secretary, formerly a secretary at his law firm, and it gave Cheramie pleasure to spend time at campaign headquarters and order the woman around. She paused in front of Nan Benton's desk.

"Hello, Mrs. Walcott," Nan said coolly, pushing her hair away from her face. "Everyone is really busy."

"I can see that. Will you tell Phillip I'm here?"

"I think they're having a meeting," she said as she stood

up with an obvious air of reluctance. Her green skirt was tight, and her white blouse unbuttoned one more button than it should have been to Cheramie's way of thinking. In anger, she watched the woman's hips sway.

In minutes Nan returned. "He said to come in," she said stiffly.

Cheramie walked into the room as William Gaffney, Phillip's press secretary; Todd Patton, his speech writer; and Gerald Thornton, his accountant, gathered up papers to go.

They greeted her, Todd stopping to talk a moment. "This is the big night. He's going to win."

"I hope so. All of you have worked hard."

He smiled and moved out, closing the doors and leaving her alone with Phillip. She leaned back and slipped the lock in place, glancing around the office. The utilitarian space held a metal-and-wood desk and metal file cabinets and was a startling contrast to his plushly carpeted law office with its Chippendale tulipwood leather-topped desk and original oils.

"Seems like ten million things to do, and today I didn't think I'd have anything to do except vote."

"Does it remind you of Rutger's election?"

"Somewhat. Except I'm three times busier. Honey, I'm swamped. I'll be home by half-past four. You can take this box home for me."

"Sure, Phillip," she asked, knowing his secretary and ex-lover sat only feet away on the other side of the door. Phillip had his tie pulled loose and his shirtsleeves rolled up; his hair was tousled, a lock falling across his forehead. Cheramie pulled down the neck-to-hip zipper and stepped out of her dress. Wearing only garter belt, hose, shoes, and bra, no panties, she crossed the office to him. He had turned his back to her and was bending over, and she slid her arms around him, unfastening his pants and reaching inside to touch him.

"God, Cheramie!" He turned around and drew in his breath as he looked down at her. He blinked. "Damn, the office is full of people! Someone will want me in the next thirty seconds."

"Sure, Phillip," she said, kneeling in front of him.

"Someone can walk—"

"I locked the door."

"Cheramie! Listen—" She heard his deep intake of breath and knew the moment he capitulated. He pulled her up to seat her on the edge of his desk. He was throbbing and ready for her, and she spread her legs as he stepped between them and pulled her to him, thrusting into her. She could hear people talking on the other side of the door. The risk exhilarated her. She opened her eyes for a second to find Phillip watching her, desire burning in his eyes. She moaned softly and moved her hips, clinging to him, climaxing at the same time he did.

He moved away, and Cheramie slid off the desk, picking up her dress. She pulled panties out of her purse while he tucked his shirt into his pants and pulled out his handkerchief to wipe off the desk as she backed up to him.

"Zip me, honey," she said softly.

He leaned down. "You're a hot bitch, Cheramie. Suppose a reporter had wanted in?"

"You would have thought of something." She turned around and smiled, straightening his tie. "You love it," she said, flicking her tongue at him. He leaned forward to kiss her. He looked smug and satisfied.

She smoothed her dress. "See you later."

Laughing, he picked up papers, and as she stepped through the door and looked back, he was seated behind his desk, a pencil in hand. When she met Nan's angry gaze, she smiled, feeling intense satisfaction. She smoothed her skirt, giving Nan a look. The secretary looked away quickly, her lips thinned and spots of color in her cheeks.

Wanting to laugh, Cheramie pulled a letter from her purse. "Nan, would you type this for me, please? If that's too much bother on election day, do it in the morning."

"Yes, Mrs. Walcott," came the abrupt answer. Cheramie dropped the letter and went out the back door. As soon as she was in the car, she laughed, thinking about the look on Nan's face. "Serves you right, you little bitch," she said softly as she drove away.

That night Phillip pulled ahead in the first thirty minutes as the returns started coming in, and within hours he had an overwhelming victory and a party was in full swing in the

Walcott Inn ballroom. Rutger was beaming, as close as Cheramie had ever seen him come to being jovial. Aubrey and Pat Reiner stood talking to Alette. The family was gathered together for pictures, and as they broke up both Cheramie and Aubrey turned to Alette.

"Wait a minute, Alette, before you get lost in the crowd. There's someone here who wants to meet you," Cheramie said.

Aubrey laughed. "Hey, that's what I wanted. I have a friend who's asked for an introduction. One of Phillip's staff, as a matter of fact."

Cheramie's eyes widened and she laughed. "So is Todd."

"Will you two please decide what you're going to do," Alette said, amused and curious.

"Ahh," Cheramie said in satisfaction. "Here's my sister, Todd. Alette, this is Todd Patton, Phillip's speech writer, who has been wanting to meet you. Todd, meet Alette Lachman, and this is my brother, Aubrey."

Aubrey and Todd shook hands as he nodded at Alette. "I hear you're in landscape architecture. That's my uncle's business."

"Maybe I've heard of him?" Alette asked, and Todd laughed.

"I doubt it. Herschel Patton in Orlando, Florida."

"There you are," came a deep male voice, and a tall, brown-haired man joined them, looking questioningly at Aubrey.

"I need to find Pat."

"Aubrey—"

He grinned. "Alette, this is a fellow boating enthusiast— Bill Gaffney. Bill, this is my sister Alette Lachman. And you know Todd."

"By this time too well. I've wanted to meet you. Todd, would you excuse us? Aubrey was leaving anyway."

"Look, Gaffney—"

"Maybe I should leave," Alette said with amusement.

"Well, we'll both leave in just a minute. Todd, I want to show Alette my new boat."

For an instant Bill Gaffney received a glare, and then

Todd Patton grinned and winked at Alette. "Never let it be
said that I caused a scene at my boss's victory party. I'll
call you."

She nodded. "It was nice to meet you."

"Sure. Gaffney, I want a word with you tomorrow."

Bill smiled and steered Alette away from Todd toward
the door. He paused after a moment. "I'm not usually that
aggressive, but Todd can be pretty persuasive. I don't really
have a new boat, but I'm dying to get out of here. I've been
talking, writing, and sleeping political campaigns for the past
six months. Would you go have a drink with me, or would I
be pulling you away from your family too soon?"

Alette was intrigued by him, curious why he wanted so
badly to meet her when he didn't know her. The room was
stiflingly hot, and she was ready to escape the party, too.
"I'm ready."

"Great. I suppose you have to say a word to family, etc."

"No. I've congratulated Phillip, talked at length to Aubrey,
Cheramie, and my father. I'm free to leave."

He grinned and took her arm to lead the way through the
crowd. They stepped into the hall, and the cool air was a
welcome relief.

Bill wound her arm with his, and she glanced at him again.
He was brown-haired, handsome, brown-eyed, and she
couldn't remember anything about him except that he was
Phillip's press secretary.

As he fished keys out of his pocket, he exhaled deeply.
"Does this air feel better! I've had so many beers and glasses
of champagne with those guys, I feel as if someone pumped
my head full of helium."

He drove to the Cliff House. "It'll be cold and quiet, and
we can listen to the waves hit the shore," he said. "You
probably did enough volunteer work on Phillip's campaign
to know how hectic it can be. Actually, I've seen you at
headquarters and wanted to meet you, but either you were
just leaving or I was. Same with Todd. It became kind of a
joke once we both found out we were each trying to meet
you."

She laughed as they entered the restaurant. "I'm flattered,

I think. There must be some particular reason you both wanted to meet me.''

He gave her a surprised look. "Sure. You're a beautiful woman. That shouldn't be so hard to figure.''

The hostess came forward to seat them, and Alette didn't have to remark on his answer until they were seated and had ordered coffee.

"Thank you.''

"For what?''

"The remark about being pretty. How'd you meet Phillip?'' she asked, changing the topic.

"We went to Dartmouth together. I was a freshman when he was a junior, but we played on a water polo team together. My home is in Baltimore.''

"And this job?''

"Phillip called and asked me to take it, and I said yes. Pretty simple. I want to be in politics.''

"You and half my family. My father, my brother-in-law—''

"For a moment there I thought you started to say 'your brother,' and shock was about to set in. Aubrey seems like the last person on earth to want to win votes.''

"You really do know Aubrey.''

"Sure. He's raced back east, and he's damned good. You know he wins lots of big races, don't you?''

"I know he races and sometimes wins, because I've read about him occasionally in the paper, but I don't know much about how big the races are.''

"The modest soul. They're big. Take my word for it. Do you sail?''

"I'm learning, but I'm not very good at it yet. I'll never be like Aubrey.''

"Not many sailors are. But I didn't ask you out to talk about Aubrey. What do you like to do for fun?''

She shrugged. "I'm easy to please. I love snow and mountains, opera, gardens, antiques, art shows. Occasionally I used to dabble at watercolors, but I kept them hidden. I'm not good. What do you do for fun?''

She listened to him talk, thinking he was easy to be with.

He sat back on the seat, his tie loosened, his coat open, and she discovered they liked many of the same things. His hands were delicate for a man, well shaped with long, slender fingers. If she had to guess his occupation by the look of those hands, she would have said an artist or musician.

"What did you do before you came out here to be press secretary?"

"I was in my father's law practice. Cohen, Waterhouse, and Gaffney. You've probably never heard of them in California."

They talked about their backgrounds, and he amused her with tales about his college days and escapades with Phillip. She felt relaxed and realized they were alike in many ways—neither one was drawn to the limelight like Cheramie or Phillip. Once, when she laughed at something he said, he grinned.

"Nice laugh. I take it there isn't any one man right now?"

"No, but what made you decide that before you asked?"

"You would have brought him with you tonight, or I would have heard about him from Aubrey or someone else."

"You're right," she said. She realized she had worked so much lately that it had been two weeks since she had gone out with anyone or done anything that was purely for fun. "I've been really busy lately with my work."

"Ditto. I'd like to fly to Colorado and have nothing but solitude for the next week. Want to?"

She laughed, knowing he was teasing. "I'd have to cancel so many appointments it makes my head swim, but thanks anyway."

"Shucks. I had hopes for a moment there. We could go into town once to a flea market," he said in a mock persuasion.

"Sorry. As much as I would love that—"

"So I just have to start my new job tomorrow. I quit this and start that. Phillip has hired me as his press secretary when he moves."

"You'll be close to your home. I didn't know you had to officially quit and then start again."

"Sure. Keep things separate and clean." He stretched out his long legs and ran his hand over his thick, wavy hair. She realized he was really quite handsome, with his firm jaw and symmetrical features. "Now I'm disappointed to be leaving San Francisco. Any chance you'll be in Washington soon?"

"After Phillip and Cheramie move, I'm sure I'll go see them."

"Ah, so I can take you out when you're there. And we'll go to an antique store I know."

"Sounds great," she said, thinking it highly unlikely they would ever keep the date. It might be months before she went to visit Cheramie and Phillip. Yet the thought of seeing Bill Gaffney again was a pleasant one, and for a moment she wished he weren't leaving San Francisco tomorrow. The realization startled her, because although she enjoyed the friendship of several men acquaintances, there really hadn't been anyone she had been eager to date since Paul.

After his third cup of coffee, she glanced at her watch. "I have an appointment at eight in the morning, and I really intended to get home by eleven tonight."

"Hey, it's after one." He glanced around. "Okay, home it is."

She smiled as they stood up, and when they reached his rental car, he held the door for her. She watched him as he walked around the car. He was slender with broad shoulders and narrow hips.

He went to the door with her and stopped on the lower step. "I wish the victory party had come three months ago on my first visit to San Francisco."

"I do, too. It was fun to talk, Bill. And thanks for the coffee."

"I can cancel my flight if you can go out to dinner tomorrow night."

"Thank you," she said with real regret. "I can't."

"Well, we have a date when you come to Washington. Don't forget."

"I won't," she said, thinking she might go to Washington far sooner than she would have if she hadn't met him. "It was fun. Glad your man won."

"Yeah. Glad your brother-in-law won." They laughed, and he leaned forward and kissed her lightly on the mouth.

"Good-bye," he said softly, watching her while she entered her hallway. As he drove away, she wondered if she would ever see him again.

11

August 1985

Heads turned in the crowded Maryland restaurant, men's gazes following the dark-haired woman's progress across the room. As Cheramie approached the table, Alette realized her sister had changed slightly. Her breasts were fuller, her waist smaller in spite of the month-old twins, Phillip Cade IV and Brian Donovan. Cheramie had her curly hair straightened and swept back from her face, giving her a more sophisticated appearance. Only when she sat down and Alette gazed at her closely did she see the faint lines of strain around Cheramie's mouth.

"Sorry," she said as she settled on her chair. "Babies change your life totally! I don't care if I have an army of help, I have to be there. Don't get married." She ran her hand across her brow. "Sometimes I think I don't know a damned thing about being a mother."

"As long as you love them," Alette said quietly, staring at Cheramie. She'd seldom seen her distraught.

Cheramie lit a cigarette and blew smoke away from the table. "Sometimes I think Phillip just wanted them because of the image it gives him. The family man."

"Cheramie, Phillip looked proud enough to pop at church yesterday, and the babies were perfect for their christening. You have all kinds of help with them. They have a nanny, you have a maid—"

"Phillip's mother was at their side—one of those hovering

mothers who isn't satisfied unless she's supervising. He expects the same of me. He says I'm neglecting them when I turn them over to a nanny. Neglect! I might as well be chained to them."

She gave Alette a weak smile. "Enough about me. Rutger tells me your business is extremely successful."

"I've been fortunate. I have the Loomis Gardens."

"My God, the Loomis Gardens! You must be good!"

Alette laughed at the shock in Cheramie's voice. "I won the bid, at any rate. I'm doing the Gene Merriams' lawn— remember them?"

"Of course."

"And I have two more lawns with people who are new to San Francisco, so you wouldn't know them."

"I'm surprised you got away for the christening."

"It's nice to get a few days' vacation. I've been working weekends."

"Are you dating anyone in particular?"

"I've been too busy."

"Alette, you keep a fence around yourself."

"Don't be ridiculous."

"Aubrey can't make a lasting commitment, and you won't let down the barriers. The two of you can live together in your old age. Two old spinsters."

She laughed again at the thought of anyone referring to Aubrey as a spinster, yet beneath her amusement was a current of surprise, because Cheramie had changed. Differences were subtle; she was more acrimonious, less relaxed.

"You just haven't met the right man, I guess."

"Cheramie, please don't fix me up with anyone!"

"Don't worry. I can barely keep my wits about me to get through each day. We have Senator Carnes's party tonight— and I wish you'd come with us."

"No. I can entertain myself in Washington."

"Phillip has parties constantly. I'm having a dinner for twenty-three tomorrow night, and another dinner party for twelve next Thursday, and we're going to a party in between. The twins need to start their shots. Listen to me—babies, babies! I wish you'd stay longer."

"Thanks," she answered, thinking that Cheramie sounded as if she truly meant what she said. "My plane leaves Saturday morning and I need to get back."

"Lord, I wish I could get on the plane with you Saturday, although when we go home to California, Phillip is as involved in politics there as here."

"Phillip and Governor Giavotella have about come to blows over the environmental issue. Giavotella is an environmentalist. Save the mountain lions, stop offshore drilling. That alone gets Rutger irate. Everyone wants to save the lions. Rutger is supporting Nelson Crown. The party is grooming him to run against Sal in the next election."

"Nelson is leaving Lachman for politics?"

"Yes, Rutger persuaded him," Alette answered, thinking about the tall, gray-haired man who had successfully run Lachman Real Estate for over ten years now and was a close family friend.

"Phillip thinks Giavotella has his sights set on Washington."

"While I was shopping this morning, I found a gorgeous red dress at Valentino's and I thought of you. Come look at it after lunch."

"Okay. I have two hours before I have to start home. You have your car, so you can come home when you want."

They shopped, and in the evening Phillip and Cheramie took her to a German restaurant in Chevy Chase. The following night was the dinner party.

Ten minutes before the guests were due to arrive, Alette heard Phillip call to his wife.

"Cheramie! The twins need to be tucked into bed."

"I have to see about dinner, Phillip. Guests are due in minutes!"

"This is more important, and Marla can handle the kitchen, Amos has the door!"

"I have to see if everything is ready!"

Alette listened to the shouted argument from the top of the stairs to the hallway below. She gave one last look in the mirror and hurried into the hallway, the green silk skirt of her dress rustling slightly with each step. "Let their aunt Alette tuck them in tonight, Phillip," she said, smiling at him.

His scowl vanished. "Okay. Sure, Alette." His gaze swept over her. "You look pretty."

"Thank you," she said, thinking the only time she had seen Phillip turn off his charm was in his clashes with Cheramie. Alette went to the nursery, where Gretchen was holding a baby. Alette scooped up the twin.

"These babies get their loving," Gretchen stated with an indignant sniff, and Alette suspected Phillip had aggravated more than his wife.

She smiled, remembering the times Gretchen had taken care of her. "I'm sure they do."

"You look very pretty, ma'am. You risk little Phillip spitting up on your good dress."

Alette rocked the baby gently in her arms. "I think he's about to go to sleep."

Phillip entered the room. "Ah, Gretchen, let me have my son and I'll tell him good night."

"I think he's almost asleep, Mr. Walcott," she said with a frown, and from years with Gretchen, Alette knew she wanted Phillip to leave the baby alone. But Gretchen handed her bundle to him.

Alette looked at the tall man across the crib from her. Phillip was strikingly handsome in his dark suit, and it was startling to see him bounce the baby lightly in his arms. Alette had never in her life seen her father holding a child, nor could she remember Rutger holding her, and she felt a rush of tenderness that Phillip loved his sons. She wondered if Cheramie fully appreciated his feelings toward the babies. Gretchen had left them alone, and for a moment, in the intimacy of the dusky nursery, Alette felt closer to her brother-in-law than she ever had. "Phillip," she whispered. His head raised, and his gaze met hers.

"Be patient with Cheramie. We didn't have a mother to set an example. All we had was a very cold father."

He frowned. "It seems as if some things should come naturally to a woman."

Alette looked at the sleeping baby, dark lashes feathered on his soft cheeks. "They're both asleep." She placed the baby in his bed and looked at Phillip leaning over the other bed. He straightened and left the room ahead of her, going downstairs as the chimes rang and Amos admitted the first guests.

Cheramie appeared with a smile, looking as radiant as sunshine, as if nothing amiss had occurred. Yet within minutes Alette realized there was a definite coolness between Phillip and Cheramie. They avoided talking to each other if at all possible. Alette forgot about their quarrel when she looked up to see Bill Gaffney walk through the door.

She stood in a cluster of people and couldn't easily break away, because someone was in the middle of telling a story. When her gaze met Bill's, she saw his brows arch. Cheramie took him by the arm to introduce him to someone, and the next time Alette looked around he was out of sight. In minutes she broke away and drifted across the room.

"You came for the christening," he said at her elbow.

Laughing, she turned around. "Hello again."

"I've asked about you, and the times you've been in Washington, I've been out—or you had just left town when I asked. It's good to see you. You look great."

"Thank you. So do you," she answered lightly, feeling a rush of warmth as she looked up at him. Even though she hadn't thought about him before he walked in the door, she was glad to see him. She had forgotten how tall he was— almost four inches over six feet. He had changed little since the last time she saw him. "How's the political life?" she asked.

"Very political," he answered. "I still like it. Has Cheramie taken you to any antique shops?"

"Yes, of course. I always go to Duncan and Duncan and to Nannie's Attic when I get time."

"I know a great antique shop that's not so well known by the public. Have you ever been to Gillman Carver?"

"No, I haven't," she said, wondering whom he dated.

"I have certain periods I prefer. I collect things that appeal to me. I have a penchant for Georgian furniture, and I collect lamps. Look, I have one appointment tomorrow afternoon. Let me see if I can change it—''

"No, don't do that!"

"I want to," he said with a finality that ended her argument. And she wanted to go. She was on vacation, away from work for the first time in a long while, and his suggestion sounded like fun.

"We can go to Carver's, and I seem to recall promising to take you to dinner when you're here, so let's go to dinner tomorrow night unless Cheramie and Phillip expect you to join them. I've got tickets to the musical *Dreams*."

"I'd love to go. Cheramie and Phillip have a party to attend."

Bill caught her hand and held it in his to look at her fingers. "No wedding ring yet, I see. Is there any certain person?"

"No," she said, shaking her head. "I don't see a wedding ring on your hand, either. Any certain person?"

"Judith Lane. She's in France right now," he answered lightly. "She just got a job at the U.S. embassy."

Alette expected only friendship from Bill Gaffney. She barely knew him, and the fact that there was a woman in his life should not have been a disappointment, but she did feel oddly let down at his words. Still, she enjoyed Bill and looked forward to antiquing with him.

"Phillip is doing a great job," he said.

"I figured he would."

"Oh, I mean better than expected. He's on good committees—chairman of the House Military Construction Subcommittee, on the Committee on Public Works and Transportation, on the Senate Committee on Appropriations. He's building up strong ties. He's young and full of energy."

"Are you trying to persuade me to vote for him?" she asked, laughing at Bill trying to impress her with her brother-in-law's accomplishments.

He grinned. "I guess I don't have to tell you about him."

"So I take it you plan to continue to work for him."

"Yes. We work well together, and I intend to make a career of politics. How's the landscape business?"

"Very busy. It has really been good, and the few days'

vacation while I'm here are welcome. I've been working weekends."

"Alette, I have someone I want you to meet," Cheramie said, interrupting them with a cavalier grasp of Alette's arm. "I see you've met Bill. Will you excuse us, Bill?"

"Cheramie, I'll be along in a minute," Alette said, extricating herself gently. "Bill and I are discussing a very important nineteenth-century Biedermeier *secrétaire*."

Cheramie frowned. "If you insist. Bill, how is Judith?"

"Fine. I talked to her last night."

"You give her my love and tell her she should get back here to work. Bill's girlfriend is in France right now," Cheramie said to Alette, who bit back a smile.

"I know, Cheramie. He told me about Judith. Cheramie and Phillip have a gorgeous Louis Quatorze Boulle bureau *plat*. Have you seen it?"

"No, I haven't," Bill answered, his eyes twinkling as he looked at Cheramie. "You're the one into antiques, not Phillip."

"Phillip relies on our decorator or my choices most of the time, but he might surprise you with what he knows about furniture," Cheramie said.

"I'll show it to you," Alette said. "Want to come, Cheramie?"

"No, I see Al Winthrop and Dottie motioning to me."

They left Cheramie, moving into the quiet hallway, and Bill grinned. "You handled that rather nicely. Cheramie isn't easily sidetracked when she makes up her mind to do something. Now where is this gorgeous desk?"

"In Phillip's study." Alette led the way, and they crossed the empty room to the recently acquired treasure. Bill moved around it, his eyes lighting with pleasure as he rubbed his hand across its leather-topped surface.

"It is beautiful!" He knelt to study the cabriole legs.

"It isn't marked," she said, noticing his thick brown hair. He glanced up.

"None of the pieces from Boulle's workshop was marked," Bill said, standing up. They admired the desk, and after a few minutes Bill waved his hand. "This is nice. I can have you to myself and find out what's been happening in San Francisco. Want to sit down in here for a few minutes?''

''Yes,'' she answered, sitting down on a deeply cushioned wing chair and crossing her legs, knowing Cheramie would find them eventually. ''We should go back and join the others in a few minutes.''

''Sure. Tell me about landscaping.''

They talked, and the time slipped by until she heard the sounds of voices as guests moved toward the dining room. ''It's time for dinner,'' she said, rising.

Bill grimaced. ''I'm sure Cheramie will have me seated between two impossible politicians whom Phillip is trying to win over.'' She laughed and moved into the hall with him.

They were seated at opposite ends of the long crystal-and-silver-ladened table, and Alette didn't see him when they returned to the living room after dinner. As she moved away from a cluster of people, Cheramie appeared at her side.

''Where did you find that gorgeous dress? Green becomes you, and you seldom wear it.''

''Thanks. You look pretty, too,'' she said, thinking Cheramie did look beautiful in a dramatic red silk with a high, flaring collar.

''Alette, Bill Gaffney and Judith are all but officially engaged.''

''We're only friends, Cheramie, don't matchmake. I've only seen the man once before at Phillip's victory party, and I'll go back to San Francisco Saturday. We're both interested in antiques.''

''How do you like Lou?''

''Is that why he was seated beside me? I actually forgot why you arranged to have me between two single men.''

''You should think of marriage.''

''After all you said at lunch?''

''I was harassed,'' she said, taking Alette's arm. ''Lou, come here.''

A thin, dark-skinned man sauntered toward them, a faint smile coming as he saw Cheramie standing with Alette. ''Tell Alette about your vacation in Tibet. I think it would be a marvelous place for all of the Lachmans to go on a vacation.

A retreat. Just think about it," she said, patting Alette's hand and leaving the two of them alone. Alette gazed up into his dark eyes and saw a twinkle.

"I can tell you're breathlessly awaiting to hear about Tibet," he said with sardonic amusement.

"Cheramie can't resist. The Lachmans don't vacation together or go on retreats, except to get together at home in San Francisco or come here for a christening."

"Tibet is beautiful, but not a place I would pick for a family reunion."

"Who's having a reunion?" Bill said, joining them. "Am I interrupting anything?"

"No," Alette said as he draped his arm casually across her shoulders. "Lou was telling me about Tibet."

"If you two will excuse me, I'll refill my drink, because I know Bill can wait to hear about Tibet." Lou walked away, and Alette looked up at Bill, laughing with him.

"Alette probably doesn't want you wasting time with me. She and Judith are friends."

"Well, I told her that's all you and I are, just friends. I'm leaving for San Francisco Saturday."

"I have to go now, Alette. I'll call you in the morning around nine and let you know what time I can pick you up."

"Fine."

"It was good to see you," he said, turning away to find his host and hostess.

The next day they went to antique shops, to the play, and back to the Walcotts' for a drink. They sat in the study and talked; the babies and the servants were asleep, and the Walcotts were out until one. When Cheramie and Phillip arrived, they paused to talk briefly and then said good night and went upstairs, leaving Bill and Alette alone to talk. It was almost three in the morning before Bill stood up.

"Lord, I didn't realize the time! You're easy to talk to."

"So are you. Time fades when I'm on vacation."

"Unfortunately I'm not on vacation, and tomorrow is a busy day."

At the front door she looked up at him. "It's been a fun day and evening. I loved the antique hunting and my new lamp. If you come to San Francisco, I'll take you to the shops there.''

"Hey, that's great." His gaze lowered to her mouth, and he placed his hands on her waist. "I've had fun."

She nodded, wanting him to kiss her.

"Judith and I are pretty serious. We plan to marry."

"I understand." She nodded.

"But even so," he said softly, leaning closer and sliding his arms around her waist, "I'd like to kiss you good-bye." He tilted her chin up and leaned down to kiss her. In seconds his arm tightened and he pulled her close against him, kissing her harder. Her hands rested lightly on his arms, but in minutes she slipped them around his neck.

His kisses were passionate and ignited desire, and she knew she should stop, that he expected her to stop, but neither of them pulled away as their kisses became more tumultuous. Her heart pounded violently, and she felt his erection when he turned to lean against the wall and pull her tightly against him.

He raised his head and glanced beyond her at the stairs. "I can show you my place," he said softly, desire burning in his eyes.

He had kindled desire, but she was accustomed to being cautious. "Bill, you're in love with Judith."

He gazed at her with blatant desire, a smoldering speculation that was as searing as his kisses. "All right, Alette. Things got a little out of hand for friends. Good-bye."

He opened the door and crossed the porch before he turned to look back. "Good night."

They gazed at each other solemnly. "Good night, Bill," she repeated, and closed the door. She went upstairs, closing the door to her room and leaning against it. She knew she could have gone to his place and he would have made love to her. And it probably would have meant very little more to him than a pleasurable evening. What would it have meant to her? After Paul she had felt cautious where men were concerned, even vulnerable the first year. Now she was more relaxed about dating, but she still was a very private person. She couldn't casually enjoy sex and forget partners easily, so it was less complicated to abstain. But Bill Gaffney stayed in her mind long after she returned home.

At Christmas Alette met Judith when she was in Washington for a family gathering. She learned Bill and Judith were engaged, and although she dated several men in San Francisco, she resolved to take her social life more seriously in the new year.

She was surprised, then, when in August of that next year, 1986, she received a phone call from Bill Gaffney.

"How are you?" he asked in his deep voice.

"Fine."

"I'm sorry I missed seeing you when you were in Washington when Matthew was born."

"I'm sorry, too. Cheramie told me you were in Europe. It's difficult to imagine my sister as the mother of three now."

"I'm coming to San Francisco tomorrow on business, and you said you'd show me antique shops."

"I'd love to," she replied quickly, pulling her calendar in front of her. "How about if I pick you up at the airport? I'll show you the fabulous yard I'm doing, and then we can go antiquing."

"Sounds great. I arrive at ten," he replied.

They hung up and she stared at the phone a moment, wondering if he was married now.

As he walked off the plane at the airport, he grinned at her. "I'm glad you're here, but you must have had god-awful traffic," he said.

"Not so bad," Alette said, glancing at him in his navy suit. She wondered if he had caught the plane straight from his office.

"How's the election shaping up?"

"Everyone is hopeful."

"I'll get a more definite answer at dinner. And speaking of dinner, I'm starving. Gee, it's good to see you. You haven't been to Washington in a long time." He gave her a friendly hug as they walked and left his arm draped across her shoulders.

"No," she said, thinking how good it was to see him. "I'm busier than ever."

"I've found a new antique shop in Bethesda, and you'll love it."

"Maybe I'll get to Washington soon," she said, laughing. "How's Judith? How're the wedding plans? The last time I saw you, you were deciding wedding cake and music."

"I'm not seeing Judith any longer."

Startled, she looked up as they went outside. When they were into the flow of traffic, she glanced over at him. "I'm sorry."

"Better now than later. You should know. She wanted me to settle into Dad's practice at home, give up politics. She hates Washington, hates politics, doesn't want to leave her parents or her friends. I've longed for politics since I was a kid. I like Washington."

"Didn't this come up long ago?"

His jaw jutted out in a stubborn manner. "No. It would come up and die down, and she would say, 'Okay, I'll live in Washington.' " Then in the past six months, she put her foot down. Her parents got into it, and that was the final straw."

"I'm sorry. Since she lived in France, I'm surprised she's so tied to home."

"She says that's why she is. She quit that job and went home to Richmond and said she never wants to leave it again. She can give you over one hundred reasons she doesn't want to leave Virginia." He looked at her. "So how's your love life?"

"Nonexistent," she said lightly. "I'm working. This is the first time in two weeks I've taken off from work. I have a date with a nice guy tonight—"

He groaned. "A nonexistent guy is taking you out! I wanted to take you out. How serious is it?" he asked, studying her.

"Not serious." She gave him a quick glance, surprised at the look of relief in his expression. "We go out several times a month."

"Does he like antiques? Sailing?"

"No, but there are nice people who don't like either antiques or sailing. You'll see. Give Gary a chance."

"I already have a mental image," he said darkly.

"Cheer up. I have a new shop to show you. I found one north of here in a small town, and it's a jewel."

"And I can drive us up there in the morning. How's that?"

She thought about the appointments she had. Her gaze raked over his lanky body, his long fingers splayed on his knee.

"Let's make a day of it. Come on, it'll do you good to take the day off," he urged.

"I have appointments," she said.

"Change them. It isn't often you get to spend the day with a Washington, D.C., antiques expert."

She laughed and nodded, glancing at him again. She was aware of him as a handsome man, but her pulse didn't race at the sight of him as it once did. Yet until today she had always known he was committed to Judith.

They had the same friendly time together, each purchasing a new antique—Alette, a small Chinese bronze; Bill, a seventeenth-century Spanish vargueno. When he took her home that night and wanted to come in, their good-night kisses lengthened until she pushed him away.

"Bill, you've just broken up and we've always been good friends, but we don't really know each other so very well."

He studied her, sliding his hands along her rib cage. Finally he nodded. "I suppose the answer to that one is to get to know each other better." He kissed her lightly and left. They went out the next day and each night until he flew back to Washington, and then he called her three or four times a week. He was easy to talk to, but Alette felt a deep-running caution. She knew he was on the rebound from Judith, and she didn't want to get hurt. She promised herself she would not become solely involved with Bill, but his ardent pursuit left her little chance.

12

November 1986

By November Alette had spent one weekend in Washington and Bill had been to San Francisco three times. His fourth trip coincided with election day. She met him at the airport and drove him to his hotel, where he had a meeting, but before they parted they made plans for his stay.

"All tomorrow afternoon is free, so I can be with you and go to dinner and the watch party."

"Any chance of getting free in the morning?"

She drew a deep breath while she ran over the appointments in her mind.

"You'll only have me here a short time," he said with an appealing grin.

"Come by the office in the morning and I'll either change the appointments or you can look at some pretty yards with me."

"Good!"

"I hope our men win." She slowed at the entrance to the Walcott Inn, a forty-story hotel, named like all the others in the chain, that was on the site of the original Walcott Hotel where the chain started. Bill climbed out and leaned down. "See you tonight. I wish I could take you out, just the two of us, but this is one of those necessary political functions."

Promptly at half-past seven the next morning Bill arrived; they went to the polls so Alette could vote before going to her office, where Bill looked at some pictures of her work and blueprints while she changed appointments. He lounged on the chair across from her desk.

"I really interfered in your morning, didn't I?"

"I'm ready for a vacation," she answered lightly, thinking he looked handsome in his navy sweater and khaki pants.

"Ready to go?" he asked, and when she nodded he slammed shut a catalog and stood up.

They spent the morning driving north to an antiques shop, then eating in a small restaurant, and when they started home Bill took the ocean highway. It was overcast and windy, clouds racing overhead while foam-topped breakers rolled in and smashed on the sand. When he turned off and parked and suggested they get out and walk down to the water, she went readily. After weeks in the city it was fun to feel the wind buffet her, to listen to the crash of the waves and forget landscape problems.

After tromping in wet sand for ten minutes, she stopped, shivering and hugging her arms to her body. "I'm freezing!" she exclaimed, amazed at how much he seemed to enjoy himself. He kicked through the pickleweed and the cordgrass, studying debris washed up on the beach. He tried to dodge waves, walking out as the water receded and then racing back when a wave came rushing in. His khakis were rolled up beneath his knees, and his deck shoes were wet.

"Coward. This is invigorating," he said over the roar of the ocean. "I love it. It's primeval, and it clears my mind." He stopped, coming back to her. "Hey, you really are freezing!"

"What have I been telling you!"

He scooped her up in his arms and climbed the dunes swiftly, heading back to the car. At the car he set her on her feet, reached inside to get a jacket, and helped her into it. She looked up and found him watching her intently. "That was nice, carrying you up here," he said solemnly.

The moment changed, and she became intensely aware of him. She gazed up into his eyes, and desire replaced her chill.

"Alette?" he whispered, and it was a question. Longing showed in his expression as he bent his head to kiss her. His lips brushed hers, and he paused. "Put your arms around me," he commanded softly.

When she did, he pulled her against him while his head

tilted, his mouth slanted over hers, his lips opening hers and his tongue thrusting into her mouth to kiss her. She returned his kisses eagerly.

When they moved apart and climbed into the car, both were silent. As soon as they were on the highway, he turned on the heater. She was surprised by her reaction to him, a reaction that had been more intense than ever before.

He reached out to squeeze her shoulder. "Warmer now?"

"Yes, I'm finally warm."

He caught her hand in his, holding it in his slender fingers as he rested his hand on his thigh. "Maybe the cold was a good thing. It changed our relationship."

"Maybe," she said guardedly, looking out the window at the breakers smashing on the sand. As she stared at the surf, all she was aware of was his presence and her hand resting on his warm thigh, her fingers locked in his.

"Back up go the barriers," he said quietly.

"What are you talking about?" She faced him again.

"You know the answer. You keep a wall around yourself. If someone gets too close, up comes the wall. I suppose it's because of Paul."

"Actually, Aubrey has accused me of that, and he blames it on Rutger," she said, finding it a simple matter to be candid with Bill now that he had brought up something sensitive.

"Excuse me?"

"My brother the boat broker and his amateur psychology— he says that we're all compensating for the lack of love as children. That Cheramie has to have approval, he has to avoid commitment, and I have to keep everyone at a distance."

"I don't know about Aubrey or Cheramie, but I think he's right about you."

"I didn't do that with Paul. Aubrey says the time I let down my guard, I expected too much, I'm too vulnerable." She glanced at the dashboard clock. "My word! Look at the time. If we're late tonight, we won't be forgiven," she said.

"We won't be late." They were quiet going back, and he stepped out in front of the hotel. "We're going to be on time."

"You're already almost there," she said. "Your hotel is only across the street from where we'll have the watch party. I have to go home and change."

"You'll be here when you're supposed to be. See you soon." He gazed at her intently, and her heart seemed to stop.

"Good-bye," she said softly, and drove away. She showered and dressed in a brown-and-white silk dress and high-heeled brown sandals. She pinned her hair back from her temples and wore diamond studs in her ears.

The moment Bill turned around in the crowded ballroom to look at her, she was glad of the choice she had made, because she could see the pleasure in his slow appraisal. When he joined her, it became difficult to remember the election. Nelson Crown, the Lachman candidate who had been strongly backed by Rutger and Phillip, pulled ahead early and kept his lead.

"Phillip predicted a big win."

"I thought Sal had been popular enough that the party would stay in office."

"Sal Giavotella was popular, but Nelson learned from Rutger and they've put on a hell of a campaign, from what Phillip has told me."

Alette's awareness was of Bill. It was the first time since Paul that she was acutely conscious of a man and drawn to him.

And she knew Bill felt the same thing. He brought drinks and moved her to a corner as far from the crowd as possible. They sat beside a window overlooking the lights of the city while they talked and forgot everything around them.

"Remember the last election—when Todd and I both wanted to take you home?"

"You don't know he wanted to take me home."

"Oh, yes, I do! Speaking of leaving—let's get out of here."

"Now? You think we should go?"

"Nelson has victory in his hip pocket. C'mon. We'll give the Crowns congratulations." Bill took her hand, and she went with him. They were at the Fairmont, and he linked her arm through his, walked out into the cool night and down the hill across the street into the lighted lobby of the Walcott Inn, where he crossed to the elevators.

In Bill's suite a light was still burning in the bedroom and the drapes were open, giving a view of the city, but Alette didn't notice. She went into his arms as he bent his head to kiss her. He leaned against the door, pulling her tightly against him.

Desire fanned like flames between them; it had been so long since she had been loved, and this was a man she enjoyed and knew well. When he twisted free the tiny buttons down the back of her dress, she unfastened the buttons on his shirt and pushed it away along with his coat, running her hands across his broad, muscled chest, relishing the feel of his body. As her dress fell around her feet, he held her away and gazed at her, his eyes burning. He slid his fingers beneath the straps of her lacy bra, bending his head to kiss her, his tongue flicking over a taut nipple while she gasped with pleasure and wound her fingers in his soft hair.

They undressed each other swiftly, and he picked her up to carry her to his bed and pull her down on top of him. He was hard, thrusting into her as she settled over him and they began to move, his hands playing over her. She was rocked by passion until a bursting climax, and then she sank down into his arms. He stroked her damp hair away from her face.

"I think I'm in love, Alette. Don't shut me out."

She smiled and played her fingers lightly over his shoulder and throat and along his jaw. "Have I shut you out tonight?" she asked with amusement.

He rolled over to look at her solemnly. "I love you."

She gazed into his eyes, her heart beating quickly. "Don't rush things, Bill. Let's make sure of what we feel. You broke up with Judith last summer, and your emotions may be on a roller-coaster."

"I know what I feel, and it's not because I broke up with her. Maybe I broke up with her because of what I feel for you."

She shook her head. "There hadn't been anything between us. You know that."

"No, I don't. We've had a growing friendship for years now. This isn't something that came up all at once."

She stroked his hair back from his face and nodded. "We haven't really gone together," she said, remembering she had a similar relationship with Paul—the deep friendship and the fact that after his graduation they never lived in the same town and saw each other only on occasional weekends. "I don't want to analyze it, Bill. Not tonight."

He grinned and rolled her over so he was on top of her. He came down kissing her wildly on her neck, tickling her, making her squirm and laugh until suddenly they were kissing and lost in an embrace. Desire fanned to white-hot heat again.

She spent the night in his arms, and when morning came she moved away after lovemaking. "I have to go home."

He shook his head. "I don't want to share you with the world."

"The world goes on. We don't even know absolutely that Nelson won."

"Of course Crown won! He had it in his pocket when we left last night. I'll get my crystal ball," Bill said, climbing out of bed. "You just stay right where you are." His voice changed to an exaggerated leer as his gaze swept over her. "And stay just like you are—naked and beautiful. I'll be right back with results."

He was back in minutes with a newspaper, and they sat up in bed reading together.

"You're right. Nelson Crown is the new governor of California," she said, knowing how pleased Rutger would be. "This will be a setback for Sal Giavotella and Jeff O'Neil."

"You don't like either one of them. I can understand with Giavotella. He's an arrogant bastard, but I don't know what's wrong with O'Neil. God knows he was a great baseball player, and it was a bum deal to have his arm injured when he was rising like a shooting star. What the hell don't you like about him?"

She wanted to retort it was the way he looked at her, but she knew that sounded absurd. "He's tough."

Bill laughed. "He's *tough*? That coming from a Lachman?

He must have given you a hard time, hon. I didn't think you knew him very well."

"Let's talk about something besides Jeff O'Neil."

Bill's smile faded as he scanned the front page, and he groaned. "Jesus. Here it is. Phillip said he thought this would be the reason Sal Giavotella didn't run again. He's announced he'll be going to Washington with a presidential appointment. He'll head the president's new National Institute of Coast and Resource Conservation."

"How much can that interfere with Phillip? I'd think he would hardly see the man."

"I hope not, but if he's ambitious, Giavotella can make his presence known. Phillip hates Sal Giavotella, and now they'll be right under each other's noses. You talk about tough—that word fits Giavotella. When he wants something, he goes after it like a barracuda."

"So does Phillip. I don't see why there's so much animosity."

"Sal is working for environmentalists—he interferes in Phillip's interests. When he was governor, he pushed for the government to pass legislation for cost-sharing provisions for water projects. He's fought at home to push for a moratorium on drilling offshore. They're poles apart."

"Rutger just hates Sal because he beat him in the election." She laughed, and Bill tilted his head and looked at her quizzically. "I just thought about Rutger. He's going to be delighted you're in my life. You're all the things he'd want in a man who would date his daughter."

"Don't say it like you've discovered I have three heads. This sounds ominous."

"Not so ominous. Just surprising." A knock interrupted them, and Alette sat up. "Who's that?"

Bill laughed. "Relax. You look as if the FBI is here. I ordered breakfast."

Later, when she dressed to go, Bill watched her. "I can arrange to stay the rest of the week. Can you take time off?"

"I have an appointment Thursday afternoon that I must keep."

"We'll work around that," he said softly, running his hands across her shoulders and down her back, gazing at her with warmth as he pulled her to him. "Maybe this is what I've been wanting all along."

She looked at him and wondered how important they would be in each other's lives.

Two days after the elections, shadows slanted long across the paving in the deserted parking lot of the white stucco building that was the headquarters of Jayton Foods. The air was clear and cool, without a breeze stirring. Jeff O'Neil opened the car door and picked the frail man up in his arms to carry him through a door held open by his mother. He set his father down in the wheelchair and pushed him along a silent, lighted corridor.

"This is all yours, Jeff? This is all your office building?"

"Yes, sir," Jeff said, feeling a rush of pleasure and love, gazing down at the strands of gray in his father's hair. He looked up. "Are you coming, Mom?"

"I'm right here," she said, following him. Her blond hair was short and curly, her figure still trim, and Jeff always marveled at how well she had weathered the years and the physical and financial problems. He pushed the wheelchair in and out of rooms, explaining what each room was used for. Earlier he had shown them the warehouse.

"Here's my office," he said quietly, giving his father a moment to look around. "It's pretty simple, but it's comfortable and practical."

"It doesn't look so simple, Jeff," Nadine said, walking around. "It's gorgeous."

Jeff gazed at his broad ebony desk, the beige upholstered chairs, the oak paneling and cabinets and deep green carpet. He opened louvered doors. "Here's a small bar. Here's the bathroom. Here's a room where I can really have some privacy and sleep if I want," he said, motioning toward the ten-foot-long beige sofa.

"Jeff, it's so nice," Nadine said, and he detected the note of dissatisfaction.

"Mom, something doesn't suit you."

"Of course it doesn't, Jeff," Barney said mildly. "Mom wants you married. She wants grandbabies. She doesn't understand your generation."

"I just want to see you happy," Nadine said. "You work so hard and you live alone."

"I'm okay, Mom. I'm busy doing what I want to do." He moved back into his office and around behind his desk to wave his hand at two maps on the wall behind his desk. One was an enlarged map of San Francisco. The other was a map of the United States. Between the two was a framed, floor-to-ceiling list of product names with red lines drawn beneath them.

Jeff pointed to the San Francisco map. "The yellow areas are places handling Lachman products. The red are places handling Jayton Foods. The orange are the ones we've taken over," he said with satisfaction, looking at a map filled with orange areas.

"What do you mean, 'taken over'?" his mother asked. "You're not doing anything violent, are you?"

"Mom!" Jeff said, laughing. "This is me, your son. Of course not. We've built up the sales force; they get big bonuses for every Lachman account they acquire. Nothing violent or illegal. I'm just a businessman out there hustling and trying to grow." He waved his hand at the list between the maps. "The products underlined in red are the ones we've taken from Lachman."

"Mother, let me talk to Jeff."

She left the room, and Jeff sank onto his chair and propped his feet on the desk. "Okay, what is it?" he asked.

"Jeff, I didn't want to worry your mother. Rutger Lachman isn't going to give up that much business, brush his hands off, and say 'Oh, too bad.' He'll come after you sooner or later, and he'll put you out of business and ruin you completely and take every penny of your savings."

"No, he won't," Jeff said quietly. "There's no way. A little price war has started, but it will hurt him just as badly, and I'm big enough to hold out as long as he does."

"I don't want to see you hurt."

"I won't get hurt."

"Anytime you fight the Lachmans, you'll get hurt," Barney O'Neil said.

Jeff heard the pain in his voice and saw it in his defeated expression. His father was stooped, crippled, and had long ago given up on life and withdrawn from society. As the years had passed, he had developed a hobby of pottery, and when he worked with his hands, he seemed contented. Jeff wasn't surprised that the thought of the Lachmans brought up painful memories, but he was surprised at how unhappy his father looked.

"I'm careful," Jeff said quietly. "He should have come after me when I started. Now he's going to have a hell of a fight if he does."

"I raised you to hate him. I shouldn't have. Hate consumes people and warps them. I know why you came back," he said softly, looking down and running his thin hand on his bony knee.

Jeff felt a knot in his throat. He put his feet on the floor. "Dad—"

"You've done all this for Mother and me," Barney said, wiping his eyes. "We're glad to have you back; we hated that you were hurt and couldn't play ball, because you had a God-given talent. But we don't want you taking on Rutger Lachman."

"I would have gone into business somewhere, and home is the best place. I did it for myself and for both of you."

"Just don't get so wound up in revenge that you change or get hurt. I'd lose twice, you know."

Jeff nodded. "You've always been positive that it was Rutger Lachman in the factory the night of the fire. How do you know for sure?"

"I saw him, and he saw me."

"Why the hell didn't you tell the police?"

"I was too hurt that night. I couldn't talk for a long time. My lungs were damaged from smoke inhalation. Then in the hospital . . ." He paused and looked away, finally facing Jeff. "I guess greed got me. I thought whatever he got from the fire he would share. I kept quiet. And then it was too late. The insurance paid the company, and I got my half. Rutger brought the money. He said we had a failing business and he wanted out of the partnership. I had the insurance money, and I finally gave in and accepted, letting him buy me out of the partnership for what I put in originally. What I didn't know was that an account I had called on before the fire agreed to do business with us. Rutger rebuilt with new machinery that could handle the account, opened again with triple the business we had before the fire. I never got a commission, even though I was the one who got the account in the first place.

"I was ill, unable to cope with Lachman. If I had been well, maybe I could have thought clearer and fought him. And of course, I should have turned him in for the fire the moment I could."

Jeff bit back any comments. It was over and done, and both his parents had suffered from it.

"Just don't forget and let your guard down, Jeff. He's going to fight. I can promise you."

"I'm not afraid of the Lachmans."

The next morning in his office, Jeff crossed the room to shake hands with Sal.

"Damn, you look like a movie star! No wonder you get such great press," Jeff said, his gaze sweeping over Sal's swarthy skin and gleaming white teeth, his hair growing a fraction longer than the fashion, a thin gold chain around his thick neck. He dropped onto a chair, and Jeff sat behind his desk. "I guess you won't be coming back into the business since you have the appointment to Washington."

"That's right. We'll move as soon as I can wind things up here. Of course, we'll keep the home here, but I want to sink roots in Washington. Besides, as far as this business is concerned, I have you," Sal said with a smile. As Jeff rummaged in the desk and produced a folder, Sal leaned forward. "What's this on a price war?"

Jeff grinned. "We've got a little margin and we've picked up some big accounts. We'll be all right."

"I'm glad you're not my political opponent. As long as you keep a profit margin like we've had, I can't complain."

"There's another reason I wanted to see you. I want to change the executives' stock plan. I want to arrange it so they own a little more of the company. I want them to have a percentage of stock based on their salaries and a bonus plan."

"You increase the stock owned by executives and you'll decrease your own profits."

"If they earn more, I'll be happy to pay out more. I think if a man has a share of the company, he'll have a vested interest in the company's growth. Here's what I have in mind." Jeff shoved a folder across his desk. "Take that home with you. I know you're busy, but when you can, read my suggestions."

Sal leaned back and pulled out a cigar. "Mind?"

"No. I thought you gave it up."

"I did, except for occasions like this where I have complete privacy. Gina nags hell out of me. She says it's bad for kids, bad for my image to have a cigar or cigarette hanging out of my mouth, and it annoys the nonsmokers, so I just do this when I can get away with it in private and I'm away from her." In minutes his head was wreathed with smoke. He waved the cigar in the air. "This is changing the subject for a minute—there are a lot of men who want you to get into politics."

"Roy Stoddard talked to me last week about the gubernatorial race," Jeff said, leaning back behind his desk. "At the moment I have all I can handle here."

"Nelson Crown is ensconced as governor. They'll need a strong man next time to fight him. He was head of Lachman Real Estate. Think about it, Jeff."

Jeff laughed. "Isn't this a little premature? Crown just won."

"No. We want you to start thinking. You can't imagine how early I started. And I've got my sights set on climbing the ladder in Washington."

Jeff didn't doubt the last statement at all. "The party has Loren Waterville. I'm not ready to leave Jayton Foods," Jeff said, rubbing his hand across the nape of his neck. "I'm flattered anyone wants me, but this company holds my full interest now."

"I'd like to change your mind. As you said, the next election is far away. Just think about it now." Sal leaned forward. "Jeff, this is the way if you want revenge. Not just one big company battling another big company, but two men who have run for the same office and only one of them has won. If you think that wouldn't enrage Rutger Lachman, then you don't know much about your man."

"I'll think about it, Sal," Jeff said, his gaze shifting to the window momentarily as he thought about how restless he had felt this past year. The business had grown until it was a formidable competitor of Lachman, yet he knew he could never put Lachman out of business. He was satisfied with the results he had achieved; the few times he'd attended the same party as Rutger Lachman, he'd seen the anger in the older man's eyes at the sight of him.

"This is why you keep inviting me to the political bashes, isn't it?" he asked Sal. "You want me to meet the right people."

"Yes, I think you'd make a good candidate. Hell, with your ball background and your charm, the voters would melt like hot butter. And you don't have a wife and family to slow you down."

Jeff studied Sal, wondering if his friend felt Gina and the kids were a burden. "I thought they were supposed to give you stability and reassure the voters," he replied solemnly. "How is Gina?"

Sal's gaze slid away, and Jeff felt a flicker of disappointment. "Hell, same as ever, bitch and nag about politics."

"That isn't the answer you would have given four years ago."

Sal looked at him sharply. "She wasn't meant to be a politician's wife."

"What about the move to Washington?" Jeff asked, wondering how much Sal had changed or if the four years in the governor's mansion had changed Gina.

Sal shrugged. "Where I go, they all go. You're lucky you're single. Gina's not an asset in politics, and I belong there," he said, and Jeff thought he sounded as if he were remarking that his Cadillac didn't run as well as it should.

"What about the new truck stops?" Sal continued, changing the subject. "You were going to look into it, go to Kansas City."

They went back to talking about business, and it was five before Sal left. Jeff worked for another half hour and then left to take his boat out for a sail before dark.

There was a brisk wind and a small chop. He spotted the familiar colorful red-and-blue sails of the small sailboat that belonged to Alette Lachman, and as he passed he saw she had a man with her. Later, when he passed the breakwater, he sailed close enough to see she was with someone he knew. He tried to place the face and remembered it was William Gaffney, Walcott's press secretary. Jeff's thoughts went to politics, and he mulled over Sal's arguments that he run for governor.

The idea appealed to him. Sometimes he wondered if he was always striving for something more as a gift to his father. Barney was growing weaker with each passing year. If Nelson Crown, a Walcott-Lachman man, ran again, it would be satisfying to go up against him. Right now Jeff didn't feel the business was strong enough for him to step down, but a lot could change in the next few years. He didn't like Crown, who had already been vocal over several hot issues, including reapportionment and medical care. Jeff thought of the florid, gray-haired man who was an ultraconservative businessman with his eye on the dollar only. Crown had fought environmental projects, medical projects, and minority rights.

Later in the berth, as he secured the bow line, Jeff turned to look at Alette Lachman as she walked past with Gaffney. She glanced around, saw him, and nodded curtly.

There was something about her that always jarred him. He raked his gaze over her shapely long legs, because he suspected it made her angry to be looked at so blatantly. She lifted her chin, and as he tightened the line, he watched the sway of her hips, speculating whether she was capable of passion. His gaze lingered on her rounded behind, and he acknowledged ruefully that he would like to find out.

13 ∽

For three days snow blanketed Washington and the surrounding countryside. Cheramie's nerves were stretched taut, because in addition to the weather, the boys had chicken pox and couldn't go to play school. She stood in the big bedroom she shared with Phillip and gazed angrily at the pile of clothing on the floor. Phillip Cade and Brian had both been sent to their room under Gretchen's sole supervision. They knew they weren't supposed to play in their parents' bedroom, and they knew better than to get into the drawers. Phillip's clothing was in a jumbled heap on the floor, and Cheramie had personally to sort it all out before getting ready for her luncheon date in three hours.

She couldn't wait to escape the house. Phillip was out of town on a senatorial jaunt to a military base in Kentucky. Sometimes she suspected he had deliberately selected committees that required him to travel. That left her shut away with the boys and no adult company for weeks instead of days.

She replaced underwear in neat stacks and was thankful Phillip was orderly, because it made life easier. He kept few things he didn't use, and he was not a sentimental man. He remembered all the anniversaries and birthdays and holidays, but it was because he had them recorded on his calendar, and his secretary saw to the gifts. Cheramie noticed two old billfolds that he no longer used, and she debated whether to discard them or not. Beneath a pile of handkerchiefs on the floor, a small package caught her eye. She pulled it out and stared at two packages of condoms.

Phillip never used condoms. She had always been on the Pill except when he had cajoled her into getting pregnant. She stared at the packages, reading the label, then tucked them away in the drawer and stacked the handkerchiefs neatly on top.

Credit cards and gasoline tickets were scattered about, and she picked them up, knowing he kept meticulous records of their bills. She put the cards in a stack the way he kept them at the front of his drawer. She sat cross-legged on the floor and studied the tickets, going through the dates. One particular date made her pause. The first of December Brian had had his tonsils removed. He'd been an outpatient, in the clinic only a few hours and then back home. The procedure had been routine, and he had recovered quickly, but Phillip hadn't been able to get home. He had been in Florida for a speaking engagement. He had called her to make sure Brian was all right. He said he had flown down. She didn't think he had rented a car. And whether he had or not, it didn't matter. The gasoline ticket read Baltimore. The date was stamped by a machine, and Phillip's scrawling signature was on it.

Her first thought was that the date was wrong. She put it back in the stack and replaced the tickets in the drawer and changed for lunch.

During the next few days she thought about the condoms and the gasoline ticket. She paid closer attention to Phillip and his schedule. She hadn't suspected any cheating on Phillip's part since they had moved to Washington, but she wasn't going to ignore the obvious clues.

She hired a private detective from Baltimore for the next month. Knowing she would have to be careful, she drove there herself to hire him and never spoke to him on the phone. If the press picked up her tail, Phillip's career would suffer. She paid the detective out of her separate account. She would sleep better once she had a report that showed exactly where Phillip had been.

Three weeks after she hired Donald Plymouth, she received her first report. At a restaurant on the highway back to Chevy Chase, she sat in a corner booth while she ordered coffee and pulled out the report. As she glanced down the page, she stiffened and her heart pounded.

The words seem to leap up at her. A motel in Baltimore, one in Leesburg. Her ears roared as she read the dates. Breathing deeply, she stared across the empty restaurant. She wanted to pick up her cup and saucer, smash them, and scream. She doubled her fists and shook, unaware that her nails were creasing her palms. They had made a deal, forgiving each other and swearing to be faithful. She read through the report again and focused on one date: the first of December.

She thought about going to the clinic with Brian, juggling schedules, and caring for her son. The next day Phillip had breezed in carrying presents for the boys and one for her, a solid-gold bracelet with three golden hearts, one for each boy. And while she had been in a clinic holding Brian's hand after his surgery, Phillip had been in a motel with another woman.

"Anything else? Ma'am, are you all right?"

She became aware of the waiter speaking to her. "I'm fine. I want my check."

"Yes, ma'am." He placed it in front of her. She left the restaurant without knowing what she was doing. She wanted to drive the car into something, to smash something. And she wanted to go home and destroy Phillip.

As she swept onto the freeway, a horn blared. A car crossed to the other lane, and she realized she had pulled in front of it and crowded him over. When the driver shook his fist, she shook hers in return as she burst past him. In minutes she glanced down at the speedometer. The needle was past ninety. Instantly she took her foot off the gas. She didn't want to wreck the car and hurt herself.

She was long experienced in watching Rutger keep an iron control on his temper while coolly, effectively killing his opponent. Another wave of rage engulfed her when she thought of Rutger. He hadn't stopped Phillip's affairs, yet he would disinherit her if he found her unfaithful. She hated them both. She felt trapped by babies and the men in her life. Her mind raced as she drove home, and by the time she swung up the driveway she had come to some decisions. She would get back at Phillip, and Rutger, too, for interfering in her life. But this time she wouldn't get caught. She had learned her lesson. Phillip hadn't.

Three nights later they had a large dinner party to attend for the Swedish ambassador, at the home of Senator Clay Wilson. Cheramie was close friends with Janet Wilson, his wife. She had spent the day at Elizabeth Arden's, trying to look her best, and she wore a dress that cost Phillip, a Gianfranco Ferré shocking pink silk organza with a high neck in front and a back that was open to the waist.

It was a mixed crowd with people from both parties, and as Cheramie paused in the dining room, she saw Sal Giavotella standing in a circle of guests. His dark-eyed gaze raked over her in a purely masculine appraisal, and as his eyes raised, he looked into hers. She stared back with a faint smile of amusement. And then, as she looked at him, she realized that not only was Sal Giavotella a handsome man, he was the man Phillip hated most. And Rutger hated him almost as much as Phillip did.

She let her gaze drift down over Sal just as blatantly and back up to meet his gaze. His brows arched, and he tilted his head and laughed. He moved away from the cluster of people, and she turned to join him when he strolled outside on the patio, where two men played violins.

"It's nice outside," she said softly.

"Nice night, nice music, and you're bored with the party," he replied. "And what's sauce for the gander is sauce for the goose," he added. "Or something like that."

She smiled. "I couldn't resist temptation."

"Do you often yield to it?"

Glancing at him, she felt her pulse skip. He was really quite appealing. "It depends on how tempting something is," she answered him in a coy tone. "And how much fun I might have."

"This is a night I'll remember. It's the first time a Lachman or a Walcott has ever socialized with me."

"Sometimes it's interesting to learn a little about your enemies."

"Enemies?" he asked, arching his brows again. "That's too strong in our civilized world."

"You know you would do anything to beat my father or my husband in politics. You take opposing stands on every issue."

"Perhaps we do. But as for the senator's beautiful wife— I have no quarrels whatsoever. I've always had a deep appreciation for beautiful women."

"Thank you," she said, laughing. "I think you must want something from Phillip."

"No. If I could have a wish, I'd wish him home with some hefty senate problem. I didn't know a Lachman could be so warm and charming."

"Thank you. I didn't know a Giavotella could be so entertaining, but then I've never met your family. Is your wife here?"

"No. We have six children, and she's too busy to make all the social functions I attend."

"I didn't know you had such a big family," she said, momentarily taken aback to discover that he was the father of six.

"I know you have a father, a brother in the boat business, and a sister who is a landscape architect."

"And a husband and three children. Now you know all about me."

"*Au contraire!*" he said. "I know almost nothing about you, Mrs. Walcott—"

"Please, it's Cheramie," she said, lowering her voice and moving a step closer, deciding he must not be totally devoted to the wife and six children if he was mildly flirting.

"Cheramie. Charming. It's a beautiful name for a beautiful lady who must like Washington as well as San Francisco."

She shook her head. "No. I like Washington, but I *adore* San Francisco."

"What do you like best in San Francisco?"

"I like the restaurants, the view, the fog, the bay."

"There are good restaurants here, good views, on occasion fog, and we have an ocean."

"Windswept beaches."

"We have that, too. You're one of the organizers of the arts ball each year. You must like museums, since the proceeds go to art. And Washington is tops for museums."

"You're right. And as I recall your name is always on the list, and you always attend the arts ball and the black and white ball."

"I'm interested in the arts. What artists do you like?"

"Titian, El Greco."

"What contemporary artists?"

"John Marin and Jackson Pollock."

"Ah, there's one of my favorites. Pollock, Kandinsky. I like Robert Rauschenberg's social protest. I like Chig Dorian's bright pictures."

While they talked about art, Cheramie was aware of Sal's proximity. She could catch a scent of his after-shave. His hair was thick and curly, his nose slightly hooked, giving him an imperious look that was offset by the flash of white teeth and a winning smile. His remark about Chig Dorian triggered a memory, and without stopping to weigh right or wrong, she made a decision.

"Dorian has a showing at a small gallery, Green Gate, tomorrow night at seven," she said casually, her pulse racing because she was taking risks. "I plan to attend, because I've followed his career since his California days."

"You're in the enemy camp, talking to me," he said quietly, glancing over her head.

"Phillip won't care. It's a party. You're just as much in the enemy camp talking to me."

He shrugged a thick shoulder. "A husband might be more sensitive about it than one of my fellow politicians. Has Phillip taken a stand yet on the commercial fisheries appropriation bill?"

She laughed. "I don't know much about my husband's business."

"You know his political stands, what he intends to release to the public."

"He's not on the side of the environmentalists. You already know that. Not if it hurts business. He's firm about keeping

California's economy strong." She smiled up at him. "I better go back inside, away from the enemy camp."

His dark eyes held a curious gaze. She turned to walk away, swaying her hips and hoping it was provocative. An artist liked by Sal Giavotella had a showing tomorrow night. She knew he couldn't mistake her purpose in telling him she was attending. Now, would Sal Giavotella rise to the bait? And if he did? Possibilities floated in her mind. There was no man she could have an affair with whom Phillip would detest more . . . than Sal Giavotella.

She glanced over her shoulder. Sal raised his drink to her. He stood watching her. She gave him another smile and turned away. Sal Giavotella was exciting, risky, sexy, and he would be the perfect revenge. He was also safe. He would want to keep an affair as quiet as she would.

That night in bed after they had made love, she lay beside Phillip's heated body and stared into the dark. "The party was fun tonight."

There was a moan from Phillip, and she knew he was almost asleep.

"I met Henry Pierce. What's he do?"

"Congressman from Maine, Cheramie."

"And who was the blonde, Gloria somebody?"

"She's married to a senator from Wyoming. Go to sleep."

"I met Sal Giavotella, but I didn't meet his wife."

"She doesn't get out much. Too many babies, and she's a homebody."

"Does he sleep around?"

"Hell, how would I know?"

"You'd know."

"He likes women. He's as slick as they come, and he's one of the smart ones. He wouldn't fuck up and get caught. He'd keep an affair hidden so well the CIA couldn't unearth it."

She turned to look at Phillip, wondering if he thought he was one of the "smart ones" and had his affairs so hidden no one would discover them. For an instant she wanted to scream at him that she could name every little cheap piece of tail he had fucked the past month. A wave of rage buffeted her as she looked at him. He lay with an arm outflung, his head turned away from her and his eyes closed. The sheet lay across his middle, leaving his chest bare, and when Cheramie thought about Phillip with another woman, she burned with fury. She wanted to pommel his chest and face and shout at him, curse him for his unfaithfulness. Instead she stared at him and retained her composure.

"I've never heard one scandal about Giavotella," Phillip continued sleepily. "The day I do, I'm running to the paper with it. Lord, he's a tough bastard!"

"Who was the tall, black-haired woman in the Dior dress?" she asked quietly.

"Hon, I wouldn't know a Dior dress. Cheramie, I'm bushed. Let's rehash the party over breakfast."

"Then you'll be in a rush to go. She had long black hair."

"Tomorrow, Cheramie," he said, turning his back to her.

She raised one finger to Phillip.

Phillip was leaving for three days to go to a military base in Arizona.

She spent the next morning at a spa in her routine exercise, and from there she went to her salon to get her hair and nails done. She had a new red dress she had worn only once. She told Gretchen that she was going to a gallery showing and out to dinner with friends. She drove to the gallery and parked, her pulse quickening as she climbed out and entered the small shop. Piped-in music played softly in the background, and she was greeted at the door and given a list of paintings and offered champagne by a waiter.

Sal was standing across the small gallery, gazing at her with a faint smile. Her eyes met his, and she felt a tingle and a surge of triumph. She felt daring and reckless and eager for revenge. Again the thought came that Sal was perfect—handsome and needing secrecy as badly as she did. She nodded to him and turned away to look at the nearest paintings.

"It's a nice showing, isn't it?" Sal asked several seconds later, and she turned around to face him.

"Yes. I'm glad you came."

"Phillip isn't interested in art?" he asked mildly, glancing around.

"No. Phillip is out of town for three days," she answered. "I wanted to see the paintings. My father has a birthday soon, and I'd like to get him something special. Tell me which ones you like. You know what appeals to a man," she added in a breathless tone, touching his arm lightly.

She was aware of the intensity of his gaze, the way he stood close. It added a sensuousness to his physical presence. She could smell his after-shave, see the faint shadow of stubble on his jaw.

"Yes, I know what appeals to a man," he said with a faint smile. "It depends on the man. Beauty appeals to some. Fire, a hint of excitement, can appeal to another. A silent promise of hidden pleasure," he said in a voice that held its own hint of excitement.

Her heart beat faster as she listened to him, finding him not only the perfect man for revenge, but also more exciting than any man she had met in a long time.

"You're poetic. Beauty, fire, excitement, and hidden pleasure. You think there is a painting in this room that will fill that bill?"

"A painting?" he asked, and gave an inflection to the word that made her certain he was flirting. "Perhaps. We'll look."

He took her arm, and they moved to a large painting of abstract expressionism in bold strokes and splotches of primary colors. While Sal talked about the painting, she gave him her full attention. Unless she was misreading signals, Sal Giavotella wasn't as circumspect as Phillip thought. And there had to be a good reason. She was honest enough with herself to know that he was not swept off his feet by his brief meeting with her last night at the party. Washington was filled with beautiful women and with beautiful younger women. They paused in front of the next painting, and Sal still held her arm. He stood close beside her, her arm pressed against his side.

As she listened to him talk and stared at an abstract painting of lines and colors, she realized what he wanted from her. He had asked her last night. He hoped to get information about Phillip. He had said it himself—he was in the enemy's camp. She realized they were both playing a game. No doubt

Sal Giavotella was intrigued with her because she was married to a powerful opponent, and Sal had political ambitions.

They moved around the room slowly, looking at each painting, discussing its merits. Her father's birthday wasn't for two months, and she hadn't thought of giving him a painting, and if she did, he would not like any in this gallery.

She debated between two paintings for a time, and they argued about which one would appeal more to a man. She bought one for her bedroom, because Phillip would see it constantly and when she looked at it she would think of tonight. With every passing minute, she knew this was the man she wanted to use to betray Phillip. And Rutger.

The picture was marked for delivery, and when she had obtained a receipt, Sal took her arm. "Let's have a drink and celebrate that you found such a marvelous painting."

She gave him a level look. "I don't usually have drinks with other men when my husband is out of town."

"And I don't usually have drinks with other women when my wife is *in* town! We aren't doing anything scandalous, and my wife won't care if I have a drink with you. Will Phillip care if you have a drink with me?"

She laughed. "I suppose not," she replied, knowing that Phillip would more than care simply because it was Sal.

"Good. See how old-fashioned you are—worrying about something that ninety percent of the population wouldn't give a thought to doing. If it's any consolation to you, I know an out-of-the-way spot where you won't see anyone you know."

It was a small, dark bar that had few customers, and she felt secluded and wondered if he had ever brought a woman there before. When he got to questions about Phillip, she answered forthrightly, because she knew little about Phillip's business. She tried to be her most charming. Sal Giavotella was playing a game with her, trying to learn more about Phillip, and to her surprise, some questions were about Rutger. Sal may have wanted to learn something about the opposition; she wanted it to become more than that. Vastly more. And to try to charm Sal Giavotella was not an irksome task. She felt sparks ignite between them. When he walked her to the car, he held her elbow.

"I'm glad you found a painting for your father."

"I like it so much, I'm tempted to look for another for him and keep it for myself. If I do, every time I look at it, I'll remember your help in selecting it."

He laughed softly. "You'll forget me and tonight and ever talking to me except in the most casual memory."

"You make me sound doddering."

"No," he said, shaking his head. He touched her collar. "You're not doddering, Cheramie."

She gazed at his mouth. His lips were full, his mouth wide, and his lips held a sensuousness and a hint of cruelty that she found exciting. She wondered how he would be in bed, and it made her pulse quicken. He touched her constantly, and he continued to flirt. She kept her gaze on his mouth, hoping he would notice, wanting to set him aflame.

"Thanks for taking time to go for a drink," he said, and she thought there was a huskier note to his voice.

"Thanks for buying drinks. I had fun, Sal," she said.

"I hope you enjoy the painting if you keep it."

She climbed into her car. She kept expecting him to say more to her, but he stepped back and watched her drive away. And she wondered how she could arrange to see him again without it being an obvious ploy.

For the next few weeks they saw each other at parties, occasionally in the halls of various buildings. Cheramie got out more, took more interest in what Phillip was doing, and visited his office more. Once at the symphony she saw the Giavotellas enter, and she studied Gina Giavotella, thinking she was the last woman Cheramie would have picked to be married to a man like Sal. She was dark-haired, looked slightly older than her husband, although Cheramie knew she wasn't. Gina Giavotella had the same dark coloring and curly hair that Cheramie did, but the similarity ended there. Cheramie's gaze shifted to Sal, and in seconds he turned his head and looked directly into her eyes. He nodded, and she didn't acknowledge his nod except to gaze back at him before he turned away.

Frustration built, because their paths crossed only at public places and parties. Cheramie was chairman of Town Forum, a civic organization that had monthly speakers talking on topical subjects. She phoned Marge Butler, the program chairman, and talked her into inviting Sal for two sessions to talk on conservation and the laws before Congress regarding the nation's coastline. Before the conversation ended, Cheramie convinced Marge she should call and ask him since she knew him well and he was so busy.

She stared at the phone, knowing that if he agreed, it was still only two meetings. Shrugging, she realized it was better than seeing him across the room at the opera.

The day before the first meeting she spent the morning trying on dresses, finally deciding on a navy Oscar de la Renta. She spent the afternoon at the salon and the next morning dressed with infinite care.

The meeting was to begin with coffee at half-past ten and would be over by noon, so Cheramie had already invited Sal to lunch afterward.

"Good morning," she said when he came striding through the auditorium door. She moved forward and extended her hand. He glanced at the empty room and laughed. "Do we have the right day?"

"The others will be here any minute now. If I invite a speaker, I want to make sure I've allowed enough time to handle an emergency."

"Are you the program chairman?"

"Actually, no. I told her I knew you well, so I was the one issuing the invitation. And as long as I'm confessing— I'm the only one going to lunch with you. That really isn't part of your speaking obligation."

He laughed and arched his brows. "It promises to be an interesting morning. And you've rescued me from a dull meeting discussing hydroelectric facilities."

"Good! You've rescued me from listening to a tedious speech and spending a boring lunch at home."

She picked an imaginary speck of lint off his suit and smoothed his collar, looking up at him and moving an inch closer. She smiled at him. "Maybe you'd rather I didn't do that. It's a wifely habit."

He looked amused. Somewhere down a hall a door banged.

"I don't mind; I think I'm going to mind ending our conversation."

"We can pick it up again at lunch."

He smoothed her collar, amusement lighting his eyes. "I have the same habit." He stepped back a few inches as the click of heels sounded in the hall. Two women entered, and Cheramie took his arm to introduce him to her friends.

She introduced him during the reception time as well as for his speech, and she sat in the front row, gazing into his dark eyes while he talked.

When they finally left the building, she paused on the front steps. "We can each take our cars, so we can go our own way after lunch. Have a suggestion for a restaurant? Somewhere I won't run into Phillip. He always wants me to stay home."

To her surprise she saw his brows arch as he gave her a quizzical look. "He wants you *home*?"

"He thinks I should be like his mother as far as the children are concerned," she said, her curiosity rising, because she suspected she had struck a nerve and she wasn't sure why.

"Damascus isn't really far. I know a great restaurant there." He glanced around. "Let's take our cars as far as the mall and park there. We can ride together from there."

"Sure," she said, her pulse skipping, because he could easily have gotten out of going to lunch with her. Damascus wasn't far, but it wasn't close, either.

"Park at the southeast corner," he said as they parted.

She felt a race of exhilaration because he was taking care that they not be seen leaving the meeting together. As she drove to the mall, she was aware he was only a car length ahead. He drove slightly over the speed limit, whipping into the mall, and she followed. In minutes she was seated in his black car and they were back on the freeway. She settled on the seat to watch him drive. His hands were big and he wore a heavy gold ring with three large diamonds.

"Your talk was interesting, and you spoke in terms we could understand."

"And your husband wouldn't agree with half of it. If he could wipe out my committee, he would. Where is he today?"

"In Virginia, as a matter of fact. He'll be back at the office this afternoon."

"He's at a base, no doubt. He's dedicated to a strong military."

"He thinks it's an absolute necessity."

They talked about politics, and Cheramie had more to say about Phillip's latest concerns. She had started discussing politics with him and with Rutger, learning what she could, deciding which items she would share with Sal and which she wouldn't.

The restaurant was across from a Sheraton Inn on a state highway. Set back in the trees, the place had only a few customers by the time they arrived. It was elegant, with oak paneling, linen-covered tables, and fine crystal and china, and she suspected it catered to the dinner trade more than business lunches. She didn't see anyone she knew, nor did Sal.

Through lunch, over trout and lobster, she flirted, gazing at him intently, smiling, giving him all the charm she could while trying to impart enough morsels about Phillip to whet his interest. She was constantly aware she might have only this lunch and another alone with him unless he made the next move.

"Why were you shocked Phillip wanted me to stay home?" she asked while she sipped a martini.

"Because you're a beautiful, vivacious woman who could be an incredible asset to him as a politician. Why in hell would he want you under wraps at home?"

"Thank you! My, I'm flattered. I've never thought of myself as an asset," she said, lying, because she considered herself a major asset for Phillip.

"I can't get my wife out of the house."

"Too bad we can't trade," she said, looking him directly in the eye. Their gazes locked, and she held her breath because there was no mistaking the blatant look of speculation in his eyes.

"Maybe we'd all be happier," he said softly, studying her. To her annoyance the waiter appeared to take their plates. They both ordered coffee, and when they were alone again he said, "I heard your father will run in the next gubernatorial race."

She laughed. "No, he definitely won't! After you so soundly defeated him, he will always take a backseat in politics. He doesn't like defeat."

"He's championing Hal Rainey, who is going to be a strong contender for Congress. Rainey supports offshore drilling, the oil companies, the big money, and he's going to make it an issue in the campaign."

Cheramie knew they were quietly beginning to organize for the campaign, and she also knew the party was arguing with Rainey for his strong stand on reducing county funding to cut the state's budget deficit. "It'll be interesting."

"And I've heard Nelson Crown intends to run for a second term."

"I don't know much about Nelson's intentions."

"No comment, eh?" he said, smiling.

"My remarks don't carry much weight. I'm out of the political scene."

"Not very far out, Cheramie. You know a lot about the current issues."

"And if I didn't, would you be having lunch with me?" she asked, giving him a questioning stare.

He chuckled and gazed back at her. "Yes, I would," he replied. "Do you think I'm with you to get information?"

"Partly."

"And the other part?" he asked, tilting his head and arching his dark brows.

"Because you were a speaker for the Town Forum," she answered carefully.

"You think I'm here because I spoke this morning?" he asked, and his voice lowered. He pushed away his plate and leaned forward, reaching across the table to touch the back of her hand and draw his finger over her knuckles. She was intensely aware of his touch, but it was the look in his black eyes that made her lose her breath and held her mesmerized. "Do you know how often I give speeches like this morning and then go to lunch afterward with members of the club?"

"Only during political campaigns."

"No, Cheramie, not this kind of speech. Not twice to the same group. I accepted because of you."

She felt as if she couldn't catch her breath. She had cheated with other men, but none of them had stirred her like Sal. They weren't as powerful, and she suspected they weren't as ruthless, and if he were single, she would never do more than the most harmless flirting with him, because she sensed he was a man who could not be easily controlled. She had started flirting with Sal out of revenge and anger, a deliberate stalking to get back at Phillip, but now she wanted him and was excited by him, and it no longer was just revenge.

"That's what I wanted," she whispered, and he drew a deep breath. A sheen of perspiration showed on his brow, and her pulse jumped with excitement as she saw the effect she was having on him. It gave her a heady sense of power, made all the more delicious because Sal Giavotella was no timid Bryce Wolfe. He was quick and dangerous and powerful.

"Let's get the hell out of here where we can really talk," he said.

She nodded, and he motioned for the waiter. In minutes they were in the shaded parking lot.

"Cheramie," Sal said when they were in the car. He turned her to face him, and her heart pounded with anticipation as his arms went around her.

He pulled her to him, his head coming down and his mouth covering hers. His tongue thrust into her mouth, and she returned his kiss with an eagerness that made her tremble. He was all she had suspected. His kisses were wild and passionate, his hands caressing her expertly.

She leaned back. "Sal, we're in a parking lot. Anyone could come out. Someone who might know you."

"Cheramie, there's a Sheraton across the road."

She nodded, placing her hand on his muscled thigh and stroking him. He drew in a sharp breath and started the car.

He checked into the Sheraton, driving to their room and stepping aside for her to enter. The moment the door closed, he caught her and pulled her into his arms again. "God, how I've wanted to kiss you."

"Sal, there can't be any ties, any commitment," she said. "We both have families. Careers would be at stake."

"I think that's my speech, Cheramie." He lowered his head to kiss her. His kisses were searing, and she wound her arms around his neck to return them. In seconds he tugged her zipper, and her dress fell away. She hadn't expected him to move as fast as he had, but she had dressed to be ready. She wore a black bra and garter belt. She hadn't worn panties.

"God, you're bare!" he whispered.

"I don't like to be constricted," she said, trying to sound seductive, wanting to shock him and make him desire her. It gave her a delirious, heady feeling of being wanted and of power to know that she could have an affair with a handsome, powerful man who risked so much to have her.

He pushed a strap off her shoulder, pulling down the lacy bra to cup her full breasts and flick his thumbs over her nipples. She gasped and tilted her head back, her hands moving over him, unbuttoning his shirt and pushing it away, unbuckling his belt, her fingers stroking his throbbing penis, discovering he was more amply endowed than Phillip.

"You're big!" she whispered, her hand sliding between his legs until she bent her head to kiss him, her fingers kneading him.

She had thought Phillip an expert lover, but Sal was even more sensuous, wanting to touch and kiss and taste, driving her to heights of ecstasy, until finally he moved between her legs to thrust into her. She wrapped her legs around him, clinging to him while he filled her and thrust his hips. She opened her eyes to look up at him, watching him when he climaxed, tightening her legs around him while she thought of Phillip.

"Now!" she gasped, clinging to Sal. She knew Sal would never guess she wasn't crying out because of her climax. Her thoughts were on revenge, on Phillip's infidelity. She had paid him in full.

She lay in Sal's arms, his big body so different from Phillip's long lean frame. Sal was covered with hair; his thick chest had a mat of black curls that tapered down and swirled around his navel. His thighs and legs were covered in thick curls, and it was sensuous and arousing to move against him or touch him. In spite of his size, he was hard muscle and trim in the waist with a flat stomach.

"I want to see you again."

She raised up to look down at him. "You're busy, and you draw attention everywhere you go. We'll have to be careful."

"I can get away next Thursday afternoon and night. I exercise and play handball. Gina has a sewing club then."

"I'll have to wait until closer to time to know Phillip's schedule," she said.

"I'll call you from a pay phone. We should arrange a time when I can call. We'll both find pay phones."

As they made arrangements, she understood why there had never been a word of scandal about him. He was cautious to the extreme.

"I wish we had all night," Sal said, running his hands over her, sliding one hand up to her soft breast to stroke her. "How long can you stay tonight? You're fabulous, Cheramie," he whispered, kissing her breast, teasing her nipple with his tongue. His big dark hands cupped her full breasts, pale in his grasp. "God, with you, a man could go to the top."

She trembled, feeling more appreciated than she had with Phillip. He desired her, loved her, but he wasn't awed by her in the manner that Sal seemed to be.

She didn't shower but went home to crawl into the big bed she shared with Phillip, her body still musky from Sal's lovemaking.

A week later, as she watched Phillip climb out of their big tub, her gaze drifting down over his lean body, she knew that all Sal Giavotella would be to her was fun and revenge. She wanted her marriage to Phillip, because in spite of his infidelities, he was everything she needed in a husband; he was wealthier than Sal, and at present he was more of a power in Washington than Sal.

And now when she hurt, she would turn to Sal to seek relief from anger and pain. He was the perfect lover—masculine, virile, handsome, and needing secrecy as badly as she. They went to secluded restaurants, out-of-the-way lone motels on interstates. The relationship satisfied her boredom, her need for adoration, her smoldering anger over Phillip's affairs.

Four months after the affair started, Sal took her to a cabin he leased. It was isolated, beautiful, in a rustic area along a stream, and she suspected the lease was in a name other than Giavotella.

In addition to the cabin, he had rented an apartment minutes away from his office. It took her longer, and she hated driving through a bad part of town at night. The area worried her. Once she voiced aloud her concern, Sal gave her a pistol.

She gazed at the Smith & Wesson and laughed. "Sal, I don't know anything about guns."

"Then you should learn. Tell Phillip you feel the need to be able to protect yourself. I insisted Gina learn years ago."

"Gina knows how to shoot?"

"She hates it, but, yes, she does. You put this under the front seat. When we're at the cabin, I'll teach you to use it."

"Do you carry one?"

"Always," he said, going to his briefcase and producing a heavy revolver larger than the one he had given her. "This is what I carry. If anyone threatens you, don't hesitate to pull the pistol."

A cold chill seemed to rush across her nape as she looked at him holding the revolver. There were moments that came briefly when he frightened her. She hadn't ever seen him lose his temper, and she hoped she never did, because there was a rough element in Sal that showed up sometimes in their lovemaking, in his conversation. He wasn't as predictable as Phillip or as civilized.

He hefted the revolver, turning it and sliding his hand over it. "It's a Webley-Fosbery .455-caliber. It'll stop anyone." He placed the weapon on a table and drew her into his arms. "I've thought about you all day," he whispered, kissing her throat and unfastening the buttons of her blouse. In moments her fear was gone.

Cheramie ran her hands over him, trying as much when she was with him as when she was with Phillip to bind him to her. She wanted both men to want her. She knew from the

private detective that Phillip was still having affairs. They
were brief, with no particular woman, just a string of beauties
to satisfy his insatiable demands. And always, when the
knowledge brought hurt and anger, Cheramie had Sal for
consolation, because if the day came when she would want
to fling her affair in Phillip's face, she knew it would devastate
him to find that Sal Giavotella was her lover.

14

1989

Alette landed at the airport and walked into Bill's waiting
arms.

"Gosh, you look great," he said, wrapping his arm around
her and taking her bag as they strode through Dulles. She
kept up with his long stride, and she clung to his narrow
waist, falling into step beside him.

"We can celebrate tonight," she exclaimed eagerly.

"How's that?"

"The California legislature voted to build a new governor's
mansion, and I won the landscaping bid!"

"Hey, that's really great, Alette. I'll bet your father is
tickled."

"I haven't told him yet. It'll be a while before I get to
start, but I'm the contractor."

"Good for you. Same old rat race here. My folks want us
to come out Monday before you go back to California."

"Fine," she said, remembering her last visit to his Baltimore home. His parents were pleasant, polite, and warm; Bill
resembled his mother, Evelyn, who was tall with thick wavy
brown hair and deep brown eyes.

"I'm glad you're here." Bill hugged her tightly against him.

After dinner and dancing, they went to his Georgetown home. He poured glasses of wine and built a fire, pulling her down on the floor beside him while he kissed her. He had shed his navy blazer and wore gray slacks and a white shirt. He pulled loose his tie and unbuttoned the collar of his shirt, gazing at her with desire evident in his eyes.

"Alette, this long-distance romance is not the greatest."

"It's that or nothing," she said, leaning back. She trailed her hand over his shoulder and down across his chest, unbuttoning his shirt.

"There's another possibility."

"You're moving to San Francisco?" she asked.

"No. Let's get married."

Shocked, she stared at him. She dated him, loved him, but hadn't really thought beyond the relationship they already had.

"Damn, you've never given it a thought!"

"I guess after Paul I just never expected to marry."

"Well, I'm asking you now," he said.

He gazed at her solemnly, and she realized how perfect they would be for each other. They liked the same things, did the same things, were both quiet and controlled, and she knew him well.

"Alette, are you going to think about it all night?"

She focused on him. "It's a big step, Bill. We live in different cities, and I know you absolutely don't want to leave Washington."

"No, I don't. You could move your business here."

She studied him, thinking about all the contacts she had built. She leaned forward, wrapping her arms around him and kissing him soundly before she pulled away. "You're very important to me, and I love you."

"Is this a polite no?"

"There's a lot to consider," she said solemnly, thinking that he was all she could want in a husband and they were compatible. "Bill, I made a mistake in judgment before, and you did, too. We both were hurt. I have to be so sure."

He traced his finger along her ear and throat. "All right. You make sure. I know what I want. I've been thinking about it. I've talked to my parents about it, and I've talked to Rutger."

"Rutger!" she exclaimed, shocked that he would discuss marriage with Rutger before he did with her.

"The groom-to-be usually asks the father for permission."

"I'm just surprised you've already talked to him."

"He's all for it, which of course, is not a plus in your books."

"I won't hold that against you," she said, nuzzling his neck and kissing him, tilting her face up. "Give me a little time. Let me be very certain."

He bent his head to kiss her hard, crushing her in his arms and leaning over her so they stretched out. He fitted her against his long length, his hands roaming over her, and in minutes marriage plans were lost to passion.

They talked about it over the weekend, yet Alette knew she had to go home and think it over. As the plane lifted off the runway, she gazed down at the Potomac and thought about Bill, and for the first time she acknowledged there was a tiny kernel of reluctance.

She didn't know if it was foolish, ungrounded fears, or too high expectations. Her misgivings were nebulous and slight, and she wondered if she hoped to be swept off her feet or was still afraid of making another ghastly mistake. They were compatible, as much as she had been with Paul, but Bill was much more of a man than Paul, much more ambitious, and much stronger.

She didn't care to discuss it with Rutger, because she knew exactly what he would want her to do, but she did want to talk to Aubrey, because she had always valued his opinion.

Thursday she opened the door of his shop and peered into a cluttered office. "Aubrey!" she called

"Hi," he said, coming up behind her and startling her. "Let's go on the boat. I'll get us some pop." He jerked his head, and she followed him to the *Easy*.

"Have a drink," he said, offering her some cold pop. She accepted a bottle and leaned back.

"What's up?" he asked, lounging back and gazing at her with mild curiosity.

"Not much. I haven't seen you for a long time. Any races lately?"

"As a matter of fact, there's the latest trophy," he said, and pointed to a large shining silver cup.

"Aubrey! It's beautiful! What did you win?"

"A boat race."

"Where do you stash the trophies? I never see them."

"Do you think I want to keep polishing? And there's no room on the boat. I give them to the yacht club, and they have mine in a case."

"You might want them someday. If you have children—"

He grinned. "Don't hold your breath on that one."

"How's Pat?"

"As a matter of fact, I haven't seen her for a while."

"Oh, Aubrey. She was so nice. Listen to me! I sound like Rutger."

He laughed. "You sound as if I gave her the heave-ho. She's the one who gave me the good-bye speech."

"Yes, and I'll bet I can recite it. She's tired of waiting for a commitment from you."

His face flushed, and Alette regretted her words. "I'm sorry. That was tactless. At least you always know what you want."

"You weren't tactless. You were a concerned sister." He looked down at his drink. "When they go all clinging and possessive, I just want out. I guess I'm claustrophobic about relationships."

"So what happens when Pat started to walk out of your life? She's not clinging then."

"No, but if I crook my finger and say 'Come back,' they turn all clingy and busy with my life again. I feel caught," he said solemnly. "I just have to have independence, and there's a point where women can't bear it."

"So you want an independent woman. So independent she won't have a relationship with you."

He grinned and took a long drink. "Catch-22. What brings you aboard the *Easy*?"

She looked down at her hands, turning the large diamond
given to her long ago by Rutger. "I may get engaged. Bill's
asked me to marry him."

"Do I sense a bit of reluctance?"

"I just don't want to make the same mistake I did with
Paul."

"You want advice?"

"Yes."

He gave her a level look that startled her, because Aubrey
rarely made any kind of commitment involving others, even
down to giving advice. He turned his head to stare outside,
and her surprise deepened.

"You're obviously not wildly in love."

"I do love him. I just don't want to rush foolishly into
something like I did before." She had expected enthusiasm,
because Aubrey always wanted good things for her. Instead,
to her surprise, he stared at her with his lips closed tightly.
For a moment she couldn't guess why, and then she realized
there could be only one reason.

"You don't like Bill! But you barely know him," she said
before he could reply to the first statement.

"You're right. I barely know him. You say you're in love,
but you're sure as hell not wildly in love."

"Well, maybe not wildly. Well, yes, I guess we are wildly
in love. I love him very much," she said, beginning to feel
a twinge of annoyance. "Why don't you like him?"

"I think Bill Gaffney is nice, bright, ambitious," he said
carefully.

"And?"

"Alette, you may marry the guy. I don't want to say
something I'll regret later. It's not my place—"

"You're my brother, and it is your place, and we've always
been honest with each other."

"He's social and shallow and not as strong a man as you
should have, Alette," he said, rushing the words.

Momentarily speechless, she stared at him in shock. "Bill?
Shallow? God, that's what Rutger said about Paul! What do
I need, Goliath?"

"No. But you need someone you don't have to carry."

"Carry!" she exclaimed, growing more astonished. "I won't ever have to carry Bill! He's educated, ambitious, successful. And he isn't shallow."

"It's glitter on the surface."

"You don't even know him," she said, growing angry and deciding Aubrey had changed more than she realized. She stood up. "I should make my own decisions. Bill is nice, very nice. He's down-to-earth, pleasant, ambitious."

Aubrey came to his feet at once. "Hell, I'm sorry. I want you to be happy, but marriage is so damned permanent. I was on a team with him once at Dartmouth, remember? I know him well enough. He's impressed with Rutger, impressed with Phillip, impressed with you. I think he's selfish and spoiled and a weak sister."

"Aubrey! That's dreadful! He isn't any of those things. We're so well suited. We like antiques, we read the same books, like the same movies, eat the same food."

He leaned down. "Another one of those gentle, weak guys who may be fun to date once or twice a month, but in the daily grind, I think you deserve better."

"That is the most ridiculous thing I ever heard!"

"You have misgivings, or you wouldn't be here discussing this with me. You know you're not deeply in love."

"Said by the expert on love!" she flung back at him, her anger mushrooming. "You've never really been in love in your life!"

"Maybe I haven't, but I have sense enough to face the fact that I haven't found a woman who makes me want to wake up with her every day for the rest of my life and give up my life-style for her."

She put her fists on her hips. "Aubrey, someday you're going to fall in love, and I just hope I'm around to see it! You're wrong about Bill. He's a wonderful man. You can take your opinions and go to hell with them!"

She spun around and left the boat and stormed to her car, shaking with anger. Along with anger was hurt that Aubrey thought so little of Bill. She had always had Aubrey's support, and she loved him and felt closer to him than anyone else, and it hurt to have him put down Bill. She felt he was wrong, but she valued Aubrey's opinion highly and knew he had her interests at heart. She backed out of the parking lot, admitting she was not ready to accept Bill's proposal.

15 ~~~

January 1990

Sal Giavotella's San Francisco business office always reminded Jeff of a hotel suite he had had once in Chicago. A giant television screen filled one corner; plush red carpeting and oak paneling were as luxurious as the tan velvet furniture. The bar glittered with crystal-lined shelves, and a rowing machine stood in a corner. An oil painting hung behind the mahogany desk, and strung up on another wall was a map with crisscrossed lines showing truck routes of the western half of the United States.

Looking full of vitality, fit, and deeply tanned, Sal came around the desk to greet Jeff. The smile he flashed was pearly against his swarthy skin. He gripped Jeff's hand and shook it vigorously.

"It's good to see you."

"Washington agrees with you."

"I love it there. How's it going here?"

"You get the reports," Jeff said, trying to bite back a grin.

"You're being modest. You're frying Lachman's tail. I didn't think you could do it, but you've made an impressive cut in his business. And profited well."

"I've got some good men working for me. So do you. I've been pleased with it. I know I'll never put him out of business. He's too big, but I can annoy him. His methods are out of date."

"You're doing that. And you've got a strong business.

Strong enough that it can do without you. I came home to get you into politics. I've talked with party people who want you to run.''

Jeff looked out the window. He had given long and serious thought when others had discussed it with him. He had made his decision, and it was time to announce it.

"Jeff, you'd win. And you'd be good for the party. You're new, you're young, you're a dynamo."

Jeff laughed. "I'm an old ball player with a bum arm."

"Sure. And I'm an old ball player who dabbles in politics," Sal said with sarcasm. "C'mon. We need you, and you'd like the challenge. You could do some good."

"I told Rupert Collins I would think it over. To tell you the truth," Jeff said, grinning, "I'm going to call him with my answer, but I thought I'd tell you first. Yes, I'll run."

"Hot damn!" Sal slapped his desk in glee. "That's really great news, Jeff."

"I want your help. I want your suggestions."

"Right off, get Howard for your press secretary and Blake Dorth for a campaign manager. You can't beat them. Let's celebrate!"

Jeff laughed as Sal went to the bar and poured vodka and tonic into two glasses. He handed Jeff one. "Here's to the future governor of California."

"That's premature."

"It's a good excuse. I don't usually get to drink this early." They talked through the drink, and Sal fixed a second round.

"Skip mine. I'm driving. How's Gina?"

Sal sobered and looked away. "It hasn't been good between us."

"Damn, I hate to hear that," Jeff said, thinking this had been coming since Sal's election as governor. "Politics?"

"Life changes. I've changed. She's changed. We married so damn young. She'd like all my time. I can't stay home and hold her hand."

Surprised by Sal's statements, Jeff felt a rush of sadness. "Maybe she needs to get away from the kids for a while."

Sal shook his head. "No. That wouldn't matter. Jeff, it's me. I've changed."

"I hope you two can work things out. You have so much between you."

"I don't think so, Jeff. The rift has been widening for a long time now. We've really grown apart."

"You sound as if you've made up your mind."

Sal shrugged and sipped his drink. Suddenly Jeff realized there might be another woman in his friend's life. He stared at Sal, taking in the elegant suit and gold cuff links, the deep tan that didn't come from an office.

"There's another woman," Sal admitted before Jeff could ask the question.

"I'm shocked," Jeff admitted, studying Sal intently. "Sounds as if you're having a damned midlife crisis."

"No, it sure as hell isn't," Sal replied. He stood up and moved the picture to open a safe. He took out a Cartier box and raised the lid. A magnificent necklace sparkled in the light, the large diamonds dazzling, the smooth round emeralds like tiny tropical pools. Jeff knew he could buy a new yacht with the money the necklace cost.

"That's for her."

Stunned, Jeff stared at the opulent jewelry. Sal returned the box to the safe and replaced the picture. "I just had it made for her."

"Jesus . . ." Jeff didn't know what to say. Sal glowed with happiness, and even though they were best friends, Jeff hurt for Gina and the kids. "Sal, you have six children."

"I know, I know, but it's over with Gina. I haven't rushed."

"You're getting a divorce?" Jeff asked in shock.

"Yes. I've filed, and I told Gina when I got to town. I've bought a condo, Jeff."

"I know Gina doesn't like politics and things haven't been the greatest, but isn't this separation sudden?"

"No. I've thought about it a long time. You haven't been around. I outgrew Gina."

"The hell you did!" Jeff said, knowing he should keep quiet. "You didn't outgrow her fast enough to keep from fathering a child only a couple of years ago. What the fuck are you doing?"

"I need this woman like I need air to breathe. She's brainy, she's beautiful, she can manage anything. She's a sophisticated woman of the world—and I need that kind of woman in politics. Gina pulls me down."

"Get a live-in nannie and let Gina join you at more things."

"She's not the type. She wouldn't do it. Those kids are her world and her life."

"You sound like they're no part of you. It's not my business, but damn—don't six kids warrant trying to work things out?"

"We'll all be better off. Six kids shouldn't be raised in an atmosphere of tension."

Jeff stared at Sal and bit back a comment. "It's none of my damn business."

"Let's forget it and go to lunch. Come on. I shouldn't have had two vodkas on an empty stomach."

Jeff stood up. "It's your life, but from where I stand, I think you're making a mistake," he couldn't resist saying, knowing Sal's bulldog stubbornness. "Did you give Gina a chance to talk it over?"

Sal's jaw thrust forward slightly, and Jeff had his answer. And he wanted to plant his fist right on that solid, stubborn jaw.

"Sal, if Gina did something terrible, I'd be all for divorce. If she ran around or drank too much . . . but she's a good woman and she adores you."

"Jeff, ol' buddy, I don't want a fucking lecture. Do we go to lunch or not?"

"C'mon. I'll drop the lecture," he said, but he knew it would be hard to keep his promise, because his thoughts returned constantly to Sal's dissolved marriage. And as they ate, he realized that Sal was exuberant and in love and almost as silly about it as a teenager in a first romance.

When they were ready to part, they stood in the sunshine in front of the office. Jeff was leaving for an appointment, but he went inside to get some papers and Sal walked back out with him.

"Thank God you'll run for governor," Sal said. "You're what the party needs, and you can afford a campaign."

"Does she live here or in Washington, Sal?"

There was a pause. "She's a Californian," he answered, his gaze sliding away, and Jeff wondered if Sal was lying, something his friend had never done before with him. "I love her more than I thought possible. She's gorgeous, and she has terrific contacts. You'll see."

"Oh, shit. Are you doing this because you're in love or because of what this woman can do for you politically? Can she give you six good kids?"

"If we hadn't been friends for so long, you'd be flat on your back now. It's over with Gina."

"It's none of my damned business, but you're like a brother to me." He gazed into angry dark eyes and knew he should drop the topic. "I guess I know you well enough to know when you make up your mind, it's set. It's a good thing the lady feels the same way you do."

"Give me a call when you're ready to sit down and talk about campaign strategy." The anger left Sal's expression. "Wait until you get to know her. Someday you'll apologize and tell me how glad you are for me."

"I hope so," Jeff said, thinking that would be impossible. He climbed into his car and hurt for Gina and the six kids while he wondered about the woman. Sal was a charismatic, appealing man who had always attracted women easily, but he had never strayed that Jeff knew about, and Jeff suspected it was a spectacular woman who had wrecked the Giavotella marriage.

"I wear the chain I forged in life." The line from the high school Christmas drama kept echoing in Cheramie's mind as she paced the floor and bit her lip. Her mind raced over her dilemma. Sal was far too serious, and she intended to end the affair. She knew it would be sticky and ugly, because Sal was growing more earnest all the time. And now the damned divorce! She'd wanted to scream when he'd told her he had moved out and filed for a divorce. She rehearsed her speech, going over it again, wanting to be free of him. She glanced at her watch and saw it was time to go. She was dressed in a business suit with a hemline that struck below her calf. Her

hair was fastened severely behind her head, and she hoped there was nothing seductive about her appearance.

She looked around the living room of their Maryland home, at the antiques, the Queen Anne furniture, the oil paintings she and Phillip had acquired. When she returned home, she would be free of Sal. Only a few hours of argument and anger and it would all be over. She opened the door to go meet him.

When she entered the apartment Sal kissed her long and hard. He was wearing a dark charcoal suit and had shed his coat and loosened his wine-colored tie. He released her slightly and looked down at her. "I thought we'd eat here in the apartment tonight. I have champagne, dinner cooked, and we can be alone. Cheramie, I'm releasing this apartment. Gina has no interest in the Washington house. I'll give her the house in San Francisco."

"We need to talk about that, Sal."

"I brought something for you." From his briefcase he produced a carved box and handed it to her.

Cheramie's interest heightened at once, and she was torn between curiosity and the wisdom to refuse a gift.

"Sal, let's talk first."

"Open your present and we'll talk all you want." He gave the box to her and slid his big hands beneath the lapels of her suit coat, removing it.

"Sal," she said impatiently, trying to wriggle away while she stared at the box in indecision.

"Open it, Cheramie," he coaxed. "It's special."

She untied the red silk ribbon and removed the lid of the box. Stunned, she drew in her breath sharply as she gazed at the spectacular necklace. Phillip never had given her anything so grand.

She stared at it, touching one of the diamonds with her finger. The stones glittered. The emeralds mounted in fili- greed gold were like ocean depths, the diamonds as brilliant as sunshine. "Sal, this belongs to a queen. It's like the crown jewels," she said in awe, suddenly in a quandary. She wanted the necklace.

"It's yours, Cheramie, with my love," he said, caressing her throat. "I love you and want you. I want you to be mine.

I want you to wear it tonight." He lifted the necklace and looked at her silk blouse with the tie beneath her chin. "This wasn't meant for a suit and blouse. Take off the blouse."

Her debate with her conscience lasted only seconds. She would break off with him next time. Watching him, she unbuttoned the silk blouse, moving with deliberation because she could see the effect she was having on Sal. His eyes burned with craving, and the sense of power she felt aroused her. She removed first one shoulder of the blouse and then the other, finally dropping it on a chair.

Sal drew a deep breath, his chest expanding. He draped the necklace around her neck. The jewels were cold against her skin, and she looked down at their dazzling sparkle as they lay above the soft rise of her breasts.

"This is the most beautiful necklace I've ever seen," she exclaimed, in one of the rare occasions in her life when she was overwhelmed. She turned around and stepped back, relishing the moment. "Do you like it?" she asked in a throaty voice. His gaze was on her breasts, and her nipples hardened in anticipation.

He groaned and pulled her against his chest, crushing her in his arms. She twined her arms around him, twisting her hips against him, and in minutes passion engulfed them. Clothes were strewn in a path that led to the bed. Cheramie did everything she knew would inflame Sal, teasing him until he finally thrust into her soft warmth. Unable to resist her own desire, she let Sal bring her to a climax first.

He rolled over beside her, turning to stroke her. "Divorce Phillip, Cheramie."

She became still, staring at him in the dusky light of one lamp. "We've been over that. I won't leave my children, and you shouldn't leave yours. They're all at an impressionable age. It would hurt them terribly."

"Children adapt. And they sense it when a parent isn't happy. You're not wrapped up in your children's lives, and you know it."

"I can't leave them! You didn't tell Gina about me, did you?" She moved away impatiently.

"I haven't told anyone, Cheramie, but I want to tell the

world. I'm tired of hiding and seeing you only briefly. I want you at my side for parties and meetings. I want you in my bed every night. You drive me wild," he said in a husky voice.

"I won't divorce Phillip. It would tear everyone's lives apart, and when it was all over, I don't know that we'd feel the same. I didn't want you to divorce Gina. I wish you'd go back to her."

"Never," he said flatly. "She's held me down long enough."

"I'd have to fight Rutger as well. He would disinherit me, and that's not something to take lightly."

Sal rolled over. "Why would he disinherit you? Because I beat him and was elected governor? You've always said you're his favorite child."

"You made an enemy of him, Sal, and you know it. Besides, divorce is not something Rutger would tolerate from anyone in his family, regardless of the circumstances."

"You're going to be mine, Cheramie. I want you more than I've ever wanted anything or anyone in my life."

He kissed her, winding his hand in her hair. As he crushed her to him, the necklace bit into her soft flesh. She struggled fleetingly and then responded.

That night as she drove home alone, she had the necklace in her purse. Her elation over it was dampened by fright over Sal's divorce and his wanting her to get one. She had long ago decided which man she wanted to spend the rest of her life with, and it wasn't Sal. It was Phillip. She had thought she was safe with Sal. She laughed aloud in the darkness of the car.

"Fool," she admonished herself. She knew he had married Gina in high school, and she suspected he had been true to her through all the early years of their marriage, but politics had changed his values. She would have to do something about Sal when they met the following Thursday.

A guilty twinge plagued her when she thought about the necklace. Whatever happened, he had given it to her, and it was hers to keep. It was the most spectacular piece of jewelry she owned.

She drove down the dark, empty street to their home in

Chevy Chase. Street lamps shed circles of yellow light, and lawns had recessed lighting in the trees. She reached her block, and at the edge of the property through the trees, she glimpsed their sprawling Georgian house. All the lights glowed when she turned up the drive, and her heart slammed against her ribs.

16 ～⌒⌒⌒

Every light in the house and six-car garage blazed. First Cheramie wondered if something had happened to one of the children. Then, as she drove closer, she saw cars everywhere, including Phillip's, and her heart plummeted. She thought of the necklace in her purse and realized she hadn't showered after leaving Sal. Fear shook her, and she wondered what to do. Phillip was supposed to be out of town until noon tomorrow.

She slipped through the kitchen door. Walking through the hall, she saw men standing and talking in the two large living areas on the west side of the house. She moved casually up the stairs, expecting to hear Phillip call to her at any moment. At the head of the steps she hurried to their room, gasping with relief when she stepped inside. His coat was over the back of a chair, and his suitcase was on the stand at the foot of the bed. She wondered what was happening downstairs. She showered quickly and dressed in green slacks and a green blouse. Then she balled up her clothes with her purse and stuffed them at the back of her closet.

Downstairs, Phillip stood beside the fireplace, and he spotted her when she entered the room. He crossed to her, holding a drink in one hand. "I came home early. I guess I surprised you."

"You did. Courtney and I went to a movie. If I'd

known—'' His hair tumbled over his forehead, and his cheeks were flushed; he was obviously excited and jubilant. "Phillip, what's happened?"

"Hey, Cheramie! We thought you'd run away with another man," Todd said jovially, and she laughed, gazing at Phillip and Todd with perplexity. Then, to her dismay, she gazed beyond Phillip and saw Rutger watching her. He smiled and approached them, and her heart beat with pure terror for a moment, because whatever had happened, if the truth were discovered about her evening, she would face a divorce and disinheritance.

"Tell her, man," Todd urged, and she looked at Phillip in question.

"I'm going to run for president, Cheramie."

Dumbfounded, she stared at him. He had said he wanted to run someday, and she knew it was the goal of his political aspirations, but she hadn't really expected it to happen so soon.

"He's told you the news," Rutger said, joining them. "I flew in today."

"I tried to call you," Phillip said, "but I gave up after calling Marge and Janice and Helen. I didn't think of Courtney."

She felt weak with relief that she hadn't picked one of the other names for her lie.

"Cheramie, are you all right?" Rutger asked, staring at her intently, and in that moment she knew she had to end her affair with Sal immediately.

"I think, for once, I've shocked my wife," Phillip said, giving her a squeeze.

"I'm overwhelmed," she said. "I can't believe it."

Rutger grinned, chuckling softly, and she could guess how much Phillip's nomination would mean to him. Phillip turned away to talk to someone, and in spite of Rutger's good humor and Phillip's acceptance of her lie, she couldn't relax. "I'd like a drink," she said, and Todd went to get her one.

"I knew this was coming," Rutger said. "It was inevitable. You've surely known there has been a movement under way to get this started."

"I knew it was what Phillip wanted, but I didn't expect it to happen so soon. I thought he was working for the next election."

"He was at first, but party members talked him into going for it now. He's young. Whatever happens, it will be good for his career. He's an excellent choice. He'll be another Kennedy. You seem shocked."

"I am. Phillip didn't prepare me," she said, wishing Rutger would go talk to someone else. He was shrewd, and he knew her as well as he knew himself. Guilt and fear plagued her. The moment Todd handed her a Scotch and soda, she took a long drink.

"Whether he wins or not, it'll change all our lives."

She looked across the room at her tall husband. "He never told me," she said, tingling with fear, realizing how deeply involved she had become with Sal.

"Cheramie," Rutger said softly, "has it dawned on you yet that you could be First Lady?"

She gazed up into his blue eyes dancing with elation and thought about the White House. And the power and position that went with it. It was as if she looked into the sun. The prospects were more dazzling than the necklace, than anything in her life.

Rutger leaned forward. "You help him get there. He'll need you."

"Of course," she said, turning to look at Phillip. Suddenly she wanted to ask Rutger about Phillip's affairs. Would he give them up for the presidency?

She knew she had to get Sal Giavotella out of her life immediately, and she would have to part on good terms with him because now she had given him power over them. He could ruin everything.

When at last the door had closed behind the last man and Phillip and Cheramie were alone upstairs in their bedroom, he caught her to him. "We're alone."

"Mr. President," she said, the possibilities looming larger by the second.

"It sounds impossible. They pointed out that even if I get wiped out early in the campaign, I might be a good candidate for vice-president. Whatever happens, it won't leave me where it found me.''

"Phillip, you should have told me," she said, realizing they had grown apart in the past months.

"I didn't know if everything would work out."

"It's wonderful. I'll do all I can."

"Oh, yeah?" he asked in a husky voice, and all political talk ended as he pulled her closer.

As Phillip became busier, Cheramie wondered if she would ever have time alone with him again. But she knew that no matter how lonely she felt, she had to tell Sal flatly that their affair was over. She also knew Sal well enough to realize she had become involved with a man as determined as Rutger.

They ate in a secluded French restaurant, and only when she was alone in the apartment with him did she turn to face him. "Sal, we have to talk. Sit down, will you.''

"Sure," he said, sitting down and pulling her onto his lap.

She moved away quickly. "I need to sit over here. Sal, we have to break this off for a while.''

"How long is a while?"

She couldn't tell him Phillip was going to run for president until the knowledge was made public. "I'm afraid Phillip suspects something, so I have to break off until things change.''

"Cheramie, this is the perfect time. Ask him for a divorce.''

"Are you listening to me?"

"Of course I am. Now is the time. Don't patch things up.''

"Sal, I'm *not* leaving my children, and I've told you that from the first. Don't hurt me.''

"I won't let you go. You're just frightened. You know you don't love Phillip.''

"I love my children.''

He moved swiftly to scoop her up and sit down with her on his lap, reaching out to unbutton her blouse. "We can have children, Cheramie. Our children.''

She wiggled to get free, but he held her. "I won't do it. I'm going home, and we can't see each other.''

"Like hell. There's something between us and you know it."

"I know we've had fun. We said when we started there would be no ties, no commitment," she said, pushing his hands away, becoming impatient with him. She had never tolerated anything standing in the way of something she wanted, and now Sal's stubbornness angered her.

"We didn't know what it would be like and what we'd mean to each other. You drive me crazy," he said in a husky voice. "You're in my blood. I can't live without you."

"I have to stop seeing you!" she exclaimed. "I don't want to be disinherited."

"I'll make it up to you. We have too much between us. You've told me over and over what I mean to you."

She scooted off his lap and paced the room. She wished she hadn't done half the things or said half the things she had. "We've had fun, but it's over. I have to stop seeing you."

"I don't want to go a few weeks without you."

She had never learned patience, and it was impossible now. She faced him. "Sal, I'm going home. I'll call you when I feel like it's safer."

His dark eyes sparked with anger, and she felt as if she faced an enraged tiger.

"You're mine, Cheramie, and I know you better than Phillip. He's wound up in his political career and he'll never have time for you."

"Good-bye, Sal," she said, meaning it absolutely. She turned to go, but he caught her arm.

"Come back here." He held her tightly, and all her diplomacy vanished.

"Get your hands off, Sal!"

"I know what you really want, Cheramie. You're not dealing with a well-mannered society man now. Phillip's not man enough for you."

"Neither are you! I'm going."

"Like hell."

"I want to go home! Dammit, Sal. I know what I want."

He shoved her around and leaned forward to sweep everything off the round table between two stuffed chairs. A book and glass ashtrays and a lamp hit the wall while Cheramie struggled to get out of his grasp, her anger transforming to rage.

"Dammit, you let go of me! I'm going home now!"

"No, you're not." He spun her around and pushed her down, shoving up her skirt. She realized what he intended.

"Sal, let me go!" She struggled as he yanked down the silk panties and moved between her legs. She struggled uselessly while he held her pressed against the table, his hand hard against the small of her back. He pulled down his zipper and entered her from behind.

She gritted her teeth and swore at him and called him names while he called her names in return, but he wasn't hurting her; he was tormenting her, trying to overcome her anger with passion. She fought, struggling to resist him, but he knew how to arouse her. Her body responded and her protests ended, and at the edge of a climax Sal pulled away.

She gasped and tried to move her hips against him.

"Say it, Cheramie, say you want me." He released her.

"Damn you, I want you."

He thrust into her hard, and she cried out, jammed against the hard table, the slate top cold against her cheek. She knew she had made an incredible mistake in her affair with Sal.

She felt his shuddering release, and finally he moved away. Exhausted, dazed, a slow-burning anger replacing passion, she turned around to look at him. "You raped me."

"The hell I did. You clearly asked me. I want you here next week, Cheramie. You will be, if I have to come get you."

"After tonight, do you think I want to get near you again?"

He stared at her and suddenly picked her up. "Come here, baby. I know you. I'll show you how much I know you."

She swore and beat her fists against him uselessly. "I want to go home, dammit! You bastard!"

He put her down on the bed. "I'm not going to just let you walk out of my life. You're mine."

And she realized he meant it. She talked to him, arguing, trying to reason, trying to push his hands away when he caressed her.

"Sal, I hurt from what you've already done."

"Shh," he said, covering her mouth with his while his hand slid between her legs. Her protests died at his sensuous stroking.

She cried out when he entered her, but in minutes her hips moved wildly as she climaxed. She moved away and showered and dressed in silence under his smoldering gaze. He frightened her. She had known rough and powerful men, but aside from Rutger, she had never known a man she couldn't handle.

She returned home with nothing resolved and knew she would have to see Sal again the following week. Each visit now was more dangerous, and sometime before Phillip publicly declared himself a candidate, she would have to get rid of Sal permanently, even if it meant telling him Phillip's political plans. She soaked her sore body in a hot tub of water for an hour that night while she tried to think of a way out of her predicament.

17

March 5, 1990
San Francisco

A black circle was drawn around Tuesday, March 6, almost five months after the devastating quake that had destroyed three yards Alette had landscaped. Busier than ever, Alette gazed at the notations for the week. It was Monday, March 5. Tomorrow night was the kickoff dinner in San Francisco for Phillip's campaign, and the entire family was in town for the event. Bill was arriving at four in the afternoon today, and she would pick him up at the airport. He had to get back to Washington immediately after the dinner, but Cheramie and Phillip were staying in San Francisco for a series of fund-raisers and parties for the following two weeks. Bill would be back next week on Wednesday.

She glanced at the folded newspaper on her desk, scanning an article that said Jefferson O'Neil, formerly a Houston ball player, CEO and owner of Jayton Foods, was planning to run for governor of California. Beside it was a picture of Jeff smiling at the camera.

Her thoughts jumped to her contract to landscape the grounds of the mansion being built for the next governor. The job had been delayed, yet she still held the contract. She stared at O'Neil's picture, thinking she didn't want to work with him but convincing herself that Nelson Crown was thoroughly entrenched and would win again.

She glanced back at the calendar, and her thoughts returned to her schedule. She penciled in dates, planning to fly to Reno next Monday to visit a hotel site she had planned.

The bell jangled and she glanced up, surprise lighting her features as Aubrey sauntered into the office.

"Good morning. I came to talk about olive branches."

She laughed and went around the desk to hug him.

"Hey!" He held her away and studied her. "I thought it would take persuasion on my part for you to forgive me."

"I forgive you. I guess because I love Bill, I want you to love Bill."

Aubrey looked at her hand. "No engagement ring yet."

"No. I value your opinion, and I don't want to make a mistake."

"And?" he asked, looking at her intently.

She shrugged. "I guess you were right—I'm not *wildly* in love, so I want to wait and make sure."

"And I really am forgiven for having a big mouth and a frank tongue and for being damned choosy when it comes to my sister?"

"You're definitely forgiven. Have lunch with me."

"I can't, but I'll take a rain check. I have an appointment."

"A new lady in your life?"

"Sweetie, why is it you want me to be married so badly, yet you don't care to rush into it yourself?"

"I worry about you. I'm not as alone as you are."

"I'm doing fine. I can cook. I sail. I even know how to do my laundry."

"Pat isn't back in your life?"

"No, and she won't be." He moved away restlessly, staring out the front window with his hands in his pockets. "I'm just not meant for marriage."

Alette nodded, knowing that she liked her independence and the thought of moving to Washington and becoming the wife of a career politician wasn't the most appealing idea.

"I'm glad you came by the office."

He grinned. "We can't have fights and harsh words between us. If we've settled that, I have to run. I'm off to see a man about a boat." He crossed the room and held up his hand in the age-old sign of childhood. She placed her palm against his and kissed his cheek.

"Thanks, Aubrey."

She watched him go with a warm satisfaction, feeling better that they had patched up their quarrel, knowing that his opinion of Bill mattered to her. As she went to the back room to get blueprints, she heard the bell over the door and wondered if Aubrey had forgotten something.

A man stood with his back to her, and when he turned around she was taken aback to face Sal Giavotella.

With a flash of white teeth, he smiled and extended his hand. "Hello, Miss Lachman. I haven't seen you in a long time."

"No. I read about you in the papers," she said, feeling her fingers gripped in his large hand. "Your institute occasionally makes the news. May I help you?"

"I'm sure you can," he said, studying her. Silence lengthened, and she felt a twinge of curiosity.

"What can I do for you?"

He looked as if he were weighing his words before he replied. "I thought we might talk about landscaping."

"Here in San Francisco? You won't be staying in Washington?"

"I'll be back and forth, but I'll always keep a home here."

"Sit down, and we can talk about it," she said with a

strange, intuitive feeling that landscaping wasn't why he had come to her office.

He glanced at his watch. "It's half-past eleven. Want to talk about it over lunch?"

"I need to be back shortly," she said, feeling an uncustomary reluctance to have lunch with him.

"I'll get you back as shortly as you want. Come on. I won't bite."

Knowing old prejudices bothered her where he was concerned, she nodded. "I'll get my purse."

He drove to Cassady's, and beneath skylights and floor-to-ceiling glass, as they ate green salads, he asked questions and talked without ever getting to the topic of landscaping. Again, she wondered why he had asked her to lunch.

"Mr. Giavotella—"

"Please, Sal."

"You mentioned landscaping some grounds."

Again she received an inscrutable look of amusement, and she had a feeling that there was more to the luncheon meeting than business.

"It's nice to get to know the youngest Lachman."

"That surely wasn't why you came to my office."

He smiled. "I'm building a six-bedroom house on a lot I've bought. It's in a hilly, wooded area. I plan to marry. This house is for my fiancée."

"I didn't know you were engaged. I didn't know you were divorced," she said bluntly, remembering he had a large family.

"Yes, I am. And I'm engaged to an absolutely wonderful woman!" he said, and laughed softly. "Can we keep this deal confidential for the time being?"

"Yes, of course, but if I get a contract with you, I'd like to work with your builder—"

"I just meant telling friends, etc. I want to surprise my fiancée, and word gets around quickly."

"You'll surprise her with a house?"

"Yes," he said, his eyes sparkling. Alette realized Sal Giavotella was wildly in love, but she couldn't understand why he had come to her for the landscaping job. San Francisco had fine, established landscape architects who had been in business longer than she had and had no past history of campaigning against him. He puzzled her, and she had a feeling he wasn't telling her everything she should know. She wondered who his fiancée was.

"We can keep it confidential. That's very easy. Do you have anything particular in mind?"

"Yes. I want something formal. Actually, the garden I like the best is the one in the British embassy. Have you ever seen it?"

"Yes, it's lovely," she said, "but, remember, that's in the D.C. climate. We have little microcosms of climate here. What grows one place may not grow in another. I'll do what I can. Roses are hardy. Do you like the three levels like the embassy?"

"Yes, and the rose beds with one kind of rose in each bed. I want trees, but I know the roses will have to have sunshine."

"You can have trees and roses. Particularly if the yard is large."

"I have a blueprint," he said, unrolling it. He leaned close over the table, and she was aware of a scent of cologne, of his large dark fingers pointing to different areas on the paper. When he looked at her his gaze held a disconcerting intentness.

"I'll have to go out and look at it, and I won't be able to . . ." She paused and looked at a small notebook she carried in her purse. "I can't until Thursday next week, the fifteenth."

"No hurry. That's fine. I plan to be here for three weeks. I'll fly back to Washington sometime during the three weeks, but I'm sure I can meet you."

"Actually, since this is an undeveloped area and large grounds, I think I'll have aerial photos as well."

"You look like your sister, Cheramie," he said softly.

"People say we look alike."

"You don't act alike," he said, surprising her.

"I didn't know you knew Cheramie," she said.

"We've talked. We move in some of the same circles in

Washington. I don't suppose you could be persuaded to come over to our side in the governor's race.''

"Hardly," she said, wanting to be finished with lunch.

"You don't like me, do you? It goes back to the campaign against your father, I suppose, because this is the first you and I have ever had more than a mere greeting between us.''

She was startled by his frankness and wondered why he cared. "Perhaps you'd rather have someone else do your landscaping.''

"Oh, no," he said, smiling slyly, and Alette felt another ripple of distaste. "I want you, because you're damned good at what you do and you have a sterling reputation.''

"There are other good landscape architects here—we are blessed with them.''

"You don't want the job?''

"I am a professional. Yes, I'll do the job if you want.''

"But you will still dislike me.''

"Mr. Giavotella—''

He leaned forward, interrupting her, amusement burning in his dark eyes, his gaze raking over her briefly in a disturbingly bold manner. "Miss Lachman, there hasn't been a time in my life I've had an enemy of a beautiful woman. I find this a challenge. Before the landscaping job is finished, I intend to take you to dinner and I intend to win your friendship.''

"I don't see why. It's getting late, and I need to get back to the office.''

He laughed softly, a throaty sound that made her look at him sharply. "I want to be friends. I want you to meet my fiancée, and I think you'll like her very much. And I'll try to make a better impression.''

Later in her office, she watched him climb into a convertible and wondered again why he had selected her for the job. She looked down at her calendar at the date, March 5, and didn't realize then it was one she would remember the rest of her life.

On the fourteenth of March Alette flew back to San Francisco from Reno and arrived home at six o'clock with barely enough time to shower, change, and get to the gallery opening on time. When the phone cut into the quiet, she was surprised by the heavy breathing and threats to Cheramie's life. Her sister's whimpers in the background left her cold and shaking, unsure what to do or whom to call first.

Slowly reality intruded on her fears, and she caught her lower lip between her teeth. She had listened to the whispered instructions but had remained staring at the phone as if she had imagined the call. She had been given a bizarre plan to follow immediately and the warning not to call Bill or her father or even Phillip.

She started out of the room, stopped in indecision, and looked at her watch. It was six after six. The eerie voice sounded through her mind again. She was to take fifteen thousand dollars to the address she had hastily penned on her desk calendar. It was a Russian Hill address—one of the best in town and only minutes from her home. She was to take the money inside a third-floor condominium and leave it in the bedroom. It sounded like a trap to kidnap her. She didn't want to do what she had been told, but she couldn't risk Cheramie's life, and every minute counted.

She rushed to her safe and counted out fifteen thousand dollars.

18

Fifteen thousand dollars was a paltry sum for a Lachman. Anyone who knew much about Rutger and Lachman Real Estate and Lachman Foods would know that fifteen thousand was a ridiculously low ransom. That made Alette worry even more, but after debating whether or not to call the police, she hurried to the phone and punched out Rutger's number. The harsh whispered warning about Cheramie's life echoed through her mind, and she slammed down the receiver. Warning or not, Rutger would handle things as he saw fit.

She glanced again at her watch and saw that it was sixteen minutes after six. She picked up her purse and sweater and strode out the door.

The address was in a block on a steep slant. Holding her wrist close to the dash, she read the time: 6:24. Fog had closed in, a soupy mist that heightened her fears and hid everything from sight. Wanting to drive away and get the police, Alette sat in her car, not entirely convinced the woman's voice on the phone had been Cheramie's. It had sounded like her, but it had been too brief to be certain.

With trepidation she climbed out of the car. Mist swirled around her, and she watched her steps in the darkness. Inside, she studied the row of boxes with addresses. The staircase was empty. Shivering, she pulled her sweater around her. Somewhere on the dark street a car door banged. With the money in a packet in her hand, she slowly climbed the stairs. At the top she looked back over her shoulder. The hall held potted palms, gilt mirrors decorated the walls, and a faint trace of tobacco smoke was in the air. She wondered if anyone was home in the other condominiums.

When she glanced at her watch it was twenty-seven after six. She was to take the money into the bedroom, and everything in her cried out to run—except she couldn't desert her sister. Now she wished she had left a note at her apartment, telling where she was going. If she disappeared, no one would know where she went or what had happened.

She stopped in front of the door and stared at it. She was tempted to open the door, toss the money inside, and run, yet the voice had emphasized that she was to take it to the bedroom. Her heart pounded violently when she reached for the knob. It was cold and smooth in her hands.

Reluctance and fear held her immobile. *Get help. Go home. Cheramie.* The words taunted her. She turned the knob and pushed. The door swung open on a dark entryway and living room beyond it. She reached inside and flipped a light switch. The decor had a decorator's touch and was masculine with rust and brown colors and heavy furniture; the room was devoid of anything personal. There was a bouquet of red roses on a coffee table. She stepped into the room, and the floor creaked. In the distance she heard the faint wail of sirens, and she wanted to be out on the street.

"Cheramie," she said, her voice faltering in the empty silence. She was supposed to leave the money and be out of the apartment by half-past six, and it was almost that now. Why did she have to leave by a certain time? She felt as if she were not alone. She couldn't take her eyes off the room to look at her watch. The kitchen was on her right, while to her left was a short hallway and the darkened bedroom door. Her feet seemed rooted to the floor, as if unable to take another step. Instinct urged her to fling the money into the room rather than go in there herself.

Two tentative steps, three steps, and her heart beat so loudly she was afraid she couldn't hear anything else.

The noise of sirens grew, yet she was isolated from the cars racing past outside. She reached the doorway, grasped the knob, and opened the door. Braced for a violent confrontation, she found herself looking into an empty room. Her hand hit the switch, and a ceiling light came on. Her gaze ran over the rumpled bed covered with black sheets. A long-stemmed rose lay on the floor.

The money was to be placed on the bed. She entered carefully, moving on tiptoes. The red caught her eye first.

Blood was splattered on a wall. A blood-spattered male body clad only in shorts was stretched beside the bed. Her heart seemed to stop and then pound violently. She couldn't move; she couldn't breathe.

A scream started deep in her throat as panic washed over her. Sirens wailed loudly somewhere outside. Dropping the money, hundred-dollar bills fluttering out of her hand, she ran blindly, striking the door, dashing down the short hall and across the living room.

When she spun through the open door into the hallway, she collided with a man.

She screamed, and he yelled. Another man rushed past her with a drawn gun.

It took seconds to register that the two men were uniformed

policemen. Her voice seemed to come from far away, and she tried to control her emotions. "Find my sister! A man's been hurt!"

He attempted to quiet her, and the next few minutes passed in a blur while they tried hopelessly to communicate.

"You've got to find my sister!"

"Lady, calm down. I'm Officer Palley. You say a man has been hurt?"

The other policeman reappeared. "I've radioed. They're on their way. He's cold."

She grabbed one by the arm. "You've got to try to find my sister! Cheramie Walcott! She's in danger."

"Calm down, lady, and try to tell me. Do you know the dead man?"

"No! I don't know him. I don't know who's in there. I went in the bedroom like I was told and saw the body, and I ran."

"Someone told you to go in there?"

"Yes! I had a phone call."

"Who called you?"

"Please, listen to me! My sister may be in danger."

"Let's go inside and you sit down. Just calm down."

"Will you find my sister?"

"How long have you been here?"

"I don't know. Only a few minutes. Can't you get on your radio?" One panic was exchanged for another.

"Look, lady, calm down. Try to tell me what happened. How long have you been here?" he repeated, taking notes.

"I just got here. I've been here several minutes, maybe. I don't know. Have someone look for my sister," she said, gulping for breath, feeling that every second was dragging, terrified for Cheramie's safety, dazed by her discovery. "You're wasting time!"

"What's your name?" he asked, his brown eyes watching her intently.

"Alette Lachman." She looked at her watch and almost sobbed. "It's over half-past six now. Please try to find her."

"What's her name again?"

"Cheramie Walcott. Mrs. Phillip Walcott."

His eyes narrowed. "Senator Walcott's wife?"

"Yes!" she exclaimed, shaking and relieved that he was finally paying attention to her.

"Dan, get on the radio. Find the senator's wife. Miss Lachman, sit down. Tell me again about the phone call."

"A whispered voice told me Cheramie was in danger and to bring fifteen thousand dollars to this address."

"How long ago did you arrive?"

"I got here just before you did. I looked at my watch in the hallway. It was"—she went blank, trying to think—"it was not quite six-thirty."

"Do you know the man?"

"No! I don't know him," she said, shivering, hoping they wouldn't ask her to go back into that bedroom and look at the corpse. *Where was Cheramie?*

A detective swept into the room. He had sandy hair, a pug nose, and hazel eyes with a no-nonsense look to his expression. He talked briefly with the officers, then came over to introduce himself. "Miss Lachman, I'm Lieutenant Harberger."

"Are you trying to find my sister?"

A blurt of static interrupted them, and the detective listened to a voice over his radio. "They think your sister is with the senator on their way to a campaign fund-raiser dinner. We'll find them within a few minutes if they are."

She sagged against the arm of the chair, rubbing her hand across her forehead. Maybe Cheramie was safe with Phillip. Maybe she'd been with Phillip all along. Alette felt limp with relief. Words swirled around as they talked, and she heard snatches—"TI's will be here . . ."—"blood . . ."—"time of death. . . ." She overheard Officer Palley tell the detective she said she'd arrived just before half-past six.

"Miss Lachman." She looked up at Lt. Harberger.

"Do you know the dead man?"

"No. I don't know—I didn't look. I just saw blood and a body, and I ran."

"Do you know Sal Giavotella?"

Alette stared at him as her ears began to buzz and she felt faint. She gripped the chair. For the first time she stopped thinking about Cheramie and thought about herself and the phone call. It had been a hoax to get her to the scene of the murder.

"Are you all right?"

His sharp voice brought things back into focus. "It was Sal Giavotella?" she asked.

"How well did you know him?"

"I just barely knew him."

"You aren't close friends?"

She blinked and looked around. Two uniformed policemen were waiting to hear her answer along with the detective. As she looked into their eyes, she was afraid she was the prime suspect.

"I don't want to answer any more questions without counsel," she said stiffly. "I want to leave. May I go?"

The detective glanced beyond her at the officer. "Yes. Do you want someone to drive you home? You've had a shock."

The radio came on again, and he picked it up. She caught some of the words and listened closely, because she heard the word *senator* mentioned. Lt. Harberger turned away, and with others talking in the room, she couldn't hear what he was saying. The technical investigators, the coroner, uniformed policemen, were on the scene now. Harberger turned to her.

"Your sister is with her husband, and they just arrived at the dinner party. We have officers at the party, so she'll be under close supervision and we'll give them an escort home."

"Thank you," she replied stiffly.

"Miss Lachman, you'll be a material witness. You'll be in town where we can find you, won't you?"

"Yes," she said, gazing into cynical hazel eyes that seemed to hold accusation. If she weren't a Lachman, she wondered, would she be walking out of the condominium to go home or headed for the police station?

As she went downstairs uniformed men passed her. A gray-haired woman stood in the hallway on the second floor and stared through thick bifocals as Alette walked past. Outside, people clustered on the porch beneath a bright light. Alette saw the television van pull to a halt outside while policemen strung yellow tape and mist swirled around them. She put her head down and hurried to her car, climbing in and pulling away swiftly.

When she reached home, she was shaking violently. She entered her house and switched on every light. She looked at her kitchen clock. It was twenty minutes after seven o'clock. Feeling a sense of panic overwhelm her, she called Abe Swan, the Lachman family attorney, who listened to her story and said he would be right over. She called Aubrey and left a message on his answering machine. For the first time she thought of Bill. It was twenty minutes before eight when she called the gallery. Bill had already been there and gone. She called his hotel and had him paged and left a message. She had left the call she didn't want to make until last. She stared at the phone and lifted the receiver with reluctance and dialed Rutger. He was out, so she left a message with a servant.

Unable to sit still, she paced the floor until Abe appeared. Balding, under five feet eight inches, with black eyes, he had a presence and matter-of-fact manner that was reassuring. He slipped off a topcoat and handed it to her. "Your house is being watched."

"Someone's watching me?" she asked in surprise.

"Police. Let's hear your story."

"Come in and sit down." She led him to the living room and sat on a wing chair while he sat on the sofa and placed a yellow legal pad on his knees to make notes. He turned on a recorder and listened while she talked.

"Do you know Sal?" he asked.

"I've met him, but no more than that."

"You've never dated him?"

For the first time she remembered the lunch with Sal, and she told Abe.

"You told the police you barely knew him, yet you had lunch with him recently?"

"I was in shock and didn't think about the lunch. It was brief, about his landscaping. I don't know the man."

"Tell me what happened when you had lunch."

"Nothing happened. We just ate, talked about what kind of yard he wanted—"

"Tell me exactly what you remember. When he came to your office, what kind of yard he wanted, everything."

Worried now about giving the police a misleading answer, she told Abe everything she could remember. She ran her hands across her forehead, feeling caught in a nightmare.

"Alette, this phone call—someone set you up. Who would know you had fifteen thousand dollars you could get easily?"

She shrugged. "My family. My close friends—"

"How would friends know?"

"Some of them have been here at the house and seen me put jewelry and money away. They didn't know the location of the safe, but they knew I had one." Besides there was still time to go to a bank, for that matter."

The phone interrupted them, and she picked it up to hear Bill's voice.

"Sorry I didn't meet you. Something's happened," she said.

"I thought maybe you had a lawn problem. What's happened?"

"Why don't you come over so we can talk? Our family lawyer is here now."

"Jesus, what happened? Never mind. I'll be right there."

She returned to sit down facing Abe.

"Has Sal Giavotella ever been here?" he asked, adjusting the long yellow pad on his knees.

"No! I didn't know him. I just had one brief lunch with him. Only my contracted clients would have a reason to come to my home. Sometimes I get more work done here than at the office."

"Why fifteen thousand? That's a damned odd sum."

"I worried about it."

The questions went on until Bill came. She met him at the door and introduced him to Abe, who folded up his things.

"I think that will do for tonight, Alette. If you hear from the police, refuse to answer any questions without me and call me at once. Don't go with them unless they have a warrant. Tell them you want your attorney present. Make sure they Mirandize you. I'll be right down and get you bonded out." He turned to Bill. "It was nice to meet you, Mr. Gaffney."

As soon as Abe was gone she rushed back into the living room to Bill, expecting finally to be able to throw herself into someone's arms, to receive some kind of reassurance. Although Abe had been calm and matter-of-fact, he hadn't been comforting, and even if the encouragement turned out to be false, she wanted to hear it. "Thank goodness you're here!" she said.

"What the fuck happened?" he asked stiffly. He stood by the mantel with his hands in his pockets, and she stopped her rush toward him.

His question, his attitude, made her feel alone. As her gaze swept over his features, she realized he was furious. Surprised, she sat down and went through the whole thing while he paced and swore and frowned.

"You don't believe me, do you?" she asked quietly.

"I want to believe you," he answered.

"You don't sound as if you do."

"Well, hell," he said, running his fingers through his hair, "you're in his place, money is all over, he's almost nude—" He looked at her sharply. "The big rumor in Washington was that he had a mistress. That's why he got divorced."

"Then why don't the police find the mistress and talk to her?"

"No one knows who she is," he said with accusation in his voice.

"It wasn't me! Lord, how can you think that! I'm seldom in Washington unless I'm with you," she said, dismayed and angered by his attitude.

"You fly everywhere for business. How the hell do I know where you are or what you're doing?"

"How can you believe that?"

"There's a lot of fucking evidence!"

"I thought you'd give me some support," she snapped, her anger rising.

"Support! For chrissakes, Alette, you've bombed Phillip's bid for the presidency and my political future! The scandal will fry us!"

She stared at him, seeing a side to him she hadn't been aware of before.

"Jesus, Alette. Some voice calls and says take fifteen grand—that's peanuts to a Lachman—and you *go*?"

"I thought Cheramie's life was in danger," she replied, keeping her voice level and controlling her temper.

"That sounds so damned flimsy. You got an anonymous phone call that said to bring fifteen grand because Cheramie was in danger and you didn't call the police?"

"Maybe if you'd had the phone call, you'd understand why I did what I did," she retorted.

"No kidnapper would ask a Lachman for fifteen thousand. Oh, God! I have to get in touch with Phillip. How could you go without calling the police or me or Rutger?"

She blinked and stared at him as he ran his fingers through his hair. His face was flushed and he was scowling, and her patience grew thin.

"Bill, I thought my sister's life was in danger!"

"Hell, she's out with Phillip and forty other people!" He jabbed the phone and in minutes talked softly, asking for Phillip. He kept his voice as low as possible, but she could hear him, and with every word she grew more angry with Bill.

"Phillip, Sal Giavotella was murdered tonight." There was a pause. "Early in the evening. Alette's implicated.

"Look, I think when you both get through there and go home, we ought to get you out of here. Get you as far from this as possible. When the news breaks, if you're here in town, you may not be able to recover from the damage."

Feeling as though she viewed a stranger, Alette stared at Bill while her love for him crumbled. Aubrey's words came back, and she realized her brother had been right. And for just a few seconds she forgot the murder and the predicament she was in. She felt an enormous relief she hadn't rushed into another engagement.

"I'll make the arrangements," Bill said into the phone. "I hope to hell both of you can account for your day. I know you can, what about Cheramie?" There was only a brief pause. "You do. I'll get the flight arranged and get in touch with your dad and Rutger. Call me the minute you get home.

"Have you talked to Rutger?" he asked when he replaced the receiver.

"You think I killed Sal Giavotella?" she asked Bill, ignoring his question.

"No. I believe you, but I've got to get Phillip away from this. You're involved. There's no need to drag him down into it and ruin his chances. Oh, damn, it's like someone did this to keep him from the race!"

He called the Lachman pilot and made arrangements for a flight to leave around midnight. "I'll go, too, Alette. I'll call you from Washington."

She nodded, trying to keep her anger in check, knowing she was on edge.

"I better get back to the hotel," he said. "I hope they catch who did it tonight." He stared at her. "You didn't know him except through politics?"

"No! What do you think?"

"I just wish to hell you had called the police," he said, and she stared at him, knowing she would never date him again, no matter what the outcome of the night would be. Bill wasn't the man for her, and she guessed that she had always felt that deep down.

"We need to get a press release out for Phillip tonight," he continued, talking more to himself than to her. "Thank God his father is a prominent judge." He walked to the door. "I'll be in touch." He closed the door and was gone.

"Good-bye, Bill," she said to the empty room, feeling no sense of loss.

Sleep was impossible, and she didn't care to hear the news.

At eleven o'clock the next morning, she heard the doorbell. When she opened it she faced Lt. Harberger and another man, who introduced himself as Lt. Rosenberg.

"Miss Lachman, we have a warrant for your arrest," Lt. Harberger said, handing her the warrant.

Alette was read her rights, a search warrant was presented, and within five minutes they found a revolver behind the front seat of her car.

19 ～⌒⌒

It was almost midnight when the police car drove down the steep hill, leaving the three-story house behind. The moment Cheramie and Phillip were in the privacy of their bedroom, Phillip reached for the phone.

"I want to call Alette," Cheramie said, rubbing her arms.

"Let me find out what the hell has happened," Phillip snapped waiting for an answer on the other end of the line. "Your sister is involved in Giavotella's murder, and that's all we know. Bill was—Hello, Bill? What the hell happened tonight?"

Cheramie stared at him, her heart pounding while he swore and asked questions and finally made arrangements to get to the airport at once. He slammed down the phone.

"There goes the fucking campaign!"

"What's happened?"

"Alette is involved."

"I can't believe it. You know my sister."

"She was at the scene, Cheramie." He ground out the words angrily. "My sister-in-law was at Giavotella's place, and that was where he was murdered." He slammed his fist on the headboard of the bed with a bang that made Cheramie jump.

"Has she been arrested?"

"No. She's home, and she has some kind of story. She had an anonymous call and was told you were in danger. Bill said we better be able to account for our time. I was with people every minute of the day. What about you?"

"I had lunch with Darcy and Linette. We shopped and then I shopped."

"Hell, you can't prove that!"

"Yes, I can. I bought an expensive dress at I. Magnin's, and I'm sure the clerk will remember me. Besides, why would I have to account for my time?"

"If Alette is drawn into this, we will be, too. And the caller said you were in danger. That puts your name in it. Oh, damn. If I survive this, it'll be a fucking miracle."

"You'll survive, Phillip."

"It depends on how bad it is, how fast they find the murderer, how much Alette was involved."

"I know my sister. She couldn't be involved!"

"No one knows another person that well. You bought a dress. Where else were you?"

"I had my hair done, finished just in time to get here—"

"Can the hairdresser verify it?"

"I'm sure they can. It was a walk-in salon, where you sign in when you arrive. I signed in at five o'clock, and you can verify that."

"Thank God. That puts you and me in the clear. Get the kids up and let's go. Bill has talked to Derek. They all agree you and I need to get the hell out of here for Washington."

"I want to talk to Alette."

"Not now. Call her from Washington. If I save my ass, I'll have to be as far away from this as possible. I'll get my papers. Call my folks and we'll pick up the boys on the way to the airport."

Cheramie called the Walcotts, and when she got off the phone, Phillip was out of the room. She picked up the receiver again and punched a number. Phillip came into the room and yanked the receiver from her hand to slam it down.

"Dammit, are you calling Alette?"

"Yes!"

"I told you—stay away from her."

"She's my sister! This whole thing is because of me."

"Oh, the hell it is! You don't even know if she was Giavotella's mistress."

"She wasn't." Cheramie leaned forward, fear and anger making her shake. "I know Alette. Alette was never Sal Giavotella's mistress."

"You're her sister, so I know you don't want to face the

facts, but we're staying away from her and we're flying to Washington tonight. We're getting the hell away from California and this murder!''

"We can't abandon her.''

"Abandon!'' Phillip's face was red, his hair tousled and his shirt rumpled. "Alette has the full battery of Lachman lawyers behind her. My father is already working his ass off to pull strings on this, and Rutger will spend all the money necessary. They'll get her off, there's no doubt about that. My presidential career is what's fucked up.''

"Phillip, I can't leave without talking to her.''

"Oh, yes, you can, Cheramie. My father said to go; Abe Swan said to go. So we go if I have to slug you and carry you over my shoulder.''

"You really think she'll be okay?''

"She won't have a problem. You and I are the ones with problems.''

Within the hour Cheramie looked down as the lights of San Francisco receded in the background while the Lachman jet gained altitude. The first thing she intended to do when they reached Washington was call Alette. "Tell me again, Phillip. You don't think she'll have any trouble getting cleared?''

"How could she with my father, your father, and Swan and Oakley?''

"I'll be glad when it's over.''

"I hope you're talking about Alette and not my campaign. God, I hate to see the press in the morning.''

20

Alette was taken to the station, allowed to call Abe, and booked. She was fingerprinted and had a mug shot taken. With strangers, she stood in a lineup. She had to hand over her jewelry, her purse, her belt, and her high heels. The nightmare became worse when she had to change from her white blouse and navy skirt to a prison jumpsuit. As she gave up her street clothes, she felt as if she were giving up her freedom. She sat in a holding cell with eight other women. One had thrown up on the floor, and the smell made Alette queasy. Two eyed her, and she stood at a corner in the front by the bars, wondering how long she would be there.

A woman leaned against the bars only a few feet away. She reeked of whiskey and had a bruise on her cheek. "Why're you here?"

"They think I killed a man," Alette answered, staring the woman in the eye. The woman shrugged and moved away. Alette looked around the cell and hoped they didn't realize how terrified she was. Three of them stared back at her. One woman was stretched on the floor, and Alette didn't know if she had passed out or was asleep.

The time was interminable. Her legs ached, but she wouldn't go farther into the cell and sit down with the others. And all she could think about was the damning evidence, her presence at the scene, the revolver found in her car. She must have made an enemy of someone, yet she couldn't think who or why.

A deputy appeared, and the door slid open with a clang. "Alette Lachman."

Dazed, thankful to escape the cell and terrified of going back to it, Alette hurried along with him. When she spotted Rutger's blond head and Abe Swan, she squared her shoulders. Last night when Bill had arrived she had anticipated some comfort. She knew better than to expect any from Rutger.

He looked at her with a cold gaze that stirred her anger, and she guessed that either her father suspected she had murdered Sal Giavotella or he was enraged that she had involved the family in scandal.

"Alette," Abe said, "we have hired a fine criminal lawyer. She was in Mexico, but she's flying home. I'll be with you for the arraignment."

"I want out of here, Abe," she said firmly. "I don't know how that pistol got in my car."

"We'll go over everything later. What's important now is to get you out of here if we can."

"I want to stop in the ladies' room a moment."

"You'll be brought into the courtroom by the deputy."

By the time she walked into the courtroom, she was coolly composed. A man in a black suit sat at a table in front of the bench—a veritable bulldog with heavy jowls, a pug nose, and round brown eyes that glanced at her impassively. She had read about him in the newspaper and knew he was Mel Cipresso, the district attorney.

Rutger sat in the back of the courtroom while she went forward to sit beside Abe. A nameplate read "Judge Bertram Klein."

The judge shuffled papers and read, "The State of California *versus* Alette Lachman. Is defendant represented by counsel?"

"Yes, Your Honor," Abe answered, "I am counsel for Miss Lachman."

"You may approach the bench. We will proceed with the arraignment at this time."

Alette stood between the two attorneys, and all she could think about was the holding cell. She didn't want to go back to it. She didn't want to be incarcerated for even one night. Her life had turned into a nightmare of unreality. A steady flame of anger burned, because someone had set her up for the crime, and as soon as possible she wanted to find out who and why.

"The Superior Court in the state of California charges Miss Alette Lachman of San Francisco County, California, with the crime of manslaughter for having shot and killed Salvadore Giavotella on March 14, 1990, at a residence located in San Francisco, San Francisco County, California."

"How does the defendant plead?"

"Not guilty," Alette answered clearly.

"Your Honor, the State asks bail be posted at one million dollars," Mel Cipresso intoned nasally.

Alette felt as if she had turned to stone. She wouldn't be allowed to leave the jail. She didn't hear what was being said until Abe moved forward, and then she caught snatches of his low-voiced words.

". . . excessive, Your Honor. There's no reason. She is an upstanding citizen of the community, she would not flee the state. We ask that bond be set at a reasonable amount, whatever is the pleasure of the court."

"Bond is set at two hundred thousand dollars," Judge Klein said. He turned to the prosecutor. "The court is cognizant of politics involved. I am going to set the time for the preliminary hearing for Monday, April sixteenth. I will expect counsel to be prepared at that time . . ." His voice faded as Alette thought about the date. After an hour in the holding cell, jail had become a terrifying threat.

"Yes, Your Honor," both attorneys said, and the judge rose.

"That's all," he said, and left the courtroom. Alette let out her breath, because it meant she had to return to the cell.

"I'll post bond immediately," Abe said.

She wanted to scream that she didn't want to go back to the cell. Instead she moved quietly along with the deputy. There were two new prisoners in her cell, one talking constantly to the other, a steady stream of foul words emitted in a whine. She walked over to Alette. "I'll bet it's the first time. Why ya here?"

"Manslaughter."

"No shit. Manslaughter. I solicited a stonie. Dude's a cop." She trailed her fingers along Alette's arm.

The slight stroke made hairs rise on Alette's nape. It was a faint touch, but it goaded her past endurance. Rage fanned in her, and she turned to look the woman in the eye.

The woman blinked. "Shit," she muttered, and walked away. Alette stared at the hall, hearing the woman talking with another again about her arrest.

The deputy returned to get her, and she walked away, ignoring the woman's call. As soon as she was dressed again in her navy skirt and white blouse, she joined Abe, whose beeper sounded almost immediately.

"Alette, Rutger has gone to see about transportation. He's called his chauffeur to come pick us up. I brought your father down in my car, but we think it's better to have a driver pick us up—there are reporters gathered outside now. I've got a call coming in I have to answer. Come here."

He walked down the hall and found an empty room. "Just wait here and don't go anywhere or talk to any reporter until I make my call and get back. I don't think anyone will find you in here." He hurried away, and she took a deep breath, staring out the window at the back lot, at parked cars, at a bird in the tree, thinking she would never view the world in the same manner as she had before, still puzzling over who hated her enough to set her up for the murder.

People strode rapidly down halls, briefcases in hand, others leaning against walls or sitting on benches, waiting, staring vacantly into space. Jeff barely noticed his surroundings. His thoughts were on Gina Giavotella and the children. He felt a hatred for Alette Lachman that went far beyond what he had ever felt for Rutger. He had friends in high places, and he promised Gina he would do all he could to see that the Lachman power didn't let Sal's murderer go free.

Intent on seeing Harberger and then Mel Cipresso, Jeff stepped out of the elevator. He passed an open room and glanced in. A woman stood by a window. She had black hair fastened behind her head in a barrette, and she wore a tailored navy skirt and white blouse. He took a few more steps before he realized it was Alette Lachman.

Rage flared, and he spun around, striding back to the room. He would tell her what he was sure Gina and the Giavotella children would say, given the opportunity.

When he entered the room Alette Lachman turned, and her gaze narrowed.

21 ∽

She expected Abe. It wasn't Abe, and she panicked at the sight of the angry man striding toward her, because there was no mistaking the fury in his blue eyes and the set of his mouth.

Jeff O'Neil stopped only a few feet away from her. "I was at Gina Giavotella's this morning," he said, jamming his hand in his pocket. His other fist was clenched.

She drew herself up. "You have no business in here. I'm waiting for my lawyer."

"I know you'll use all the Lachman and Walcott connections, but, lady, there's justice."

"In this country you're supposed to be innocent until proven guilty," she retorted. "You've tried and convicted me without knowing one thing about me or where I was or what happened that night."

"I can read the papers. I knew Sal and I know Gina. There are six children and a widow, a fact you seem to hold in little regard."

She drew a deep breath, because beneath the anger she could hear the pain in his voice, and she remembered he had been close friends with Sal Giavotella and his family.

"I didn't kill Sal Giavotella," she stated firmly with a quiet dignity. "I barely knew him and saw him only on rare occasions."

"I'll bet your lawyers have rehearsed your story so much you could recite it backward and in your sleep."

She gazed into fiery blue eyes and felt a tenseness between them. "I didn't kill Sal Giavotella," she repeated. "That's the truth. I wasn't his lover." She leaned forward, anger sweeping her again, because she didn't have to answer to Jeff

O'Neil about anything. "And if I had done it, I would have picked a better way to do it. Get out of here, Mr. O'Neil."

"I'll go when I damn well please. I know you'll get off easy because of the Lachman-Walcott ties, but I hope to hell you don't walk without some kind of sentence." He leaned closer to her until they were only inches apart, glaring at each other. She refused to back up. "Six children!" he snapped. "Doesn't that matter to you?"

She felt engulfed in a strange mixture of sorrow for his pain and anger with his arrogance. "I didn't know him. Do you know anything about the circumstances involving his murder? You assume my guilt! You assume my involvement with him!"

A noise came from the doorway. "What the hell?" Aubrey stepped inside the room. "Where's Abe? Jeff?" He looked back and forth between Alette and Jeff and scowled. "What are you doing?" Without waiting for an answer, he looked at Alette. "Is he harassing you?"

"He's tried and condemned me."

"Damn you," Aubrey said without slowing his stride. He crossed to Jeff and swung, catching the other man by surprise, connecting with his jaw and sending him staggering backward. Alette yelled. To her horror, Jeff regained his balance without falling, and she suspected he had barely been containing his temper before the blow.

He lashed back at Aubrey, slamming his fist into her brother's jaw. Aubrey sprawled over the table and sent a chair crashing to the floor. Without stopping to think about it, Alette stepped between them.

"Stop fighting!" She faced Jeff, who had his fists clenched and raised. His eyes were dilated and his face had paled, and for a moment Alette wondered if he really saw her or if he would hit her because she blocked his way.

He drew deep breaths and dropped his hands, looking into her eyes. "Sal was a good man."

"I barely knew him," she said in the same quiet, emphatic manner.

She received a curious searching stare, which she met

without wavering, understanding how Jeff O'Neil must be grieving for his friend.

"Get the hell out of here, O'Neil," Aubrey said gruffly, moving beside her.

Jeff O'Neil turned on his heel and walked out, and she turned to look at Aubrey. "Are you all right?"

"I just found out," he said. She thought she would faint with relief when his long arms wrapped around her.

"The message was on my office recorder."

"I left it there last night. Aubrey, I didn't do it."

"Good God, I didn't think you did!" He leaned back, and she gave him a squeeze before moving away.

"Thanks for coming. Abe had a phone call, and Rutger went to see about transportation. They didn't want to ride home in Abe's car because of the press outside."

For the first time in the encounter, Alette really noticed Aubrey. Shocked, she tried to think of the last time she had seen him in anything but casual clothes. He wore a navy wool gabardine suit, a button-down cotton-and-linen white shirt, and a conservative navy silk tie. Gold links were fastened in the cuffs.

"You shaved your beard!" she exclaimed, looking at the trim sandy mustache and smooth jaw. He dabbed at the blood in the corner of his mouth. He looked handsome and had that same commanding air as Rutger. It was the first time she had ever noticed it about him. "And a suit?"

"I figured I better be presentable when the press sees your brother beside you. Presentable, wholesome, upstanding—a brother who is a credit to you."

"Oh, Aubrey, you shaved your beard for me," she said, feeling a lump in her throat. "I not only have a presentable brother, I have the most wonderful brother in the whole world!" She hugged him tightly and stepped away. "Thanks."

She heard footsteps and looked up as Abe and a willowy, beautiful black-haired woman entered the room.

"Alette, I'm sorry. Victoria just arrived," Abe said, frowning as he looked at Aubrey. "What happened?"

"Jeff O'Neil came in here," Aubrey answered, shaking hands with Abe.

"Damn. What did you do to him?"

"About the same."

"No police interfered? Are we going to have an assault charge?"

Aubrey shrugged. "Alette stepped between us and stopped the fight."

"I'm sorry I was late. This makes it worse. Your father is coming. I told him where we are, and he's already met Victoria. Alette, I want you to meet your attorney, Victoria Steiner. This is Alette Lachman and her brother, Aubrey Lachman."

As they all shook hands, Abe said, "Victoria is one of the best criminal lawyers around."

Alette gazed into the blue eyes of a woman who looked little older than she was and wondered how competent she would be in the courtroom.

"Abe, what brought this change about? I thought your firm would represent Alette," Aubrey said belligerently, making no mistake about his unhappiness with the change.

"The limo is waiting," Rutger said, striding into the room. "Aubrey, what are you doing here?"

"I got Alette's message. Why the fucking hell didn't you send someone after me last night?" he asked in a tight voice, turning on Rutger.

"I didn't see how you would be any help. You avoid all family matters," Rutger replied coldly. He turned to Alette. "There are newsmen in the lot. I've got a limo waiting at the back, but I know there will be some reporters no matter which way we go."

"When you leave here, I'd like you to come to my office, Miss Lachman," Victoria said quietly, and Alette nodded.

"When you're finished with Miss Steiner," Rutger said stiffly, "you can come home to stay with me until this is over. You won't want to stay alone at your place and have to contend with the press and cranks."

"She's staying with me," Aubrey said, and gave her a questioning glance. She nodded, thankful that he wanted her.

"That's what you want?" Rutger asked.

"Yes. I'd like to stay with Aubrey."

"I'll drive her to Miss Steiner's," Aubrey said, his distaste obvious when he said the lawyer's name. "Give me the address."

"I'll go with Aubrey," Alette said, feeling reassured when he draped his arm across her shoulders.

Victoria handed Alette her card, and Alette left with Aubrey, striding away without waiting for the others. They went outside, and as two men hurried toward her, Aubrey opened the door to a four-door blue sedan. She slid in. He slammed the door and hurried to the other side. A camera flashed as they drove away.

Dazed, Alette rode without thinking, relishing the quiet, wanting to shut out everything that had happened in the past hours. "Where's your Jaguar?" she asked finally.

"I bought a new car," he said, turning onto Market.

"This is your car? A four-door sedan?"

He took a deep breath. "I thought it would give me a degree of respectability. Listen, I'm going to check into this lawyer," he said tersely. "I don't know what Rutger and Abe are trying to pull—"

"Abe wouldn't get anyone except the best he could find."

"Hell, I'll bet she isn't one day older than you are. And she's a woman! There are no women criminal lawyers."

"I don't know about women in criminal law, but I know women lawyers win cases. I'm surprised at you." She studied him as he concentrated on driving. "You're my liberal, open-minded brother."

"I'm not a damned bit liberal or open-minded when it comes to my sister's future. For chrissakes, have you ever heard of her? Is this a name like Melvin Belli or Stanley S. Arkin? Hell, no. Victoria Steiner. Who the hell is she?"

"I trust Abe's judgment," she said, astounded by Aubrey's belligerence. "I trust his judgment."

"I don't trust Rutger. Abe will do exactly as Rutger wants him to do. I'm telling you, Alette, there are no women criminal lawyers. And look at her! The men will be thinking about bed, and the women on a jury will hate her!"

"We can find out what cases she has tried and what she has won."

"And what she has lost. Damn well we'll find out! I intend to find out all I can about Miss Victoria Steiner."

When they entered the law offices, a receptionist asked them to be seated. Five minutes later Victoria appeared. "If you'll come in now, Miss Lachman. Mr. Lachman, if you'll just have a seat, please. I need to talk to Alette alone."

Alette squeezed his arm and followed Victoria Steiner into a small room lined with shelves of law books and containing a long narrow table, on which rested a tape recorder, a yellow legal pad, and a pen.

"Have a scat."

"My brother usually is very pleasant."

"I understand. Pressure sometimes destroys polite manners. I'm going to tape our conversation, so I can be sure I get everything correctly. Now it's imperative that you tell me the truth. I'm your lawyer, I'll be defending you. I can go in the courtroom and do the best for you if I have as much information as possible. It's your life that's at stake. No matter how painful, now is the time to tell the truth and tell it all. Do you understand?"

"Yes," Alette said, sobering as the grim truth of the predicament was brought back full force.

"Will you go through the whole story, please."

She told about flying home, receiving the phone call, and her visit to Sal's condo and finding his body. Victoria wrote on the long yellow table, taking it all down while the tape revolved. When Alette finished, Victoria looked up.

"Were you Sal Giavotella's lover?"

"No," Alette answered calmly, feeling none of the resentment she had felt with her family. Victoria Steiner was a stranger and had no way of knowing the truth without asking.

"Had you ever seen him before?"

"Only through politics and at parties, with one exception," she answered, and proceeded to tell Victoria about the business lunch she had with Sal.

"Do you think he had talked to other landscape architects?"

"He didn't act as if he had."

"Why would he pick you when your family had opposed him and you've campaigned against him?"

"I don't know. I didn't understand why, and at one point I suggested he find another landscape architect."

"Someone saw to it that you were in his condo with the victim; someone placed the weapon in your car. You must have a powerful enemy somewhere."

"I've thought about that constantly, but I can't come up with an answer."

"Abe already has the information about the murder. Sal Giavotella was shot with a Webley-Fosbery .455-caliber revolver; the bullet matches the weapon found in your car. Time of death was a few minutes after five. First, where were you at five o'clock?"

"I was alone at my office. My plane arrived after four o'clock. I had my car at the airport and went to my office to take messages and check the mail. There were no witnesses that I can account for, because I was alone."

"You don't own a revolver?"

"No. I've never owned one. I don't even know how to shoot."

"Does your father own one?"

"Yes, my father has a pistol, but I haven't seen it in years, and I have no idea what make it is. Why do you ask?"

"Because you have access to it." She made a note on the pad. "Let's go through it again, and this time I'll interrupt when I have a question."

Alette started a second time, with Victoria interrupting constantly, asking questions, jumping back and forth, going back to the first time Alette had ever met Sal Giavotella, to the hatred the Lachmans felt toward Sal.

"What men are you dating?"

"Only Bill Gaffney."

"Are you sleeping with him?"

"Yes. Bill has asked me to marry him."

"Are you going to?"

Alette took a deep breath, and Victoria's head raised, the

pencil poised in her hand. "No. I haven't given him an answer yet, not a definite one. There were a lot of things to consider—my moving to Washington, closing my business here."

"You've decided now?"

Alette gazed into Victoria's blue eyes. "As you said, pressure destroys polite manners. I thought I loved him, but with this happening, I've seen a side to Bill I hadn't seen before, and I don't like it. He doesn't believe my story. And he doesn't want this scandal to wreck his career. Last night he flew back to Washington, and I haven't talked to him since."

"Are you sleeping with any other men?"

"No."

"Have you while you've dated Bill Gaffney?"

"No."

"Please understand, Alette, why I'm asking these questions. I need to know everything about you, because the prosecuting attorney is going to do anything he can to point up to the court that you're lying. The crucial thing with jurors is who is telling the truth."

"Will I have to answer the same questions in the courtroom?"

"I imagine you will."

Alette leaned back in the chair, crossed her legs, and answered questions through two more hours.

"Were you not dubious about someone wanting a mere fifteen thousand dollars in exchange for your sister?"

"Yes."

"How old do you think this person was?"

"I couldn't tell, it was just a whisper. I don't even know whether it was a man or a woman."

"Did it remind you of anyone?"

"No, the words were garbled, difficult to understand, a slight southern accent. Something kept scraping the phone. What is a manslaughter charge?"

"Voluntary manslaughter means intent to kill or to cause great bodily harm. The accused caused the death of another under circumstances of extreme emotional distress. Extreme emotional distress can mean the accused acted in the heat of passion caused by sufficient provocation to lose normal self-control."

"But I didn't act in the heat of passion. I wasn't present when the shot was fired."

"We'll try to prove that. Should I tell your brother we'll be finished in another hour? He's already vented his hostility once today, so I assume he's impatient."

"He usually is a very nice guy. He usually charms every woman he meets."

"Your brother?" Victoria asked, raising her head.

"Yes. Evidently I've finally found one who is immune."

"Yes, you have."

Alette spent three hours with Victoria while Aubrey waited outside. As soon as they were in the car, Aubrey asked, "What did she say?"

"She listened to my story and asked me questions, and we went over everything. Rutger had hired a private detective who is working on what happened to Sal Giavotella."

"So have I."

Startled, she looked up at him. "You shouldn't do that, Aubrey."

"I don't know why not," he said in an unyielding voice.

"With the police and two private detectives, it seems as if they might get in each other's way."

"They might. I'll talk to Rutger and see what's going on. Someone ought to unearth some facts. Where the hell is Bill?"

"He's gone back to Washington with Phillip and Chera-mie. You were right about Bill. He suspects I was Sal's mistress."

Aubrey swore, a long monotone of names and curses.

"He hasn't called since he flew back to Washington. I'm glad you told me your honest opinion."

"Bill's got all the trappings of a great guy. I just happened to have been with him when he was in tight situations in sports, and he didn't come through so well. Now he's in another tight situation."

"Rutger looks at me as if he's sure I did it. And the

evidence is incriminating. I fit the neighbor's description of a black-haired woman; I had the murder weapon in my car.''

"You have a cockeyed story for that night. And it was known in Washington that Giavotella had a mistress. But he wouldn't divulge her identity, and he hid his tracks damned well.''

"How on earth do you know that?'' she asked, amazed by him. "You don't get near D.C. And when did you hear my side of the story?''

"One of the detectives on the case has a sailboat.''

"Victoria Steiner is coming by this afternoon or tonight. She wants to get some family pictures of Cheramie, Phillip, Bill, and everyone else I know well. I have to stop at home and pick them up.''

"She's coming to my boat?''

"Yes. She won't contaminate it, Aubrey. I really don't think you're viewing her in the right manner.''

"No, I'm not. I want her off the case, and I want someone really sharp and tough on it.''

"She's fine, Aubrey.'' After a moment she added, "I've ruined your friendship with Jeff O'Neil.''

"It wasn't important. He bought a boat from me, and we compete in races. The bastard better not come near you again.''

"He was close friends with the Giavotellas. Remember there are six children without a father.''

"That doesn't give O'Neil the right to decide you're guilty and come after you.''

"I don't think, with the exception of you, he has a high opinion of the Lachmans.''

"Well, to hell with him. He better keep out of my way.''

"Don't hit him again! I'm seeing a side to you I haven't seen for years. I think he was really hurt over Sal.''

"That still doesn't give him a right to condemn you.''

She sat back and gazed out the window as they took a steep hill so fast it made her stomach drop. Aubrey slammed on his brakes, and they had to wait for a cable car to pass. Then they swooped over another rise and down another long slant. She watched a ship in the bay and thought about Jeff O'Neil, remembering the pain in his blue eyes, wondering if anyone except Aubrey would ever believe her story.

"Aubrey, if Rutger and Bill don't believe me, how can I expect the police and a judge and a jury—"

"You'll have the Walcott connections, and you'll use your head, Alette. If you didn't know Giavotella except casually, the truth will come out. They'll find who hated Sal Giavotella enough to murder him, and that will be all there is to it. A nightmare that is gone and over."

"Aubrey, someone must hate me terribly," she said in a low voice.

"That's why I want a detective on it now. There are some other possibilities."

"What?" she asked, unable to think of anything except the damning involvement she was caught in.

"Someone might hate you. Or someone might hate the Lachmans and not care which one they hurt or which one they hurt *first*. Rutger's made a hell of a lot of enemies."

"No one would kill Sal Giavotella and frame me to get at Rutger."

"Someone may have hated Sal and the Lachmans. His father once worked for Rutger years ago, so there are some ties."

"I can't see that at all."

"Okay. Another possibility is that you're a convenient scapegoat. You don't have an alibi. You live close to Sal. You were available; you fit the description."

"I've thought of that," she said quietly. "But I can't think who could be involved."

"Keep working on it," Aubrey said tightly, and turned his head away, a muscle working in his jaw.

They stopped at her place, and Aubrey came in while she packed. When she was ready, she returned to the living room, where Aubrey stood by a window.

"Should we go now to talk to Rutger? I'll have to sometime."

"Why will you have to? I don't want to talk to him again today. I would hate to slug my father, but if he looks at me and tells me he doesn't believe your story, I will."

He said it quietly, yet she knew he meant it. "All right. Let's go to your boat."

A reporter was outside when they returned to the car. Aubrey sent him scurrying while he rushed Alette into the car. As soon as she was settled on his boat, she found him in the salon. He had changed to cutoffs and was mixing drinks. He handed one to Alette.

"I hope it helps me forget. That place was so terrible this morning."

"Sorry. You won't have to go back."

A retort came, but she bit it back, because Aubrey was trying to help.

"Why don't you tell me your side?"

She repeated the story, and he gave her his full attention, his eyes widening when she told him about Sal Giavotella coming to her office for a landscaping job.

"Why the hell would he pick you to do the job?"

"That's what I can't figure. He had a fiancée he was building the house for."

"The mystery mistress. The police are digging on that one."

"And they think it's me," she said grimly. "I travel back and forth between here and Washington. That's one more damning thing. I had the opportunity."

Aubrey paced restlessly, stopping in the center of the salon and rubbing the nape of his neck. "Why would he come to you? That's weird as hell."

"I thought so at the time. I almost refused the job. He looked amused about it, Aubrey."

"Who knew where you were yesterday afternoon?"

"Lots of people. You probably did. Friends did. Rutger, Cheramie, Bill, and Phillip all knew. The maids knew. Business connections knew."

"It still narrows things down a little. The murderer is tied to you in some manner."

She felt a chill across her nape as she returned his solemn gaze.

"You take care. Be careful where you go and what you do, will you?"

"Yes. That might hold true for you and Cheramie and Rutger as well."

"It might." He became silent, pacing the salon, staring outside, then sitting down and finishing his drink. She couldn't think of any answers. She had clients to contact, yet the thought of business was impossible.

"Alette," he said, his voice sounding peculiar. She looked at him sharply.

"Is there any chance Cheramie was the woman in his life? She lives in Washington and San Francisco."

"Cheramie? With Phillip running for president?"

He sighed. "I guess not. She wouldn't run that risk for any man. No one man is that important to Cheramie."

"Besides, her time is accounted for, Aubrey. She was with Phillip the night of the murder."

"Sal died right after five o'clock."

"Rutger said she was having her hair done when I got the call. I've been thinking about it. I've seen Gina Giavotella, Sal's ex-wife. She has black hair and dark eyes. She's a little shorter than I am."

"I've seen her, too."

"She would fit the same description. Suppose she was so jealous she killed him?"

"I imagine the police are aware of the possibilities. Have you talked to Cheramie yet?" he asked.

"No. Bill and Phillip's campaign manager are concentrating on political strategy. They don't think Cheramie or Phillip should see or call me. By putting distance between us, they hope to salvage his campaign."

"Well, fuck them. Cheramie goes along with that?"

"She may not have much choice."

"Lon, my detective friend, said Cheramie and Phillip were at a dinner party."

"Yes. She never was in any danger. I tried to find her, tried to call her, but no one answered."

"Let me talk to her about this."

"No. Rutger said to avoid calling her. The phones might be tapped, and any conversation won't do us any good."

Aubrey swore again, flopping down and stretching out his

long legs. "I can't imagine she won't call you. I'll tell you one thing," he said, leaning forward, "I intend to find out exactly where Cheramie was when Sal Giavotella was murdered."

"Cheramie would never kill a man. Never. You know she wouldn't."

He rubbed his forehead again. "I know, but I'm going to check anyway. She fits the description, too. Surely she'll call you."

"I don't expect to hear from her."

"Well, to hell with that," he said, crossing the room to the phone to punch a number.

"Aubrey—"

"I want to speak to Cheramie Walcott. This is her brother, Aubrey." He held the phone out to Alette. "Come talk."

In the Hall of Justice, Jeff entered the district attorney's office. Mel Cipresso waved him to a chair while he finished a phone conversation. As soon as he replaced the receiver he gazed at Jeff. "Someone must have slugged you on the way in here."

"I was going to see Harberger. I got a sucker punch."

"Honest to God? Who the hell? Did they arrest him?"

"No. I hit him back. What's happening on the Lachman case? Is all the influence going to take the heat off her?"

"I'm fighting it, but they wield a lot of power. You don't go against Rutger Lachman and Judge Walcott without big guns."

"Who's her lawyer?"

"Victoria Steiner. She's good. Only lost one case. They'll have everything at their disposal, and they've hired two detectives."

"Two? Why the fuck two?"

"The brother hired one, the father hired the other. I don't think brother and father communicate, from what I hear."

"What do you have?"

"You read the papers."

"Come on, Mel."

"We have a damned good case. Victim shot point-blank

with a Webley-Fosbery .455. There's a black-haired mistress, a mystery woman.''

Jeff wanted to say she was already under arrest, but he kept quiet and listened.

"We have two descriptions from neighbors. Black hair, dark eyes, slender.''

"I take it Alette Lachman's been arraigned. What do you have to take into court? You must have something good," Jeff said, seeing a satisfied smile come to Mel's face.

"Alette Lachman fits the description of a woman seen going into his condo with him before the murder. The little old lady neighbor was confused at the lineup and couldn't pick her out, but Alette Lachman fits perfectly. Then we got a hit this morning when they searched her place. The murder weapon was found behind the front seat of Miss Lachman's car. Also,'' he added with smug satisfaction, ''the night of the murder, she said she barely knew Giavotella. When we picked her up, she remembered that she had lunch with him this past week. Said she was in shock and forgot about the lunch.''

"That's possible, Mel.''

"Give me a break. She lied.''

"So tell me something new with the Lachmans,'' Jeff remarked dryly, thinking how honest he had thought she sounded.

"Jeff, I'm going to go into that courtroom with the world watching me and nail her!''

"You sound damned sure. It better be good, with a Lachman.''

"She told Harberger she arrived at Giavotella's condo around six-thirty. We have a neighbor witness, Mrs. Haskell, who said a black-haired woman arrived at four-thirty. Mrs. Haskell was out looking for her cat. Alette Lachman is lying about the time she arrived. She came back to town right after four. The Lachman pilot verified that. There was time for her to drive straight from the airport to meet Giavotella. She said she went to her office alone—no witnesses.''

"Were her prints on the weapon?''

"No, it was wiped clean.''

"Okay, how good is the witness?"

"Good enough."

"Suppose she sticks to her story. It's one woman's testimony against another."

"The murder weapon was in her possession. That's enough."

"What about DNA?"

Cipresso shrugged. "We don't need to run expensive tests with all the rest we have. This isn't a rape, and that's where DNA becomes so important."

"This will be a plum for you, Mel."

"She cleaned the condo. The only prints were on doorknobs, the front door, and the bedroom door. Alette was caught at the scene, in hysterics. Her story about a mysterious voice over the phone is screwball. The money is paltry for a Lachman."

"What about Washington?"

"No leads. Giavotella covered his tracks damned well."

"Gina doesn't know one thing about the woman except Sal told her she was beautiful and she could be the kind of wife he needed. Sal told me that much himself."

"Yeah, what else did he tell you?"

"Nothing specific. Told me to try to like her."

"Why wouldn't you like her?"

"Because of Gina Giavotella. And because I hate the Lachmans."

"He didn't give you a name?"

"No. Sal knew how to keep a secret. He didn't talk."

"You'd think the wife would have found out who the woman was. My woman would hammer at me until I confessed."

Jeff gave him a fleeting smile. "Most women, maybe, but not Gina. She adored him. She would have taken him back without a word of complaint."

"How's she doing?"

"She's strong and she'll be okay. The divorce had already separated them. This is clear-cut, and she can grieve and hopefully heal. Death is more final than divorce."

"There are a hell of a lot of people who would argue with

you on that one. I think Alette Lachman is guilty as hell, and I hope I can get some kind of conviction. The right kind of jury won't have any sympathy for her, especially when I put the widow on the stand. I want every one of the Giavotella kids at the trial.''

"When did Sal die?" Jeff asked quietly. It hurt to think about Sal; the violence made it even worse.

"Death occurred shortly after five o'clock. Alette Lachman was running out of there at half-past six.''

"What did she do in the time in between? That's a long time with a dead body.''

"Who knows? Wipe away prints. Get dressed.''

"How long would it take to wipe away prints?''

"It depends on how many places she touched. She came at half-past four and was there until half-past six. She must have gone over the place thoroughly.''

"She can look you straight in the eye and swear she didn't know him well at all and she didn't kill him.''

"You haven't looked into as many lying eyes as I have. People get on the stand and swear to tell the truth and then lie with every breath. Sit on this side; see how much you believe.''

Jeff had one foot propped on his knee, and he ran his finger along his ankle. "I came up here believing her guilty, but damned if she didn't sound like she's telling the truth. The brother believes her.''

"That's who hit you.''

"Yes. Aubrey's all right.''

"The bartender at Cassady's read about it in the paper and phoned us.''

Jeff rubbed the back of his neck. "Doesn't it strike you as odd that someone who had kept an affair as well hidden as Sal had would one day take her to lunch at a place like Cassady's?''

"What the hey? He's divorced now, she's free, and he wants to marry her. Why not come out in the open?''

Jeff sat in silence, staring at Mel.

"You don't like it.''

"I knew Sal as well as a brother. If he kept her a secret

from the world, there was no way he would take her to a restaurant like Cassady's for lunch. That's showing her to the world.''

Mel leaned forward, his jaw thrusting out. ''Well, we're going to take it into court, because one thing is a fact. She was found with the murder weapon. That makes my case. The rest is icing on the cake.''

''You're probably right. It just doesn't fit with Sal. But then, I never thought he'd divorce Gina. Do you have a motive?''

''A love triangle. Alette Lachman is going with William Gaffney, who is press secretary for Phillip Walcott. We figure she wanted to break off the affair because it would ruin things and William Gaffney is moving up in the world. He's from wealth; he's young and ambitious, and Phillip Walcott wants a presidential nomination.''

''There should be an easier way to end an affair,'' Jeff said, ''except Sal was wildly in love, and I know he wouldn't let her go.''

''There you are,'' Mel said with satisfaction. ''Giavotella was recently divorced, and his wife said he intended to marry another woman. We've already checked into Giavotella's background and have concluded that when the guy wanted something he went after it tooth and nail. He was obsessive. I can remember his gubernatorial campaign. When he tossed his hat in the ring, no one thought he could win.''

He tilted his head to study Jeff. ''Would you have called him obsessive?''

''Yes, if he wanted something, he went after it with everything he had. He was single-minded about achieving goals.''

''There you have it. He wouldn't let her go. She wanted out.''

''There's sure as hell better ways to do it than put a slug through him, hang around the place for an hour and a half, and then run into the arms of the police,'' Jeff insisted.

''She didn't know a neighbor called the police.''

''What time did the call come in?''

''Not until six twenty-six. It was a little old lady who didn't want to give us her name. She said she thought she heard a gunshot and her daughter told her to forget it. When her daughter left, she called to tell us.''

"Which neighbor?"

"There's two of them. An old lady lives to the east, another to the west, and neither one admits the call, and both have daughters. They all deny a phone call, but there are two old ladies living close enough to have heard the shot and made the call. Whoever called said she didn't want to get involved.''

Jeff stared at him. "That seems unlikely. Most little old ladies I know when confronted by a man in uniform spill their guts. Two mothers and two daughters who won't acknowledge a call?" He stared at Mel. "Alette Lachman said she went to Sal's because of an anonymous call. The police went because of an anonymous call. Mel, that fucking stinks.''

"Don't make too much out of it, Jeff. You were the one all steamed up to have us prosecute and see justice done and not let the Lachmans and Walcotts escape behind a screen of power and money. Now you encounter Alette Lachman and she wags her pretty little ass and bats her big brown eyes at you and says she's innocent and you *believe* her?"

"I don't want to, but you've got some holes. . . .''

"Nothing is ever all neatly tied up except the one I had where the wife blasted six holes in the guy with a Remington and then called us.''

"Two anonymous calls. I'd think a lawyer could make something out of that.''

"Let her try. I have a witness who says Alette is the woman and she arrived at four-thirty.''

"The fifteen thousand is too small.''

"Jeff, you aren't accustomed to being lied to on a regular basis.''

Jeff gave a rueful laugh and smoothed his hand on his knee. "I guess not. If she did it, can you get a conviction? Can you fight the Lachman-Walcott power?''

"I sure as hell can. I intend to see it all the way. I don't know what kind of sentence she'll get, but I'm going to get a conviction. She was present at the scene, a witness has a description that fits, she lied about her arrival, conveniently forgot about lunch until the next day, the murder weapon was in her possession.''

"Thanks for telling me," Jeff said, and stood up. "I know Gina wants the woman caught and punished for her crime."

"Give the widow my regards."

"Sure thing." Jeff walked out and down the hall.

While he drove to the office, he thought about Alette. Having talked to her, he wasn't as firmly convinced of her guilt. Her straightforward declarations hadn't sounded like lies. And the phone call tipping the police bothered him. These little discrepancies could add up to an overall innocent impression, and her story was too dumb to be a lie.

At the same time, Mel had the facts. Lunch with Sal. He stared out the window, remembering vividly her dark eyes and full lips. She was a mixture of contradictions from the way she walked to her story about the murder.

Almost six hours later he was still mulling it over when he saw her dark head in a bobbing sailboat on the bay.

22

Waves slammed against the boat, and black clouds boiled in the sky, the first light rain falling while Alette struggled to start the motor. She was soaked from spray and had worn only shorts and a blue shirt. The storm had come up swiftly, and she wasn't experienced enough to cope with getting back without a motor. The boat bobbed and rocked, and she expected any moment to be dumped into the bay. Two boats had passed, and she had tried to flag them down. One had ignored her, and on the other everyone had waved.

"Trouble?"

She heard the yell and looked up to see Jeff O'Neil sailing

in close. A wave caught her boat and tossed it high. She lost her balance, grabbed the gunwale, and clung.

Jeff maneuvered his boat and came alongside, tossing her a line. "Secure it to the mast," he yelled, and for an instant, in her relief to be rescued, she forgot her animosity. Knotting it tightly around the mast, she turned to him.

"Get on board!" he yelled, holding out his hand.

Her boat banged against his, and she didn't pause to weigh the decision. She grabbed his hand and jumped. He caught her around the waist and swung her on board. He wore a sweatshirt and cutoffs, and when he scooped her up, her hands connected with his warm, solid chest and shoulder; her bare legs rubbed against his, and she was inordinately conscious of the contact. He released her and tightened the line, securing it swiftly around a cleat.

"I don't know if that will hold or not, but we need to get back to shelter," he shouted over the noise of wind and rain and the boat's motor. She scurried through the hatch into the cabin.

"The storm came up so fast," she said. He revved the motor and stood at the wheel. The little boat bobbed behind them, and they were almost to the breakwater when the clouds opened. Rain poured down in driving sheets, dousing Jeff at the wheel. He steered into the berth, secured a line, and came in out of the rain, yanking off his soaked shirt.

Inside, the cabin was steamy, and Alette was acutely aware of Jeff's fine-honed, athletic body. Two scars ran along his arm, white lines against his dark skin, and she guessed it was from the injuries to his arm. He was quiet while he peered outside. The rain became a deluge, a solid sheet of gray drumming on the boat.

"We'll have to sit it out. There's no need to go out in this."

"Thanks for coming to my rescue. I don't know what would have happened out there if you hadn't."

"You didn't see the clouds coming up on the horizon?"

"Not until I was too far out," she said, thinking how restrained and polite they sounded. "When I left here, the day was clear, unseasonably warm. I was lost in my thoughts.

The wind came up against me, and I'm not that good a sailor. Aubrey has gone, or he probably would have come out to rescue me. It's the first time I've had trouble." She realized how ridiculous the last sentence sounded. "I guess I should correct that," she said quietly. "It's the first time I've had trouble sailing."

"I've never seen you sail alone before. You're usually with Gaffney."

She gazed beyond him at the rain. "Bill is in Washington."

"You've broken off with him?"

When she looked back at Jeff O'Neil, she saw the searching questions in his eyes and his anger. He had one hand resting casually on the bulkhead, the other on his hip, his fingers splayed out as he studied her.

"He went back to help Phillip."

"You didn't answer my question. Have you stopped dating him?"

"Probably, but he doesn't know it yet," she said, looking away, wondering why she felt compelled to answer Jeff O'Neil's questions.

"So when you went to lunch with Sal, you intended to break off with Bill Gaffney?"

Startled by the question, she looked at him. "Actually, no. At the time I went to lunch with Mr. Giavotella, I was thinking about accepting Bill's proposal. I don't know why I'm answering your questions. I didn't kill your friend."

"The DA says they all say they're innocent."

She knew so little about Jeff, and he looked like a man on the edge of violence. She felt out of her element, uncertain about what he might do. "I'm surprised you stopped to help me."

"I almost didn't," he said, a muscle working in his jaw. "If you weren't a Lachman, you wouldn't be out on bond to sail around as you damn well please."

"I didn't come on board to be questioned or badgered."

"You're on my boat, and the captain is king," he said with an arrogance that intensified her anger, even though she suspected that was exactly what he hoped to achieve.

"Have you always been so damned certain of your decisions? And made them with so little basis of knowledge?" she snapped. The rain was a drumming hiss, the boat had steadied, rocking only slightly, and thunder rumbled. The cabin was stifling; steam heat permeated the air. He stood too close; he was too masculine, too challenging. And too sure of her guilt.

"I talked to the prosecutor. He has a case."

"He may have a case, but in your eyes, Mr. O'Neil, I'm guilty because I'm a Lachman," she retorted. "If I were Jane Smith, you wouldn't have condemned me out of hand, and you know damned well you wouldn't have!" She leaned forward. "It's your prejudice that is eating away at you. You don't know anything about me and your friend, yet you believe the worst because my name is Lachman. It's your father's old hurts that you're angry over."

"You killed Sal," he replied tersely. "You were his lover and you killed him when it interfered with your future."

"With my future?" she asked in amazement, her anger diminished by surprise. "How could Sal Giavotella have interfered in my future?"

"You said it yourself—you were thinking about marrying Bill Gaffney. Sal stood in your way."

"You really believe that," she said, blinking and studying him, seeing herself as he saw her, understanding more clearly now why he blamed her.

"Yes, I do. Sal had a mistress—and he kept her well hidden. You've been going back and forth between D.C. and San Francisco for a long time now. You fit the description. You had the gun. You were *there*."

"I was there because I had an anonymous phone call—" She went through the whole story again, giving him all the details. He was a good listener, giving her his full attention, hearing her out without interruption.

"I don't know who placed the gun in my car," she said, knowing it sounded flimsy, seeing the disbelief clearly evident in his expression. "I barely knew Sal Giavotella. He came to the office and asked me to have lunch with him to talk about landscaping property here he had bought for his fiancée."

"You tell a good story," he said with cynicism. "You were in his condo; you left fifteen thousand dollars scattered in the bedroom and hall—money Sal could have given you—Sal had been shot at point-blank range and the bed was rumpled. The mistress had black hair and brown eyes, and you fit the description. You flew to Washington often, and Sal flew to San Francisco, making you both move in a damn small world." Anger tinged his voice. "You were the mystery lover, the woman he hid from the world because you made him hide you! He told me about you!"

She stared at him in shock. "You're lying. I didn't know Sal Giavotella well at all. I was not his lover. And you're lying if you stand there and tell me Sal Giavotella said I was his mistress." She realized she was breathing hard and her pulse was racing. And she was surprised by Jeff's reaction.

The anger had gone out of his expression, and all that was left was perplexity. He turned away and stared outside.

She gazed at his broad back, noticing a smattering of freckles across his shoulders. His cutoffs rode low on his narrow hips; the white waistband of his briefs showed above the waist of the cutoffs. She jerked her gaze away to watch rain pouring on the boat.

"That sounds like a giant, prefabricated lie." He turned around and gave her a raking glance.

"You'll believe what you want to believe. I've told you the truth."

There was a tense silence, and then he moved restlessly. "Want a cold beer?"

"Yes, please."

He removed two bottles of beer from a small chest, opened them, and handed her one. He took a long drink, tilting his head, his Adam's apple working as he swallowed.

He glanced outside. "I didn't think it could rain this hard for so long. . . . You're staying with Aubrey?" he asked a few minutes later.

"Yes."

"Why not your father?"

"I need Aubrey's support," she answered with a lift to her chin.

"When will Aubrey be back?"

"He said not to wait up," she replied, and the moment she said it, she wondered if she should have. There was a wild element to Jeff O'Neil that made her uncertain about him.

"Are you afraid of me?" he asked, startling her, because he was close to the truth.

"Should I be?"

He arched a brow and gazed at her in the intense manner he had that could change the atmosphere between them from cross purposes to a disturbing awareness. She stood up and turned her back to him to lean against the bulkhead.

"I misjudged you on one thing," he said softly.

She turned around in exasperation over his scrutiny and her reaction to him. "Maybe you misjudged me in everything."

"That's a hell of a story."

"And you don't believe a word of it," she stated. "It doesn't come as a surprise." She gazed beyond him. "The rain has let up. I can see the dock."

He fished in a bin and pulled out a dry sweatshirt, offering her one. They emerged on deck. "Your slip is close. Get in and I'll paddle us over there."

He helped her into her boat and tried the motor unsuccessfully. He rowed toward her berth, and she noticed he knew where it was without asking. As soon as they had her boat secure, he helped her out. "Have you eaten dinner?"

"No."

"Neither have I. Want to go with me?"

Again she paused only a moment, caught between a strange choice. She was curious about Jeff O'Neil, attracted to him, and was honest enough with herself to acknowledge that she wanted him to believe her.

"Yes, I'd like that," she answered. "I've been alone all afternoon, and it's better to be with someone."

The corner of his mouth lifted in a lopsided grin that made her draw a swift breath, because it was a winning smile.

"You don't have to rationalize why you're accepting. We can take my car." They walked along the dock, which smelled like the sea and wet wood and rain. Drops fell from the roof and off the pier in a background of plops and drips. He caught her arm lightly. "Look, a rainbow."

Intensely aware of his slightest touch, she turned to see an arc of color high over the bay. "When I was little, I thought rainbows were good luck," she said.

"Most kids think they have a pot of gold at the end of them. That's what I thought, and I wished I could go get it."

"I prefer luck."

"What the hell could a Lachman want?" he asked.

"Love." The word was out before she thought. She glanced at him.

"There were three of you."

"Rutger kept us split up as much as possible after our mother died. He wanted to foster independence."

"He succeeded," Jeff said dryly, and she had to smile.

"You don't really know if I'm independent or terribly clinging."

"A clinging vine wouldn't have been out in the bay sailing alone." He grinned. "There are other little signs."

For a moment the animosity lifted, and she liked him. "I don't really know much about you in spite of the past and politics."

"I lead a pretty simple life."

They walked in silence to the parking lot, and he led her to a black BMW.

"What sounds good to you? Anything in particular?"

"No, it makes no difference," she said. "The choice is yours."

"Well, I prefer good food over atmosphere." He drove to a wooden building on a pier. Inside were tables covered in red-checkered tablecloths. They were seated beside a window, and Jeff seemed to know all the help.

She took his suggestion, and they ordered prawns and calamari in tequila with green salads; Jeff ordered a Michelob, and she ordered tea.

"We don't have many topics of conversation that aren't touchy as hell. We can't talk about your situation, my campaign, my business—"

"Boats are safe. How do you like the boat you bought?"

"It's great. Aubrey found just exactly what I wanted. Well, that isn't right. He found what I could afford. I have something else I want."

"What's that?"

"A bigger one, of course. Something I can take out on the ocean. Not a sailboat. A cruiser."

"Do you want to live on it like Aubrey?"

"No. I have a beach house south of Carmel. It's roomier than a boat and the view is great and it's out over the water, so I have that feeling of being surrounded by the sea. Are you an ocean lover?"

"Not so much," she said. Their conversation was ordinary; the tension between them was not. She knew he was still speculating about her. At moments she felt his anger surface, yet she also sensed he was wavering in his opinion of her guilt. And somehow it was important to Alette that Jeff believe her.

She tried to avoid looking at his mouth, to keep her gaze from roaming down over him, but she had never been as physically aware of a man in her life. He wore a shirt now; he had pushed the sleeves above his elbows.

"I like the mountains," she said. "That's what I'd like someday—a cabin somewhere on a mountain. I love aspen and spruce and cool air and mountain flowers and clear streams. Oceans smell fishy, and beaches are flat. The sea is all right, but I prefer mountains."

"I guess we won't ever be neighbors," he said, leaning back as salads were placed in front of them. He took a long drink of beer. She could see lights reflecting on the water as darkness came.

"You're a landscape architect, aren't you?" he asked. "Tell me some jobs you've done."

"I did the Magellan Building, the Waterville Turnpike, the Loomis Gardens. Of course, most of my projects have been residential. I'm getting more commercial jobs now than I used to when I started. Or I was. With this, my jobs are fading like snow under a hot sun. People have all sorts of reasons and excuses to put off the work. I didn't dream I'd become such an instant pariah. The calls started this morning.''

''I'm surprised the Lachman name doesn't protect you. Surely some of the jobs are for people who know your father.''

''At the moment, no. The only ones that haven't been postponed or canceled are out of state, and I can't leave. And state jobs. I won the bid for the new governor's house.''

''You did?''

''Yes.'' She had to laugh at the startled expression on his face. ''Change your mind about running?''

He gave her a lopsided grin. ''Not over the landscape architect. I can live with that if I win. You just took me by surprise.''

''Well, you might as well be prepared. We may work together if you win, because the job has been postponed repeatedly. I don't know when they'll tell me I can go ahead. Funding ran into red tape.''

''Maybe you'll end up working for me,'' he said, and momentarily his voice lightened.

''Maybe I should get boxing gloves.''

''I don't get physical,'' he answered with a twinkle.

''My job is safe,'' she said with mock relief, making him smile.

''The Loomis Gardens are spectacular,'' he added, paying her a compliment, but in a grudging tone of voice. ''I want to know what the tree is in the southeast corner behind the arboretum.''

She thought a moment. ''It's an Italian stone pine. It's an old tree indigenous to the eastern Mediterranean and can get seventy to eighty feet tall.''

''I liked it. All I've got in my Carmel yard is cypress.''

''Cypress are beautiful trees.''

''These are,'' he said matter-of-factly while the entrées were placed before them along with a basket of sourdough bread.

They talked about trees and her landscape jobs through dinner, and she found that even though she had more appetite than usual, she still couldn't eat quite half of the salad or dinner.

"Is that because you don't like the prawns or because you just don't eat? Or am I disturbing you?"

"The choice of entrée was grand. Actually, I've eaten more tonight than I usually do. And to answer the last—not as much as sometimes."

"Where did you go to college?"

She answered him, and they talked about college and his ball team and topics far removed from their prime concerns. Once they strayed to politics, and her curiosity stirred about what Jeff really wanted, what drove him into the campaign.

"Why are you drawn to politics? I know why my father was, but I can't imagine you have the same goals."

"I sure as sweet hell don't, I'm sure," he said mildly. "I have environmental concerns. I think we need a strict lead-content bill. Tableware doesn't have strong controls now. Lead leaches out of tableware, and children shouldn't be consuming it."

"I'll agree with you there."

"I'll bet you agree with me on something else," he said. "We need better flood control; we need to preserve wetland habitats in the central valley. It would be even better to restore some habitats."

"Yes, I agree with all that."

"What do you know," he said with a touch of amusement, "we're not poles apart."

They talked about politics, and he told her his views on other issues. She didn't realize the time until she noticed they were the only people left. Jeff nursed a beer, sitting back, half-turned on his chair with his back against the wall while they talked. She felt mired in something she couldn't cope with as she talked to him. She had to admit it to herself— she liked being with him; she wanted him to believe her. At the same time, she felt the clash between them, a tension that at moments sparked their conversation and brought an angry look to his eyes.

"I think we should go so they can close."

"Hank won't care, but we can go."

Outside, the air was cool, the fresh smell still hovering from the earlier rain, but now stars twinkled in the sky. He drove her back to the darkened boat. "I'll come in with you."

He strolled with her to the boat and followed her on board. She switched on lights in the salon.

"See, everything is fine," she said, rubbing her arms. "Thanks for coming with me. My nerves aren't as steady now."

"Aubrey have any beer here?"

"Oh, yes." She got two beers and handed him one. His fingers brushed hers, and he gazed steadily into her eyes.

"You still don't believe me," she said, moving away from him to sit down. He sat down across from her, studying her in the intent manner he had.

"I'll have to admit, you've given me doubts."

She felt a ripple of elation that surprised her. "I'm curious about what's caused you to doubt my guilt."

He shrugged, studying her closely. "Your story is too dumb to be a lie. The anonymous calls bother me. I knew Sal as well as I know anyone else. He wouldn't have taken you to lunch that day if you were his mistress. As crazy as your story sounds, it could fit."

"I can't figure out why he did take me."

Jeff rubbed his jaw. "Maybe if you figure that one out, you'll have a clue to his murder."

The look he gave her made her pulse jump. "For a while there at dinner, I forgot our family's old quarrels. And actually, I know you weren't involved. You weren't even born when our fathers were partners. On the other hand, how do I know you aren't just like your father and I'm being royally conned?"

"What do you mean?"

"We've reached some sort of truce. You've made gains on winning me over; I've made gains in getting to know you, Alette. Let's leave it that way for tonight. The old stuff can't ever be resolved." He stood up to go. "I'm glad we talked."

"Wait a minute! Don't go now. I want to hear about the old stuff. Maybe I was young, but maybe if you tell me what you think happened, I could understand better."

"*What I think happened?*" he asked with a sardonic inflection in his voice. "Let's take the pluses we have now and leave it that way. I'll see you around."

"Wait a minute," she said, catching up with him outside on the deck. She took his arm, feeling the solid muscle. "Sit down out here. We might as well have as clear an understanding as possible—"

"I don't think it will help feelings between us."

"You think they can get a whole lot worse?"

"Yes," he said flatly. "Yes, I do. I'm beginning to believe your story. If I tell you what your father did years ago—and I'm sure you've never heard the other side of the story— you'll hate me on sight."

"Try me, Jeff," she challenged. "I want to know. I answered your questions."

"Oh, hell. All right. Your father was less than truthful where his business dealings with mine were concerned. Your father has always lied. He has always denied he set fire to the Lachman-O'Neil warehouse."

"Of course he has. He didn't set fire to his own business."

"My father doesn't lie to me," Jeff said. "He said your father set that fire."

"My father says he didn't."

"Mine says he saw your father. He caught up with him and Rutger hit him. Then a beam fell on my dad."

She drew a sharp breath, staring up at him. "Rutger couldn't have! He's always said he didn't know how the fire started," she whispered.

"What did he get out of that fire?" Jeff snapped, leaning closer. "Go ahead, answer me! What did he get out of it?"

She knew exactly. Enough insurance money to build a new plant, buy out Barney O'Neil, and have a good start again. She had heard the fire discussed and mentioned several times in her life. She gazed into blue eyes that were filled with contempt.

"If that's true, why didn't your father tell the police? I've never heard of any official accusations. Why did he sell to Rutger?" she asked, yet she could imagine how difficult it would be to hold out if Barney was hurt and Rutger was pushing.

"Dad was too hurt that night, and by the time his lungs had recovered and he could talk and think and remember, he said he wanted to bide his time and see what Rutger would do. He expected to be cut in on the new business, to be recompensed for his damages. At that point in time, they were on even footing."

"He's never gone to the police."

"There was a time to do so. When it passed, it would have been ridiculous to show up with accusations. You should understand that. It never occurred to my dad what your father would do to him. They had been partners."

"Your father got his half of the insurance money, plus a payment for the business."

"That's right, but the payment was ridiculously low. And they each always took a commission on any accounts sold. Dad was calling on a good one; they weren't going to do business with the company and then after a few months decided they would. When they called, Rutger took the call and didn't tell Dad. Later Rutger closed the sale. The account was too big for the old plant to handle. He kept that account hidden from Dad. The only way they could take on the account was to improve the plant. It burned. After he got out of the hospital, Rutger came to Dad, who expected to be cut into the deal—he gave him his half of the insurance and said the business was failing. He offered to buy him out at what they had each put in to start, which was only a few thousand dollars. Rutger said he couldn't work with a partner. Dad was crippled, sick, and willing to sell his part to get out of the partnership."

"He still could have gone to the police."

"He was getting what he thought he had coming to him from the fire, and he was glad to get that. They had only a small insurance coverage for injuries. Rutger took his half of the insurance money, rebuilt, and opened with old accounts and a dandy new one that Dad should have received a commission on. And Dad was out of a booming business. By then he didn't have the will to fight Rutger, and he knew it would be a hopeless cause."

She understood why Jeff O'Neil was so angry with the

Lachmans. "That's why you're in the food business, isn't it?"

"Yes, it is. I can't drive your father out of business, but I can annoy him. It's an old incident; my father has lived with the results, but he no longer cares. I've grown up seeing what happened eat at my dad."

They stood facing each other, the water lapping against the pilings accompanying a rhythmic clink of rigging of other boats. "Your father was absolutely sure it was Rutger in the burning building?" she asked quietly.

"If I punched you in the face, would you know whether it was me or someone else?"

"I know Rutger can be ruthless when he wants something," she said, still shocked by Jeff's revelations. "So I suppose I have to believe you, but that wasn't the version we grew up with."

"I didn't figure it was."

"Rutger and I haven't always agreed. But just because he's ruthless, don't attribute that to me. I did not kill Sal Giavotella."

He gave her a level look. "Want to talk about it some more over lunch Saturday? I'm taking my boat out for a run before the next race, so I'll be here anyway."

"I'm surprised you want to be seen with me," she said, feeling a sudden lifting of worries.

"I'll take you to a cubbyhole," he answered lightly.

"Yes, I'd like that," she said, wondering what he really felt, realizing he must believe her now to ask her to go to lunch. Either that or he was still trying to sort out her story and decide.

"Half-past one too late?" he asked.

"No, not at all," she said, knowing Aubrey would be in for a shock. Jeff O'Neil stood with arms akimbo, staring at her a moment in silence, and they both laughed. He shook his head.

"I never thought I'd see the day I really get along with a Lachman, and now there are two of you I like."

"I'll be glad when like changes to trust," she said quietly.

"Sure, Alette," he said, sobering. "See you Saturday."

He turned away, and she stood on the deck and watched him. His hands were jammed in his cutoffs, his long legs stretched out.

Aubrey climbed out of his car in the parking lot and strode toward his boat. He was almost there when he realized he heard voices and then saw someone striding toward him. He recognized the lanky shape and golden hair of Jeff O'Neil.

"What the hell are you doing here?" Aubrey demanded.

"I had dinner with Alette."

Aubrey stared at him, suddenly at a loss. "You and Alette ate together? What brought that on?"

"I'm not sure either of us could answer you," Jeff replied, tilting his head to study Aubrey. "She said Bill Gaffney doesn't believe her story."

"I think the asshole is scared shitless the scandal will fuck up his career."

"I haven't seen Cheramie around giving support, either."

"Phillip is following advice. He's gotten the hell away in Washington, and he's told Cheramie to break all contact."

"So it's just you and Rutger who are standing beside her and believe her."

Aubrey's patience was wearing thin. "Rutger will try to do all he can to protect the Lachman name."

"He doesn't believe her, either?" Jeff asked, and Aubrey detected the surprise in his voice.

"I'll see you later, O'Neil." He brushed past Jeff.

"Aubrey. I hear you hired a private detective."

"That's right."

Aubrey hurried to his boat and entered the salon. Alette was seated in the corner, huddled up, looking worried.

"I just saw O'Neil. He said you ate dinner together."

"We did. Did he tell you he rescued me?"

"No! What happened?" Aubrey shed his suit coat and untied his tie. "Dammit, I hate neckties."

"I was sailing and didn't realize how far out I was, and the storm came up quickly."

"I heard it rained here."

"Where were you?"

"In San Francisco. I've been with the detective."

"I thought he reported to you."

"I wanted to check out some things on my own. So how did O'Neil come to your rescue?"

"I couldn't get the motor to start."

Aubrey swore and went to the refrigerator. He poured milk and made a sandwich while she told him about her evening up to the time Jeff returned to the boat with her.

"I told him he didn't believe my story simply because I'm a Lachman. One thing led to another, Aubrey, and he told me why he's hated the Lachmans all these years."

"It's because Rutger bought out Barney and Barney didn't want out of the business."

"Jeff said Rutger set the fire to the Lachman-O'Neil plant."

"Rutger?"

"He said his father caught Rutger, and Rutger struck him. Rutger ran, and a beam fell on Barney."

Aubrey paused, his knife in the air and a slice of bread in one hand. "Why the hell didn't O'Neil tell the police?"

"He was too hurt to talk, his vocal chords were damaged by the fire and smoke, and he wanted to wait and see what he got out of the deal. Then it was too late. Rutger gave him his half of the insurance money, told him he wanted to dissolve the partnership and either go on his own or get out. He bought Barney out. He cheated Barney out of a commission, and he opened a new plant with better accounts. The partnership was worth more than he paid Barney."

Aubrey lowered the bread and knife and leaned his fists on the counter, staring at her while he weighed what she said in his mind. "Do you believe him?"

She drew a deep breath. "Yes."

"I've raced with O'Neil. He's honest. Rutger probably did run his partner out of the business! Why the hell didn't Barney turn him in later?"

"Jeff said his father was crippled, sick, and he knew he couldn't beat Rutger. He waited too long to go to the police about the fire. He couldn't prove that Rutger didn't tell him about the account before he sold his part of the business."

"I can see that."

She picked a piece of lint off the settee. "I believe Jeff."

"It sounds like Rutger. To think he got away with the fire, though, and started his new company from the proceeds—O'Neil got out of the business and has never had two cents to rub together until his son got into pro ball. No wonder Jeff hates us." They both sat in silence while Aubrey made a sandwich of cheese and sliced turkey. He sat down to eat and propped his feet on a table.

"Do you think Mom knew the truth?" Alette asked.

"You're thinking the same thing I am. It was drilled into us not to ask questions about that time, but it was Rutger who taught us the subject was forbidden. I remember how pained she always looked if anything was said about the fire."

"She never complained that it was unfortunate that Barney hated Rutger for something he didn't do," Alette said.

"I asked her once where Rutger was when the plant burned, and she said he was in bed with her. She said they slept through part of the fire and didn't know about it until minutes before the fire department arrived."

"She told me that, too."

"I was older than you, Alette. I think she was covering for him, because you know how she would say what he wanted her to say, but whenever it went against her principles, she always sounded as if she were giving a rehearsed speech."

"It's all far in the past now. But I see why Jeff hates us so and why he didn't believe me."

"If he ate dinner with you, he's probably trying to sort things out."

"It doesn't matter what Jeff O'Neil thinks," she said, but even as she made a firm declaration, she knew that it did matter. "I'm having lunch with him Saturday."

Aubrey lowered his sandwich, and his brows arched. She blushed and shrugged. "He said we could discuss it some more."

Aubrey nodded. "Good. I'd rather Jeff believed you. I don't want to get punched again."

"He didn't start it."

"Are you defending him?" Aubrey asked, and she knew he was teasing her.

"I want him to believe me, Aubrey."

He nodded. "He will if he talks to you about it. I'll look at your boat tomorrow. Maybe I can fix it. Did you find out anything about Victoria Steiner's background?" he asked.

"No, I didn't. She picked up the pictures before I went sailing."

"Well, I don't trust Rutger's choice. I'm going to find out exactly what cases she's won and what cases she's lost and who else is in her firm."

They sat and talked while he ate his sandwich, and when Alette went to her cabin, Aubrey switched off the lights and went to his, stripping and climbing into his bunk to fall asleep instantly.

At ten the next morning, wearing a new gray suit, Aubrey was ushered into the office of Victoria Steiner. She came around her desk and extended her hand to him. She was a knockout in a red dress that complemented her dark coloring, and her breathtaking looks made Aubrey's temper rise. The skirt swirled slightly around her shapely legs as she walked toward him, and a belt emphasized her tiny waist. She had a firm grip and a faint smile. As soon as he released her hand, she sat down on a chair and motioned him to another one. She sat on the front side of her desk only a few feet from where he sat. "What can I do for you, Mr. Lachman?"

He glanced around the office. It was fairly bare, with a standard-size desk, bookshelves lined with law books on two walls, a floor-to-ceiling view of the city, and three file cabinets. There were no plants, no pictures, and everything, including the desk, was immaculate. The thick dark blue carpeting muffled sounds, and the chairs were comfortable, but her office did not convey a silent message of success. His concerns deepened.

"You look as if you detected a foul odor. Is something in my office disturbing you?"

"No. It's very neat."

"You say that in the same tone someone would describe a two-car pileup. Are you opposed to neatness, Mr. Lachman? Is that another one of my sins?"

"No," he answered stiffly, his patience wearing thin, something that he experienced rarely with a beautiful woman.

"Good. I'm glad to hear you approve of neatness," she said with cheeriness that he found annoying. "So what may I do to help you? I know you're here for a reason."

"I want to know about your background," he said abruptly. "What cases you've won. What cases you've lost. I think my sister is entitled to know."

"Amazing as it is," Victoria continued in the same happy tone of voice, "I rather suspected you might pay a visit for that reason." She leaned forward to retrieve a folder off the desk. As she stretched out her arm, the high V of her dress puckered open slightly, and he glimpsed smooth flesh. He drew a deep breath while she opened a folder on her lap. "So here's a list," she said, handing him a paper outlining cases with dates, results, settlements, and judgments.

His annoyance deepened to have her second-guess him so accurately. He ran down the list, and amazement came. He turned to the next page and looked at her. She gazed back blandly. He scanned the second page and turned to the third.

"One defeat since you started practice."

"I'm glad you didn't faint."

She irritated him, and he had to hold his temper. "That's a good record."

"Thank you, Mr. Lachman. Your father thinks so."

Aubrey smoothed the papers impatiently while he thought about her record. "Don't you find some prejudice in the courtroom toward a woman lawyer?"

She tapped the papers in his hands. "Doesn't my record answer your question? Mr. Lachman, I don't particularly care for you, either, but I've been hired for the case, and I can defend your sister. She seems satisfied with my firm and my legal expertise."

Aubrey took a deep breath. "Okay. You're it. You damned well better get her off."

"Threatening me, Mr. Lachman?" she asked brightly.

"Hell, no," he said in annoyance. She was a good-looking woman, and she looked much younger than she really was.

"God, you look gorgeous! You look like a model or a singer, or something besides a brainy lawyer."

"Thank you, I think," she said, her eyes dancing with amusement. "There's something about the tone of your voice that makes me a little uncertain that was a compliment."

"Wouldn't it be better if you wore fake glasses and did your hair in a bun and wore practical shoes?" he asked in exasperation. Her cheer was grating on his nerves, and in spite of her record, she looked like a featherweight when it came to brains. "I'd think a jury would give you about as much respect as a teenager."

You're a real doll, Mr. Lachman." She tapped the papers again, harder this time, so her finger thumped his knee each time. "Once more, let me point to my record in answer. Sufficient jurymen must have taken me seriously in those cases."

"I find it damned amazing."

"You can come watch."

"I intend to do exactly that."

"And I know you'll look your usual dignified self. I won't have to coach you on how to dress, as I do some relatives."

"All right, dammit! You're our lawyer and you must be good. You and I better declare a truce." He held out his hand.

She shook hands and smiled blandly at him. "I'll sleep better nights now."

In spite of his trepidation, he laughed as he fished in his pocket. "Look, I hired a private detective. He's been talking to neighbors, lots of people, and he flew to Washington to talk to people there. So far there's nothing, but here's his name and number if you want to talk to him." He pulled out a slip of paper.

"Thanks," Victoria said, taking the paper from him and placing it in a folder on her lap.

"I'll get out of your way," he said, standing up. She stood with him. Maybe she would be good for Alette, he mused. Her record was strong. Under any other circumstances, he thought he would be charmed by her.

"If you really want to help," she said, and he paused,

placing his hand on his hip. "It wouldn't hurt to have Bill Gaffney here for the trial. It would help if she's seen with him by the press."

"Did she tell you why he's in Washington?"

"Yes. She doesn't want to ask him to come back to California during the trial, because it'll make it more difficult for her brother-in-law, but politics won't let this die a quiet death anyway, and any show of support by the family and friends will be good."

"Bill Gaffney will be there," Aubrey said with alacrity. She placed her finger alongside her nose, ducking her head, and Aubrey wondered if she were laughing at him. It was a novel experience, and he felt a mixture of exasperation and curiosity.

"I don't want to have to defend you for coercion or assault, Mr. Lachman."

"I won't force Bill to come, but I'll damn well ask him. And stop calling me 'Mr. Lachman.' Aubrey will do."

"I seriously doubt that you and I will ever be on closer footing than Mr. Lachman and Miss Steiner."

"Suit yourself," he said airily, but her cool answer intrigued him, and he felt a subtle challenge. He left without looking back, but it was an effort to keep from turning around to look at her again. And the fact that Victoria Steiner had found him amusing rode like a burr beneath his toe.

The green tent flapped slightly as a breeze swept up the hill and shook it. Jeff stood behind Gina, his hands on her shoulders, while the priest said rites over the casket. The children were lined beside Gina, each with a rose in one hand. Finally the service was over, and they returned to the house that was as much an extension of Sal's personality as his bold handwriting and stylish clothes. Jeff stood by the gun rack, looking at the rifles and pistols, thinking how Sal loved guns and had died by one.

Gina came back into the living room, and he crossed to her, moving among a crowd of relatives, both hers and Sal's. He caught her hands. "I'm going now. You know I'll do anything I can to help."

She nodded, tears coming to her eyes. "We have to talk, Jeff. I have to get rid of Sal's business."

"Gina, you have an accountant and an attorney. Don't rush. You have time. We'll sit down and talk about it." He hugged her and left, climbing into his car and pulling away, his thoughts shifting to Alette. He had spent two restless nights thinking about her, remembering her denials that rang of truth.

The more he talked to her, the more drawn he was to her. His doubts were fading, and he wondered if he was being a fool, conned by big dark eyes he had dreamed about in the night. Yet she sounded sincere and earnest.

And he had to admit, there was an attraction that was physical and intense, a curiosity about what it would be like to hold her and kiss her that gave him a sleepless night. He had misjudged her there. There was nothing cold about Alette Lachman once he was with her. All the haughty arrogance vanished when he'd pulled her on board his boat last night.

She was an enigma, mysterious, contradictory, and he was drawn by an attraction that kept him tossing in bed until dawn. He couldn't stop thinking about her. He swore and realized he had taken the wrong turn and was in a suburban area, wandering aimlessly.

Once home, he changed clothes and left again, on his way to Sausalito, feeling an eagerness he wished he could better control.

23

Alette sat at Aubrey's chart table with a set of blueprints spread before her. She had worked for two hours on plans for a job that was still pending. Just when her concentration was shot, she heard a deep voice call to her in greeting.

She recognized Jeff O'Neil instantly and glanced at a mirror. She had dressed hours earlier in a yellow cotton dress, which she now smoothed before rubbing quickly at a spot of ink on her face.

Jeff O'Neil stood in the bright sunshine on the dock, wearing jeans and a T-shirt. His golden hair was tangled by the breeze.

"You've been working?" he asked, touching her jaw.

"Do I have ink on my face? I thought I got it off."

"It's just a spot," he said, stroking her jaw lightly. "It doesn't detract. Where's big brother?" he asked, his thumb still rubbing her jaw, his steadfast gaze altering her heartbeat.

"Out doing something. He doesn't tell me where he's going, and I think it has to do with me. He never goes anywhere on land if he can avoid it. I left him a note where I'll be."

Jeff nodded and helped her to the dock, although the boat was tied so close she couldn't have fallen into the water if she had tried. He released her immediately, but she was aware of his touch even after his hand was gone.

"I hear you have a lady lawyer."

"Yes, Victoria Steiner."

"I don't know her, but that doesn't mean anything. It's unusual to have a woman criminal lawyer, isn't it?"

"All things change."

"I'm surprised your father would allow a woman lawyer."

"She was the Lachman lawyer's choice, so Rutger went along. Aubrey doesn't like her at all."

"So you're taking your father's choice over Aubrey's."

"Actually, Aubrey hasn't made an alternative suggestion, and I like her. She's lost only one case."

"That sounds good, but do you know what the cases were that she won?"

"Oh, yes. Aubrey's already checked into that. We have a notarized printout of just about everything Victoria has had a hand in." With a smile, she looked up at him. "Have you seen her?" she asked. "Aubrey says she'll make all the men on the jury think about sex, and the women will hate her upon sight."

"I can't wait to meet her," he said with an inviting grin.

"You can have a ringside seat soon," she said.

"Scared? Or is that word unknown to a Lachman?"

"When I was charged, it seemed unreal, like a dream. Then when I was taken to jail before the arraignment—well, that will always be too real. I only spent a little over an hour in the cell, but it was enough. This is one Lachman who knows fear," she admitted. "When I think of prison, I'm terrified."

They stood on the dock in the sunshine with empty boats all around them, several boats going out into the bay, people moving around farther down the dock. Wind caught a lock of his hair and curled it over his forehead while he studied her.

"You stick to the truth and your fine lawyer should be able to get you off."

"How's your father?" she asked.

"He's all right. Mom keeps him going, and now they have a covered pool and she teaches kids swimming lessons year round. Both of them enjoy it. She should have had six kids. She's great with them." He held open the door to his car and drove a short distance to a restaurant overlooking San Francisco Bay. Sailboats were out, the sunshine bright, and talk wandered from the trial to random topics until Alette glanced at her watch and saw it was half-past three.

"My word! I thought you were going to practice for a race!"

"I can do that another time," he said blandly. "I wanted to talk to you. I've been thinking about what you told me." He studied her as if he were thinking about a knotty problem. "If you're telling the truth, you were royally framed. Someone hates you or someone who knows you well used you."

"I realize that. I have friends and clients who know me well and know my schedule. And of course my family knows. I don't have any enemies that I know about. No one who might go to such lengths."

"If you had someone who was an obvious enemy, they probably wouldn't take the chance to pin this on you, but you might have made an enemy of someone without knowing."

"Sal Giavotella's companion was described as a black-haired woman with dark eyes. That description fits Gina Giavotella."

"No. I've known her for years—since they were dating. It wasn't Gina. Gina would have placed the gun at her heart and pulled the trigger before she would have hurt him."

"You think you know her, but her marriage had broken up, he had a mistress."

"No. I'd bet my soul on her," he said with intensity, and Alette wished he felt that way about her.

"You're loyal," she said, studying him, realizing she enjoyed being with him in spite of their differences.

"It's more than being loyal. I just know Gina. For that matter, your sister fits the same description."

"She was with people all the time."

"I know. I talked to Mel Cipresso again."

"They checked on Cheramie?" she asked in surprise.

"They check on everyone who could be involved. She fits the description, so they checked. Her name is the one that brought you into this. Someone may hate you both."

"I've thought about it endlessly, but I can't come up with answers."

"Maybe you need to stop worrying for a little while." He nodded toward the bay. "Let's go sail. I can get in a little practice, and I'll keep you too busy to worry."

"I'd like that," she replied cautiously.

"Nickel for your thoughts?" he said in the car.

"I've had fun."

"Surprised?" he asked, grinning. "I'll have to admit, I have been. And maybe I've learned a lesson about prejudging things. How's it feel to have a brother-in-law trying for the White House?"

"Knowing Phillip, I think he's been aimed that direction all his life. I hope this doesn't ruin his race."

"I didn't mean to stir up the worries again."

"It's not something I can forget."

"Yes, but worrying won't help. Easy for me to say, I know."

"I pray I don't hurt Phillip. I know this scandal won't

help his campaign. I imagine that's what makes Rutger so furious.''

Jeff turned his head, and she realized she shouldn't have said the last. "Your father is furious?" he asked.

"He'll help me all he can," she said. "I'm not doing the family name much good. You understand politics."

When they reached Aubrey's boat, he was lounging on a chair on deck. He looked up in surprise.

"We're going sailing," Jeff said. "Want to come along?"

"Sure," Aubrey said, surprise still arching his brows. "Yeah, sure. I'll get some beer."

"I need to change," Alette said. Within half an hour they pushed away in Jeff's boat. He manned the tiller while Aubrey helped with the sails. It was a perfect day for sailing, with a brisk wind and warm sunshine. The three took turns at the tiller, and for a few hours Alette forgot the trial, losing herself in laughter with two men who were good company, both turning on the charm. When the dock loomed in sight, she was sorry to return home.

Jeff took the boat in, sliding into the berth with competent ease while Aubrey told them to come back for sandwiches.

As they sat around his table, he lowered a cup of coffee. "I got a report from Mort Edwards, the PI I hired." He glanced at Jeff. "I might as well discuss it now, because you talk to someone at the Hall of Justice, so you're probably aware of various aspects of the case."

"What is it, Aubrey?"

"I had Mort check on Cheramie that night. She fits the same description. Cheramie has ironclad alibis for the time of the murder. She was in I. Magnin's, and a clerk has verified it and said she was there until four-thirty. The beauty shop operator has told the police Cheramie arrived at five and signed in. The time in between when she said she was shopping wasn't enough to tie her to the crime. Also, she has a cellular phone and when the police checked, no calls were made that day."

"I didn't think Cheramie was involved in any way," Alette said, feeling a sense of relief to have it absolute. "I'm glad she has witnesses."

"I am, too," Aubrey said solemnly. "Alette, it's someone who knows you well." He turned to Jeff. "You knew Sal. Do you have any possibilities? Do you know who the mystery woman was?" he asked blandly, as if Jeff had never accused Alette of being the woman.

"No, I don't. He talked to me a little about her. All he said was that she could open doors for him." He looked at Alette, and she felt drawn to his probing gaze. Yet now it held no anger. It took an effort to attend to what he was saying.

"He said she's a Californian, so it was someone from here, but she also was in Washington."

"And I fit that description," she said. She searched his gaze but couldn't find anything accusatory in his expression. "He was madly in love with her. She had to be special to make him abandon Gina and six kids."

"God, when you put it that way, it seems impossible that he kept her such a secret!" Aubrey exclaimed. "She must move in his social circles if he said she could help him."

All three were silent until Jeff looked at her. "We're not helping you with this. It was better out sailing when you could forget. We can't guess the woman, so let's do something to take your mind off the problem. My folks have a heated pool." He glanced at Aubrey. "Why don't we all go swim? A good workout will help drive away worry."

"Good idea," Aubrey said, standing and gathering up the dishes.

"That's nice," Alette said, not wanting to meet strangers and go swimming, "but—"

"Come on, Alette. The man offered, and he's right. You can't swim and worry at the same time. I'll accept for her."

"Aubrey!" She looked at both of them and realized they were trying their best to help. She held up her hands. "Swim it is." She placed her hand on Jeff's arm, and the moment she touched him she drew a breath, feeling a swift awareness from the contact.

"Jeff, we're Lachmans. Will your folks—"

He shook his head. "You weren't born when the warehouse burned. Aubrey must have been a baby. My dad will adjust quickly, and my mom loves the world," he said, but again she received a look that met and held hers.

The O'Neils lived in a large two-story house. They were warm and gracious, and when she saw how frail Barney was, she felt a twist of sorrow. He looked years older than Rutger, too frail to have ever worked with her ruthless father.

The three of them swam, and Alette had to struggle to keep a respectable pace with two strong, fit men who were determined to exhaust her. When they drove home, Aubrey asked Jeff inside. As if there were a silent conspiracy to keep her mind from wandering back to the arrest, Aubrey suggested cards, and Jeff accepted instantly. They played rummy, and time seemed suspended, the interlude surreal—a simple card game that for seconds at a time could take Alette's mind off the fact that she was accused of murder. Accustomed to taking charge and getting things done, she wanted to do something to clear her name, yet she had to wait and let the investigators and police dig for the solution.

Knowing the effort Aubrey was making for her sake, she tried to keep her mind on the game. Once she glanced at Jeff in the warm light. He was studying his cards, and his presence added to the unreality of the night. He looked up and met her gaze.

"It's your turn to play," he reminded her quietly.

"Sorry."

They played until one in the morning, when Jeff announced he had to go. Aubrey said good night at once and vanished to his stateroom, leaving her alone with Jeff.

She walked outside with him, standing on the deck, listening to the gentle slap of water against the hull, the jingle of halyards. "Thanks for the day. It did take my mind off things a bit."

"Good," he said, reaching out to place his hand casually on her shoulder.

"Your folks are nice, Jeff," she said, aware of his touch and his proximity, wishing circumstances were different.

"I hope something turns up."

She nodded as he dropped his arm. "Good night, Alette."

"'Night.'" She watched him walk away, seeing him move from the shadows to the circle of light from a pole on the dock. He waved before he climbed into his car and drove away.

He called two days later, and they talked for an hour that night. He was busy with his campaign, busy with work. The phone calls came at odd intervals; occasionally he would appear, and the three of them would sail again. Twice they all went swimming at the O'Neils again, and as the weather warmed they were able to swim in the ocean, able to surf. In the times with Jeff and Aubrey, Alette did forget the coming trial. In the wild ride on a surging wave, she could forget that she was no closer to knowing who had committed the crime than she had been the night of the murder.

One afternoon as she came out of Victoria's office, Aubrey was waiting. They both had business in town and had ridden together.

"How are you, Mr. Lachman?" Victoria asked.

"Same as ever. Here's the latest report from the PI. No news, but I thought you might want to look it over."

"Yes, I would like to. I want to see you again Monday, Alette."

"The closer it gets, the worse everything seems to be," Alette said. She felt drained, worried about the trial.

"Hey," Aubrey said gently. "I just saw Jeff O'Neil, and we're going sailing."

"That'll be good for you," Victoria said to Alette.

"Why don't you come with us?" Alette asked. "It's Friday afternoon."

Victoria glanced at Aubrey and he smiled. "I won't push you overboard. Come on, counselor. It's the weekend."

"If I can go, you can go," Alette said, and Victoria nodded, capitulating.

"I'll close up and drive to your yacht," she told Aubrey.

The four of them sailed south. The first few minutes out of the berth and harbor into the bay sent Aubrey scurrying to Victoria, who worked alongside Alette and was trying to untangle knots in the line.

"You know how to sail," he said.

She smiled. "I haven't spent all my time in the law library."

"Here, want some help?" he asked. He reached for the knots, but she moved them deftly out of his reach and stood up to untangle them. As they slipped loose, she rolled up the line and moved away.

Alette laughed at the expression on his face. "There's an independent one, Aubrey."

"Yeah, you're right. I think she'd reject my help if the boat went down and I had the only life jacket," he said, moving away and studying Victoria.

They anchored offshore and ate on a rocky beach, then sailed back before dark. To Alette's relief, Aubrey was being his most charming, and Victoria seemed to be having a good time. They carefully avoided all talk of the trial, and Alette hated to see the evening draw to a close. She walked to the car with Jeff in the late hours of the night.

"The PI hasn't turned anything up about the mystery woman, has he?"

"No. It seems impossible for two people to have an affair and keep it so well hidden."

"If you had known Sal," he said, and she realized he had come to believe her completely, "you'd know how secretive he could be. He didn't talk. He could hide things like a squirrel. He would have made a good spy."

Jeff's voice was deep in the quiet night. His car was parked in the shadows out of the perimeter of light. Victoria and Aubrey had already told them good night and had gone.

"Sal probably used another name or names, but how the hell anyone can find out now, I don't know."

"The trail has grown colder," she said.

He touched her shoulder lightly, squeezing it while he gazed beyond her, looking lost in thought. "There has to be a trail, though. And the woman is from here. Someone black-haired in society."

"The PI has checked out so many people—all to no avail."

"I like your lawyer. I hope she's as good in court as she is on a boat. The woman knows how to sail."

"I heard Aubrey talking to her about racing. It's a relief to get out like we did tonight."

"Good," he said, focusing on her. Their gazes held. He looked at her mouth and leaned down, his lips pressing hers lightly, then with more force. After a few minutes he moved back. "Good night, Alette," he said softly.

She stepped away from his car and watched him drive away. He was as expert and thorough about kisses as he was about sailing. The next time she saw him was in the courtroom at her trial.

24

Elevator doors parted in the Hall of Justice, and two uniformed deputies fell into step on either side of Alette. The lights of minicams and the flash of bulbs were blinding, although Alette managed to stare straight ahead. She swept past them, and the ordeal of getting into the courtroom was over.

Sunlight came spilling through the long windows, and lights shone brightly on the high ceiling. It was an ordinary room with a flag, the necessary railings, chairs, tables, and benches. The institutional room represented a cold, calculating force that she never expected to be a part of her life. Wearing a navy wool gabardine dress with a white collar, her hair cut shorter and turned under to curl just below her ears, Alette entered with the deputies.

It had been agreed that Phillip would not attend the trial. She had been told Bill and Cheramie would arrive immediately preceding the trial. They sat in the front row behind the railing. Wearing a navy pinstripe suit, a starched cotton shirt, and a conservative navy tie, Bill stared straight ahead. To his left was Cheramie, who smiled at her. Her hair was cut shorter than it had been in years, a tight cap of black curls that emphasized her dark eyes. She looked beautiful, but Alette was surprised at how much weight her sister had lost. Rutger sat beside Cheramie. He was handsome, aloof, his face set like that of a granite statue.

Her gaze moved over the rows of people. There were strangers, reporters, and her friends. She wanted to squeeze the hand of each friend who was there to give support. Wearing dark glasses, Alette's actress friend, Christie, nodded. Barker Chapman, another landscape architect, was present as well as Homer Murphy, an engineer she'd known for years. Teeky, Pat Kincaid, Francie McIntosh, Mary Jenkins, Ralph Lansing—all her old friends—were at her side.

Jeff O'Neil sat at the far end of the first row on the side of the courtroom opposite her family. She looked into his solemn blue eyes, and for a long moment they both stared at each other, and then he winked. She didn't acknowledge it, but it made her feel better. On the front row at the opposite end of the aisle from Bill, Aubrey nodded, and she was thankful for his presence. Alette knew he would be sitting in judgment on Victoria during the trial.

Victoria Steiner wore horn-rimmed glasses. Her hair was pulled into a bun behind her head, and her plain navy suit deemphasized her figure. Her shoes were thick-heeled oxfords, sturdy and sensible; she looked as if she could tramp across the city in comfort.

"All rise," the bailiff announced amid the scraping of chairs against linoleum.

"The Superior Court for the county of San Francisco is now in session. The Honorable Reed Chapman presiding."

Alette had seen his picture but didn't know him. Victoria hadn't said much about him except that she was pleased. His long thin face was devoid of expression. Rimless spectacles rested high on his nose.

"The State *versus* Alette Lachman." Alette shivered at the words.

The district attorney stood. "Ready for the people, Your Honor," he said.

Victoria rose. "Ready for the defense, Your Honor." Her voice was low, well modulated, with quiet assurance.

The attorneys began voir dire. Victoria watched the jurors intently, never taking her eyes off them. Alette wondered what she searched to find as her basis for removing them with preemptory challenges. There were five women and seven men. One woman was young, with a yellow low-cut dress and dangling earrings that jingled slightly when she turned her head.

Victoria finished her questions, and counsel advised the court that they were satisfied with the jurors as called.

The first witness for the prosecution was Officer Palley. He had been first on the scene and described Alette running from the condominium. He also explained the identification of the body.

The next witness, Dr. Herman Harris, a forensic pathologist, described the cause of death from one shot fired from a Webley-Fosbery .455 with a clip to modify it for regular .45 bullets. The revolver was presented, ownership given as belonging to the deceased.

When Lt. Harberger testified, the prosecutor confirmed that Cheramie Lachman was with her husband at a party and safe, never threatened, never in danger, during the day or evening. He also established that the Webley revolver was found behind the front seat of Alette Lachman's car.

Gina Giavotella was called to the stand next. In a halting, tearful voice that was barely audible, she told how Sal had asked for a divorce and had a mistress he intended to marry.

"Did you learn her identity?" Mel Cipresso asked.

"Never."

"Did he tell you anything about her?"

"Yes. He said she was beautiful, intelligent, sophisticated. He said she would fit in his world better than I did," she said, looking at Alette. "He said she had been raised in a world of high society."

When Gina Giavotella stepped down, Alette noticed one of the jurors staring at her with a frown.

During a half-hour recess, Alette sat in silence while Aubrey stood nearby, staring out a window. He gave Victoria a stormy glare as they reconvened.

It was half an hour before the neighbor, Mrs. Haskell, was sworn in. "Mrs. Haskell, will you tell the court what you saw on the afternoon of the fourteenth of March," Mel Cipresso asked.

"I was in my yard getting my cat when I saw Mr. Giavotella. He always spoke to me," she said, the light reflecting off her thick bifocals, "and a woman was with him. She never spoke. She had a scarf tied around her head this time, but her black hair stuck out—I could see it where the scarf had slipped back."

"Mrs. Haskell, take your time. Do you see that woman in this courtroom?"

Alette gazed at her impassively.

"Yes, I do."

"Where is she seated?"

"At the table behind you," she said, pointing her finger.

"Can you describe her clothing so the jury can see to whom you're pointing."

"She's in a navy dress, and she has black hair."

"Do you know what time it was when Mr. Giavotella spoke to you?"

"Yes. It was half-past four. I know because I was missing my favorite soap while I tried to get my cat back into the house."

"Did you ever see this woman with Sal Giavotella any other time?"

"Yes, about a month before. Right after he moved in, I saw them together. She didn't have a scarf on her head that day."

"Thank you. No further questions, Your Honor."

Victoria stood up and moved forward. "Mrs. Haskell, you've pointed out the woman you think you saw. I'd like you to look at the fourth seat from your right in the front row of the courtroom."

Alette didn't need to turn her head. Yesterday she had seen the model Victoria had hired, and the woman was as good a look-alike as Alette would ever see. She could be the third sister in the family. She wore one of Alette's dresses, and her hair was worn long the way Alette's had been at the time of the murder.

"Take your time and look carefully." Victoria moved back a step and waited while the jurors looked at the audience, looked at Alette, looked at Mrs. Haskell.

"Oh, my."

Alette heard the worried note in Mrs. Haskell's voice, and her pulse beat faster. She had argued with Victoria over the ploy. She didn't think Victoria could sway the testimony if she had a row of identical models.

"Please remember you are under oath, Mrs. Haskell. Will you point out the woman you saw with Sal Giavotella?"

"Well, there's more than one who looks like her."

Alette wanted to let out her breath. Score one for Victoria Steiner. She knew it would take more than this to crack the prosecutor's case, but it was a start.

"Mrs. Haskell, will you identify the woman you saw with Sal Giavotella? What color dress is she wearing?"

"Well, that woman in the front row looks like her, too. As a matter of fact, so does the woman at that end of the row in the navy dress," she said. Alette followed her finger and saw she pointed to Cheramie.

Mrs. Haskell turned her head. "And so does the woman in the third row!" she exclaimed. "The one in the green dress." Alette looked around at Gina Giavotella, who had gone pale and was shaking her head while there was a murmur from the spectators.

"So there are four women who look like the woman you saw with Sal Giavotella?"

"Yes," she said in a worried voice. "I don't know. They all look like the woman I saw."

"That's all, Your Honor. No further questions."

Gus Longmeadow, the bartender at Cassady's, was called to the stand. He was burly, walking with a swagger, raising a beefy hand to be sworn in. Thick black hair curled above his narrow forehead.

"Where do you work, Mr. Longmeadow?" Mel Cipresso asked.

"At Cassady's. I tend bar."

"Do you have regular customers?"

"Yes," Longmeadow said, lounging back and looking relaxed.

"And you know them by name?"

"Yes, and by drink."

"On the fifth of March, do you remember seeing Sal Giavotella?"

"Yes, I do. He came in to have lunch with a woman and ordered his usual Scotch and soda."

"Do you see the woman in this courtroom who was with him?"

"Yes, Miss Lachman." He pointed to Alette.

"Do you know Miss Lachman?"

"Sure. She eats at our place a lot. Doesn't drink much, though."

"And she was with Sal Giavotella for lunch only nine days before his death on the fourteenth? Is that correct?"

"Yes, it is."

"Look around the courtroom and look at the front row. Are you certain it was Miss Lachman rather than the woman in the third seat on the front row?"

"Sure. It was Miss Lachman."

"Thank you. No further questions, Your Honor."

Victoria moved forward to cross-examine. "Mr. Longmeadow, when did you see Miss Lachman with Sal Giavotella?"

"On Monday, March fifth."

"Does she look exactly the same?"

"Yes, she does."

"Does her hair look exactly the same?"

He frowned and shifted on the chair. "Sure, I think so."

"Is her makeup the same, to the best of your memory?"

"Yes, I think so," he said, frowning. "I don't know much about makeup, but, yeah, she looks the same."

"How do you know that the witness on the first row is not the person you saw?"

"Well, I know Miss Lachman personally, and I know that woman isn't her," he answered.

"Mr. Longmeadow, do you know all customers personally?"

"No, just some of them."

"What was or is your *personal* relationship to Miss Lachman?"

"Well, she eats lunch at Cassady's."

"Have you ever had a conversation with Miss Lachman?"

"Well, yeah," he said, scowling at Victoria. He shifted again, clamping his lips together.

"If you had a conversation, what was it about?"

"Objection!" Mel Cipresso came to his feet. "Counsel is harassing the witness."

"Let the witness answer."

"Well, I asked her what kind of drink she wanted." Someone in the courtroom laughed, and Gus Longmeadow's scowl deepened.

"What other women who have lunched at Cassady's do you know personally?"

"Well, hell—excuse me. I just talk to customers. Say hello. Nice day."

"No further questions."

That night as Alette sat with Aubrey rehashing the day, they heard footsteps outside. Jeff appeared.

"I was here to check on my boat and thought I would stop by. Is this a bad time?"

"Come in," Aubrey said. "I'll get you a beer."

"No, thanks. I'll just be here a minute." Jeff crossed the room to sit down while Aubrey disappeared outside.

"How're you doing?" he asked solemnly.

"I think all right. I feel numb. Too scared to think about tomorrow," she said, feeling an inordinate pleasure that he had come to see her. "I thought you'd be sitting with Gina Giavotella."

"No. I talked to her."

"Were those her children with her?"

"The two oldest. Jeff and Doreen. You looked great today, composed and cool."

"I hope I looked innocent. Victoria has warned me about

juries. It's peculiar to have my life so much in the hands of others. The real contest now is between your friend Cipresso and Victoria.''

"They're both pretty good at what they do," he said. He sat close to her, and his voice was low, his gaze intent.

"You give all the evidence of finally having accepted my side of the story."

"I think I did that a long time ago."

Impulsively she reached out and squeezed his hand. "I'm so glad! I know how you hurt over Sal's murder."

Jeff caught her hand as she started to withdraw it and held it, turning it in his, gazing into her eyes, and she forgot the trial. The attraction was tangible, obviously mutual from the way he was looking at her.

"I may be gullible as hell," he said softly, "but I believe your story. Since I've gotten to know you, I don't think you're the woman." He rubbed her knuckles along his jaw, and she wished circumstances were different. She wanted to be in his arms.

"I can't think about tomorrow. All the damning testimony was today—right now I can't look too good to the jury."

He nodded. "Tomorrow you testify?"

"Yes." She pulled her hand away from Jeff's as Aubrey entered the room.

"Tomorrow will be Alette's day," he said with a cheer she knew was forced. The phone rang, and Aubrey crossed to the bar to answer it.

The moment he started to swear, she turned to look at him and tried to make sense of his conversation. He scowled, and she had a sinking feeling. She glanced at Jeff, who was watching her. He reached over to hold her hand again.

Aubrey replaced the receiver. "That was that son of a bitch Bill, who still can't understand why you didn't want to go to dinner with him tonight."

"That can't be the only thing wrong," she said.

"No. Hang on, Alette, for a shocker. This will fry Rutger's ass. The Washington press got hold of information that Phillip has been having an affair."

"Phillip?" Shocked, Alette stared at her brother. "He wants the nomination—"

"He hasn't thrown in the towel yet, but you know he can't weather the scandal. Who would want to give him the nomination?"

"I'll be damned," Jeff said softly, and Aubrey focused on him.

"I forgot—politically, you're in the enemy camp as far as Phillip is concerned. It can't mean a lot on the home front though, because he won't have anything to do with the gubernatorial campaign anyway."

"I'm astounded. I would have guessed Phillip Walcott would have done everything possible to keep his record clean."

"Yeah, like running out on his sister-in-law in a crisis and then keeping Alette and Cheramie apart. The hypocritical, perfidious son of a bitch can hang it up now. Damn, it serves him right!"

"I suppose he'll campaign against me."

"Hell, he ought to crawl in a hole and hide. I'm going to call Victoria and tell her. Your attorney needs to know everything about us."

"I have to go. You have a long day." Jeff stood, and Alette walked out with him as he waved to Aubrey, who was talking in a low voice on the phone.

"Thanks for coming by," Alette said. "It helps."

"Good. You hang in there."

She looked away, momentarily thinking of prison.

"Alette—"

His voice was low, with an uncustomary warmth. She met his gaze, and he looked caught in indecision. "Good luck tomorrow," he said finally, and leaned forward to brush her lips.

"Thanks, Jeff," she whispered, wanting him, knowing she faced an ordeal and shouldn't complicate it, wondering if he had thought the same.

She watched him walk away, and when she returned to the salon, Aubrey was stretched on a settee, his feet propped on the bulkhead, talking to Victoria. Alette waved good night to him and went to bed, only to lie awake and stare into the darkness, thinking about Jeff and Phillip and the trial.

The following morning Alette took the stand. She wore a brown linen dress without jewelry. The same people packed the courtroom. Jeff O'Neil gave her another wink. Looking at ease, Aubrey sat with a faint smile on his face, and she knew he was doing it purposely to put her at ease. She told her story as she had done so many times with Victoria Steiner. She told about lunch with Sal Giavotella, that she didn't own a gun, didn't know how to use one, and didn't know how the Webley came to be in her car. When she glanced at Cheramie, she saw her sister's face pale.

When Mel Cipresso questioned her, he asked her to repeat almost everything.

"Was Sal Giavotella a political enemy of the Lachman interests?"

"Yes, he was."

"Miss Lachman, when you had lunch with Sal Giavotella, what did you discuss?"

"Objection, Your Honor. The question is irrelevant."

"Your Honor, the State does not consider the question irrelevant."

"Objection overruled."

"What did you discuss with Sal Giavotella?"

"He wanted his property in Orinda landscaped, and I told him I would take aerial photographs of the land, then meet with him later to get measurements. He talked about roses and said he wanted something like the British embassy grounds," she said, turning to look at Jeff O'Neil.

"Was there any talk of romance between the two of you?"

"No."

"Do you have a contract for this job?"

"No. We merely discussed the property preliminarily, and it was the only time we talked about it."

"Miss Lachman, are you telling this court that you had a single date with this man? You didn't meet him on March fourteenth?"

"Objection, Your Honor!" Victoria Steiner was on her feet instantly. "That's harassing the witness. I would like to approach the bench."

Alette couldn't hear Victoria's statement, but the judge asked the prosecutor, "Do you have any evidence whatsoever that she has dated this man?"

"No."

"I want to caution you against harassing the witness."

The objection gave Alette time to become more composed. She answered carefully, and finally Mel Cipresso sat down and Victoria stood up.

"Miss Lachman, I'm a little confused. Would you clarify this for me? On the night of the murder you told the police that you did not know Sal Giavotella. Is that correct?"

"Objection, Your Honor! It's already been covered."

"I'm going to allow her to answer for the purposes of clarification," Judge Chapman said. "Go ahead."

"That night I just didn't remember the lunch with him. I was in shock. I remembered later and told the police the next morning."

"Is your makeup the same as you wore on Monday, March fifth, when you had lunch at Cassady's?"

"No. I'm wearing a different eye shadow and blush."

"Is your hair exactly the same as you wore it on Monday, March fifth?"

"No, it isn't. I've had it cut. It's several inches shorter and styled in a different manner."

"Have you ever owned a revolver?"

"No."

"Did the deceased show you a revolver?"

"Never."

"Where do you park your car?"

"On the street in front of my home."

"Do you keep it locked?"

"No, I don't."

"Was it locked when you parked in front of the home of Sal Giavotella after you received the anonymous phone call?"

"No, it was not."

Point by point, Victoria went over every detail with her as she had told her she would, until finally Alette was finished and stepped down.

Victoria then qualified a ballistics expert, who testified as to how far, with the windows open, a shot from a .45 could be heard by neighbors. Alette could remember Victoria sitting back in her chair and saying, "I've subpoenaed every neighbor in the whole area who could have heard the shot and made an anonymous phone call."

"Were you home at this time?" Victoria asked the first neighbor.

"Yes," said a gray-haired, bespectacled woman who was tall and gaunt.

"Did you hear a shot?"

"I heard a bang and thought it was a car backfiring."

"Did you phone the police to tell them?"

"No."

"Were you paid by the defendant to give this testimony?"

"No."

Have you been paid by anyone to give this testimony?"

"Lord, no. I don't know any of these people."

One by one she went through every witness, until the jurors were fidgeting and the judge called a recess. When they reconvened, Victoria began again, until the last person who could possibly have heard the shot had testified and no one admitted making a call to the police.

They were through, and it was time for the summations. Mel Cipresso stood up to talk to the jurors.

"The State has presented testimony that indicated the defendant was present at the scene of the crime and was found with the murder weapon. We have put on a witness who saw the two together within nine days of the murder, yet the defendant," he said, pausing, his soft voice gradually gaining intensity, "the defendant was dating a man who has political ambitions. Evidence shows that Sal Giavotella was having an affair with a 'beautiful, sophisticated woman of society.' Witnesses have testified that when Sal Giavotella wanted to become governor, he campaigned night and day; he relentlessly pursued whatever he wanted. When he wanted to marry another woman, he divorced his wife and told her he would *have* the other woman.'' Mel Cipresso's voice rose slightly.

"The bed was rumpled, the deceased in a state of undress, and he was shot with his own gun—a revolver later found in the defendant's car. You have heard the testimony of a witness who saw Sal Giavotella enter his condominium with a black-haired, dark-eyed woman thirty minutes before the fatal shot was fired. The defendant was found running from the condominium by Officer Palley. You have heard the defendant's own testimony. She was at the scene. We submit that the defendant had a chance to marry an ambitious, wealthy man with a bright future, and a man—unlike Mr. Giavotella—approved of by Lachman interests. Clearly the lady seen entering Mr. Giavotella's apartment, not only immediately prior to the murder, but on one other occasion, had to rid herself of him. The State asks you to find the defendant guilty of manslaughter as charged.''

When it was Victoria's turn, there was a subtle change in her appearance. Her hair was still pulled behind her head, but instead of the severe bun, it was clipped with a barrette. Her suit fit better than the one she had worn previously. The sturdy shoes were replaced with high-heeled pumps, and she wore a slight bit of makeup. She still wore the horn-rimmed glasses, lending her an attractive and authoritative air. Her voice was low-pitched and carried conviction.

"May it please the court, ladies and gentlemen of the jury, it is the State's responsibility to prove beyond any reasonable doubt that this woman shot Sal Giavotella. There is no evidence that she shot him. The State's own witness no longer could identify the defendant as the woman who entered the condominium. It reasonably could have been the estranged wife.'' Victoria moved closer to the jury box. She spoke slowly, and each juror watched her. She went through each point of the case briefly and efficiently.

"The defendant has told us in her own words the horror she felt upon discovering the body, and in this state of shock and fear, she did not tell the police about the lunch with the deceased on March fifth, but she volunteered the information the next morning.''

"Ladies and gentlemen of the jury, this woman is not a hardened criminal. She has no former record, no more violations than a traffic ticket when she was twenty-two years old. She has never been involved in anything other than her family life and her business. Imagine a woman with this background finding a murder victim. She was shocked, frightened, unable to think clearly. Under the circumstances, would it be possible to forget one business lunch? After all, this was no date. Sal Giavotella walked into her office, and they went to lunch to talk business. And that is the only time the two of them were together. The defendant does not own a gun; her family has no history of owning guns or hunting as a hobby. Her unlocked car was parked on the street, accessible to anyone."

Victoria moved slightly, edging toward the opposite end of the jury box, and still all eyes were riveted on her. "The defendant has told you she received an anonymous phone call to go to the condominium to save her sister's life. Another anonymous call is logged on police records, a call telling them about a gunshot. The fact that no one within hearing distance will come forward and state that he or she made this call is not rational. You have heard testimony from every witness within hearing distance, and no one"—Victoria paused a moment—"not one admitted to making the phone call.

"This indicates to me that someone made an anonymous tip who had a very good reason to do so. Someone wanted to get the police at that condo the very moment that Alette Lachman was there.

"It is not a question of whether you politically support the Lachmans, whether you like or dislike this family and all they represent. The question here is whether or not Alette Lachman killed a man. Is there evidence supporting this claim? We submit there is none," Victoria said in a firm voice. "This is a woman who has been an upstanding member of the community, who has worked on charity events, who runs her own business. Her mother died when the children were small, and these three children were closer than many brothers and sisters, an intimacy that has carried over into their adult lives. They have all been present throughout this ordeal, because they are so close. Alette Lachman is involved in this because she went to the aid of her sister." Victoria's voice gained intensity and was filled with assurance.

"We would ask you to place yourselves in her shoes. Think about what you would do if a member of your family's life was at stake. Would you go? Or would you wait, call the police, and risk the life of your family member?

"Can anyone in good conscience incarcerate Alette Lachman for life because she ran to the aid of her sister?" Her words slowed as she spoke with fervor. "There is no evidence here that anything other than what she has told you is not what has occurred. What the evidence smacks of is a frame.

"Bear in mind, as you deliberate, that you must live with your decision."

There was a pause, with complete silence in the courtroom. Victoria's voice became lighter and warm. "Thank you, ladies and gentlemen of the jury. I speak for the judge, the State, and all the members of this court. You have been attentive, good, kind jurors. We appreciate your attention." Alette saw three smiles appear. A fourth person smiled. Victoria turned around and sat down.

The jurors received instructions from the judge and filed out. To Alette the time between the moment they left the courtroom and when they returned seemed suspended. She sat without looking around, without moving. When they were told the jury had their verdict, she looked at Victoria, who gazed back solemnly. She watched them file into the jury box.

"Miss Lachman, would you please rise?"

Alette stood up and faced the twelve men and women who would decide her future. While she stared at them, she was aware of many things, the silence, the important people in her life who were close at hand.

The clerk's voice was flat, almost bored. "Mr. Foreman, has the jury agreed upon a verdict?"

Alette's insides seemed to draw up into a knot, and she hoped she was absolutely impassive. Her gaze ran across the jurors, and as the woman with the bangles and dangling earrings smiled, Alette knew the verdict as it was spoken.

"We have, sir. Not guilty."

She leaned against the table and turned around to smile at Victoria, her heart pounding as the silent courtroom erupted in noise. Aubrey let out a whoop and vaulted the railing, swooping her up to swing her around. As soon as he set her on her feet, he caught up Victoria in the same sweeping spin. Her glasses were knocked off, and she looked taken by surprise. Alette looked into Jeff O'Neil's eyes. He smiled and gave her a thumbs-up sign, and she smiled in return. And then Cheramie threw her arms around Alette and sobbed.

"They wouldn't let me come see you, and they wouldn't let me call. Thank God it's over! I knew you'd get off."

"Cheramie, don't cry. It is over. Completely over. And I understand."

Cheramie couldn't get her emotions under control, and Alette patted her and stared at her sister in shock. This was the first time she had ever seen Cheramie lose control when she wasn't deliberatly acting to gain something.

"We'll have to talk," Alette said.

"Cheramie." Rutger's voice stopped her tears, and she stepped aside. Alette looked up at her stern father.

"Congratulations."

She nodded and turned away. Aubrey grinned from ear to ear as he placed a hand on Victoria's shoulder. "Come here, counselor," he said, taking Victoria's arm and pulling her away. Laughing, Victoria picked up her briefcase, and Alette knew that her attorney was as keyed up as she felt.

25

Sunshine seemed brighter, the air clearer, as Aubrey dashed outside and down the steps, pulling Victoria with him.

With traffic streaming past only a few yards away, he faced her and grinned. "I apologize. You did a great job."

She laughed. "Thanks. Right now everything is great."

He laughed and scooped her up again, swinging her around as he let out a whoop. Laughing, she clung to his shoulders.

"Don't you feel like yelling? You just beat the socks off the prosecutor! My dad said that simply because she was a Lachman, there was no way Alette would walk. You just stand there and smile. But I feel like turning cartwheels! Don't you want to shout for joy?"

Victoria laughed at his exuberance. "Maybe. It would be a little unseemly if the winning attorney did cartwheels."

"Oh, to hell with that!"

"Miss Steiner?" Victoria turned to face a reporter with a mike. "Can you tell us about the trial? Did you expect to win?"

"I thought my client had an excellent chance. She was innocent, she merely told her story, and the jury gave their verdict."

"Are you the brother?" he asked, turning the mike to Aubrey.

"Yes," Aubrey said, placing his hands on his hips.

"Did the trial go the way you wanted? Did you expect an acquittal?"

Aubrey looked at Victoria, whose eyes sparkled. "Yes. I knew my sister was innocent, and I knew we had the best attorney possible." He took Victoria's arm, and they started to walk away.

"Thanks," the reporter said, turning toward a minicam.

Victoria burst out laughing. "I expected a bolt of lightning to come out of the sky and strike you for that one!"

"Do you think I ever doubted your ability?" he asked. They looked at each other, and both laughed. "Let's get a couple of beers and a couple of joints—"

"You're talking to a lawyer at the Hall of Justice! Are you crazy?"

"Yes! I'm so relieved. Ah, Victoria. I'll bet no one ever calls you Vicki."

"Never. I don't want to be called Vicki."

"Okay, Vic. You were fabulous!" He caught her around the waist and kissed her. He meant to kiss her lightly, unable to contain his joy, but when he pulled her close and his mouth covered her soft lips, Aubrey forgot the trial. He inhaled a whiff of a sweet scent as his lips pressed hers. But she resisted his kiss. He traced her lips with his tongue, and finally her mouth opened. He tightened his arm around her, realizing now how long it had been since he had held a woman in his arms.

Hugging her slender form, he deepened their kiss, pressing her body against his. His erection came swiftly, and he wanted her to know what effect she was having on him.

Her body softened, molding against his. He wanted more than he could have from her in a public place, so he released her, stepping back and studying her as if he were really seeing her for the first time. Her eyes were closed, and he had never noticed how thickly lashed they were. They rose slowly, and when she focused on him, he felt hot with desire.

"We're going to know what it's like," he said softly.

Her lashes fluttered, and she gazed at him in a wide-eyed look that conveyed mutual curiosity.

"Let's go find your client," he said in a husky voice.

Inside the courtroom, Alette turned to face Bill. "Thank God you won," he said.

Before she could answer him, reporters surged forward, bombarding her with questions. Aware of Bill at her side, she answered their questions and looked across the courtroom. Jeff was standing with his hands on his hips, his gaze directed on Bill. He glanced at her, and she wished he would ignore Bill and join her. Instead he turned and left the room.

As she spoke, reporters became silent, some writing furiously, some taping while lights shone brightly in her eyes.

"I'm grateful for the outcome and the decision of the jury. I'm innocent; I told the truth, and you know the verdict. Now I want to go home for a rest."

The questions started again, but Bill and Rutger walked on either side of her, and Abe took Cheramie's arm and stepped in front. They made a wedge through the mass of bodies that surged forward with them. She felt Bill's arm tighten around her, and finally they were in an elevator, Bill and Rutger blocking the doors so no one else could enter until they closed.

"Your father arranged for limos waiting outside," Abe said. "We'll go out the back way. I don't know what happened to Victoria and Aubrey."

The elevator doors opened, and the men rushed Alette and Cheramie down the hall to a back entrance, outside, and into their cars. Abe, Rutger, and Cheramie took one limo while Bill and Alette shared another. Victoria motioned them on, thrusting her head into Alette's car.

"I'm riding with Aubrey. We'll see you in a few minutes."

Mystified as to where she would see Aubrey and Victoria in a few minutes, Alette nodded as Victoria closed the door and hurried across the parking lot. At that moment a reporter rounded the corner, a cameraman lagging behind him. The limos pulled out of the lot and entered traffic. Thinking they resembled a funeral procession, Alette sat back in a corner.

"Your father has reserved a private room at the club for a quiet celebration," Bill said. "I'll take you to dinner afterward, so you can celebrate your victory."

"Bill, you sound as if you're announcing we'll go to the cemetery after the club. I can't go to dinner," she said, wishing she had talked to Jeff. She wanted to get away from Bill, who seemed distracted and tense. "You don't sound like a man about ready to celebrate. Do you still think I'm guilty? Is that it?"

"Hell, no!" He glanced at the back of the driver. "I want to take you to dinner. Rutger won't expect you to eat with him. We can discuss everything later. This isn't the place, Alette," he said sharply in reprimand.

They rode in silence. Alette felt keyed up and excited, a heady sense of relief that made her want to jump and shout. Instead she was with Bill, who acted as angry as if she had received a guilty verdict. Rutger would be as controlled as ever, and even Cheramie seemed sobered and distraught, as if her nerves were completely frayed. Perhaps the whole ordeal had been harder on others than she realized, but she didn't see how it could be.

At the club she walked down the hall with Bill in silence, wondering how they could be so much alike and yet so little attuned to each other's needs. She thought of Jeff again and wanted to get away from the family gathering.

When she and Bill entered together, applause erupted, and Rutger raised his glass in a toast.

"Here's to Alette—congratulations!"

"Hey, wait for us!" came a shout from the hall as Aubrey swept into the room. He was exuberant, breathing vigor and life into his surroundings. Victoria looked radiant at his side.

"Here's to the best damned criminal lawyer in the state," Abe said, raising his glass in another toast. They all applauded again.

In minutes more people arrived, and Alette realized Rutger had invited every friend who'd sat through the trial with them. Except Jeff. But then Rutger didn't know about her friendship with Jeff. Victoria joined her after a few moments.

"I can't ever thank you enough," Alette said.

"Oh, yes, you can. You'll get a bill that will adequately show your gratitude."

Alette laughed. "It won't, really. I'm indebted to you all my life. I imagine there are people in prison who have told the truth."

"It's over. That's what's important."

"How do you unwind?"

"You begin with skipping out early on my sister's victory party," Aubrey said, sliding his arm across Victoria's shoulders. "And then you go to dinner with a grateful relative. And then you take a sail on the bay and watch the sun go down and the fish swim and the seaweed grow."

"If I didn't know better, I would think you had been drinking all day long!" Alette exclaimed.

He held up a glass. "This is it. I'm delirious with your verdict and with your brainy, persuasive lawyer," he answered, looking at Victoria as she gazed into his eyes.

"I'm glad, Aubrey. You see, this one time you should have trusted your little sister's judgment."

"I suppose so, Alette." He dropped his arm from Victoria's shoulders and gave Alette a hug. "Congratulations."

"Can a big sister get in on this?" Cheramie asked while Alette hugged Aubrey. She got a knot in her throat as she squeezed him. He was the one person who, without question, always stood by her. She stepped back and blinked, smiling at Cheramie, not trusting her voice.

"Come join us. Cheramie, I don't think you've met the brilliant Miss Victoria Steiner. Victoria, this is my sister, Cheramie."

"You did a wonderful job," Cheramie said.

"Let's let the sisters talk," Aubrey said, steering Victoria away.

"I wanted to come home, Alette," Cheramie said.

"It's all over now, and it doesn't matter. And I knew why you didn't."

Cheramie looked down at the floor. "It's over now, and we're moving back. Phillip withdrew from the race."

"I'm sorry."

"You know why, don't you?" Cheramie asked too brightly. Her voice was low and tense. "He can't resist. He's a congenital cheat. He's got to fuck every little piece of tail in Washington. He would have lost the chance to campaign regardless of your situation."

"I'm sorry, Cheramie."

"I don't know what Rutger will do."

"He won't do anything that will hurt you."

Cheramie took a long drink. "I know he won't, thank God! Judge Walcott and Katherine are as angry as Rutger, but they'll all stand behind Phillip. At least your ordeal is over forever."

"I don't know why someone picked me. It's never made sense. Aubrey has a private detective looking into it all."

"He does?"

"Yes. He'll let him go now, I'm sure. The detective hasn't found anything, but he's convinced it had to be someone who knew me."

"It's over, and the campaign is over. We're all victims," Cheramie said. "There are worse things than dropping out of a presidential campaign. Honey, do you mind if I leave early? find Rutger and his lawyer less than jolly, and I talked to

Leslie Joan and she said we could go to her home on Pebble Beach so I can forget some of this. I have a sixty-year-old nanny with the boys, and Phillip can just go screw the dog for all I care! Anyway, do you mind if I leave?''

"Of course not. I'd like to slip away myself," Alette said, "and I think Aubrey already has."

"So he has. And took the pretty lady lawyer with him. Anyone that bright has no right to be so beautiful. When Phillip sees her on television, he'll wish he had come to the trial."

"Let's go to lunch soon, Cheramie."

Cheramie turned away, and Alette noticed her walk was slightly unsteady and that she bumped into the door as she left. Alette hurried after her. "Cheramie, wait. Would you like me to call a taxi? You're not driving, are you?"

Cheramie laughed, a loud braying sound that bordered on hysterics and startled Alette. "You don't want me to drive because I've had a few drinks. I'm fine. I can take one of the limos. Dammit, don't worry about my welfare!" She walked down the hall in her unsteady gait.

"Alette." Bill joined her. "I told Rutger we were leaving. My car is here. Why don't we go to dinner now?"

"Was Cheramie like that in Washington?" she asked, distracted by her sister.

"Yes. Phillip was the devil himself, and she's drunk from sunup to sundown. But under your father's watchful eyes she'll sober up fast enough."

Downstairs, Alette took Bill's arm, but when they stepped outside she faced him. "I'm not going to dinner. We can talk right here."

A muscle worked in his jaw. "I suppose you're angry because I stayed in Washington."

"It wasn't that in itself so much as what that meant an represented. You and I are very much alike and we like th same things, and I think that blinded us to other things. Thi has caused a rift. I think it's over."

"Look, Alette, I've had so damn many screw-ups in m life lately, and I know I haven't done what I should whe you're concerned. But the end of my political career has also been staring me in the face.''

"Because you worked for Phillip? It can't have repercussions that far-reaching!''

"Yes, it does. I'm moving back to Baltimore to go into my father's firm. I've been busy making all the arrangements." He grabbed her by the elbow. "Why do you think someone set you up?" he asked abruptly. "I mean, if you're innocent, that's what it had to be!"

Alette heard the anger in his questions, and she realized that in his eyes he was still unsure of her innocence.

"I don't know. All that matters is that I'm free. And this is good-bye."

"Alette—"

"And I was telling the truth. I've never known Sal Giavotella except in the most casual way. I was never his lover."

"Alette, wait a minute." He caught up with her. "I'm sorry. Everything has been pure hell. Let's not do anything hasty."

"I've had a long time to think about this. Since March fourteenth. I couldn't be more certain, Bill."

She turned to walk away, and he followed, catching her arm and spinning her around. "Alette, please. Listen to reason."

"I'm surprised you're arguing. You still think Sal was my lover! The answer is irrevocably no." She walked away from him without looking back. She climbed into one of the limos and gave the driver her address, knowing that Rutger would find some way to get everyone else home.

She entered her quiet house and switched on lights—and gasped in shock. Balloons and streamers of paper and confetti were everywhere. Two huge bouquets of flowers were in the living room, and a banner that read "Congratulations!" was stretched over the sofa. She laughed as she picked up a note:

"Congratulations on the court victory again. I wiped all the messages off your recorder except the five most recent, which came today. See you in a few days—A.''

She laughed again, feeling better. She kicked off her shoes, unzipped the dress, and dropped it in a heap. She wanted never to wear it again. She took a hot bath and then wrapped herself in a thick towel to listen to her messages.

The first was from Christie, with a throaty "Congratulations," and the next three were from business acquaintances, all happy for her and ready to resume business where they'd left off before the trial. Alette's hand paused in midair as she brushed her hair when she heard the fifth voice.

"Hi, Alette. Jeff. I caught Aubrey and asked where I could find you to congratulate you. He said you might come home tonight. If you do, I'd like to say congratulations. My number is 555-8382."

She lowered the brush and turned around to stare at the phone. She picked it up, punched the numbers, and heard his voice say, "Hello."

"This is Alette. I'm home now, and I got your message."

"Congratulations. Innocence won out."

"Thank goodness!" she said, brushing her hair slowly.

"I suppose you two are celebrating."

"Aubrey has escaped," she answered, laughing. "He—"

"I didn't mean Aubrey. I saw you with Bill."

"I told Bill good-bye forever," she said. There was a long pause.

"If Aubrey is gone and you told Bill good-bye and your family celebration is over, would you like to go to dinner with me?"

"I'd like that," she answered, thrilled at the idea.

"Good. I'm ready now. How about you?"

"I'm in a towel. How long will it take you to get here?"

"I wish ten seconds, but it'll take ten minutes."

"I'll be ready."

"You can stay in the towel if you want."

She laughed. "See you soon."

She replaced the receiver and hurried into her bedroom, humming a tune. She looked at her closet. She didn't have what she felt like wearing and knew she'd better decide or she would still be wearing the towel when he arrived. She picked a fuchsia miniskirt she had worn once for a Valentine charity event in a shopping center. It had a matching fuchsia silk shirt trimmed with white piping. She wore the highest-heeled pumps she had, the biggest hoop earrings, and some sheer black hose.

When she opened the door, Jeff stepped back to look at her.

26 ⌒ᴗ⌒ᴖ

Stopping in a cove up the northern shoreline, Aubrey and Victoria had eaten sandwiches he had taken on board and roamed the beach as the sun slanted low over the water. Wind blew off the ocean, and Victoria turned to lift her face to it.

"This is the way to celebrate winning a case."

Aubrey turned to face her. "I think it's time for this to come down," he said, unfastening the barrette. Long raven locks cascaded across her shoulders, the wind swirling a lock across her cheek. Aubrey studied the effect. "Better, counselor," he said, thinking she was the most beautiful woman he had ever known. She was fastidious, brainy, orderly—all the qualities he usually avoided with a vengeance. She had shed the suit coat, and the mist from sailing had dampened her blouse, molding it to her breasts. She looked ridiculous on the beach in her suit skirt and white blouse, as he did with his rolled-up suit pants, unbuttoned shirt, and uncuffed shirtsleeves.

"Now you can get rid of your detective," she said.

"I suppose, but it still worries me that someone set Alette up and that someone knew her," he said absentmindedly, wondering what it would take to get Victoria in his bed and what she would be like if he got her there.

"It's going to get dark fast. We better get back."

"There's nothing to be afraid of if the sun goes down."

"We have about two yards of ocean to wade through to get to the boat. I want to see what I'm stepping on."

"Ah, the unshakable Victoria Steiner is afraid of squashy creatures. There's a flaw."

"There's a flaw all right. I'm definitely afraid of them."

"What else is flawed?" he asked in a low voice. "You look like perfection. Except after that brief moment in front of the Hall of Justice today." He moved closer.

"Aubrey, I don't mix—"

"I'll bet you sure as hell don't," he said, sliding his arm around her narrow waist and pulling her to him. He was aroused, growing hard, and he wanted to kiss her. He wanted to touch her, to make her lose control.

She started to say something; he imagined it would be a protest. He placed his mouth over hers and kissed her, his tongue thrusting deeply. He held her head with one hand, his other arm tight around her waist and pressing her against him. At last he raised his head. "Let go, Vic," he whispered.

He kissed her again until he felt her body soften and her hips move against him. Aubrey thought he would burst with longing.

"Aubrey, let's go back to the boat," she whispered.

He didn't want to move or break the spell or do anything but touch her and possess her, and he didn't care if they were on a rock or in the ocean or in ankle-deep sand; so he continued, and her protests died.

Their voices mingled as they climaxed, and then he held her close while their hearts slowed to a normal beat. She murmured in a sign of contentment as she stroked him. He kissed her shoulder, thinking he couldn't move if the tide came in.

"Aubrey, love . . ."

He wondered if his throbbing pulse had warped his hearing. "Yes, Vic?"

"Mmmm. You know how to celebrate."

He gathered the remnants of his strength and rose up on his elbows to look at her. She had her eyes closed, the fabulous long lashes feathered on her cheeks and a smile on her face. She opened one eye to stare back at him, and her smile widened.

"You're full of surprises."

"Is that right?" he said, thinking he could say the same of her.

"I won this afternoon, but we both won tonight."

He grinned then. "All right, Vic." He put his head down close to hers. "When I get the strength, I'll carry you back to the boat, but not yet." He chuckled and blew in her ear, and instead of feeling as if he had discovered all he wanted to about her, his curiosity increased. He wanted to hold her and see what else she responded to, and already he was beginning to want her again.

He rolled over and looked up at a sky twinkling with stars. "You forget how many stars you can see when you're in the city."

"It's fantastic," she said in a tone of voice that made him turn his head and study her and think it wasn't stars she had on her mind.

He stepped into his trousers, tied his shirt around his waist, and scooped her into his arms. He carried her through the icy water to the boat.

When they sailed home they decided to eat breakfast in the slip at Sausalito. Victoria didn't have anything planned for the day, so they spent it together, sailing north, returning at a leisurely pace, spending the night on the *Easy* in its berth at Sausalito. The next morning, as she walked around the cabin, Victoria turned to him.

"I guess our idyll is over, and now I really do have to get back to my car and drive home," she said. "It's been a delightful celebration, and I've really enjoyed getting to know you, Aubrey. Really."

"That sounds like good-bye."

"No, not good-bye. It's just time for me to go home."

"After last night? I'd like you to stay longer," he said, wanting to keep her with him, surprised at his own invitation. "We can get your things tonight."

"I don't think so, Aubrey," she said cheerfully, shaking her head, her long hair swirling behind her. "I have to work on a ton of other cases. My life-style is too hectic to lounge on your boat forever.''

He stared at her in dismay, thinking this was the one time in his life he wished a woman would cling.

This boat . . .'' She paused and seemed to be searching for a word. ''Is rumpled.''

''Rumpled?''

''I like order. You like chaos. Most people can tolerate or work out little differences like that. I can't.''

He couldn't believe what he was hearing. ''Isn't what we've found special?''

''Very special,'' she said in a throaty, warm voice that made him want to reach for her.

''Then let me pick you up after work.'' To his amazement she shook her head. ''Why not?''

''We're compatible; we've had fun, but I have to return to my orderly life before I let this go too far. Otherwise we'll never be able to turn back, and I fear we'd be at each other's throats before long. We have very different life-styles.''

He felt as if he were arguing with a rock. And it was a unique and disturbing experience. ''I think we're great together.''

She smiled, but Aubrey knew he hadn't convinced her. Yet. ''Victoria—'' He felt at a loss. ''I want you to stay.''

''Now is the time to stop. Before we're all entangled.''

She turned to pick up her purse. ''You were great to stand by your sister. I'll always remember and admire you for that, as well as our time together.''

He stared at her in stunned disbelief as she headed for the door. He caught her arm. ''You're just walking out?''

Her gaze went over the boat again. ''Aubrey, you can't imagine how I feel right now. Please drive me back to my car.''

He patted his pockets and turned to hunt for his keys. After five minutes of hunting and swearing, he saw her reappear in the doorway. ''What's wrong?''

''I can't find my damned keys.''

''You should have one place to put them—but I don't suppose you want to hear that.''

"No, I don't," he said tersely. He spotted them under a cushion and yanked them up, trying to get a grip on his temper. He *cared* if she walked out of his life. That was amazing in itself. But he couldn't force her to stay any more than any women in his past could have forced him. "Let's go, Victoria."

She laughed and walked out with him, chatting about the weather and the show she was going to see on the weekend.

With the first streaks of sunshine slanting up over the roof-tops to the east, Aubrey drove back to the deserted Hall of Justice. The streets were empty, the air fresh; Victoria's car was the only one in the lot. As he pulled to a stop beside it and switched off the ignition, she turned to wrap her arm around his neck. "It was fun."

He slipped his arm around her waist, leaned over, and kissed her, putting heart and soul and anger into the kiss, wanting to make her change her mind and say she was wrong. She kissed him back, her leg moving up over him.

Desire consumed him, an urgent need that shut out the world. He pulled her head to him, settling her hips over him. When she moved away, she gave him a sultry look that set him aflame while she straightened her clothes.

"God, you'll ruin me. Suppose—"

He turned her head to look at her. "You had fun."

They looked into each other's eyes, and he drew a deep breath, unable to understand what it was about her that made his pulse pound, made him want to reach for her.

"I do have to go. I have to be at work. Good-bye," she said in a breathless voice. Straightening her clothes again, she got out of the car and walked away.

Aubrey stared after her. He imagined her without the skirt and blouse, he remembered her crying out his name, her hands moving over him, later in the cabin how she had gone down on her knees and kissed him with her black hair falling over her shoulders. And now she was walking out of his life and there wouldn't be other nights like the past two.

"She is Victoria Steiner. Stick Steiner. Compulsively neat. 'riggin' lawyer Steiner," he grumbled. He watched her climb ito her car, catching a glimpse of fabulous long legs. "Fuck

you, Steiner," he said, yanking on the gears and making the
tires squeal as he pulled out of the lot, talking aloud to himself. He was better off without her in his life because she
would try to change it. She would want it orderly. He was
lucky. He had always wanted an independent woman, but
now that he had found her, he didn't want her to be so
independent that she wouldn't be able to spend time with
him.

"Serves you right," he said to himself. But it wasn't any
consolation. He hit the steering wheel with his fist. There
were lots of beautiful women in California, women more
amply endowed than Victoria Steiner. The thought wasn't
much consolation.

After pacing the *Easy* for half an hour, he cleaned the
salon.

Jeff waited, and the door swung open. As his gaze swept
over Alette, he felt dazzled and elated, and he could see the
joy dancing in her eyes, a sparkle he had never seen before.
Impulsively he held out his arms, and she walked into them.

"Congratulations," he said, moving her backward into the
room and kicking the door shut behind him. She laughed as
she held him.

"I feel like a caged bird set free. I'm so *happy!*"

He wanted to crush her in his arms. "We'll celebrate," he
said, his voice husky. He pulled her to him, watching the
change come to her eyes before he bent his head and covered
her mouth with his.

He meant to go slowly, but the moment he felt her full
soft lips part beneath his, hunger consumed him, a desire to
know her, to taste and possess. He bent over her, holding he

tight against him, his tongue playing over hers while his kiss lengthened.

He was hot, hard with desire, when she pushed away and looked at him breathlessly, dazed; yet there was no mistaking the joy in her eyes.

"We need to slow down," she said. "If I can. I feel as if I could open the window and fly."

He laughed, trying to control his longing to reach for her again, knowing she stirred him in a manner no woman ever had. None had given him sleepless nights or worries or this fiery longing that could ignite when she crossed the room. And he wondered if she even saw him as more than a friend who had been an enemy.

She moved away from him, and he took a long look at her, thinking she seemed different somehow. "Wow!" he exclaimed, making her laugh.

"I found the wildest clothes I own. I can't tell you how I feel, Jeff."

"I'm damned glad. You had a terrific attorney." To his delight, the cold aloofness Alette always exhibited was gone. Even in friendly moments he always had a feeling she was keeping a guard on her emotions. Now she looked as if she wanted to let go. He glanced beyond her and entered the living room. It was all white and filled with priceless antiques. It was what he might have guessed her home would look like. Beautiful, flawless, and remote except for the balloons and streamers.

"Do you like balloons?"

"Aubrey's been here."

"Aubrey did this?" Jeff turned to study her again, his hands resting on his narrow hips. All he could do was grin when he looked at her infectious smile. "I think I feel a vicarious victory."

"Good! That makes me feel good to know you're happy for me and you can stand it if I spend the evening grinning like the Cheshire cat!"

"It's a glorious smile," he said, curbing the urge to reach for her again, wondering how he could have ever thought her cold.

"Ready to go?"

"I'll get my purse," she said, kicking balloons out of her way as she went to the bedroom.

"May I see your place?" he asked from the doorway.

She looked startled, as if she hadn't realized he had followed her upstairs. Balloons were scattered around the bedroom, and helium-filled ones hung from the ceiling. "This is nice," he said, thinking that without the balloons it looked like a hospital room, sterile enough for surgery.

"It feels good to be here. I haven't been back since the night I received the phone call."

"Still no leads about who called you?"

"No. And tonight I don't care. The main thing is—I'm free."

"I'd think you'd want to know more than anything on earth. Whoever it was tried to pin the murder on you."

"Aubrey let the investigator go, but I've hired him, because I do intend to find out. I don't see how two people could hide their tracks completely. This man is good, he's patient, and I'm patient." She crossed the room, and Jeff stood watching her. The tight miniskirt revealed her long legs as she approached him.

"Any choices for tonight?" he asked, inhaling a fragrance that was subtle and inviting.

"I'll leave it up to you."

He had no idea what she would like to do to celebrate acquittal on a manslaughter charge. He ran through choices as he walked with her to his car.

They went to a Greek restaurant close by. The tables had white cloths and candles, and there was a narrow dance floor at one end of the room. Jeff ordered a bottle of champagne to celebrate, and as soon as they were alone, he raised his glass in a toast. "Congratulations. May the truth always win!"

"Thanks," she answered with amusement, touching her glass to his and gazing at him over the rim as she sipped. Her hair fell loose in a swinging pageboy. The candlelight was reflected in her dark eyes.

When she took the first spoonful from a bowl of avgolem-

ono, she sighed with pleasure. "This is wonderful! I don't
think I've eaten a full meal since this all started. Time seemed
to stand still. Your campaign is in full sway now," she said,
changing the subject abruptly. "I wish you luck."

"Thanks," he said with a grin. "You'll be with the opposition election night."

"I don't know. You've talked about the environment so
much—I'm beginning to be swayed."

"I can't think of a voter I'd rather sway," he said, teasing
her, pleased that she might switch because of his platform.

"So much about my life has changed." She put down her
spoon. "I think Cheramie is having a difficult time with
Phillip's withdrawal, but she'll get along. She always does.
She's tougher than I am."

"That I doubt," he said. "I heard he's back here to practice
law."

"Yes. They kept the home here, so they don't have to hunt
a place to stay."

He had asked Mitzi to go out with him to the next fund-
raiser, and now he wished he hadn't, although it would send
some of his party regulars into a tailspin if he brought Alette
Lachman.

"If I win, you may be drawing up plans for the new lawn
when I move in."

"Yes, as a matter of fact."

They talked and ate Greek salads and roast leg of lamb
with zucchini. Dancing started when they were talking over
coffee, and they watched Greek dancers, who invited diners
to join them. Jeff took her hand and grinned. "You might as
well."

She came to her feet and in minutes was moving with an
easy grace, laughing, tossing her head to keep her hair away
from her face.

After two dances Jeff caught her arm, and they headed
back to the table. "Cheat! You didn't tell me you could dance
so well."

"I lived in Switzerland for two years. I learned a lot of
things over there."

"Like what else?" he asked, standing close to her.

"You'll have to wait and I'll surprise you," she answered, enjoying flirting with him, something she hadn't felt free to do before. She felt giddy, deliriously happy, and she knew it wasn't all because of the victory in the courtroom. It was also because of the man at her side.

He took her to a jazz club near the water. The crowd was a mix of boat people, sailors, locals—an assortment that jammed in a smoky frame building to dance. Gyrating hot bodies and the throbbing beat created a steamy, sexual ambience. Alette seemed to relish dancing, perspiration beading her brow while she stepped quickly in time to the music, her hips swaying seductively, her breasts bouncing slightly in the thin blouse.

Jeff wanted her badly, and he wanted to know her more than he did now. He danced around her, moving, watching her, becoming aroused. She was moving as seductively as any woman he had ever danced with, and it was easy to imagine her without the fuchsia blouse and skirt. He unbuttoned his shirt as he danced. He was hot, burning from watching her.

His life would change if he won the election. He would become a public figure, and he didn't intend to bring notoriety to the governor's mansion. But tonight he was only a candidate and he was single and he wanted her. Fleetingly he wondered how Phillip Walcott had reasoned away his affairs.

The music ended, and the players took a break. Jeff caught her hands. "I think you could dance straight through until tomorrow night."

"I can! I haven't been able to do anything for so long!"

"Let's get away from here."

He half expected her to protest, but she didn't. When they stepped outside, the cold sea air was a welcome relief. "Some night I'll bring you down here crab fishing."

"There's going to be more nights like this for us, then," she said, arching her brows.

He looked at her and laughed softly. "Do you want there to be?"

She tilted her head and studied him. "Mr. Tough Guy.

I've been told I keep a barrier around myself. I don't think it's anything to what you keep around you.''

Startled, he looked at her. "No one's ever accused me of being standoffish."

"You were at first. You haven't been lately. You don't know how much it meant to see you sitting in the courtroom and have you wink."

He traced his finger along her jaw. "You did a great job with the trial."

"Victoria coached me for hours. Have you ever been in love?"

"Sure," he answered, amused. They reached the car, and instead of opening her door, he braced his hand against the car. She looked at him quizzically.

"I meant really in love."

"I came close," he said, gazing into dark eyes that were wide, full of curiosity. "Once I came close."

"What happened?"

"It just didn't work out. How about you?"

She drew a deep breath. "I was engaged once. It was the first time I was in love, and I was young and he was reassuring. A gentle man who was what I needed after growing up with Rutger. It didn't work out, and later I was glad. So much for the past." She smiled at him. "Let's keep tonight fun. I feel as if I've been given a second life. I had a close scrape with something terrifying." Changing the subject, she said, "I remember the first time I saw you. You've always disturbed me."

"Have I now?" he asked, curious and surprised.

"Enough said," she said, and slid into the car beneath his arm.

He drove fast, on impulse whipping up Lombard the wrong way, taking the hairpin curves as fast as he could while she laughed like a teenager. He sped away, dropping down one of the steep hills a couple of blocks later.

"If you get a ticket—you'll be in our ranks. Headlines, headlines. Politics and scandal."

"I didn't get a ticket, and here we are," he said, stopping

in front of her house. He was out before she could protest, and he walked her inside. In the entry hall she turned to face him, leaning against the wall. "Thanks for a wonderful celebration."

"Sure," he said, looking at her lips and raising his eyes to meet hers.

"Come in, Jeff," she invited. "We'll have a drink."

"I'd like that." He followed her to the bar and mixed them drinks. He turned to hand her a vodka and tonic and sipped his.

"We didn't finish our conversation," he said, trailing his finger along her slender neck. "You said I disturbed you. Why?"

Crossing to the sofa, she kicked off the high-heeled pumps and sat down, folding her long legs under her.

He crossed the room to sit down on the sofa, barely touching her legs. "Scared to answer?"

"You were always so blatant in the way you looked at me."

"Every man you pass looks at you that way," he answered with amusement.

"No, none of them do."

"The hell they don't."

"Not the way you do."

His gaze lowered slowly, drifting down over her to her toes and back up again, lingering on her blouse and seeing her nipples outlined by the clinging silk. "That disturbs you?" he asked in a husky voice, setting down his drink and taking hers from her hand. "Let me tell you something, Alette. It could never disturb you like it disturbs me."

She blinked and her lips parted, her breasts pressing against the blouse as she drew a deep breath.

"God, you're responsive when you let down the wall." He leaned forward, sliding his arm around her. He expected her to resist or protest. To his surprise, she slid into his arms, wrapped her slender arms around his neck, and lifted her face to his.

His heart seemed to slam against his ribs. He had wanted her so long now, dreamed about her, held back because of her problems. He felt he had waited forever for this moment. He placed his open mouth over her soft lips and thrust his tongue deep and released her enough to slide his hand up her ribs to her breast. He pushed the blouse off her shoulder and filled his hand with her smooth flesh, flicking his thumb over her taut nipple while she moaned deep in her throat.

He leaned back once to look at her. Her lashes raised slowly, and she gazed at him with a heated look that singed every nerve. "I've waited a long time for this, Alette." She seemed to sigh and tightened her slender arms around his neck.

His arousal throbbed. He wanted her softness; he wanted to stir her to passion, to see her let go completely. He pulled her against him.

With her heart pounding wildly, Alette wound her fingers in his soft hair at the back of his neck. His kiss was torment, his tongue cajoled and promised. He made her insides melt.

He kissed her breast, pushing away her blouse completely and flicking the catch on her bra to cup both breasts, filling his hands, flicking his thumb over her nipples and watching her cling to him while she gasped with pleasure.

"Do you like this, Alette?" he whispered, his gaze consuming her, making her shake with desire. Her hips moved as she reached for the buttons on his shirt.

He bent his head to take a nipple in his mouth, to suck and tease while she shook with eagerness.

She pushed away his shirt, trailing her hands over his muscled body, virile and strong. His furred chest was golden, and she leaned forward to kiss him, hearing his quick intake of breath, feeling his powerful chest expand.

Muscles rippled when he moved, his stomach was flat and ridged. He peeled away the miniskirt and silk blouse and bra. She was slender, smooth-skinned, with full, upthrusting breasts. He wanted to touch and kiss every inch of her.

"Lord, I've wanted you." His gaze roamed over her while he unbuckled his belt and trousers and stepped out of them. His erection thrust out of his tight shorts, and she reached out to free him, pushing them away as she stepped out of her heels.

He picked her up, heading upstairs toward her bedroom. After placing her on her bed, he kissed her again. His tongue trailed over her, making her writhe and moan and cling to him. With deft strokes he unfastened the black garter belt and peeled away stockings and belt.

His hand slid slowly up her smooth leg to the moistness between her legs, his fingers stroking as her hips moved and she clung to his powerful shoulders. His body was golden, his organ dark and thick. Hands and mouth and hard, strong body were over her, against her, a teasing, exquisite torment while she responded and gasped with pleasure and kissed him wildly in return.

He moved between her slender thighs, coming down to enter her. She wrapped her long legs around him as he thrust deeply. He slid his arm around her shoulders and kissed her while his hips moved. Hot and hard, he thrust into her soft warmth and they moved together. She knew he was trying to hold back; she strained against him as waves of pleasure washed over her. His tongue played with hers, his hips moving convulsively, his shuddering release coming, making her reach another climax that was blindingly intense.

As they became still he wrapped both arms around her and showered her with kisses. "You do know how to let go," he whispered.

She turned her head to look into his eyes, and they both smiled. He held her tightly against him and rolled on his side. He was still inside her.

"I didn't until tonight," she answered him, amazed by him and by the response he elicited from her. His forehead was beaded with perspiration, and his body was hot and damp.

"Jeff, you said you had waited so long—"

"I've known for a long time now that I wanted you. I want to know you better, to love you, to take you places, but it wasn't the right time to tell you or ask you out with the trial looming over you."

"You've really wanted that for a long time?"

He kissed her shoulder. "I could eat you, love. For a long time."

"How long?"

He grinned and she laughed, wrapping her arms around him. "You always looked at me like you were imagining me naked."

"I was."

She laughed again, burying her face in his shoulder, turning to kiss him, sliding her hands over him. "You've made me wanton. I want to touch you and kiss you all night, all over."

"Help yourself, sweetie. And return the favor. You don't know how many sleepless nights you've cost me."

She drew a breath and framed his face with her hands to study him. "Really?" she asked breathlessly.

He bent his head to kiss her, and their playfulness vanished in hungry, languorous kisses.

She slept that night in his arms, and in the morning he loved her again. Halfway through breakfast, he found her stereo, put on a CD, and caught her up to dance with her.

"What are you doing?"

"C'mon. Who says you have to dance after dark?"

"Don't you have to go to work?" she asked, watching him move around her, his hips swaying provocatively, the morning sunshine streaming through the window and playing over his golden body. Muscles rippled when he moved. His hips were narrow, a contrast to broad shoulders. The thin white scars that covered his arm in no way detracted from his overwhelming masculinity.

"Hell, no! I own the company," he said, giving her a grin that would melt a snowman in January. "I can skip one morning."

She laughed and began to move with him. "You're crazy."

"My feet are sticking to your floor. Wait a minute."

He left and in a moment returned with socks for both of them. "Put these on and we can do better."

"Jeff—"

"Want me to put them on you?"

"No!" She laughed and yanked on white socks, looking at him begin to dance again in his shorts and socks. He did know how to dance. And she realized she had never had a deep appreciation of the male body. Until now.

The second song was slow, and in seconds it became hot in the room as Alette watched Jeff move sensuously, knowing what his golden body could do to her, what his hands could evoke. Her breathing became ragged, her chest rubbed against his. Her eyelids felt heavy, and her lips parted as she gazed at his mouth.

Desire made her shake and wrap her arms around him. He caught her up against him easily, and she wrapped her legs around him. He kissed her long and deep as he walked to the living room and slid down on the floor. He pulled off his briefs and untied the sash on her short robe, pushing it away and pulling her down on top of him.

She moved desperately, needing him, wanting him, relishing the rapture and vitality he gave her.

Later, she showered while he was stretched on the bed. Then, while he showered and shaved, she took a business call.

"It's amazing," she told him when he reappeared in his slacks, his shirt open. "The morning after the murder, people canceled their jobs with me. Now my phone is ringing constantly. They've all found reasons to go ahead with their original plans."

"That's human nature."

"I've found out who my true friends are," she said.

"Did you?"

"I hope so," she said, and he walked to her to put his arms around her. She stood on tiptoe and kissed him a long time.

"If I'm going to work at all, I better go. I'll pick you up for dinner. You haven't been treated to my culinary talents."

"I'm going to miss you," she said softly, watching him tuck his shirt into his pants. She walked to the door with him.

"We'll continue our celebration tonight. One night isn't enough for a victory like yours." At the door he caught her to him to kiss her again, and when they parted they were both breathless.

"Congratulations again. It's over and you can forget now. Except I'd always wonder like hell who set me up. Did she do it to save herself—"

"What makes you think it was a woman?"

"You think Sal was in his shorts with a man when he had a fight?"

"It's possible."

"You didn't know Sal. It was a woman."

While he talked, she was aware of his proximity, his low-pitched voice, the thick golden curls on his chest. She wanted to reach out and touch him, but she resisted the urge; yet anywhere she looked, she was mired in physical longing. His mouth was sexy, appealing; his eyes were bedroom eyes, sending silent messages. Memories made her hot.

His gaze dropped to her breasts and raised. "It's going to be a hell of a long day."

He walked away, and she watched him, feeling an excitement and warmth and longing she had never experienced with Bill or Paul.

She closed the door and returned to her bedroom, looking at the rumpled bed, realizing that in spite of her relationships with the two men she had known, she was inexperienced about erotic love. She closed her eyes, remembering vividly, tingling over recollections, wanting Jeff, wanting him for more reasons than the physical.

In the next few days she became busier than ever. Cheramie had moved back to town, but Alette saw little of the Walcotts. She suspected Phillip blamed her for his disastrous campaign more than he blamed himself for his affairs coming to light. She spent every spare moment with Jeff, but her work and the campaign cut into their time together. They talked long hours into the night when they couldn't be together, Jeff discussing issues, Alette finding that she agreed with him on many. He listened while she told him about problems with landscapes. He was still a marvel to her, disturbing, exciting, more fun than any other man she had ever known.

She'd left some of her belongings on Aubrey's boat and finally called to say she would pick them up. When she arrived, he was in his office on the phone. He replaced the receiver and turned to look at her.

As she leaned against the door, she realized his office was different.

"You cleaned your office!"

"It's not that amazing."

"Yes, it is. What brought this about?"

"Not one damned thing," he said so tightly that she looked at him in shock.

"Sorry, Alette. I've had my own problems."

"Can I help?" she asked, studying him. "You know I'll do anything."

"No, but thanks. How're things going?"

"Just fine. I'm having a dinner party a week from Friday. Can you come?"

"Is this a family gathering?"

She laughed. "It's mostly in your honor for all the help you gave me, and no, I'm not inviting Rutger. I'm going to invite Cheramie and Phillip."

He ran a hand across his forehead. "I don't think I could take an evening with Rutger right now, and Phillip is a pompous ass."

"I'd think he would be a little less so now."

"I don't think Phillip will blame himself for what happened, but Cheramie probably needs some support. She was pretty rocky at the trial. Yes, I'll be there."

"Good. It'll be small, just Jeff, Cheramie and Phillip, and Victoria and her brother, who will be in town, so I told her to bring him along."

"Aw, gee, Alette. Victoria?"

"I thought you parted on good terms."

"Not exactly."

She studied him, watching him shuffle papers, and realized he was shuffling the same papers repeatedly. She looked around the orderly office. "It might do you good. You can get through dinner."

He stared into space, and Alette felt a flicker of surprise. "She's very independent," she said softly.

"She sure as sweet hell is, and I wish—" He clamped his mouth shut. "I don't know about dinner."

"Don't be ridiculous. Do you want to see her again or not?"

"I need to forget her. I'm the one who's all weak-kneed and hand wringing. She doesn't give a damn."

"You'll manage, I'm sure. And you really wanted to know an independent woman, Aubrey."

"Not this damned independent, and not this time."

"Do you ever call her?"

"Sure. We talk nearly every day, but she's busy when I ask her out, and she just keeps her distance."

"She won't be keeping her distance at my dinner; she knows I'm inviting you. Half-past seven a week from Friday."

He nodded, and she went past him to the boat to collect her things. The boat was orderly, and she wondered about Victoria. As much as Aubrey deserved what he was getting, Alette loved him too much to see him hurt, and she hoped he worked things out. After spending hours with Victoria before the trial, Alette knew he had indeed fallen in love with an overly independent woman who prized her solitary life.

28

Jeff was the first to arrive and pulled her into his arms the moment he closed the door. "Are we alone?"

"I have help in the kitchen."

"That's far away, and the door is closed," he said, pulling her to him and bending his head to kiss her. After a few minutes he shifted away. "That's why I came early," he said in a husky voice. He held her with his hands on her waist while he looked at her green silk dress. "Wow and wow. You look prettier than my boat!"

She laughed. "I know enough about men and boats to say 'Thank you'! You look rather delectable yourself," she said, looking at his dark suit. She wanted to be alone with him.

"Got time to go to the bedroom and lock the door?"

"No! Come in and we'll get you a drink," she said, linking her arm in his. "How was the talk in Fresno?"

"I think things went okay."

"How could they not go okay for you?" she asked, smiling at him, her voice soft.

"My opponent is beginning to throw a little mud."

"I can't imagine anything anyone could come up with that would do you harm."

"I'm perfect?" he asked with a grin, taking over and pouring white wine for her and mixing his own drink.

"Absolutely!"

He paused, and his expression sobered. "I can't wait for your guests to go home." His gaze shifted, and she leaned forward as he kissed her again.

"Jeff—" She picked up her wine and moved away. "What kind of mud is your opponent slinging?"

"Tying me with Sal, which I was, and bringing in all the scandal about him," Jeff answered solemnly.

"I changed my party registration today," she said.

He arched his brows. "Your family isn't going to like that."

"Aubrey changed his long ago, and I'm beginning to agree with you on some of the issues." She smiled. "Besides, I know which man will make the best governor."

"I'm glad. I'm really glad if I've convinced you of some of the issues."

"As a landscape architect, I'm more than a little interested in the environment."

The doorbell rang, and she excused herself to answer, opening it to face Aubrey, who was in a charcoal suit, looking handsome and as solemn as if he were headed for a funeral.

"Come in. Jeff and I were just discussing politics."

"Hot into an argument?"

"Actually, no," she said as Aubrey crossed the room to shake hands with Jeff. "I told Jeff I changed my party affiliation today. He's convinced me of some environmental issues, and I like his stand on taxes."

"Rutger lost another one from the fold. And the earth didn't shake today at all."

"What would you like to drink?"

"Scotch and soda," Aubrey answered.

Jeff moved past her. "I'll get the drinks," he offered.

The doorbell rang, and Alette greeted Cheramie and Phillip, and in a few more minutes Victoria and her brother arrived. Victoria wore a royal purple dress, and her hair was swept up on one side of her head in a dramatic hairdo. She looked stunning. Beside her stood one of the most handsome men Alette had ever seen, whom Victoria introduced in her well-modulated, low-key voice. "It's nice to see you, Alette. I want you to meet my brother, Jason. Jason, this is Alette Lachman."

Alette shook hands with him. Other than his black eyes, masculine features, and a cleft in his jaw, he resembled Victoria, with black hair, a deep tan, and thick lashes.

"You're the landscape architect, aren't you?" Jason asked as he stepped inside. "I'm an architect."

"I've lost my brother's attention for the next hour," Victoria said. "He could hardly wait for tonight."

"It's nice you included me in this gathering."

"I'm glad to meet Victoria's brother. Come in and you can meet mine."

Alette made introductions as Jeff poured drinks, and she couldn't help noticing Aubrey watching Victoria constantly. In minutes he was deep in conversation with her.

Over green salads Jason turned to Aubrey. "Are you in landscape architecture, too?"

"No. I'm a boat broker."

"You didn't tell me, Victoria. Aubrey Lachman. You race. Of course! You've won our big race. It was about three years ago. Remember, Victoria?"

"Yes, I do," she said quietly, and Aubrey gave her a questioning glance.

"We've grown up on the water," Jason added.

"I have a race this weekend, and one of my crew is sick. If you want to fill in," Aubrey said to Jason, "you can get a feel for the bay."

"That would be great, but I'm going home. Victoria is the one to fill in. She's an excellent sailor."

"I know she is," Aubrey said, watching Victoria. "She's sailed with us."

"There you have it!" Jason said cheerfully. "Why don't you crew for him?"

"I think the captain ought to pick his own crew, Jason," she said with amusement.

"I need someone if I hope to win the race. I'd like to have you on my crew," Aubrey said.

"And if you don't crew for him, you can for me," Jeff said.

"Sorry, Jeff, but thanks for the invitation. Aubrey asked first," Victoria answered.

"Good. We practice Friday afternoon at four"—he looked at Jeff with amusement—"and may the best crew win on Saturday."

Jeff grinned in return. "I'll be there."

"I'd like to see your boat before I go home," Jason said brightly. Alette caught the look Victoria gave him, but he seemed to miss it.

They talked about boats and politics, while Jason and Alette discussed landscapes and architecture. The time passed swiftly; Alette was constantly aware of Jeff, delighted that he was such friends with Aubrey. At midnight Aubrey suggested they all go look at his boat. Thinking she would rather be home alone with Jeff, Alette exchanged a look with him, but when Aubrey urged them to join the others, they agreed. He showed Jason the *Easy*, and then they sailed on the *Catbird*, the men peeling off suit coats and ties, keeping Victoria and Alette out of the spray and not allowing them to do any work. It was brisk with a bright full moon, and Alette felt a deep contentment.

Friday afternoon Aubrey paced the boat. He was ready, and it was almost time for his four crewmen to arrive. He saw someone approaching and squinted against the sunlight, taking in long, shapely legs and short shorts. His mouth went dry at the sight of Victoria Steiner striding toward him. She wore a tank top, short lime-green shorts, and deck shoes. He wanted to cast off, go back down to a secluded cove, and make love to her and to hell with the race.

"Hi, you're early," he said when she stepped on board

He gave her a hand to steady her, and she came down on his level.

"I finished, and the day is beautiful, so here I am. I know I'm a little early. Am I interfering?"

"You look great," he said softly.

"Thank you, Aubrey. I've been counting the minutes," she said, her eyes holding more warmth than the sunshine-splashed deck.

Desire stirred, and he drew a deep breath, taking a step away from her. "Let's get this boat ready."

As they moved around, working together, he couldn't keep his eyes off her. When they were all set, he started the motor.

"What are you doing?" she asked.

He shook his head and cupped his ear as if he couldn't hear, even though he knew exactly what she had asked. She frowned and inched her way back to sit down beside him. "What are you doing? Where's the crew?"

"They're supposed to be here at four," he said.

"It's only ten minutes until four. You're leaving without them."

"Yes, I am," he said, his heartbeat quickening. "If you'll go with me, we'll sail up the coast. I have food and beer enough for four."

She stared at him. "You planned this all the time?"

"No, I didn't. My crew is coming. This is insanity. I've missed you, and I've told you on the phone I've missed you. I'll lose the race if I don't practice. I'll lose my wits if I can't see you, Victoria." He leaned closer, inhaling a subtle perfume, wanting her. "We're close to the dock. I'll take you back if you insist."

Her wide eyes seemed to engulf him. "What about your crew?"

"They'll cuss and swear and go back to the yacht club to have a few beers, and we'll lose the race tomorrow."

She seemed to think that over. "You don't mind losing the race?"

"Not if I get to be with you this afternoon."

She looked away, and the wind caught a lock of black hair, curling it across her cheek. With long fingers she twisted it

behind her ear. "I've tried to be so practical." She swung
her head around, and his heart seemed to thud against his rib
cage. "I've really tried." She sighed. "What kind of race is
it tomorrow?"

"Tomorrow is a big race with a dandy money prize, and
I've won it every year for the past four. Victoria," he said,
his patience gone. He reached for her, and she came into his
arms willingly. He crushed her to him, bending his head to
kiss her.

Later, when he released her, he grinned. "Ah, Vic. What
do you know—the old lawyer logic can't rule your heart,"
he said, tilting her chin up, kissing her lightly. "Let's get
this baby going and get out of here before my crew sees me.
They'll hang me from the highest yardarm if they see me
lollygagging, bussin' my lawyer in the bay."

She laughed and shook her head. "I was surprised last
night, Aubrey, at how orderly the *Easy* was. It was a nice
surprise. You should have told me when we talked."

"It doesn't matter now," he said happily.

They sailed north, both enjoying the sunny afternoon and
brisk breeze. They returned to the dock at sundown. As soon
as they were on board the *Easy*, Aubrey pulled her into his
arms while Victoria moved close against him, holding him
tightly.

29 ❧

Mel Cipresso leaned back in his chair, his forehead furrowed in a scowl. "We haven't had any new developments on the case, but there's no statute of limitation or
murder."

"You can't still think Alette Lachman did it?"

"Shit, yes, I do. She had the murder weapon. She was a

the scene. The defense lawyer made a circus of the trial with all the witnesses about the anonymous phone call, the model to confuse Mrs. Haskell, so I lost my case. The fact still is, Mrs. Haskell saw a woman who looks just like Alette Lachman go into that condo with Sal Giavotella at half-past four. Alette Lachman admits she had a lunch date with Giavotella.''

"Hell, it wasn't a date, and she went over that."

"Jeff, the woman's got you ass-bomboozled."

"I don't think she does," Jeff said. "As far as that lunch was concerned, it makes her look innocent, not guilty. That wasn't Sal's way if he was hiding her. I know that."

"Her story was idiotic. I think she's as guilty as hell."

"You can't try her again."

"No, and we keep looking in case anything else turns up. The one thing in Alette Lachman's favor . . ." He paused, and Jeff listened attentively. "She hired the damned PI. That's the only thing that gives me pause. I can't figure it. I'd think the first thing she'd do would be to pull off the PI."

"That's right, Mel. What could she possibly gain from a private investigator nosing around?"

"I don't know. At any rate, we'll keep checking. You're damned fast to defend her. Are you seeing her?"

"Yes, I am."

"Oh, shit. Jeff, don't be gullible. The woman would turn anyone's head; she's damned beautiful, but there's too much evidence."

"She had her trial, and she was found not guilty, Mel. Not guilty. That's what you have to accept."

"I accept it; I don't believe it. And I hate to see you get suckered and drawn in by such a woman."

"Keep checking your leads since the case is still open. Someone set Alette Lachman up. She's doing all she can to discover who."

"That's the one fucking thing. We check on the ex-wife, on any lead we get."

"You ever tell me Gina Giavotella pulled the trigger, I'll never believe it. And I don't think Alette Lachman did it, either."

"Stranger things have happened."

Thirty minutes later Jeff emerged from the Hall of Justice, climbed into his car, and started for the office. He drove ten blocks, swore, and turned abruptly, changing direction. Nine minutes later he walked into Alette Lachman's office.

Out of the corner of her eye Alette saw someone get out of a car and cross the walk in long strides, heard the bell jingle as the door opened. Then Jeff strode into the middle of the office and stopped to face her. He wore navy slacks and a white shirt and had shed his suit coat. Wind had tangled his hair.

"Hello," he said, studying her.

"You were in the neighborhood and thought you'd drop in?" she asked dryly, feeling her pulse race at the sight of him, never able to understand the effect he had on her simply by being present. He was handsome, but San Francisco was filled with handsome men. He stood in the center of her office, and her curiosity grew as to why he was there in the middle of the day.

"I've been to see Mel Cipresso. He's keeping the case open. He knows you have the PI."

"Judging by the expression on your face, Mel Cipresso still thinks I did it."

"Yes, he does. The PI gives him pause, though."

Jeff looked incredibly handsome; his thick golden hair was windblown. She became aware of herself, her blue silk-linen minidress. It was sleeveless, with a low-cut V neckline, and when she stood up and walked around her desk, she glanced up to find his gaze roaming over her hips and legs to her toes and back up again to meet her eyes.

"Pretty dress," he said, his voice becoming warm and husky.

"Thank you. Since the trial I haven't been able to bring myself to wear the tailored work clothes I always wore before. Sometimes I dream I open the door and the two detectives are standing there again with a warrant."

"It's over, Alette. They can't try you again," he said pulling her close and bending his head to kiss her.

His kisses fanned and fed a hunger that ran deep. She kissed him passionately in return, delighted by him, joyful for their few moments together.

"Close up shop and let's go to my place," he urged, his hands sliding over her.

"I can hardly get any work done," she replied, "so I might as well go with you."

He took her arm and they walked to his car. The moment they were in the elevator in his building, with the doors closed in front of them, he took her in his arms. They rode to his condominium on the fourth floor, then rushed inside, into a room with a glorious view from floor-to-ceiling windows along one side. As soon as Alette entered the room, she faced Jeff. His blue eyes darkened, his gaze was searing, hungry, as he reached for her.

"I had to be with you. I think about you, I *need* you," he said, unbuttoning her dress, his fingers warm against her flesh. He wound his fingers in her hair and tilted her head up to kiss her, his mouth covering hers. She returned his kisses, wanting him, unbuttoning his shirt. He tugged away his necktie, and she opened his shirt to kiss his chest. He inhaled deeply, pushing away her dress while it dropped around her ankles, and she kicked off her pumps.

His belt fell away, he stepped out of the trousers, and she peeled down his briefs. She ran her hands on his warm skin, sliding them over him, feeling the planes and angles, the curly hair that covered his thighs and chest. He picked her up and carried her to his bed, spreading her thighs, moving between them and entering her, filling her, hot and thick, her softness enveloping him, holding him, as they both moved.

"Alette," he whispered, a husky murmur that made her feel wanted. His shoulders were broad and strong, and she clung to them as she kept her legs tight around him, holding him close, wanting to give and give. She cried out with each climax, and he held off, finally giving a shuddering release before his weight came down on her.

She ran her hands back and forth along his smooth back, marveling at how muscular he was. He turned his head to look at her, playing with a lock of her hair and letting it slide through his fingers. He leaned forward to kiss her cheek, her ear, the corner of her mouth. They kissed, slowly, deeply, a

satiated kiss, a kiss of satisfaction. Breathless, she opened
her eyes when he raised his head.

Her gaze roamed over his features, his thickly lashed eyes,
his sensuous mouth with the full underlip, his prominent
cheekbones and tangled, golden hair, and she knew she loved
him in a way she had never loved before.

"Want to go eat dinner?" he asked, smiling at her.

She nodded. "I'll get dressed," she said, sliding off the
bed. He caught her around the waist.

"If you can stand my cooking, we can eat here."

"That sounds best of all, O'Neil. Now I learn what kind
of cook you are." She slipped away and went to the bathroom
to dress.

When she came out, he had showered and dressed in cutoffs. His chest and legs were bare. He was barefoot and stood
by the kitchen counter. "Tonight the specialty is crab and
shrimp in champagne sauce, a loaf of sourdough bread, and
salad." He poured two glasses of Mondavi Chardonnay.

"Sounds grand. What can I do?"

"Kiss the cook."

She laughed and walked over to him. He gazed down at
her, and she could see the satisfaction in his expression. He
wrapped his arm around her neck and pulled her close to kiss
her. He kissed her lightly at first, and then deeper. When she
pulled away, she was breathless. "I think you may have
burned the shrimp and crab."

"It'll be worth it," he said, watching her. As if it took an
effort, he turned back to cooking.

She picked up her glass to take a sip, watching him, finally
noticing her surroundings. The kitchen was oak, with bright
touches of color, new appliances. The dining room held pro-
vincial furniture, and the living room was filled with color,
an Oriental carpet in the center of the highly polished floor,
deep blue furniture with bright touches in the cushions and
oil paintings. Baskets of flowers hung from the ceiling, and
there were several bronzes on the tables.

"I like your house. You like color."

"It's comfortable. This is ready. Come help yourself."

They ate beside a window with a view of the city and the

bay and watched lights slowly blink on and the sun go down.

"You're a wonderful cook," she said when she'd finished.

"I've had a lot of practice. I used to cook for my folks. Mom worked, and Dad wasn't able to get around, so I'd cook dinner after school. I've been cooking all my life." He stood up and took her hand, and they moved to the sofa, taking their drinks with them. He switched on a lamp and sat down beside her. She curled her legs under her and faced him, trailing her fingers along his cheek, unable to resist touching him.

He gazed at her solemnly. "Alette, if you get a lead from the PI, share it with me. Let me tell Mel. Don't act on it on your own."

"I won't take risks," she said, looking him in the eye. "I just want to know who did it; I can't help but want to know why she picked me," she said, realizing Jeff had convinced her it was a woman.

"Your sister fits in so many ways. She looks like you; she was in Washington and San Francisco."

"It ends there. She has ironclad alibis. It wasn't Cheramie. A dress clerk said she sold her a dress at Magnin's at four-thirty. A beauty operator was washing her hair at five minutes after five when Sal was shot. I know the police checked. The private investigator gave Aubrey sworn statements from the dress clerk and the beauty operator."

"Have you seen the statements?"

"No, but Aubrey has. He told me about them, and I believe him. I wouldn't have had the investigator check on Cheramie. I know the police checked her whereabouts. Cheramie isn't the mystery woman. There are two witnesses. She couldn't have made the phone calls to me. She was having her hair done."

"You're absolutely sure?"

"Yes. My sister never would hurt me like that. With a presidential campaign coming up, she wouldn't have jeopardized Phillip's chances. You can't imagine how socially ambitious Cheramie is."

"It goes to show how little you know about someone when

you think you know a lot. Sal was so closemouthed about his affair, never talked about any earlier ones, if there were any.''

"He seemed keyed up and excited over his fiancée and the house he was going to build for her.''

"God, I wonder who she is!''

Alette studied Jeff's profile. He stared straight ahead, lost in thoughts about Sal. She wanted to lean forward and kiss him. He was handsome, exciting. Her gaze ran down the length of him and back up, and she set her drink down carefully and leaned forward to kiss his ear. He turned his head, his arm going around her waist instantly. He swung her around onto his lap, and she wrapped her arms around him.

He pulled her to him, bending his head to kiss her, his hand twisting free the buttons of her dress.

She spent the night in his arms, clinging to him, knowing that she was deeply in love.

When morning came, they ate breakfast and he asked her for a date for dinner. "I don't have many more free nights until election. I hit the campaign trail.''

She nodded. "I understand about political campaigns.''

"Can you go to dinner tonight?'' he asked.

"Yes. You won't have this much privacy if you're elected governor.''

"No, but I'm going to have my own life. I decided that when I considered running for the office. I'm not the first bachelor to hold public office.''

He was solemn, a determined note in his voice. All she wanted to do was sit on his lap and caress him. She moved around the table, sitting down on his lap. She kissed his ear and trailed her tongue to the corner of his mouth. He turned his head to kiss her fully, his hand stroking her back until she pulled away.

"I have an appointment and I remember that you said you do, too.''

"I'll take you home.''

He drove her to her house and reached across her to open the door. "Don't forget what I said—if you learn something from the investigator—let someone else know. Don't take risks. You're dealing with a cold murderer.''

Jeff watched her climb out, his gaze going over her long, lovely legs, and he ached for her. He watched her walk into her house, her hips swaying slightly, that haughty lift to her chin, and he remembered how she was in bed with those long legs holding him tight.

He felt better, infinitely better, but he wanted to do something else. He drove away, turning toward Sausalito, and twenty minutes later he stepped on board Aubrey's boat.

Aubrey thrust his head through the doorway, saw Jeff, and came outside. "Good morning."

"Hi. Can you spare a minute?"

"Sure," Aubrey said. "Let's sit in the shade." He moved to a deck chair and motioned Jeff to one.

"I wanted to ask you a few questions. Alette said you have sworn statements about Cheramie's whereabouts on the day of the murder."

"Yes. She was with someone, a dress clerk at I. Magnin's, until half-past four. A hairdresser said she signed in at five and she was doing her hair by five minutes after Cheramie arrived at the shop. She spent the evening with Phillip at a party." Aubrey sighed, shifting on the chair. "And I can tell you, my sister would not have an affair when her husband is getting ready to run for president. Cheramie is the most socially conscious and ambitious woman I've ever known."

"Suppose she was having the affair long before Phillip announced?"

"It wouldn't take her long to break off an affair."

"Sal could be stubborn and determined."

"You think he could match the Lachmans for determination? Cheramie has been manipulating men since she was ten years old. Neither Alette nor I can imagine her in such a situation. Even if we could, she has two people who swear she was with them."

"Could she have paid them to swear to it?"

"Nope. If you ask around at the Hall of Justice, you'll find that the police have already checked this out. Cheramie's not the mystery woman. Go talk to the hairdresser yourself. She's the real clincher. You won't mind the time it takes, either.

She's a looker." He studied Jeff. "Do you know something I don't? What brings this up about Cheramie?"

Jeff shrugged. "She's a choice. She fits the description; she was in Washington and San Francisco. She would be able to contact Alette, know where to place the revolver, know what to expect from Alette."

"I've thought of all of that," Aubrey said solemnly, "but she has an alibi for every second."

"It would fit so much better if Cheramie hadn't been with someone else."

"I know. If she's innocent, it's a damned good thing she did have an alibi. She would be the next one on trial. I don't know why they don't keep after the wife."

"I can tell you—Gina is the one I know. She would never have shot Sal."

"We think we know so much about our family and friends, but there's always a secret silence in each mind that we can't know."

"There was in Sal's. I've asked Alette if the PI comes up with anything to tell me. I don't want her to take risks." Jeff paused, feeling a knot of worry whenever he thought about Alette and the investigator. "Your sister is so damned independent—"

Aubrey snorted, and Jeff looked at him with curiosity.

"Sorry, go ahead."

"I'm afraid she'll take the initiative and do something that may place her in danger."

"I hadn't thought about it, but you're right. I'll talk to Mort, because I've worked with him. I'll get him to let me know if something really hot breaks."

"Thanks, Aubrey. I'll sleep better nights."

"God, women will drive you to drink!"

Jeff laughed and looked at Aubrey. "On that one, I think I'll get up and go to work."

"How's the campaign?"

"Going strong. I'm traveling after today, making the rounds of the state. The first time I'm seen in public with your sister, you'll see another flurry of wild headlines."

"Am I going to see that?"

Jeff gazed at the sparkling water and back to Aubrey. "Yes, I imagine you will."

Aubrey grinned. "You'll give Rutger apoplexy! I'm glad, though."

He walked along the deck with Jeff. "When we were growing up, we were close as kids. Cheramie, Alette, and I are still close. There was no mother, only a glacial father. We stuck together because we were all we had."

"You had a father who provided you with everything."

"Everything but love. You didn't come out so bad when you stop to think about it."

Jeff blinked and stared at Aubrey. "I guess I didn't. I love my dad and he loves me, and I've always known that."

Jeff strode off, looking back when he was in the car to see Aubrey still standing on the bow of the boat. He backed out and turned around. Now he wanted to ask Alette to the watch party election night, and he could imagine the furor that would stir with the party leaders and with his campaign staff. They might as well get accustomed to him, because he wasn't going to change his life completely.

That night when she opened the door, Jeff's breath caught in his throat. Her hair was down, swinging free. She wore a red leather miniskirt, a black cotton scoop-necked T-shirt, and a red leather collarless jacket.

"I'm going to have heat stroke," he said, wiping his brow. "Oh, baby, do you look great!" he added with an exaggerated leer.

"I hope I get over this style of dressing soon, but I told you, I can't bear my conservative clothes since the trial."

"I hope you never get over it. You look great," he said in a husky voice, closing the door behind him and walking her back against the wall. He slid his arms around her and bent his head close. "You smell wonderful, you look delicious, and I'll take you to dinner later, but what I'd like to do right now—"

"Is probably the same thing I'd like to do," she said softly, standing on tiptoe, raising her mouth, and thrusting her hips against his.

His heart seemed to turn over as he gathered her to him.

30 ～ↄ

Three days later, late at night in a motel suite in San Diego, Jeff glared at his campaign staff. "I'm inviting her to the election watch party. I'm seeing her, and after the campaign we'll be together regularly."

"After the campaign you do what you want," Blake Dorth said, pacing the floor and raking his fingers through thick black hair. He had been Sal's campaign manager, and he was Jeff's. Until this moment Jeff had trusted his judgment implicitly.

"If you date Alette Lachman before the voters go to the polls, your chances will go up in smoke," Howard Westerman argued.

"He's not going to have time to date her a lot before election day," Clyde Taylor pointed out quietly in his high voice.

They had all flown to San Diego for a rally and speech. Jeff had arrived two days before. He had spoken to a women's group, the Rotarians, the Lions, and the California League of Conservation Voters and given a talk at San Diego State. Tonight had been a barbecue and rally of party supporters. Now his staff was assembled, and he gazed at them, knowing he was in for a fight. He had almost the same staff as Sal. Sal had been instrumental in helping organize his staff. Jeff's gaze roamed over the men. Howard Westerman had a few faint streaks of gray at his temples. Clyde Taylor was new, not Sal's man; Clyde had been Jeff's chief accountant since he'd bought Jayton Foods and Bob Knight had retired.

Jep Bradly was his pollster, and it was the first time Jep had looked badly shaken. His thick red hair was awry from constantly scratching his head as he argued with Jeff.

"Suppose she costs you the campaign?" Howard asked. "This isn't a woman you've been dating a long time and are in love with. You weren't even going out with her when you started the campaign—at least I didn't know you'd ever gone out with her."

"Well, I have."

Jep moved restlessly. "Jeff, Howard's right. You have to decide. You have an image to maintain—the ball player, Mr. Wholesome Nice Guy. If there's a little woman at your side, she's supposed to convey family and respectability. Alette Lachman may cost you the election."

Jeff looked at him, and he bit off his words.

"The press will pick this up, because you call her often," Blake said.

"My hotel phone isn't tapped," Jeff said patiently.

"Jeff, she a fucking *Lachman*. You're on opposite sides."

"That's her father you're thinking about," Jeff answered in a pleasant voice. "Alette has changed her party affiliation."

Several men exchanged glances while Blake swore softly under his breath.

"Let's get to the bottom line," Howard interjected. "Are you willing to risk election to see her?"

Every man in the room looked at him, and Jeff gazed back blandly. He had already asked himself that question. "Yes, I am. She's more important to me than becoming governor."

There were groans and swearing; Clyde's high-pitched voice rose above the protests. "You have your answer, gentlemen. I say we get down to plans for the rest of the week. Don't forget to turn in any expenses to me while I'm here. I fly back to San Francisco tomorrow."

Jeff focused on their talk, listening, contributing, but his thoughts kept drifting to Alette, and often he would glance down at his watch to check the time. When the hands read five minutes before two in the morning, he called the meeting to a halt.

"If you want me to give speeches all day tomorrow and remember names and field questions for the television interview, I have to get some sleep."

They filed out, and the moment he locked the door behind them, he went to the bedroom to stretch out and phone Alette.

She sounded sleepy, and images came and he wanted to be with her.

"I just got rid of everyone or I would have called sooner."

"How's it going?" she asked, sounding more awake.

"Fine. No tomatoes in the face so far."

"You won't have that. You're Jeff O'Neil, the all-American baseball player with a rags-to-riches life."

"I didn't know I was so great."

"You didn't?" she retorted in a throaty voice. "If I could tell the women of California what I know, you'd win! Of course, the men might not be so happy with you."

He laughed. "I want you here. Any chance you could fly down and be with me?" He knew when he asked that he would cause another wild furor with his staff, worse than before, because it was weeks until election. He didn't care. When he heard Alette's voice, he wanted her. "Are you there?"

"I'm thinking. When did you want me to fly down? And fly down where?"

"Let me get my schedule."

"Jeff, this is a spur-of-the-moment thing. Have you okayed this with your staff?"

"This is my campaign and my staff. They have to take me the way I am. I'm not going to let them run my life."

"That's not a realistic view of politics. I think we better wait to go out until you get home."

"I'm going to get my schedule. You get yours and let me worry about the voters. Do I have to fly home and get you?" He dropped the phone and went for his briefcase. "Alette. I'm in San Diego tomorrow. I fly tomorrow night to Palm Springs, then to San Bernardino. Sunday I'll be in L.A. I have to go to a private dinner, a fund-raiser, Sunday night. I can bring a date."

"I need to work."

"On a Sunday night? Come on. I don't know much about the landscape business, but I know you can juggle things around and have a Sunday free. You've put off work all through the trial. I'll fly home and get you if I have to.''

"I know what it's like to be involved in a scandal. How do you think I'd feel if you lost because you were going out with me?"

"How do you think I feel without you?" he asked quietly. "I need you here." And as he said it, he realized it was true. He wanted her with him badly. And he had never felt that way about another woman. "Alette—"

"You've really thought about the consequences?"

"Yes. Honey, this is a big state. There are other towns besides San Francisco, and you're not quite the item elsewhere. You come to Los Angeles or I come home to be with you. That will hurt my campaign."

"I gave you every out," she said quietly, and he grinned. "Your staff won't like me."

"You can handle them. They're all men except Jan, my secretary, and she's at home."

"The newspapers will have a field day."

"You go out to dinner with me. I'll get you your own suite in the hotel. I'll even get you a suite in a different hotel if it makes you feel better."

"I think that's a good idea. The press will make enough hullabaloo over our dinner date."

"It'll keep my name before the public. I wish you were here now. Tell me what you did today." He lay back and listened and imagined her in bed, and he longed for her. They talked until half-past three and she sounded sleepy, at which point he told her good night and cradled the receiver. He stripped and went to bed to stare into the darkness and think about Alette, and he knew what he felt for her ran deep. It would be a bombshell dropped on his staff when he informed them about his date. And he wondered what Rutger Lachman would think when he discovered his daughter was dating an O'Neil.

Sunday he stood in the sunshine and watched for Alette. She arrived on a commercial flight, and he met her the moment she stepped into the hall, sliding his arm around her and giving her a squeeze.

"You look gorgeous!" he exclaimed, his gaze drifting over her hot pink blouse and matching pink cotton skirt. They headed for the car.

"How come you're here? I thought you'd be giving a speech."

"I have a few free hours."

"Does the press know yet?"

"How would I know what the press knows?"

"And your staff?"

He grinned. "They won't snarl at you. You'll win them over. Did you tell Aubrey you were going out with me tonight?"

"As a matter of fact, I happened to talk to him yesterday and I did."

"And what did he say?"

"He said he thought that was nice," she said, looking up at Jeff solemnly.

"So Aubrey approved of your coming to Los Angeles."

"Aubrey wouldn't know the meaning of worrying about a campaign."

"That makes me feel good. Does Rutger know?"

"Not yet. I'll know when he knows."

"You don't laugh enough, Alette. I'm going to change that," he said in a husky voice. "Let's see if we can't find something fun to do."

They picked up her bag and went out into bright sunshine. She watched him unlock the car. "I thought you had a driver."

"Not for the next few hours," he answered. He drove fast, taking a freeway and turning into a sprawling motel with fountains in front.

"I've already registered," he said as he whipped around to the back and parked.

"Is this where you're staying?"

"For now." He grinned as he put his arm across her shoulders. He unlocked the door to a suite, and the moment he closed it behind him, he pulled her into his arms. "I have two hours until I have to put in an appearance. We have two hours to ourselves."

"This isn't where we'll stay tonight?"

"No," he said, "I rented it for now." His expression changed as he watched her. His arms tightened around her. "I've missed you," he said, leaning forward to kiss her.

"Oh, Jeff!" she exclaimed, wrapping her arms around him and thrusting her hips against him.

That night she took a deep breath when she opened the door to face him at her hotel suite. As he entered the room, his gaze went over her slowly, stirring her pulse. He looked so spectacular in a tux, she wondered if there was a female in California who wouldn't vote for him.

"I was so worried, but when I look at you and think about your record and your history, I don't think I'll hurt you."

"I don't think you'll ever hurt me," he said. "You look gorgeous."

"Thank you. This is the first time—and I did this especially for you—that I'm wearing something conservative," she said lightly, turning around for his perusal, the black puckered silk sheath clinging to her. It had a white satin collar and cuffs. Her dark hair was combed back from her face, pinned up high behind her head.

He leaned against the closed door and looked at her, a look that took her breath and made her stop and face him. "I wish we didn't have to go," he said in a husky voice.

"But we do. I'll make my debut. This is your last chance to avoid escorting a scarlet woman." She became solemn, moving closer to slide her fingers along his lapels. "Jeff, I'll understand completely. I've been involved in political campaigns. If you'd rather I stay here while you go to the dinner—"

"To hell with that," he said, sliding his arm around her and leaning forward to kiss her long and passionately, his tongue playing in her mouth, evoking a scalding response. When he leaned away, he gazed at her with blatant longing. "If we stay here, we stay here together."

"No. We go to the dinner. Minus lipstick," she said, rubbing her thumb on his mouth. He took out a folded handkerchief and carefully wiped his mouth while she moved to a mirror to repair her makeup.

"I'm ready," she said when she'd finished.

She entered on his arm and met his campaign staff, all of whom were cordial. Minicams took their pictures, focusing on her. A reporter stepped up to ask her a question. She smiled at him.

"This is Mr. O'Neil's night. You ask him the questions." She gave him her best smile, and the man smiled in return.

"Sure, Miss Lachman," he said.

When Jeff was beside her at dinner, he said, "I think maybe the wrong person is running for governor. You have them charmed."

"You know better than that. Wait until you read the papers tomorrow."

"That's all right. It'll get everything out in the open."

"Including before Rutger."

"It's time he knew about us."

They were interrupted, and she didn't get to talk alone with him the rest of the evening, and he had a meeting as soon as the party ended. At two the phone rang and she rolled over to lift the receiver and hear his voice.

"How about I come over?"

"How about you don't!" she said, coming awake and laughing. "I'll bet there's a reporter lurking on the premises somewhere."

"All right. I had to call."

She settled against the pillow and talked to him for an hour before they finally hung up. She settled to sleep, thinking that the problems with dating Jeff were small compared to the problems she had recently faced.

He picked her up for lunch the next day, and he was free to see her catch her flight back to San Francisco. On their way to the airport they stopped for lunch. She placed a paper on her lap. "We're news today," she said. "Our pictures are on the front page, and there are paragraphs about my trial."

"It got me a little more publicity," he said lightly. He drove into the lot of a restaurant and parked, turning to face her. "Look, we're going to see each other. To hell with scandal. You didn't murder Sal, you were acquitted. You'd make headlines if none of that had happened simply because you're a Lachman.''

She nodded and waited until they had ordered to bring up the subject again. "How about your staff?"

"We'll win them over. It's my staff, remember that always. I know what I want."

"Rutger will know now."

Jeff lowered his water glass and stared at her with an arched brow. "You expect trouble?"

"Yes. He doesn't like you, Jeff, and in spite of all your charm, you'll never be able to win his approval."

"I hadn't really intended to try," Jeff answered dryly.

"I think I better tell you about Paul a little." She told him briefly and quickly, getting to their breakup and Rutger's part in it.

"He's threatened to disinherit Cheramie if she ever has an affair."

"You think he'll tell you to stop seeing me or he'll disinherit you?"

"I don't know. I can handle that, because I've been threatened with that before. I have my own income."

"I want you with me election night. All right?"

"Yes," she said, leaning back while the waiter served her chicken salad.

They talked through lunch, forgot the time, and she had to rush to the airport. In the hall of the airport, he caught her around the waist to give her one long, hungry kiss good-bye.

"See you at home, honey," he said softly while her heartbeat raced. She nodded and boarded the plane to fly home.

When she played back her answering machine, she had a sexy, teasing message from Jeff and two business calls. Then Aubrey's voice came on, cheerful and lighthearted.

"Congratulations, sis! I'm no longer the black sheep of the Lachman clan. You have the distinction. Our draconian patriarch saw your picture with Jeff, and Rutger is steamed. He's so hot, he's been out to see me to find out how to get hold of you. Do you think Rutger realizes children grow up or understands that age twenty-one might mean one can think rationally for oneself? If you need me for guidance or protection, just call. Vic and I are going sailing, but I'll be back tonight.''

She smiled, happy that Aubrey and Victoria were seeing each other now. After Aubrey's message there was a curt one from Rutger to return his call the moment she arrived.

She carried her things to the bedroom to unpack and decided she would get to Rutger later.

Jeff took a whirlwind tour of the state, following Sal's strategy and going to big cities and small towns, covering the length of the state, busy night and day. Alette talked to him for over an hour every night. Rutger was away on business, and she had yet to see him about Jeff.

She rarely saw Jeff because of his campaign schedule, but one night in October he took her home with him to have dinner with his parents. During dinner, she glanced over once at Barney O'Neil, looking at his frail hands with blue veins, his stooped shoulders, as he sat at the table in his wheelchair, and she couldn't blame Jeff for hating Rutger and wanting to get back at him.

When election night arrived, she still had managed to avoid seeing Rutger.

She dressed for the evening in another conservative dress, this one a teal silk that was a little more carefree than the black. She let her hair fall free. When the phone rang, she picked it up to hear Cheramie.

"Alette? I had lunch with Rutger today."

"I haven't seen him."

"Since you haven't returned his calls, he's really angry. I just thought I'd warn you. You ought to call him."

"How are you, Cheramie?"

"I'm all right. Things are settling back to normal, thank God. Time helps."

"Let's get together for lunch. I need to run. Jeff is going to pick me up."

"If you're dating him, you're caught in politics. Shitty business," Cheramie said bitterly. "I'll call about lunch."

"Fine." Alette said good-bye and replaced the receiver,

staring at it with a frown, knowing she should call Rutger and face the inevitable confrontation.

She looked at her reflection, decided she was ready for Jeff, and picked up her purse. The bell rang and she rushed to the door, anticipation growing. She opened it wide—and faced Rutger.

31

Alette stepped back in surprise. Rutger was dressed in a navy suit with a navy tie, looking imperturbable as he stepped into the entryway.

"I'm going out," she said stiffly. "This is election night, and I'll be with Jeff."

"You haven't returned my calls."

"I returned them several times, and you were out of town."

"Alette, you know you can reach me if you want to. I came by to stop something disastrous. I want to talk to you."

"Fine, Rutger, but I have a date now."

"He's using you, Alette, to get at me. You go from one scrape to another with all the naiveté you had when you were ten years old."

The words didn't hurt as they once would have, and she wondered how much she had changed with the trial. "I don't think Jeff is using me to get at you."

"That's the only reason he could want to date you. Our families have been bitter enemies since before you were born. He came back here with only one purpose—to put me out of business. Ask him! Everything Jayton Foods does is aimed at cutting into Lachman's business. He's seen he can't put me out of business, so he's trying to get at me another way— through you. You're a lovely woman, and I'm sure he's having a good time, but I'm also sure you mean nothing to him.''

"I don't agree with you," she said, experiencing a calm she had never known around Rutger and wondering if the trial had made her able to cope with her father.

"You're being a fool. I know the man is appealing. He was a baseball player, the office of governor may be his tonight, but he doesn't give a damn for you personally. You need a man of your own type, your own class.''

"Rutger—''

"You should go out with Bill Gaffney! He comes from one of the best families of Baltimore. I know he would patch things up with you. I know he's tried to call you.''

"It is absolutely over with Bill. I will never be interested in dating him again.''

"Jeff O'Neil wants only one thing from you—to get at me. And when he does, you'll get hurt.''

"Did I hear my name mentioned?'' came a deep voice from the hallway, and Jeff strode into the room.

They both turned to look at him. He was in a dark suit and looked confident enough to have already won. His gaze went from Rutger to her swiftly, and he moved to her side.

"Okay?'' he asked softly, sliding his arm around her waist.

"Yes,'' she said, and meant it.

"I came to warn my daughter about you,'' Rutger said bluntly. "I know why you take her out. I know what you want from her. You're trying to get back in a way your father never could.''

"I'm not using Alette,'' Jeff said mildly, looking down at her.

"I think time will tell. Alette has never been wise in her choice of men.''

"That includes picking a father,'' Jeff said. "But then babies don't have that prerogative.''

"Alette, we'll talk later, but you're making a mistake you'll regret,'' Rutger said, watching Jeff.

Jeff's arm tightened around her. "Good night, Mr. Lachman.''

"I intend to do everything I can to see you defeated, or to

see you fail if you do win the election tonight,'' Rutger said. ''Alette, you know I've always been right in these matters. You'll see. He'll hurt you.''

''Sir—''

''I'm going.'' Rutger turned on his heel and left, striding to the elevator and disappearing inside. Alette turned to look up at Jeff.

''Damn,'' he muttered, pulling her to him and kicking the door closed, ''I'm going to give my dad a great big hug the next time I see him. Honey, I'm sorry you had to grow up with that.''

''Children accept their parents.''

''Lord, he's formidable.'' He tilted her chin up. ''Believe it or not, when I date you, your father is the last thing on my mind,'' he said, a smile curving one corner of his mouth.

She hugged him. ''I know that.'' She pulled back to look up at him.

''Okay?'' he asked in a soft voice, and she nodded. He held her away to look at her and whistled, a blatant look of desire in his blue eyes. ''Honey, the cameraman will be looking at you all evening long.'' He reached out and drew her back to him. ''One kiss and we go.''

One kiss turned into long, passionate, wet kisses that sent Alette back to the mirror to repair her makeup while Jeff pulled out a snowy handkerchief and wiped his mouth free of lipstick.

At the Fairmont she stood beside him, in favor of many of the issues he pushed, so eager for him to win. She watched Jeff, thinking he was more handsome than the actors present, poised, giving his wholesome grin to the camera. His parents glowed with love and pride. Jeff was talking to someone, and when she caught his eye, he winked at her.

Jeff won by a landslide, and Nelson Crown conceded defeat by ten o'clock. Even though Jeff looked exuberant and triumphant, he didn't glow with victory as Phillip had, and she knew politics wasn't the driving force in his life. And she knew he wasn't doing it for personal power. He firmly believed in the issues he campaigned for, while Phillip reveled in the glory and public light.

The victory celebration went on until midnight when the last supporters left. Jeff hugged his folks before they left, and finally she stood in the parking lot, a balloon in hand, while he talked to Howard and Blake.

And then he came walking back to her, his coat swinging open as he pulled loose his tie. He held open the car door, and she looked up at him. "Congratulations, Governor O'Neil."

"There are so many things I can't wait to accomplish."

"But you will, all in good time. I don't think this victory means as much to you as it did to Phillip when he won. He looked as if someone had given him the world."

"I'm glad to win, but there isn't any victory like slugging a ball out of the park," he said quietly. "Or pitching a no hitter. You've never seen my house at Carmel. Want to?"

"I'd love to." She knew he was keyed up, and she settled back in the car. The two-hour drive flew past, and they talked all the way. While he was on the highway, he drove fast with one hand, his other hand on her knee or his fingers winding in her hair.

He drove past Carmel to a windswept, isolated beach, turning toward the water. When they entered the house moonlight spilled through the wall of glass, and Alette could see the western decor. She kicked off her shoes and looked around while Jeff opened the doors. The crash of breakers was as clear as if they had been standing on the beach. He took her hand and led her outside on the deck built over the water. There was a redwood chaise longue with thick green padding and a redwood table and chairs, with pots of plants everywhere. Cypress, bent by prevailing ocean winds, leaned over the grounds, their branches like long, gnarled fingers reaching into the darkness.

"It's marvelous," she said, turning to look at him and finding he was watching her.

"I've never brought anyone here before," he said quietly, and her breath caught at his solemn expression. "My parents haven't seen this house, no one has."

"Why not?"

He drew her to him. "I suppose when you grow up an on

child with adults, you learn to keep part of you shut off from everyone else. Maybe you start out that way, and it becomes a habit. This is my escape from the world. I want you, Alette," he said in a husky voice, running his fingers through her hair. He leaned forward, his mouth covering hers, tongues meeting.

Later, as she lay in his arms, he shifted to look at her. "I don't feel complete without you." She kissed him, holding him while he stroked her head. "Alette, I want to marry you."

"Jeff," she said, the word coming out like a sigh of pleasure. He bent his head to kiss her throat, trailing kisses lower to her bare breast. She gasped and clung to him, closing her eyes, and it was a long time before he raised his head.

"I love you," he said, turning her head, his finger beneath her chin so he could gaze into her eyes.

"I love you, Jeff," she said, turning to him, pulling his head down to hers, her mouth covering his while his arms tightened and words were lost.

Later he stroked her shoulder, his fingers toying with locks of her hair. "I've never wanted a woman the way I want you," he said. "I've watched my folks all these years, and I know I want someone who will stand by me through thick and thin like my mom stood by Dad."

"That's a little scary to live up to"—she framed his face— "but I'll give it my best."

"I've never really been in love. Never like this."

She wrapped her arms around him and gazed at him.

"Okay, with a look like that, a quarter for your thoughts," he said.

"This is the most exciting night of my life," she said, "but it also feels so right," she said. She didn't always agree with Jeff, but she could understand his views. He was more forceful and dynamic and confident than the men she had known before. He was also sensitive in his own way, exciting, sensual, and so much fun to be with. She hated to share him with public office, but she knew that was what he wanted, so she intended to do her best to support him.

"It is right," he said gruffly. He wound his fingers in her hair and leaned over her, kissing her passionately while his hand moved along her legs.

They watched the dawn come up over the rooftop, bathing the ocean in sunshine. She moved drowsily in his arms. "This is wonderful. I feel cut off from the world."

"We are. There's no phone."

She sat up to stare at him. "Even Aubrey has a phone."

He shrugged broad shoulders. "I don't."

"Now you're going to have to. You're the governor, and people will have to be able to get hold of you. Suppose you had a robbery or someone fell off the deck?"

"Until last night the only someone to fall off the deck was me, and if I fell off, I couldn't use a phone." He grinned and stood up to stretch, holding his fists high overhead. Her gaze ran down the length of his golden body. Her mouth became dry, her heart thudding, as she looked at his body. She couldn't resist and came up on her knees to stroke his hip.

"You do that and you won't get breakfast for hours," he said, his voice changing. He held out his hand. "Let's shower."

"Talk about not getting breakfast for hours . . ."

They ate on the deck and later walked the beach, and Alette prowled through the house, sparsely furnished with a wall of books, Indian artifacts, western paintings, a bronze of a cowboy, and Navaho rugs.

"We have to go back," he said after breakfast.

"I know." She joined him, and he wrapped his arm around her waist and pulled her close to walk to the car.

"Alette, do you think your dad will disinherit you?"

"He might."

"I guess I better get a balance sheet and see if I can make up to you part of what you'd lose. I've made some money but not like your father."

"Jeff, how important do you think that is to me?"

He studied her. "I don't think it's all that important, but needed to mention it. After all, you'll be tossing aside fortune for my body."

She laughed and hugged him, and they got into his car to drive back to San Francisco. "We have to decide when we'll tell everyone."

"Let me get you a ring and you can show them."

"Sounds fine to me, except I want to shout it from the rooftops and anyone who sees me will guess."

He laughed. "I feel the same. I'll get the ring damned fast."

She slanted him a look. "You didn't propose on the spur of the moment, did you?"

"What do you think?" he asked softly, catching up her hand to rub her knuckles against his smooth-shaven jaw. "I've been thinking about it for months. Surely you have, too."

"Maybe since shortly after my trial. You never said a word."

"Did I need to?"

"No, you didn't," she said, locking her fingers in his and sighing with a contentment she didn't think she had ever felt before. "I don't care what we have, as long as there's love. I grew up with too little of it. I hope I don't smother you."

He laughed. "Give it a try, Alette. It sounds good to me."

Two weeks later on Monday morning Cheramie called. After a few minutes she asked, "How's everything between you and Jeff? Has Rutger caused a problem yet?"

"No, not really. It's nice. I love Jeff, Cheramie."

"Well, I can't blame you for that. He's so damned handsome. There are drawbacks to being married to a handsome man. Are you going to the Pacific ball next weekend?"

"Yes, we will," Alette answered.

"Good. We're going. Maybe we can get Phillip and Jeff to declare a truce."

"I'm sure they will," Alette replied. They would all be family someday, so the sooner Phillip and Jeff began to get along, the better it would be.

"Phillip has been hell to live with. Life is returning to normal, and our friends seem to forget quickly."

Two hours later Alette received a call from the Capitol and

was told they were ready to commence work on the grounds of the new mansion for the governor. With a smile she listened politely to instructions to call Governor-Elect Jeff O'Neil's assistant, Blake Dorth, about the landscape plans.

In the middle of the afternoon, she talked to Blake; they discussed plans and a time on Tuesday for her to go to Sacramento to take measurements of the grounds. Within an hour Jeff called.

"Blake told me about your appointment with him. I want to look at the mansion, so go with me to meet him. It's going to be where you'll live, too."

"I'm amazed when I think of that," she said. "I'll be landscaping my own grounds."

"Only one term, sweetie. Then we get a private life."

"A politician should never make a rash promise like that," she quipped lightly, yet she knew that was really what she hoped he wanted. "I won't hold you to it."

"I'm getting my own plane so we can get back and forth easily."

"You'll be the first governor to live in the new mansion."

"There's always been controversy about the governor's place. The old mansion is a tourist attraction now. I think the state hopes to start a new tradition here. You're to meet Blake at ten o'clock. I'll pick you up at eight tomorrow morning and we'll have some time together. How about dinner tonight, and I'll make sure you're here by eight tomorrow?"

With a bubbling eagerness she agreed, aware that time seemed suspended when she was with Jeff, became long stretches of emptiness when she was away from him.

The next morning they flew toward a blazing sun to Sacramento, passing over the tall, domed Capitol with its impressive grounds. They drove to the new location, and Alette walked through the two-story stone mansion they would occupy. The carpet was new; the furniture glistened with polish. She felt as if she were in a museum. It was difficult to imagine anyone living in it with its order and silence and newness but as she watched Jeff move through it, she could imagine him fitting in easily. He wasn't intimidated by surrounding or people, accepting either easily. He prowled through th house with the curiosity of a cat, switching lights, sitting on chairs. She watched him move with ease, knowing how fit his body was, knowing how strong he was.

She loved him wildly, passionately, and with a hunger she hadn't thought possible. He had awakened a sensuousness in her she hadn't known could exist.

At ten o'clock she met with Blake, and they discussed possible plantings. She stepped off the grounds and measured everything. She planned to keep all the oaks left behind when they built the house, and she made notes of their location so she could work around them.

Late in the day she flew back to San Francisco with Jeff. That night she lay in his arms and thought how much she loved him. He would be busier soon, leading a public life.

Both of them had appointments early the next morning, and Jeff watched her dress, his gaze following her around the room. "You're ruining my powers of concentration at work."

"Am I really?" she asked, striking a pose with one hip thrust out while she gave him a teasing smile. "That's nice. It makes me feel warm all over to think you can't concentrate because of me."

"It's not so funny, Alette," he said. "Good thing you're out of reach."

"Well, you ruined my concentration long ago, buster," she said lightly.

"That does it," he said, coming off the bed and reaching for her.

"Appointments, remember?"

He groaned. "You make me regret becoming governor. I want to book a flight to Tahiti or Zanzibar or some warm, lazy place and take you away and devour you," he said, nuzzling her neck, his voice becoming husky.

"Instead you have people to see. If I bathe again, Jeff, my skin will drop off."

"We'll see. Maybe if you don't have any skin, I can concentrate."

She laughed and looked into his eyes with satisfaction. "If you can't concentrate anyway, a little more hanky-panky won't do any harm."

"You're wanton," he said, kissing her ear and throat, trailing kisses down the open V of her blouse.

"You made me that way," she whispered, bending her head to kiss him, her hands roaming over him.

"Do we have time for this?"

"Probably not." She twisted her head to look at the clock. "It's half-past eight."

"Oh, Lord, I'm going to be late. I'm meeting a group about earthquake relief at nine."

"How nice," she murmured, stroking him. She stepped back. "Oh, Jeff, it's so much *fun*!"

He laughed and caught her up in his arms, lifting her off the floor and holding her so she was on eye level. "To hell with punctuality," he said, leaning forward to kiss her soundly. When he set her down, he smiled at her. "It is *fun*. And marvelous. We'll race to get to our appointments."

They laughed and locked up and climbed into cars, and he passed her as she drove away. She watched his car and thought how fortunate she was he had come into her life.

On the night of the ball, Jeff took one look at her in a new turquoise-blue silk dress and gave a low, long whistle of appreciation. "I want to hold you, but I suppose it would wrinkle that terribly," he said, aching to reach for her. The ring he was having made would be ready soon, and he couldn't wait. They hadn't set a date, and he had to juggle his inaugural and a wedding, but he wanted to marry more than he had wanted anything.

As they drove toward the Pacific Union Club, Alette twisted on the seat.

"Cheramie and Phillip will be here tonight."

"They're beginning to mingle in society again."

"Of course. They have so many friends here. People forgive and forget, and both Cheramie and Phillip are social people."

"I get the feeling I'm expected to be nice to Phillip Walcott," he said, hoping he could be patient.

"He's my brother-in-law."

"I try to forget that."

"Jeff!"

"Honey, it's a measure of my love that I will go out of my way tonight to be nice to that pompous ass."

"Jeff! Don't call my brother-in-law a pompous ass."

"Aubrey does," he answered drily, thinking Phillip Walcott was one of the most arrogant, pompous jackasses he had ever known.

"I can't do anything about Aubrey."

"What are you going to do about me?" he teased, finding it easy to forget Phillip.

She laughed and leaned across the seat to flick her tongue in his ear.

"Alette, I'm going to turn around and go to my place."

"No, not yet. I've promised we'd put in an appearance. I'll stay on my side of the car."

The dance was in full swing, and they joined friends of Jeff's at a long table. Most were from his campaign staff, Howard and Blake, Tim Kramer and his wife, Joan, a retired Giants player and his date. As they danced the first dance, Alette turned her head. "There's Cheramie and Phillip. When the dance is over, let's go talk to them."

"Sure. I'll start trying to adapt to my future in-law's husband."

"Phillip is charming."

"Said by a woman," he replied in a sardonic tone.

"Men!"

"The music is over and I'll drag out my best behavior with the Walcotts. Your sister will be easy. Talk about charm. She has it all."

"Depends on the viewpoint," Alette said, and waved at them.

"Then we slip out and I get to kiss you."

"You're crazy."

"Crazy for your fair white body, love," he drawled, enjoying making her laugh. He didn't want to look at anyone else or talk to anyone else, and he knew he was more in love each day.

He took Alette's hand as he spotted Phillip Walcott in the crowd. Cheramie was dazzling in a bright green silk dress that plunged to her waist. "Your sister hasn't been too intimidated by the scandal. She's wearing a dress that everyone present will remember. Half the men in the room are watching her."

"She's happiest that way."

"Thank God, you don't need that kind of adoration."

"Aubrey says it's because of the way we grew up. I shut everyone off, he can't face commitment, and Cheramie needs men's approval."

"Well, there's one person you don't shut off any longer," he said lightly.

"For that, Jeff, I'll always love you and be grateful to you. You and Aubrey and Cheramie are the only people I've ever learned to really be myself with. Maybe Victoria Steiner, too, because it was necessity at first. More than any of them, you're the one I don't hold back with at all."

"You would tell me that on a crowded dance floor," he answered just as solemnly, realizing how alone she must have been growing up.

He turned from Alette to Phillip, holding out his hand, thinking the man's friendliness was slightly overdone because if he hadn't been with Alette, Phillip would barely nod. Jeff turned to smile at Cheramie.

"How's the beautiful sister?" he asked lightly, draping his arm over Alette's shoulders.

"Thank you. I'm fine."

She looked gorgeous. Jeff's gaze went from her wide dark eyes to her full red lips, to her slender throat, the plunging neckline. His gaze returned to her throat and the diamond-and-emerald necklace that lay against her breasts. It glittered and sparkled in the light, a fabulous necklace of light and dark, a necklace fit for royalty, jewels for murder. He had seen it once before in Sal Giavotella's hands.

32 ⟿

Later, when he looked back on the evening, Jeff realized he couldn't remember anything he said or did after he noticed the necklace around Cheramie Walcott's neck. When he made love to Alette later, there was a sense of desperation in it, because he felt caught in something that frightened him.

While she slept, he sat up and gazed at her. Her lashes were feathered on her cheek, the sheet pulled up beneath her arms, her slender bare arms flung out, one across his legs. He stroked her hair away from her temple. He wanted to hold her close, to keep her, but he was terrified he was going to lose her.

He thought about the necklace glittering against Cheramie's tawny skin. It was the same necklace Sal had shown him. Cheramie had been Sal's mistress. *And his murderer.*

Jeff raked his fingers through his hair while thoughts tumbled through his mind. Mort Edwards, the investigator, Mel Cipresso and the police, all had checked her whereabouts, and she had two people who testified to being with her, one at the exact time of the murder. Mel Cipresso was satisfied; he'd dropped it as soon as the report came in from Lt. Harberger.

The case was over and done and Jeff could keep quiet and no one would ever know and Alette would be happy. But Sal's murderer would go free. He looked down at Alette, and his heart ached with love and longing. She was all he wanted in a woman. She took his breath away with her beauty, she was sensual and wanton in bed, intelligent, and a sunny disposition was beginning to surface. He knew he could rely on her to stand by him in trouble, but if he caused trouble for her sister, it would be a different matter. Aubrey and Alette both had told him more than once how the three were so close as children, how they stood by each other.

He looked beyond Alette into the darkness and thought that one of them had committed the cruelest deceit possible, a deceit as vile as the murder, because Alette could have gone to prison.

Every time he thought of what Cheramie had put her sister through, anger threatened to destroy logic.

All he had to go on was the necklace. It would be only his word that Sal had showed it to him and said he was giving it to the woman he loved. But Jeff knew it was the same necklace. Everything fit. Cheramie fit the description. She fit what Sal had said. She was the right temperament. And she had a motive.

On the other hand, she had two witnesses who could account for her whereabouts the day of the murder. So he could be wrong. If he was proven wrong, he would lose Alette. He raked his fingers through his already tangled hair. He felt restless, and sleep was impossible. It had to be the same necklace. He looked down at Alette, who rolled over. She stirred, her eyes coming open languorously, focusing on him as she wound her arms tighter around him.

"Jeff?"

He kissed her throat and the corner of her mouth, raising his head to look at her. "I love you, Alette. I don't want to ever lose you."

Drawing her hand over his bare hip, she gave a sleepy laugh. "Fat chance!"

He caught her chin and turned her face up to his to kiss her hungrily, with a longing that went far beyond the physical.

When he moved back, she looked at him in the dark. "Is everything all right?"

"Yes. I was just thinking how much I need you."

She leaned forward to kiss him in return. In minutes she put her head against his shoulder and was soon asleep. Holding her, he stared into the darkness, remembering Sal, thinking of Gina, thinking of Cheramie, who had murdered his friend, framed her sister, and flaunted Sal's magnificent gift

He remembered Sal and the last long conversation, and he could see how Sal would have been dazzled by Cheramie as much as Jeff was by Alette. Sal would have wanted Cheramie physically and wanted her to satisfy his ambition. While he mulled it over, he experienced a mushrooming hate and rage toward Cheramie Walcott.

A week later he still thought about it. He was busier than ever with the transition to Sacramento. Thoughts about the necklace nagged at him until he made an appointment to see Mort Edwards, Alette's private investigator. He sat across the desk in the small office and listened to Mort read from a report.

" 'She bought the dress around half-past four. I remember I got back from a coffee break at four o'clock, and some time passed before I waited on her. It could have been twenty past four, but I think it was four-thirty.' " He looked up, his hazel eyes bland. "Her name is Nelda Spaulding. She's pleasant. She'll be overwhelmed if the governor-elect questions her. And a bachelor at that."

"There's a chance, then, it could have been twenty past four?"

"Yes, there's a chance. She isn't absolute, but she's close to absolute. Enough the cops accepted it."

"Read the report on the other one."

"The hairdresser? Her name is Lillith Goodnoy. She said they take walk-ins. She saw Cheramie sit down, and about five minutes later she was finished with a customer and she took Cheramie. She was through with Cheramie about a quarter past six. She said Cheramie signed in at five o'clock."

"Did anyone else see Cheramie at the beauty salon?"

"I didn't ask."

"I'd like your services for a few days. Go back and ask. See if you can find anyone else who will give you the time Cheramie had her hair done, the time she left the beauty shop."

"Sure. She had to leave about the time she said—almost six-thirty—because she got home and left for the dinner party with her husband, and the police can verify that one. She has a cellular phone in her car, but she was in the hair salon when the calls were made to her sister, and no calls were made from her cellular phone. They checked.''

"See if you can find another witness for the time in the shop."

"This is kind of old business, isn't it?"

"The police won't close the case."

"Maybe you should talk to them."

"I intend to. From the testimony at the trial, a woman was seen going into his condo one time prior to the murder. Did anyone ever see her car?"

"So far, no. I haven't found any information about a car other than his. If he had a mistress, he was damned careful."

"Let me know what you find."

Mort Edwards nodded and tilted his head to study Jeff. "I'm accustomed to these cases and working with people. Something's stirred you up. It might help me to know what."

Jeff debated and nodded and told Mort Edwards all he knew about the necklace. Mort listened with impassive features, and Jeff liked the attentiveness he gave. "Any chance you can find out exactly who purchased the necklace?"

"I'll look into it," Mort said.

"I know you're on Miss Lachman's payroll and you can't violate that, but there is also a cold-blooded, dangerous killer on the loose here. Keep me apprised of what you learn. I don't want Alette in danger."

"I understand. I've got the word on that from Aubrey as well."

After he left Edwards, Jeff felt more disgruntled than before. Cheramie was with a hairdresser and a dress clerk; she couldn't have killed Sal.

He tried to forget, and another week went by. The holidays were approaching, decorations were up, and he was going to take Alette to dinner and give her the ring. He kept it in a dresser drawer at home, waiting for the right night to present it, holding back now for one reason—Cheramie's necklace. He talked to Mel Cipresso, and there were no new developments.

Finally he went to I. Magnin's and met Nelda Spaulding

She was short, blond, and eager to please. She flirted, said she voted for him, and had the longest red fingernails he had ever seen.

"You remember Mrs. Walcott?"

"Lord, yes. Do you know how many times I've been asked about selling her that dress? Now the governor."

"I'm not governor yet," he said pleasantly, "and I'm interested. I'm close friends of the families involved. You're certain she was here at half-past four?"

"Sure. I came back from break at four. I showed her dresses, she tried on the dress and bought it."

"She might have finished about a quarter after four?"

"No. She looked longer than that."

"Maybe until five?"

"No. It was shortly after I got back. It could have been twenty-five after, give or take a minute, but it wasn't much later, it wasn't much earlier."

"But it could have been twenty-five after?"

"Sure. That's almost four-thirty."

"Is twenty after almost four-thirty?"

"Yes."

"Could she have bought it by twenty after?"

"She could have. I think it was closer to half-past, though."

"Do you know for sure?"

"No. I'm guessing."

"Do you wear a watch?"

"No."

"Listen, thanks for taking time to talk to me."

"Sure. Good luck as governor. I'll watch for you on television."

"Thanks."

He left and walked out, thinking about it. If Cheramie had bought a dress at twenty after four, could she have met Sal and gone to his place and gotten there by half-past? He knew she had parked in a garage on Powell. He drove from I. Magnin's to the garage. It took three minutes. He drove from the garage to Sal's condo. It took five minutes. While he retraced his footsteps, he knew he should leave it alone.

The hair salon was busy, every chair taken and one woman waiting. He looked at the sign-in sheet, studying the names, and sat down to wait. A woman came in and signed in and had a seat. In a few minutes a customer left and the operator turned to the woman who had been there when he arrived.

"Ready?"

The woman nodded and stood up, and the operator looked at Jeff. "May I help you, sir?"

"Yes. I want to talk to Lillith Goodnoy."

In minutes an operator approached him. She was a striking blonde, almost six feet tall, with enough hair for three heads. It was crimped and thick and looked like a lion's mane. She focused wide blue eyes on him and smiled. "I know who you are. We're having an argument over it. You're Jeff O'Neil. Maybe I should say Governor O'Neil."

"It's 'governor-elect' until inauguration. I wanted to ask you about the day Sal Giavotella was murdered. Do you mind telling me about Mrs. Walcott coming in?"

"The governor investigates crimes now?"

"I'm not here in any official capacity. I was a friend of Sal Giavotella, and I'm trying to sort out what happened."

Big blue eyes gave him a message that she wasn't buying it. "Well, she signed in, sat down. I saw her come in. I finished a woman and took Mrs. Walcott next," she answered perfunctorily, as if she had said it dozens of times before.

"Do you know the time?"

"She signed in at five o'clock."

"Do you still have the sheet?"

She gave him a toothpaste-ad smile. "I should charge to show it."

He laughed as she went behind the counter and produced a stack of large sheets.

"You have a sense of humor. The police don't. Here's the famous page. Maybe I should frame it."

"For Mrs. Walcott's sake, you better hang on to it."

"She's going to need it?"

"No. I just know she has the most interest in it." He looked at the scrawling signature that read "Cheramie Walcott." In the space next to her name was printed "Five o'clock."

He looked at Leslie Keefe, the name above Cheramie's, and saw "4:56." Lois Schneider, the name following Cheramie's, signed in at 5:21. He pulled out a tablet and wrote down the other names, the one before and the one after.

"Do you know Mrs. Walcott arrived right at five?"

"It says so."

"You didn't look at a clock or a watch when you saw her?"

"No. We were busy, and by five everyone just keeps working and trying to get through. I had a date that night and needed to finish."

"Do you know what time she left?"

"That I know better, because I only had one more appointment. She left about a quarter after six."

"Tell me about doing her hair. What do you do?"

She shrugged. "Just wash hair and set it. She sat under the dryer and then I combed her out."

He turned to look at the dryers that were on the other side of a latticework partition that partially hid them from the view of the operators.

"Do you know if she left the dryer at any time?"

"No. Not that I know of. That's a new question. No one has asked me about her leaving."

"Could she have left the dryers and you might not have noticed?"

"Sure. I was busy with the next customer. I wash one while the previous client dries. My back is to the dryers."

"Is there a phone around here I can use?"

"Yes." She bent down and picked up a phone and placed it on the counter.

"I don't want to tie up that one. Is there another?"

"The hotel has pay phones in the lobby. They're right across the hall to your right. You can't miss them."

"Thanks so much. Are either one of these women repeat customers?"

She looked at the names he had written down and shook her head. "No. I don't know them at all."

"Thanks, Lillith."

A wide smile was bestowed on him. "You're welcome. Anytime. We cut men's hair, too."

He winked at her. "I'll remember." He moved to the front of the shop where women were seated beneath dryers. He glanced at his watch and went into the lobby, spotting the pay phones immediately. They were just across the hall. He drove to the Hall of Justice.

Mel Cipresso leaned back in the chair. "What the hell is this? You're detective now? Want to try another Lachman? Or do you know something I don't know?"

"Did anyone talk to either Leslie Keefe or Lois Schneider?" he asked, avoiding the last question. He couldn't bring Mel and the SFPD into it until he was ready to tell Alette. "Is everyone taking Cheramie's word that the time she signed on the sheet was the actual time? What's to keep someone from walking in there at five-fifteen and signing five o'clock?"

"Not much of anything, and we thought about that, and we can't find the woman who came in after Cheramie Walcott. Remember, that's a hotel. She could be from anywhere in the world. She could have flown in with a husband from Argentina or Des Moines. We can't find her."

"Well, hell."

"True. Do you know something?"

"I just got to thinking about the time. What about th woman who signed in before?"

"She lives in San Francisco, and by five o'clock she wa getting her hair washed, so she didn't see anything. We can find anyone who can say Cheramie Lachman did or did no arrive at that shop exactly at five. There you are."

"If the dress clerk was off ten minutes, she could hav arrived at Sal's place around four-thirty."

"Right."

"If she really arrived at the beauty shop at twenty minut past five, she could have shot him. It's only blocks from Sal to the hotel with the beauty shop. The garage where her c was parked is across the street from the shop. She had tin to drop the weapon in Alette's car and still get home to go the dinner."

"Right. But we have two witnesses who say she was the at half-past four, and she signed in at five. And we don't ha one thing to implicate her other than the description, which fits Alette Lachman, Cheramie Lachman, Gina Giavotella, and God knows how many women in San Francisco.''

''Okay. I'll get out of your way. Thanks.''

''It's against the law to withhold evidence. Let me know if you turn up something.''

Jeff went home and for two more days thought of Cheramie and the necklace. If he told what he knew, he could easily lose Alette, because she was so fiercely loyal to her brother and sister. Yet Cheramie had murdered a man, and he could see only one choice. He reached for the phone and called Aubrey.

33

Aubrey came out of his office when Jeff arrived. ''Let's go to the boat and have a beer.''

''I needed to see you,'' Jeff said when they were seated in the salon. ''Shortly before his death I met Sal at his office. He told me about the woman in his life. He didn't tell me her name, but when I accused him of a midlife crisis, he went to his safe and removed a necklace. It was diamonds and emeralds; he'd had it made for the woman in his life. The necklace would cost more than my boat.'' Jeff took a deep breath and felt as if he might begin to lose Alette in the next moment. ''At the Pacific ball, Cheramie was wearing that necklace.''

Aubrey was stretched back on a settee, his feet on a table. He lowered the beer. ''You made a mistake.''

''No, I didn't. You don't forget a piece of jewelry like this one, and I'll never forget Sal showing it to me. It was the first I knew about his divorce.''

''Cheramie wouldn't take such a risk. How could she explain it to Phillip? How could she explain it to anyone?''

"I don't know. That's why I came to you first instead of Mel Cipresso. I'm not wrong about the necklace. Everything fits. I've talked to Nelda Spaulding at I. Magnin's. I drove to the garage where Cheramie parked. I drove to Sal's. I went to the walk-in beauty shop. If Lillith Goodnoy and Nelda Spaulding don't have the time exactly right," Jeff said carefully, aware of sparks of anger showing in Aubrey's eyes, "Cheramie could have shot Sal."

"The police went over that. Mort went over it."

"I talked to those two women. They're not giving exact times. The one at Magnin's doesn't wear a watch. Lillith Goodnoy is going by the time Cheramie signed on the sheet."

"Cheramie would be crazy to wear the necklace. Except Cheramie is vain as hell and loves expensive things." Aubrey was growing a beard, and sandy stubble covered his jaw. He rubbed it with the tips of his long fingers while he thought about it. "You feel certain it's the same necklace?"

"Absolutely."

"If Cheramie could explain the necklace to Phillip, and if Sal were as secretive as indicated, she might not be afraid to wear it. Cheramie would want to wear something like that. Do you know where it came from?"

"Cartier."

"The police can check on it."

"I'll bet there is no Giavotella name. It'll be another name."

"You think he paid cash?"

"Yes. Sal was a great believer in avoiding a paper trail. know that from doing business with him."

"Cheramie wouldn't set Alette up for murder. You're dead wrong."

"Is there any way you can find out who Cheramie say gave it to her?"

"Hell, I don't see Cheramie often."

"Do you have any women friends who do?"

"We don't move in the same circles." He rubbed his jaw again. "I guess when I stop to think about it, we have mutual friends. I know someone." He stood up and finished the beer

"Let me make a call. I'll find out. This woman will notice a new bauble."

"Bauble isn't the right word. This necklace is fit for the queen of England."

"Cheramie couldn't resist wearing something like that if she thought she could get away with it," Aubrey said again, a frown furrowing his brow.

"You know what you may find out," Jeff said solemnly.

"If she shot Giavotella and tried to pin the fucking rap on Alette, then I don't give a shit. When I think how close Alette came to prison, I break out in a sweat. But I think you're wrong. I think you're dead wrong. Cheramie's selfish, but we're so damned close in some ways. She's closer to Alette." He rubbed the nape of his neck, talking as if he were thinking out loud and had forgotten Jeff, staring beyond Jeff. "Cheramie can be bitchy, so like Rutger. I hope you're wrong. I don't think Cheramie would stoop to setting up her own sister, but she didn't hesitate when we were kids if she could get away with it."

"That's a far cry from this. Go make your call."

Jeff watched sailboats glide out to the bay and others come sailing in.

Aubrey reappeared and sank down on the settee. "I found a friend who knew," he said cheerfully, and Jeff could see the relief in his expression. "Rutger gave it to her." Jeff drank the cold beer, feeling it go down, thinking about Alette.

"You don't believe that, do you?" Aubrey asked.

"No."

"Her friend was more impressed with it than you are. The necklace must be spectacular."

"It is."

There was a silence, and the look of worry had returned to Aubrey's features. "It'll be trickier to find out from Rutger."

"Would he lie about it to protect her?"

Aubrey stared at the water. "I don't know. If he bought it at Cartier, it'll be on his bill."

Jeff turned his head. "I'm going to call Cartier and tell hem I'm Rutger and my bill is screwed up—"

Aubrey stood up. "I'll do it. I can answer security questions to identify Rutger and you can't. Family friends say our voices are alike. And I know who to call at Cartier's."

He was gone a shorter time. He sat down and picked up the beer. "They're looking for the bill. I told them I wasn't at home and I'll call back in half an hour."

"Suppose they call Rutger? Just to check."

"We take that chance. I don't think they will."

They talked about baseball and the holidays. "What do you do over the holidays?" Jeff asked.

"This year I'm going home with Vic to meet her family. I'm going to ask her to marry me."

"Hey, that's great. Congratulations."

"Tell me that when she says yes. My sister is independent, but compared with Victoria Steiner, she doesn't know what the word means."

Jeff laughed. "Good luck, then." He wanted to tell Aubrey about the ring for Alette and their plans, but the necklace loomed as an obstacle that made their future impossible to predict.

In half an hour Aubrey went back to the phone. He returned and plopped down, his elbows on his knees. "They can't find the record of the sale. I asked to check if Phillip bought it and the charge got on Rutger's bill by mistake."

Jeff took a deep breath. "I didn't think they would have any record of Rutger purchasing it. Alette will hate me for this," he said, finally voicing his concern.

"God, I can't believe Cheramie would do that to her!" Aubrey stood up to pace back and forth. "I'll talk to Rutger. I don't know why they can't find a ticket, but Cheramie wouldn't hurt Alette badly. Not with a murder rap."

Jeff ran his hand over his head. "Aubrey, sooner or later I've got to tell Mel Cipresso. I can't let her go if she murdered a man."

Aubrey swore and stared at the water. "No, you don't have a choice."

"I don't want to tell him. I'm afraid when I do, I'll lose Alette."

"I'll call you as soon as I talk to Rutger."

As Jeff stepped off the boat, Aubrey called to him and he turned around.

"If Cheramie did that, she's capable of doing it again."

Jeff nodded. "I'll be careful. The minute I get something definite, I'll turn it over to Mel Cipresso."

He sat in his car a long time, debating about it, knowing Rutger hadn't given Cheramie the necklace, knowing Cartier would never find the bill under Rutger's name or Sal's name. He swore and backed out to drive to the Hall of Justice, knowing he really didn't have a choice at all.

An hour later Jeff stared at Mel's jaw, which was thrust forward, a muscle working in his cheek while he scowled.

"Dammit, I can't go on anything that flimsy. I'll check the records at Cartier, see if Sal Giavotella bought the necklace. But if there isn't a sales transaction recorded, then it's your word against hers. Even if she can't prove who gave it to her, that's not enough to take into a courtroom when she has two witnesses who say they were with her that afternoon and one of them will say she was with her at the exact time Sal was shot."

"But Lillith Goodnoy is going by the sheet where Cheramie signed in. Find Lois Schneider, who signed next after Cheramie at twenty-one after five. If she can say Cheramie was sitting there waiting to get her hair done at twenty-one after five, you have a case. Lillith Goodnoy didn't go by a watch or clock. She went by what Cheramie had signed. She saw her sit there about five minutes, and she did her hair. Later she went back and looked and saw Cheramie had signed in at five, so she told the police Cheramie arrived at five, but that's all she was going on."

"Okay, okay. Let me check, but if it comes to nothing, your word about the necklace isn't enough. I'm not taking another Lachman to court on less evidence than the first and get blasted again. My career can't take it."

Jeff left, knowing the next place he had to go was Alette's.

34

Jeff took Alette to dinner, and then they went back to her house. The moment they were alone, he pulled her into his arms to make love to her, because he was so frightened of losing her. As he was poised over her, she gazed up at him, desire burning in her eyes, her mouth red from his kisses. He thought he would burst with love for her.

She pulled him to her and he entered her, moving with her, feeling her long legs and slender arms hold him tightly while she cried out his name until he covered her mouth and kissed her as they climaxed together. He kept kissing her, wanting to hold her in his arms and never let go, declaring his love over and over.

After dinner she sat in his arms with him on the sofa. She trailed her fingers along the round neck of his T-shirt.

"Bad day at the office or bad politics?" she asked.

"What makes you think something is wrong?" he asked in surprise, because he thought he had kept his worries hidden.

"You keep watching me, like something is really bothering you."

"You're right," he said, exhaling his breath. He rubbed his hand along her arm, wanting to hold her, feeling an undercurrent of fear he had never known. "There is something wrong. Before I tell you, I want you to think about something. I love you. I love you more than I've ever loved anyone or ever will love anyone. I need you desperately," he said in a husky voice.

Her dark eyes widened as she watched him solemnly, and she slid her arms around his neck and leaned forward to kiss him a long time.

When she pulled away, she stroked his cheek. Unable to

imagine what was disturbing him so badly that would involve her, she smiled at him. "Now why the worry?"

"Remember, I told you about Sal showing me a necklace he bought for the woman he loved?"

"Yes, I remember," she said.

"I've seen that necklace on a woman."

"You have? How do you know it's the same one?"

"Because it is a magnificent piece of jewelry he had made for her. No one would forget it. He showed it to me when he told me about his divorce. I was shocked, and I can remember vividly."

Alette stared at him and sat up straighter, because Jeff was upset and had put off discussing it, so it had to involve her. And she remembered seeing a necklace recently that was spectacular. "The last time we saw Cheramie, she had on a new necklace," she said. "It was gorgeous. Phillip gave it to her."

Jeff blinked and frowned. "How do you know Phillip gave it to her?"

"I heard Rutger compliment her on it."

Jeff closed his eyes and leaned his head back against the sofa and swore beneath his breath.

"Jeff, Phillip gave her that necklace. You're mistaken. I know it's a gorgeous necklace, but it's not the one—"

"She told one of her friends that Rutger gave it to her," he interrupted her in a flat voice, raising his head to meet her gaze.

"They must have misunderstood her."

"Did you misunderstand her?"

"No, I didn't. Jeff, that couldn't have been Cheramie. That's absurd! Stop worrying about something so ridiculous. People have said they were with her when Sal was shot. There are sworn affidavits from witnesses who vouched for her time."

"They think they were with her, but the hairdresser is going on the time Cheramie signed in, not the time she actually saw Cheramie arrive at the shop."

"Aubrey went over all of that, and her time was accounted for. Just because she has a lovely new necklace—"

"Alette, that's the necklace Sal showed me. It's absolutely unforgettable."

"Men don't remember jewelry or clothes."

"This man does when his best friend produces something like that necklace and announces he has just asked his wife and mother of their six children for a divorce. I won't forget that necklace in Sal's hands for the rest of my life."

"Maybe there are two necklaces just alike," she said, sliding off his lap and moving away. Her irritation grew over his stubborn arguments. "Two people were with Cheramie; she couldn't have been the murderer." She faced him, sparks dancing in her eyes, anger slowly rising. "You've made a mistake."

"I've been to see Aubrey."

"Aubrey believes you?"

"He's listening to me. He called Cartier. They don't have a sales record for the necklace to either Rutger or Phillip."

"They told him that?"

"He said he was Rutger and his bill was mixed up, and he called later and asked if Phillip could have made the purchase, and they said he hadn't."

"Did he think to ask if Sal Giavotella bought the necklace? That seems the logical thing to do."

"Mel Cipresso will do that, but I know Sal. It won't be in his name. There will be no Giavotella name in their records, and they'll never find the man who made the purchase."

"You've been to see Mel Cipresso," she said quietly, anger increasing because she felt he was wrong. "My sister would never try to send me to prison. Never!"

"Not even if it meant she wouldn't have to go?"

"No! Cheramie wouldn't. She's in the clear, and you're doing this to her."

"For just a minute, suppose I'm right. Don't you see why I had to go to Cipresso?"

"No, all you'll do is cause trouble for Cheramie, and she'll hate you for it. She didn't commit murder!"

"Someone did who knew you well."

"That includes many people." She moved impatiently. "Why are you doing this?"

"Because I know that's the necklace."

"And I know it's not. If Sal gave her that—which is impossible—she wouldn't wear it."

"You wouldn't wear it. You sister would. She'd think she could get away with it."

"Not by telling Rutger that Phillip gave it to her and telling Phillip that Rutger gave it to her!" Alette retorted, becoming angry with him and wondering why he was persisting.

"They're not going to compare notes about the necklace."

"They could easily mention it to the other."

"I know that's the same necklace."

"Doesn't it occur to you that there is a slim possibility you're wrong?"

"I can't forget it."

Her anger grew, and she went to the telephone to pick up the receiver. Instantly he moved and jammed down the button. He was inches away, and her head came up to glare at him. "I'll call Cheramie and ask and you can have the truth," she said. "We can settle this quickly and in a minute."

"Stop and think first. If there is a chance I'm right, you shouldn't call her. She'll get rid of it or get someone to lie for her or do something. And if she murdered a man, she could do something violent again."

"Jeff, I don't believe this!" Alette glared at him, and Jeff hurt, because he had known what her reaction would be just as he knew what he had to do.

"Alette, answer one question."

"All right."

He ached, he wanted her so badly. He knew he was hurting her, and he didn't want to. He wanted her in his arms. He wanted to marry her. "Just suppose what I'm saying about Cheramie and the necklace is true. Would you want me to turn a blind eye and live with the fact that she murdered Sal?"

She blinked and stared at him. "If Cheramie murdered Sal, and you knew it, you wouldn't have a choice. You'd have to go to the police. But that isn't the case! You're fabricating this out of nothing! You've been to the DA with this! I can't believe you would involve Cheramie. There is no reason to do so. None. Unless . . ." She stared at him in stony silence.

He slid his hands up her arms to her shoulders. "Alette, I'm not doing this to discredit Cheramie."

She tried to wriggle away, and he held her. "Alette," he whispered. As he leaned forward to kiss her, she looked at him with a stony gaze.

"Maybe Rutger is right again."

"About what?"

"Revenge."

He felt as if she had slapped him. He raised his head. "You think I'm doing this to get back at him?"

"It would fit! I don't know why else you're doing it! Cheramie suffered enough with Phillip's infidelity and scandal. Now you come up with this, trying when you know she was elsewhere to tie her into a murder! You know it isn't true. So that leaves only one thing—you're going to get back at Rutger! Or get back at all of us! My sister never would do something to send me to prison! Cheramie wouldn't do that to me."

He tried to cling to patience, but he was angry with her accusations, hurt over what he knew he had to do, and frightened of losing her. He pulled her to him, one strong arm banding her waist, his hand cupping her head. She fought against him, pushing against his chest.

He kissed her, thrusting his tongue into her mouth, holding her until her struggles ended. She stood still in his arms, trying to resist, and he leaned over her, bending her backward, wanting her to yield until finally she slid her arms to his shoulders.

When he released her, they both were breathing as if they had been running. "You think that isn't real?" he asked gruffly.

"It's physical!"

"The hell it is. It goes deeper than just something physical when we kiss, and you know damn well it does!"

"Rutger was right about you. I'm gullible. I want you to go, Jeff."

He closed his eyes, because her request hurt like an actual blow. "All right, I'll go, because I know you're shocked, but you think about what I've said."

"If you stir this up for Cheramie, don't come back. Don't call me. I have to believe Rutger if you continue to pursue this, because there is only one reason for it—to hurt the Lachmans. Cheramie wouldn't frame me. Get out, Jeff."

"I'm going," he said quietly.

He left, closing the door behind him. Alette stared at the empty door without moving. She loved Jeff, and she didn't think he knew what he was talking about when he said it was the same necklace. It could so easily be similar, and a man who saw it only once wouldn't know.

For the first time in her life in a crisis, she didn't want to turn to Aubrey. She didn't want anyone except Jeff.

Jeff had gone into business to ruin Rutger; had he dated her to cause more trouble? Or was he simply mistaken? It had to be one or the other, not that Cheramie was guilty.

She had been cleared by the investigator, by the police.

Alette dropped down on a chair and rubbed her forehead, hurting badly.

Two days later she hadn't heard anything from Jeff. She was at work when the bell jingled and Aubrey entered.

"You're a stranger," she said, leaning back in her chair, scared she would burst into tears if she told him about Jeff.

"I thought you might call me."

"Was I supposed to?"

"I've talked to Jeff. You didn't believe him about Cheramie. He said you don't want to see him."

She stared at Aubrey. "Surely you don't believe him?"

Aubrey pulled up a chair and sat down across from her. "Yes, I'm beginning to."

"Aubrey! How can you! You're the one who checked on Cheramie and found out she was having her hair done when Sal was murdered. Do you think our sister would cause me to go to prison?"

"Alette, Jeff is positive about that necklace."

"He saw it only a few minutes. He's not a jeweler. Men don't know about necklaces—unless they're in the business or have a hobby or a real penchant for jewelry or clothes. A baseball player sees a necklace one time for a few minutes and later sees another diamond-and-emerald necklace and thinks it's the same one. Can't you see how easily he could be wrong?''

''He said he will never forget the necklace.''

''Rutger said Jeff just wants to hurt us—''

''Bullshit. I know you don't want to accept facts about Cheramie,'' Aubrey said tensely, ''and that's blinding you—''

''Blind! You're taking Jeff's side because he's opposed to Rutger. You've suspected Cheramie from the first, and when you got proof it wasn't her, you still can't drop it. I don't want to hear any more about it.''

''Do you miss him?''

''You know I do,'' she said stiffly.

''Alette, I know how close you are to Cheramie, and she's your older sister, but—''

''I don't want to hear it, Aubrey.''

''Okay. I'll come back when you do. Don't get as bull-headed as Rutger.''

He left, the door swinging shut behind him, and she put her head in her hands to cry.

The following week she had an appointment in Sacramento to go over the final blueprints of the landscape plans with Blake Dorth. They walked the grounds and discussed the plans, finally going to his office at the Capitol to look at blueprints. When she was finished, she gathered her things and left. Outside, she met Jeff coming up the steps and her heart seemed to stop beating. His golden hair was slightly tangled, his coat swinging open, and she longed to touch him. She felt a constriction that was painful, and she wondered if she would ever get over him.

He looked up, his gaze meeting hers with an impact that was physical. His gaze lowered slowly, drifting down over her to her toes and back up. It was leisurely, bold, arrogant, and she thought she ought to feel a stir of anger, but all she could feel was desire kindling. She wanted to walk into his arms and kiss him wildly.

''Hello,'' he said quietly. ''Have an appointment with Blake?''

''Yes. I'll start work on the grounds in January.''

"I'll be living there in January. The Governor's Inaugural Committee set the ball for January eleventh and my inaugural is January fourteenth. Want to go to the ball with me?" he asked.

"Under the circumstances, I don't think so, no," she said stiffly, aching to accept. Right now as she gazed into his eyes, she felt caught in a sensual challenge.

"How have you been?" he asked softly.

"Fine." They stared at each other, and she thought he could hear her heart thud.

Jeff nodded and gazed at her with a searching look. She didn't want to turn and walk away, because she felt as if she were walking out of his life permanently, yet she had really done so already.

"Good-bye, Jeff." She walked away briskly. The moment she was in the car, tears came, blurring her vision.

On New Year's Eve the phone rang at one, and Aubrey greeted her. "Happy New Year, Alette! This is the greatest year of my life!"

"Happy New Year, Aubrey!" She laughed. "I hope you aren't driving anywhere."

"Oh, yes. I'll drive us back to Vic's later. I'm sober. Vic wants to talk to you."

"Alette!" Victoria Steiner's voice came over the line, and she giggled. Alette couldn't imagine giggles coming from Victoria.

"The party must be great," she said dryly.

"It is! It's fabulous. Alette, I'm so happy! We're engaged. I want you in my wedding!"

"Engaged! My brother—engaged? I'm so glad, Victoria! I'm really so glad," she exclaimed with sincerity, feeling happy for Aubrey, thankful that he could finally make a commitment, hoping the scars of childhood would fade for him. They talked, but it didn't make much sense except she learned they were going to get married the last week in February. Aubrey came back on the line.

"Congratulations, big brother," she said. "I'm really happy, Aubrey. Victoria is wonderful."

"I think so. Thanks. Her parents are great, and they seem
to accept me."

"Of course they'd accept you!" she exclaimed, laughing.

"My own father doesn't. He'll accept Victoria, though.
Isn't that the crock? We get back to the city tomorrow night.
Go to dinner with us."

"I'd love to. Aubrey, I'm so glad."

"Did you see Jeff tonight?"

"You know that's over."

"Oh, hell. You know how I feel about that. You're hurting
Jeff. Vic's giving me looks. I'll call you when we get to town
tomorrow."

She hung up, smiling as she sat down, and then a spurt of
tears came, because her thoughts turned to Jeff. She thought
about Aubrey standing by Jeff so vehemently. For the first
time she considered the possibility that Jeff was right.

Alette saw him on television at the inaugural and in the
paper, a beautiful blond woman at his side, smiling at the
camera. Alette didn't know she could hurt so badly.

As the week passed she mulled over the dilemma. She
decided to confront Cheramie. She wanted to see Cheramie's
reactions, and then she could decide whether Jeff's charges
were absurd or not. And she could find out exactly who had
given the necklace to her sister.

Late in the afternoon on Tuesday, she called Cheramie and
invited her for lunch on Thursday. A suppressed excitement
tinged the hours, because Alette expected to get the truth and
eliminate the wedge that had come between Jeff and her.

Wednesday morning she was due to oversee the initial
phases of landscaping the mansion in Sacramento.

35 ⚘

Jeff barely listened to Clyde Taylor. He was due at the Capitol in twenty minutes, and it was time to leave, but he couldn't move away from the window. He stood in the large, high-ceilinged office of the new governor's mansion and watched Alette moving around the yard. A nurseryman and landscape contractor were there. She was probably talking about plants and sprinklers, and Jeff ached so much watching her, he wanted to go out and take her by the arm and pull her into the house and into his arms. And he knew it was impossible. He had seen her once at the opera with a tall blond man. She hadn't seen him. He dated, most of the time Mitzi because of their old friendship, but it was no more than friendship, and he had no interest in any other woman. He loved Alette, and she was the only woman he had ever truly loved.

"Jeff, you're going to be late."

"I'm coming," Jeff said.

"And I'm going. See you in a few minutes."

Clyde left the room, and Jeff stood watching Alette. She wore a full royal blue skirt, a tweedy jacket that swung open to reveal a blue sweater, and high-heeled pumps. Her hair was longer, caught behind her head in a barrette. Without looking around, he reached for his coat and knocked a paper-weight off his desk. He swore, picked it up, pulled on his coat, picked up a briefcase, and went back to the window. He was usually punctual, so failure one time wouldn't be the end of the world.

He thought about Mel Cipresso. They couldn't find Lois Schneider, who had signed in after Cheramie. Jeff suggested having the registers of other hotels nearby, and Harberger was checking. Jeff talked to Jay Harberger once a week, and so far nothing had turned up. Jeff swore quietly as he thought about it, damning Sal for covering his tracks so thoroughly. Two people shouldn't be able to hide from the world, particularly two who looked like Sal and Cheramie.

Jeff was half tempted to confront Cheramie and see if he could rattle her enough into making a mistake. He had talked it over with Harberger, who told him to leave police work to the police. He had discussed it briefly with Aubrey, who said it would only help Cheramie to hide things. Jeff had the ring for Alette in a box in his desk. His folks missed her and knew he was suffering. He swore, picked up the briefcase, and strode outside.

She turned before he reached her, and he looked into her wide eyes. His heart contracted violently. "Good morning," he said, at a loss for words, not trusting himself to speak for a moment. He didn't know he could want someone as badly as he wanted her.

"I thought you'd be gone by now."

"I'm going. Aubrey told me he's engaged to Victoria."

"Yes, they called New Year's Eve and told me. I'm so happy for him, and I think it's wonderful."

"How have you been?"

"Just fine."

He hated the polite conversation. He drew a deep breath, saw her gaze rake over him and swiftly jerk back up to meet his eyes while her cheeks turned pink. He wondered what she was thinking.

"I miss you," he said tersely. She blinked and paled and looked down quickly, rubbing her fingers together. He was thankful to see that she still missed him. He wanted to fling down the briefcase and scoop her into his arms so badly, he clenched his fist and gripped the briefcase tightly. He couldn't resist reaching out to brush her shoulder.

Her head snapped up, and he shrugged. "You had some lint," he lied. He would swear she looked on the verge of crying, and he wondered if he was misreading signals.

"I saw your picture in the paper. The woman with you was pretty."

"I haven't called her since." He stared at her, knowing

time was passing and he should be at the Capitol; they were still at an impasse. "I'm late as hell for a meeting," he said, and they were caught in another long, tense silence. "I thought it was bad when I hurt my arm."

Someone called to her, and she turned away. "Cheramie's coming to my place for lunch Thursday," she said in a tight voice.

He nodded, wondering if she'd flung that at him to remind him how loyal she was to her sister. He turned and strode swiftly into the house, past the startled cook, and to the library to pick up the phone and dial Jay Harberger.

"Morning, Gover—"

"Have you found any damn thing yet on the Giavotella case?"

"No. We're still trying."

"Everyone knows there was a woman in Sal's life. Surely you can find someone who saw him with her."

"We're looking. The man was as careful as they come, because everything is a dead end. We've found an apartment in Washington. It was his. It was under the name John Williams. Now we're trying the neighbors. The neighborhood is yuppie, young couples on the move, singles, people who don't stay in one place long or have time to chat with the neighbors."

"Call me the minute you learn anything."

"I will."

Jeff slammed down the phone and left for the Capitol. Between meetings he called Aubrey to see if he had learned anything new about the necklace.

"No. I'd call you if I had."

"I talked to Harberger," Jeff said. "Sal had an apartment in Washington. It was under the name John Williams. They're checking neighbors."

"I'll let Mort Edwards know. If he has anything, I'll call."

"You do. Get me out of a meeting. Tell them it's an emergency. I saw Alette this morning. She said she's having Cheramie over for lunch Thursday."

"They used to have lunch together often."

"Call me, Aubrey." Jeff hung up and looked at his calenar. He had a committee meeting in three minutes, and all he could think about was Alette.

Alette moved around the yard and knew if she didn't get out of there, she might burst into tears in front of everyone. Jeff's words ran through her mind constantly. He looked thinner and as grim as she felt. *"I thought it was bad when I hurt my arm. . . ."*

"Are you all right, Miss Lachman?" asked Chuck Price, the nurseryman.

"I don't feel well. I think I'll go now unless you have more questions."

"No."

She hurried to her car and drove back to the airport to get the Lachman jet to San Francisco. She had to confront Cheramie, to find out absolutely the truth about the necklace and resolve things with Jeff, because she couldn't stand the separation.

Thursday morning Alette finished her appointment by eleven and went home to fix lunch for her sister. She felt tense and worried, because she had to ask Cheramie some direct questions.

36 ~~~~~

Aubrey finished the contract and put it in a folder. He had an appointment tomorrow morning to sell a boat. He glanced down at his watch, pulled over the paper to scan the headlines, saw Jeff's name, and thought about Jeff and Alette. And he thought about Jeff's last phone call. Something nagged at him. He rubbed his jaw; half an hour later he sat up straight and swore. He yanked up the phone and punched a number and received Alette's answering machine at home. When the signal came on indicating he could leave a message, he said, "Alette, call me immediately. This is an emergency. It's a quarter before one o'clock. I'm in my office."

He hung up and yanked up the phone book to call the governor's office.

Jeff sat back in the private dining room that had been reserved for a lunch meeting with the head of the warehouseman's union and two assemblymen. His thoughts kept drifting to Alette while he tried to pay attention to Roger Handwier, an assemblyman. A waiter entered the room and leaned down beside Jeff.

"Governor O'Neil, you have a call. You can take it in the office. It's a Mr. Lachman, who said it's an emergency."

"Excuse me a moment, gentlemen," Jeff said, and stood up. He hoped Aubrey had a break on the case, some bit of news that would solve it and end the doubts in Alette's mind, because his nerves were frayed and his concentration wasn't on his work. His stride was long as he followed the waiter to an empty office. He closed the door, and when he heard Aubrey's voice, his breath caught and held.

"Jeff, sorry to get you out of a lunch meeting like this. Tell me again what you said about Alette and Cheramie having lunch."

"God, I thought maybe you had something!" Jeff exclaimed. "Everyone's all right?"

"Jeff, tell me quickly."

Perplexed, he said, "They're having lunch together."

"Exact words. That isn't what you said before."

"She said, 'Cheramie's coming to my place for lunch Thursday.' Those are exact words, I think."

"So they're eating at Alette's?"

"I suppose so. Why?"

"They've eaten together for years and never once at either home. Never."

"Why would——" He stopped, suddenly guessing what was worrying Aubrey. "She's going to tell Cheramie my accusations."

"I've tried to call her place. The answering machine is on."

"Surely Cheramie wouldn't hurt her sister. She wouldn't gain anything."

"I don't like the idea of Alette with her. Alette's very frank, and Cheramie is emotional and mean when cornered. Call that lieutenant you know, Harberger, and tell him to get someone to Alette's on some pretense. Anything. Just get someone over there. I'm on my way now."

"Call me," Jeff said tersely, and for once he was going to take advantage of his office to get things done. He called Harberger first and told him, then he called his office and made arrangements to go straight to the airport and fly to San Francisco. He hurried back to the table to excuse himself and left, praying for Alette's safety.

Alette opened the door to face Cheramie, who stood with boxes in her hands and looking gorgeous as usual. Her hair was still short and curly; she wore navy wool slacks and blazer and a white turtleneck shirt with a bright red scarf around her neck.

"I still say we should have eaten out," Cheramie said, sweeping in past Alette, her arms ladened with packages. "You're getting terribly domestic. One thing about having a husband caught in an affair—it gives me free rein with his checkbook. I bought the most beautiful dress today."

"The salads are in the refrigerator. Go ahead and show me," Alette said, trying to be polite, following her plans to wait until after lunch for any serious talk, because even if innocent, Cheramie was still going to be furious with Jeff O'Neil when she learned his accusations.

Cheramie spilled packages over a chair. "I want to show you everything!" She flung aside the lid of a box and lifted out a Christian Dior blue silk dress. While Alette gave appropriate comments, Cheramie went through five packages with a silk blouse, an Ultrasuede skirt, a new pair of lizard pumps, and a bottle of perfume.

"You bought all this in one morning!"

Cheramie laughed. "Shopping gives me great pleasure.

know it eats on Phillip. Rutger never cared, because he wanted all of us to dress well, but Phillip wants to know where his dollars are going. They're going a lot faster now, I can tell you!''

"Come in the kitchen. It's just the two of us, and I'll put things on the table.''

They ate chicken salads and had lemon cookies for dessert with cups of hot black coffee. They talked about clothes and the boys and harmless topics, and finally, as they sat back at the table, Cheramie studied Alette.

"You said you and Jeff haven't patched things up. I'm sorry. Why don't you come to our house for dinner Saturday night? I have three bachelors on my guest list.''

"Oh, no, Cheramie. Maybe Jeff and I will get back together. I'm not interested right now.'' As much as she hated to bring up the topic, because she knew it would unleash a storm of fury in Cheramie, she had to, and now was the time. Alette fully expected her to account for the necklace, to offer to show it to Jeff, to find that he was mistaken; but if all that proved to be exactly right, Cheramie wouldn't forgive him for a long time, and she would be in a rage. And if he were right—Alette couldn't imagine it.

"I never told you why we separated, did I?'' Alette said, studying Cheramie, knowing she had to see her face to face when she brought up the subject of the necklace. She had turned on the recorder so the phone wouldn't interrupt them, because she didn't want anything to break into the conversation. She thought she would be able to tell Cheramie's guilt or innocence if she could see her expression.

"No, you didn't,'' Cheramie replied, "but I figured it was none of my business, so I didn't ask.''

"It was over you,'' Alette said, feeling a knot of tension growing.

Cheramie frowned and stared at her. "Why over me? I don't know Jeff, and I've never gone out with him.''

"I know you haven't. Jeff thinks you murdered Sal Giavoella,'' she said quickly.

All color drained from Cheramie's face. In that one moment of silence, the change in complexion was an answer.

Alette stared at her in shock. Guilt was the only emotion that could have transformed Cheramie so suddenly. There was no surprised protest, no startled disbelief. Cheramie caught herself, but that moment of truth was impossible to erase, and Alette stared at her as if she were unable to comprehend it was her sister seated across from her.

"That's absurd! I didn't know Sal Giavotella," Cheramie said brightly, color flooding her cheeks.

"You would have let me go to prison," Alette whispered, staring at Cheramie, still in shock.

"Don't be absurd, Alette! That's why you broke off with Jeff? Why did he accuse me? He has to have a reason."

"He does. I didn't think he was right. I accused him of all the things Rutger accused him of doing—spite, revenge, hatred of the Lachmans."

"Rutger is right more often than wrong, unfortunately." Cheramie lit a cigarette and stood up, carrying her dishes to the sink. She turned around to pick up her cup and saucer. "What reason does he have to accuse me of a thing like that? I was in a beauty shop when Sal Giavotella was shot. I can account for my time. Phillip and I have already had to do that," she said sharply.

"You wore the necklace that Sal gave you."

Again Cheramie paled, drawing a sharp breath. As if recovering her poise, she blinked and gave a harsh laugh. "That's absurd!" She carried the cup and saucer toward the sink.

"You wore it to the Pacific Ball, and he's told the police you did. He's been to Lt. Harberger and—"

Cheramie dropped the cup and saucer she was carrying. The china struck the floor and splintered. Ignoring the crash, she spun around.

"God, he's gone to the police? When?"

Alette stood up. "How could you do that to me?"

They stared at each other as silence stretched tautly between them. Cheramie's eyes darted to the door and back to Alette.

"I didn't—"

"Don't lie, dammit!" Alette snapped, clenching her fists. "Answer me, Cheramie! I'm your *sister*!"

"Because I knew you'd get off!" Cheramie shouted. "Yo

were innocent, with no ties to Sal. I didn't know you'd had lunch with him. I knew you couldn't account for your time, but that's not enough for a conviction. I didn't think the old bitch could identify you. I knew you were innocent, and with the Lachman wealth and the Walcott influence, I knew you'd get off. I thought I had to save a presidential campaign! Jeff has been to the police?''

"Dammit, you would have sent me to prison!"

"You never would have gone. Rutger's lawyers got you off just as I knew they would.''

"I spent one hour in a holding cell, and it was terrifying. And for several months I thought I might spend the next years of my life in prison. I lost business. I've lost Jeff!'' Alette shook with anger. "I didn't believe him!''

"I had a presidential campaign I thought I could save. If they had known it was me, I wouldn't have gotten off like you did. It would have come out about our affair, and Rutger would have disinherited me.''

"You flew off to Washington and let me go to jail and let me take the scandal and the pressure when you killed him.''

"I didn't kill him! We had a struggle and his gun went off.''

"That makes it worse. You could have told the truth.''

"The presidential campaign would have ended then. I might have been cut from Rutger's fortune. Phillip would have divorced me. I would have lost everything. It started as a harmless dalliance to get back at Phillip, and then Sal fell in love. I didn't know until it was too late, but Sal was as obstinate as Rutger. I couldn't control him. Damn that bastard O'Neil! What's he told the police?''

"Jeff knows that Sal gave you the necklace. Sal showed it to him.''

"God, Sal was always so careful! He was more careful than I was. He showed it to O'Neil?''

"Yes. Now the police know about it. I argued with Jeff over this. I broke up with him, Cheramie, because I had such belief in the ties we've always had between us. I told him you would never do something like that to me.''

Cheramie left the room and came back holding her purse.

"I've wondered what I would do if this came out. Once long ago, Rutger caught me cheating on Phillip, and he threatened me then. I learned then to cover myself and to think about what to do if the truth came to light."

"You'll be caught. You should have told the truth."

"I'm leaving the country. I can live somewhere else. I have friends in Paris. Rutger will never completely cut me off."

"You'd leave the boys and Phillip?"

"The boys can join me in France; I won't go to prison."

"Yet you would have sent me!" Alette snapped angrily. "I trusted you!"

"You're naive, Alette. You weren't really hurt. I'm leaving, and you're going part of the way with me."

"No, I won't."

"You'll turn me in if I leave you behind."

"I don't know what I'll do, but I won't go with you. I won't help you, Cheramie. When I think how I argued with Jeff and accused him of ulterior motives—I won't help you."

"Yes, you will," Cheramie said, an angry glint coming to her eyes. She pulled out a Smith & Wesson and held it pointed at Alette.

"Sal gave me this and taught me to use it. You can take a plane ride and see me across the Canadian border, and then I'll let you go. I'm not going to leave here without you and let you turn me in to the police."

"I won't go, Cheramie." Alette burned with fury.

"Yes, you will if you want to see Jeff again. I know how to use this. Sal taught me, and I used to practice often. All you have to do is drive me to the airport and fly with me to Canada."

Tempted to challenge her, Alette studied her sister, wondering about her, uncertain now.

"I'll use it," Cheramie said. "I'd rather shoot than go to prison."

"I don't really know you. You're a stranger."

"It was a crime done in the heat of passion. Sal threatened my life. I had to escape. You're coming with me now."

"All right, but you're only making it worse."

"Don't be absurd. Let's go."

"You carry money to do something like this?"

"I carry more than you could possibly guess. I've been prepared for something to happen since that night. You know I couldn't bear to be in a jail."

"No one wants to be in a jail!" Alette retorted angrily, picking up her purse while Cheramie watched her and called to tell them to get the Lachman plane ready for a flight to Canada. They climbed into Cheramie's car and headed for the airport.

The sun was bright, the traffic arteries dotted with cars and trucks, as Jeff's plane came in for a landing. The moment he stepped out, he rushed to find the airport police. "I'm Governor O'Neil," he told a uniformed man. "I'm supposed to contact Lt. Harberger the moment I arrive."

The man nodded. "Come with me."

They went to an office, where the man talked on a radio a few minutes, and then Jeff heard Harberger's voice. The policeman handed Jeff the phone.

"She's not home. There's nothing we can do now, except look for them. The brother seems to think she'll go to the airport. I just talked to him."

"Thanks. I'll keep in touch." Jeff handed the radio back to the policeman. "Thanks," he said.

"If you need help, Governor, we're here."

"Good. Watch for this woman," he said, pulling out his wallet and flipping it open to a picture of Alette. "This is Alette Lachman's picture. I want to find her desperately."

"I'll watch for her. Give me the picture and I'll pass it round. I'll get it back to you."

Jeff pulled it out and gave it to the man. As he went through the busy lobby, he thought of the Lachman plane. He turned round and headed for the hangar with the private planes, riding through an exit door and across the tarmac. The plane was in sight, the familiar blue-and-gold stripe showing. He started to go back and get airport security to watch the plane when he saw a car slow and two women climb out.

He swore softly and stretched out his long legs, moving

toward them. They went around the car, their backs to him
as he headed toward them. He broke into a run, narrowing
the distance swiftly as they approached the plane, and then
he slowed, studying them. Cheramie's hand was in her purse,
and he knew she had a gun.

37 ~~~~~

They heard him and turned, Alette first, seeing him and
shaking her head as if to warn him away. He ran, almos
reaching them when Cheramie glanced over her shoulder
saw him, and raised her purse. "Stop where you are."

Cheramie stood beside her sister, her hand in her purse
the muzzle of the gun clearly thrusting against the soft tan
leather. He moved closer.

"Stop where you are if you don't want to get shot. I'n
going to get away from here."

"You think you can escape prosecution?" he asked, tryin
to stall for time, thinking what he could do to get the gun
moving closer.

"You move again like that and I'll pull the trigger. S
taught me how to use this. Get out of here, Jeff," Cheram
said. "You don't want Alette hurt. She's flying to Canac
with me, and then she can come back with the plane. She'
be home for dinner, but if you try to stop us, I'll hurt her
get away."

"Let me come along," he said.

"No!" Alette said. "Jeff, I'll be all right."

"You can't come along. I'm not going to worry about y
being on the plane with us."

"I don't want Alette to go alone. I'll sit where you c
watch me," he said, stalling for time, trying to think
something. There was only a few feet of space between the

He knew Sal's love of big guns. She had an unwieldy one with a long muzzle that thrust in a sharp point against the leather. If it had been a snub-nosed pistol, he would have been more alarmed, but the revolver he imagined she held would be tricky to handle in a purse.

"Jeff, do what she says. I'll be all right."

"Turn around and walk away from us," Cheramie ordered. "Don't turn us in, because you'll just cause trouble for Alette."

"Jeff, you were right," Alette said.

"I've got your engagement ring," he said. He looked at Cheramie. "Let me give her the ring so she can look at it while she's on the plane."

"Dammit! Get out of here and give it to her tonight!"

"Cheramie, please," Alette said in a voice that sounded as if she were terrified.

"Cheramie, let me give her my ring," he said in a coaxing voice. "I've waited this long to give Alette an engagement ring."

"God, you two are crazy! You have to toss it."

He reached in his pocket, saw the moment her eyes dropped to his hand. He swung his fist as hard and fast as he could, ramming it up against her arm. The gun went off, a shattering blast in spite of planes roaring on the runway.

The shot went high, and Jeff tackled Cheramie, knocking her to the pavement. She kicked and fought, but in seconds he had her pinned to the ground. A siren wailed in the distance. Alette retrieved the purse with the gun. While Cheramie swore and struggled, a car screeched to a halt. Jeff looked over his shoulder to see Aubrey and Lt. Harberger spill out of the car. He stood up, sliding his arm around Alette while Cheramie came to her feet.

"You were right all the time," Alette said to him.

Aubrey reached them before Lt. Harberger did. He walked straight up and slapped Cheramie, the sound of his palm on her flesh a sharp crack. "Damn you! I've never hit a woman, but you had it coming. *Damn* you! You almost sent Alette to prison."

Cheramie burst into tears, covering her face with her hands. "Call Rutger. Someone please call Rutger!"

"Aubrey, please," Alette said, and Jeff suspected that in another minute Cheramie would stir Alette's sympathy. He looked at Aubrey. "Can you handle this?"

"Yes. I'll call Rutger."

"They're not going to need us," Jeff said softly to Alette. "I'll take you home."

"They'll want a statement," she said, tears flowing.

"They can come get it."

"I think I have an engagement ring here somewhere."

He saw the box, picked it up, and dropped it into his pocket. Alette leaned her forehead against his shoulder. "You shouldn't have taken that risk."

"Honey, I grew up in a tough neighborhood. Besides, my reflexes are better than Cheramie's. She might as well have had a damn musket in her purse. Sal never expected she would really use that gun."

Jeff led Alette away, and when they neared the airport he steered her around to the side of the building behind a truck and tilted her face up to his. "Are you all right?"

"Yes. You were right about everything. The necklace, Sa . . . She implicated me to save herself. She said she knew would get off."

He pulled her to him and held her. "I'm sorry, Alette."

"I guess she was desperate. Cheramie never could take getting caught. She said she didn't kill Sal; they had a fig and there was a struggle and he had the gun and it went off.

"And she still tried to pin it on you!"

"Because of the scandal and Phillip."

He leaned away from her. "Honey, I want our engageme to be a happy time. I don't want you to remember the nig you got a ring was the same day Cheramie was taken in custody."

"Wait and surprise me," she said, looking at him so emnly. He leaned forward and kissed her.

"I'll try. Let's go home."

A man named Dawson Clower was hired as Cherami lawyer. Alette avoided reading the papers, which blazed w headlines about the wrong Lachman being accused the f time. A week after Cheramie's arrest, Alette was in Sacramento and had dinner with Jeff. After dinner he pulled her onto his lap and placed a box in her hands.

She opened it and smiled while he took the diamond ring and slipped it on her finger. She turned to throw her arms around his neck and kiss him.

"How soon can we get married?" he asked.

"Victoria and Aubrey are getting married in February." She didn't want to think about the trial. Rutger had already said Dawson Clower would try to delay it to have plenty of time to prepare a defense. "With Cheramie's trial hanging over us, I'd like a very small wedding with just family. We can invite more to the reception."

"Whatever you want. My schedule is getting busier, so the sooner I stop commuting back and forth, the better."

"And I feel like the whole state is watching to see whom you date and what you do."

"So marry me and they'll lose interest."

"All right. How about the third week of March?"

"That soon? We'll have to juggle schedules."

"Are you arguing?"

"Never!" he exclaimed with a grin, tightening his arms around her. "I've got a plane waiting. Let's fly home and go tell my folks and Aubrey we're engaged."

She laughed. "You can get away from here that long?"

"Try me."

She hugged him, and he called the airport. In San Francisco they drove first to see Barney and Nadine, who got teary as Nadine hugged Alette.

"Thank goodness!" Nadine said, smiling. "Now I can stop worrying about him being so alone!"

"Mom," Jeff said, laughing, "the governor is not lonely!"

"You won't be governor forever. I'm so happy, Alette. So very happy."

Barney took her hand, and she leaned down to hug him tightly, feeling his bones through the fabric of his shirt. "I'm happy, too, Alette. What happened between your father and me doesn't have anything to do with you and Jeff, and it no longer matters. I've learned a lot about love from Jeff's mother, and that's more important than hate. You're what the rascal needs.''

"Thanks, Dad!" Jeff grinned and pulled Alette to his side. "Lonely, a rascal—families keep you humble."

They talked about wedding plans for half an hour and then kissed his folks good-bye to go see Rutger. When they went into the living room and faced her father, Alette was shocked. He had lost weight and had lines in his face she had never seen before. His shirt was wrinkled; a slight stubble of beard shadowed his jaw. Alette tried to hide her shock. Rutger motioned them to sit down and sat facing them.

"We came by to tell you we're engaged," Jeff said, sitting on the sofa beside Alette, his arm casually across her shoulders.

Rutger looked away, staring at a fire burning in the fireplace; a muscle worked in his jaw, and Alette knew he was struggling. All the years she had known him he had kept his emotions locked tightly under control, and she pitied him that he had never learned to express them, to share his joy or grief, because now the burdens were his alone. Jeff's finger tightened on her shoulder to give her a squeeze.

Finally Rutger looked at them. "I'm not surprised. I can't say I'm happy with your decision," he said stiffly, and Alette knew that concession was too painful for him, but at least he wasn't going to argue or fight with her or demand that she break off with Jeff.

"I want a small wedding. We're getting married the twenty-third of March. I'll just invite family members and ask Victoria to be my matron of honor."

Rutger ran a hand across his forehead. "Whatever you want," he said, and it was the first time she had heard her father's voice laced with defeat. "You'll live in Sacramento won't you? Will you close your business?"

She looked at Jeff, realizing they hadn't discussed it. "We haven't decided," she said.

"I suppose, Alette, that I owe you an apology," Rutger said with such a grudging effort that she wondered if regretted her innocence. She realized Cheramie's crime was the one thing that had finally beaten down her father and destroyed his iron will. "I thought it was you with Sal Giavo-tella. It turns out it was Cheramie, something impossible to believe. I'll never understand why. Never."

"We're going to see Aubrey to tell him about our engage-ment now," Alette said, wanting to escape. Too long ago in childhood Rutger had separated himself from her, and she couldn't bridge the gap now. It was difficult to feel sympathy, and she knew it would be impossible to assuage his feelings.

"Have your folks accepted this?" Rutger asked, looking at Jeff.

"Yes, sir. My folks are crazy about Alette. They're gaining a daughter, and my mom is delighted."

"You were only a baby then; now you'll be my son-in-law," Rutger mused, giving Alette a start. She realized he must be thinking of the fire at the warehouse. Rutger studied Jeff. "You've done well. And now you're governor."

Alette stood up. "Rutger, we're going to Aubrey's."

"We'll have lunch and talk about the wedding, Alette."

She nodded, knowing she would pay for the wedding her-self and not involve Rutger other than to ask him to attend. Outside, Jeff pulled her close against him and she shivered, relishing his warmth. "Something has finally shaken him badly. He wasn't that undone when my mother died. Of course, he was younger. But he's always adored Cheramie."

"Try not to worry. Now let's see your charming brother."

When they went on board, Aubrey thrust his head outside. "We're in here. Come join us. We're knee deep in taffeta."

"We are not," said Victoria. "I'm showing him swatches material that my attendants will wear. What do you think, Alette? You'll be wearing this."

Alette looked at the shimmering deep green taffeta. "It's beautiful."

Victoria gasped and took Alette's hand. "You're engaged!"

Aubrey looked around at her and then at Jeff. "Hey, con-gratulations!" He crossed the room to shake hands with Jeff. "Welcome to the family," he said. "At least half of it."

"And welcome to the O'Neil family," Jeff said. "To all of it."

'Hey, now I'll have a brother! This calls for a celebration.

How about cognac instead of champagne? I gag on champagne.''

"When's the wedding?" Victoria asked.

"March twenty-third. It'll be quiet, just family. I'd love
you to be my matron of honor," Alette said.

Victoria's eyes shone. "I'd love to. Thank you, Alette.'

"You haven't seen Rutger, have you?" Aubrey asked a
he poured the cognac.

"Yes."

"I think Cheramie will be his undoing. Our perfect fathe
is finally coming apart at the seams."

"He'll rally," Alette said.

"Maybe." Aubrey passed out the drinks. "Here's to happ
families." He put his arm around Alette. "Look what we'i
getting, sis. The governor and the most gorgeous crimin:
lawyer in the state. Here's a toast to us for picking the best.

When they lowered their glasses, Jeff put his arm light!
across Victoria's shoulders and faced Aubrey and Alette :
he raised his glass. "Here's another toast to us for picki
Lachmans who transformed our lives." He looked down
Victoria. "We'll never be the same, thank goodness!"

She laughed and raised her glass. "I'll drink to that!"

Aubrey walked over to Jeff. "My dad was the cold
man who ever lived. Here's hoping the in-laws thaw the l
hint of it out of us." He gave Jeff a quick hug across t
shoulders and stepped back to raise his glass. "I'm damn
glad."

"Now come look at the picture of the dresses," Victo
said, moving to a settee and pulling out a book, and talk v
about weddings while Jeff and Aubrey moved to the bar.

"Have you talked to Harberger?" Aubrey asked Jeff i
low voice.

"No. I'm out of it. I don't want to be involved now.'

"Bad news for Cheramie. They found the woman v
came to the beauty shop after Cheramie. She said Chera
was waiting to get her hair done when she signed in at twei
one after five."

"So there goes the alibi."

"That's right. Vic said Cipresso will have the burde

proof. They've found a witness in Washington, and they are flying her out here. She saw Sal with a dark-haired woman. Cheramie has always done as she pleased and escaped consequences. This time it caught up with her.''

"It almost caught up with Alette. That's impossible to forget.''

"Cheramie and Rutger will have to live with themselves. I don't feel sorry for either one.''

"I feel damn lucky,'' Jeff said, looking at Alette.

"So do I. Be patient with her, Jeff. We don't know much about warm families.''

"I'm not worried about that." Jeff grinned. "I don't have a brother, and my dad said he wanted to sit with Mom, so would you be best man?''

"I'm honored,'' Aubrey said. "That's great.''

"It's going to seem like a year before the twenty-third of March.''

The day finally came, and Jeff watched Alette come in on Rutger's arm. She wore a floor-length pale blue dress, and her hair was caught up behind her head with a spray of lily of the valley. Her gaze met his, and all the way down the aisle of the small chapel she watched him. Cheramie sat in a pew with her boys, Phillip looking impassive at her side, and Rutger was seated in front of them. Victoria looked radiant in a deep blue dress, but Jeff barely noticed her. All he could see was Alette.

They repeated their vows and then had a reception at the Pacific Union Club. Only family came to the wedding; friends were invited to the large reception. Early in the evening Jeff and Alette slipped away to a waiting limousine and went to the airport, where they took his plane to Carmel. Jeff had a car waiting and drove to his house, carrying Alette inside.

"I offered you Europe, Mexico, Tahiti, Australia, and you wanted to come here, so here you are. Nothing new, nothing fancy, no hotel room service, although I did have a few meals prepared and put away.''

"Are you unhappy with my choice?'' she asked lightly, kissing his cheek.

"Never. I love it." He set her down, stepping back to look at her in her long dress. "Welcome home, Mrs. O'Neil."

"Oh, Jeff, that sounds wonderful." Alette looked at her husband, the most handsome man she knew. She watched him take off the black coat, and she stepped forward to unfasten the silk cravat beneath his jaw.

"Lord, you are handsome, O'Neil. Of course, you really look better naked," she drawled, teasing him, feeling excited, so wildly in love that she hadn't known it was possible.

He tilted her chin up and looked into her eyes. "Alette, I love you," he whispered, and bent his head to kiss her, his arms wrapping around her and drawing her to his heart, holding her tight.

They spent a week in Carmel and then flew home. In two weeks Alette closed her business and opened a new office in Sacramento. One night as she lay in the big bed in the master bedroom, she rolled over to look at Jeff. She brushed thick golden hair away from his face.

"Honey . . ."

"I'll bet you want something."

"I call you honey other times."

"Yes, but not in that tone of voice," he said, grinning at her, running a long lock of her hair back and forth across her bare shoulder. "I'm glad your hair is growing long again. I like it that way."

"Jeff, I'd like a family soon."

He drew a deep breath and looked at her, pulling her to him. "I'm ready when you are," he said in a husky voice, turning his head to kiss her.

Alette wound her arms around him, thinking she had everything she could want in Jeff.

Later, as she lay in his arms, she listened to him talk while she ran her fingers through the curls on his chest. His voice was sleepy and deep.

"I've cleared my calendar for the trial—the last week in August."

"I hope Dawson Clower gets her off. I know how you and Aubrey feel, but prison is so terrible."

"So is murder. Sal had six children and a wife when th

started the affair. And for what she did to you—we agreed we won't get into that. Anyway, we'll be there. It'll be a circus, and the media will want your picture.''

"Are you kidding, buster! They'll want the governor plastered across the front page.'' She lost her teasing tone of voice. "You don't have to attend.''

"I'm not sending you to the trial alone. You've had enough of that in your life.''

"Aubrey stood by when he could.''

"But he wasn't always there. I'm here, and I'm going with you. Whatever happens, I hope it's speedy.''

They arrived for the trial in limos and rushed past the throng of media people into the Hall of Justice and to the courtroom that brought bad memories to Alette. As they sat on the front row, Jeff locked his fingers in hers. Aubrey and Victoria went with them, and Rutger was already seated. Gina Giavotella sat at the back with two of her children. Phillip and the boys were there. Alette hurt for the boys, because it would be painful for them to sit through the testimonies, but Dawson Clower had been adamant that they attend.

Cheramie entered, accompanied by a deputy, and Alette was shocked to see how much weight she had lost. There was gaunt harshness to her beauty. Her gaze met Alette's, and she looked away, sitting down with her back to them. Dawson Clower wore cowboy boots, a bolo tie around his neck, and western suit and shirt. His hair was sandy and long, and he looked as if he belonged on the back of a horse and not in a courtroom.

The charge was manslaughter; the plea was not guilty by reason of self-defense.

For three days they listened to testimony. A woman from Virginia who owned a restaurant identified Cheramie without hesitation as the woman seen with Sal on three occasions.

Lois Schneider, silver-haired and self-assured, testified that Cheramie was still waiting to get her hair done at twenty-one after five.

Lt. Harberger told about Cheramie trying to get to the Beechman plane when they went out to arrest her.

Alette was not called as a witness. Finally Cheramie had to take the stand. Her black dress was tailored with a white collar and cuffs that gave her a demure appearance. Her voice was subdued, barely audible in the silent courtroom.

"I was caught in a love affair. My husband was involved in his campaign, involved in family business, gone night and day. Sal Giavotella was charming, persuasive. When I realized how deeply I was becoming involved, I tried to break off with him. And then I learned what a mistake I had made. I always loved my husband. I never wanted to hurt my family. I made a mistake. And then I couldn't extricate myself.

"Sal Giavotella divorced his wife. I begged him not to and told him repeatedly I would not leave my husband or children. I begged him to think of his children, but he would not. I realized too late that I had become involved with a man driven by compulsion. We argued and fought, and both of us became more desperate. I wanted my husband to win his campaign. I love my children.

"Sal Giavotella bought the condo here, and the day of his death I had lunch with friends. I bought a dress. I parked in the garage and met Sal there and went straight to his condo where the fight began. He shoved a gun in my ribs. He was a man accustomed to guns and always carried one. He yelled 'I'm not sharing you. You belong to me.' I was frightened and shocked and tried to get out of his embrace. We struggled. I tried to shove him away, and he grabbed my arm and shook me violently. We were seated on the edge of the bed. I thought he was going to kill me." Cheramie burst into tears. "My God, I thought he was going to kill me! I tried to push him away. I knew he was going to kill me if I didn't agree to leave my family. The gun discharged, and he was shot through the chest. I know he intended to kill me—"

Sobbing, Cheramie broke off, covering her face with a handkerchief. "I didn't kill him!" she cried. "All I did was make a mistake, and then I couldn't get out of it!"

Alette felt Jeff squeeze her hands and was startled to see the anger in his eyes. He looked down at her, and she guessed that he didn't believe Cheramie's version of what had happened.

Then Mel Cipresso began his cross examination. "Mrs. Walcott, was your sister tried for this crime?"

Alette drew a sharp breath, and Jeff squeezed her fingers.

"Yes," came Cheramie's barely audible answer.

"Were you in attendance at that trial?"

"Yes," she answered.

"Did you at any time tell the police, the court, the jurors"—he paused—"or your sister that you in fact were present when Sal Giavotella died of a wound from a forty-five through his chest?"

"No."

"Were you aware that your sister might have been found guilty of murder in the first degree?"

Cheramie looked across the courtroom at Alette and burst into sobs.

"Did you put the murder weapon in her car?"

Through her crying, Alette heard her affirmative answer.

When Alette was finally in the limousine with Jeff at the end of the afternoon, she turned into his arms. He held her close against him.

"Cipresso is crucifying her," she whispered.

"No. Cheramie is paying for what she did," he answered grimly, tightening his arms around her.

The next day came the summations. Afterward the jury was gone only half an hour.

"Defendant, please rise. We will hear the decision of the jury." Alette felt Jeff's reassuring squeeze of her hand.

"We find Cheramie Lachman guilty of manslaughter."

Cheramie fainted, toppling over, and Dawson caught her, lowering her as a deputy and Phillip hurried forward. Sentencing was set for the following week, and once again the family gathered.

Cheramie was given three years with two on probation.

Alette let out her breath. "She'll go to prison one year."

"I knew Judge Walcott would influence the decision," Victoria said.

Cheramie and her attorney approached the family. She stopped across the railing from Alette. "You got off. I don't know why I didn't." She moved away to Rutger, leaving Phillip waiting. Jeff took Alette's arm.

"Come on. We're going." Outside, the sun was bright, and they stopped to talk to Aubrey and Victoria before going to the car.

"We're leaving town," Jeff said, and Alette looked up in surprise.

"We are?" she asked, her curiosity growing.

"Great minds run in the same channel," Aubrey said lightly. "The *Easy* sails in an hour. Vic has cleared her calendar and I've cleared mine. We're going down the coast where it's warm and sunny and the music is steel drums and the tequila flows. If you smile just right, you can join us."

"Thanks," Jeff said, "but we have reservations in sunny Spain. The plane leaves in an hour."

"Jeff!"

"I think we'll go at this point and let you two discuss your surprise," Aubrey said. "Try not to worry, Alette. She had it coming, and Vic says they may get her off the one year with an appeal. We'll call when we get back, but don't look for us for a month."

They walked away, arms around each other's waists. Alette turned to Jeff. "What's this about Spain? I have an appointment to look at a lawn in the morning."

"Not anymore. My secretary took care of that. Let's get in the car and talk."

"When did you do all this?"

"I've been busy working on it." He held the door, and after he was seated he said, "I thought you'd need to get away."

She took his hand and held it tightly. Determined to forget the bad memories of the past year, Alette knew she would always cherish the strong man beside her, and together they would build a life full of warmth and happiness.